LIFELINE

* * *

LIFELINES

MICHAEL GEISOW

This book is a work of fiction. The main characters are fictional and any resemblance to actual persons, living or dead is purely co-incidental. The work does make reference to real individuals but these play no active role in the fictional narrative. The work makes reference to real places and institutions, but these are included to provide location and context. The narrative relating to these is entirely fictional and does not reflect their actual organisation, policies or actions.

Every effort has been made to obtain the necessary permissions with respect to copyright material, both illustrative and quoted. I apologise for any omissions in this respect and will be pleased to make the appropriate acknowledgement in any future editions of this work.

Faces on the cover page have been generated by Artificial Intelligence software

See: My Modern Met

https://generated.photos/

Text Copyright © 2021 Michael Geisow

All rights reserved.

ISBN:979-8460965366

This novel is dedicated to my wife Jill who has put up with me saying 'I'm going to write' for 20 years.

***

Author's note

I have written *LIFELINES*, not just as a work of fiction, but also to suggest what Artificial Intelligence (AI), could do for human healthcare and well-being. As a species we are facing a perfect storm of physical and mental dis - ease.. Pandemics, obesity, depression, dementias, addictions and the contagion of sexual exploitation and extremist ideologies. *That's* the challenge explored by characters in my book. Of course, AI is already in use in specialised branches of medicine. But. in the novel, several of my characters foresee AI as a technology with the potential to unify human therapy - both "mainstream'"(pharmaceutical, surgical and psychiatric) and the many therapies labelled by the umbrella term "alternative". I hope for two outcomes to my novel:

First; that readers will find characters who they can enjoy meeting. Their very human failings and desires for advancement, love and companionship are not neglected in my story!

Second; that ideas in this novel will stimulate discussion and even whet readers' appetites for a possible sequel! I ask for my readers' indulgence where technical ideas or terms appear. We all need to be aware, where that's not already the case, of the rapid adoption and burgeoning power of AI. It's still fiction to suggest that computers could produce a *novel* that would be judged "a great read". Many readers will be very relieved to hear that it isn't coming to a bookshop near them soon. But although they cannot give a date for that many leading AI figures think that will someday happen. When you read my novel—still written by a human—try to imagine what such a future AI might do for human ills.

Michael Geisow
August 2021

The Woodlands

Tamford, England 2021

The Woodlands is a Complementary Medicine Centre on the edge of Tamford in the UK. Offering the usual range of alternative therapies, it also provides a physiotherapy clinic. The practice, which is near the University in a suburb with many flats and other affordable accommodation, is well supported. This is not surprising as young men and women who are socially and intellectually upwardly mobile tend to suffer more mental and physical problems than the general population. General Practice does not cater well for the consequences of loneliness or inappropriate lifestyles. The Centre staff themselves are not immune from the same issues.

Part One

OFF-LINE

The real danger is not that computers will begin to think like men, but that men will begin to think like computers.

Sydney J Harris

Most of us believe in trying to make people happy only if they can be happy in ways which we approve .

Robert S Lynd

CHAPTER ONE

Martin

The rear bar of the Green Dragon pub in Tamford was remarkable in one respect. However boisterous the drinkers in the main bar became, it was possible for people sitting in that cosy area to the rear to overhear ordinary conversation. Voices from the front of the pub seemed to be sucked in by the rather stained upholstery. Martin Wright was sitting alone with a pint of Abbot Ale and had time to notice such things. He also saw that this evening most of the couples sharing tables that evening were women.

'Men seem to be an endangered species around here', he muttered, then remembering the back bar's good acoustics, quickly looked around to see if anyone had overheard. But as usual, no-one was showing the least interest in him. *Talking to yourself again* he thought. *You really have got it bad, mate.* Since leaving work, depression was slowly gathering like a fog in his head again, deadening his senses. He made an effort to lighten his mood by concentrating even harder upon his fellow drinkers. *Well at least females exchanging confidences was more interesting than listening to blokes parading their egos* he told himself.

Martin was becoming a serious people-watcher. Since his split with his partner, Helena there wasn't much else beyond his job as a physiotherapist to occupy his time. It was less painful to dissect other people's relationships than dwell upon your own failed one. There was a vicarious comfort to be had from looking for signs of tension between other couples and reflecting that he had, for now, put all that behind him. Plus he could fantasize about a relationship with some of the women in the bar, without the awkwardness and risk of actually starting one.

Two tables away a foursome were talking animatedly. Seated with their backs to him were a very vocal young man and a girl wearing a woollen hat over a shock of almost white hair. Facing him was an older man and a tall and particularly attractive woman. He closed his eyes to assist his eavesdropping and caught snatches of their conversation.

'. . .well, it's certainly a novel idea. .'
'. . .would it actually be *feasible*? . .'
'. . .intriguing! . .'
'. . .wouldn't you need Uni ethical committee approval or something? . .' The quieter of the two men was frowning:
'. . .and you *aren't* going to clear this with your supervisor?'

The tall woman glanced pointedly around the room. After a slight pause, their conversation continued at a more subdued level. Clearly, what was being discussed, was not intended for casual listeners like Martin. At that moment his attention was diverted by raised voices behind him. He looked round to see a sporty looking woman standing and arguing with another woman still seated.

When Martin turned back to the table containing the foursome, the tall woman had also risen to her feet. She glanced in Martin's direction, catching his eyes for a second, turned to give a little wave to her companions and headed out of the bar. Her companions were silent for a moment, looking at her empty seat. Martin looked down at his glass. It too was empty. When he returned after queuing for his pint, the bar had started to empty. At the table where Martin had been eavesdropping, only the man who had appeared to be leading the conversation remained. He looked up at Martin and grinned widely. He waved at the empty seats around him.

'If you're on your own too, want to join me?' Martin stood and stared. He'd suspected that The Dragon was attracting more gay clientèle and here was proof of that.

'You don't recognize me do you?' Martin clutched his glass firmly and awaited further explanation.

'Last year? Frozen shoulder? Student from Tamford Uni?' Martin shook his head, but smiled back. He couldn't remember, but the stranger had said the magic words "frozen shoulder" and that must mean *he* had been recognized by a patient and it was therefore OK to join him.

'I'm sorry, I get so many sports injuries from the Uni' The student glanced down at his own glass. Prompted, Martin offered:

'Can I get you a drink?'

'Hey great. Abbot please.'

'OK, keep an eye on mine for me.' Martin headed back to the main bar and returned with another pint.

'In case you still can't remember me, I'm Peter - *Pete* to friends and physios!' Martin sat opposite, accepted Pete's extended hand and announced himself.

'Martin - Mart to former clients.' He raised his glass slightly.

'Cheers!'

'So how's business?'

'So so. How's the sporting injury?'

'OK, but I got it from spending too much time at a keyboard – and too little doing exercise.'

'What do you do at Uni?'

'I'm a post grad – computer science.'

'Were your friends here tonight all doing higher degrees in computing?'

'Yes, all except Serena - the girl next to me. She's a mature student – doing a Ph.D. in psychology.'

'Sounds like a formidable lady.'

'She is.' Pete nodded and raised his own glass as if in acknowledgement of that. Martin and Pete both drank. It was Martin's third and he relaxed a little. Now that the back bar was almost empty of people to watch, it was more pleasant just to chat.

'What sort of computer work are you doing?'

'It's a bit complicated to explain. Do you use the Internet much in your work?' Martin hesitated. Pete had touched on his blind spot. His recent downfall in fact. It was the Internet in general and social networks in particular that had led to his break-up with Helena. That was how she'd discovered a better relationship. His immediate reaction had been to avoid the 'net. It had been the complete opposite for Helena. She'd set up her own sports coaching website and spent most of her free time on the Web promoting her new business, networking and emailing her mates. He'd had plenty of opportunity to use it, but hadn't found much there of interest to him and *his* clinic was advertised for him on the Woodlands website. But that was all in the past. Martin took a large mouthful of his real ale. Time to move on!

'You might not believe this Pete, but I'm definitely an Internet innocent - or should that be a World Wide Widower?'

'I'm not sure I get you?'

'Social networking contributed to the split with my long term partner.'

'Oh. Sorry to hear that.'

'But you can still tell me what you do – perhaps I *should* get more aware of what's going on; on-line, I mean.'

'After what you've just told me I'm not sure you'll want to hear this, but I'm studying social networks.'

'Ah. Oh well, go on.'

'Well, social networking has changed the way people start, develop and even end relationships; business as well as personal ones.'

'Tell me about it!'

'Er, yes, including your own experience, of course. Well, in short I'm hoping to guide this disruption in a good way.'

'Excuse me?'

'I'm developing new software – programmes - to build high quality networks which will recognise potentially valuable *associations* between people.'

'Not sure I understand what your programmes will actually *do*.'

'They'll get me a Ph.D. and hopefully a mega salary!' Martin nodded his head at first then smiled as it dawned on him that Pete was being cynical. Pete grinned too, then looked quite serious.

'No; joking apart, right now we've many situations where the Internet can either make all our lives better or, as you have just told me about your own experience, take us to places we'd rather not be when we get there. Here's just one example – I've friends at Uni who're all fired up about genetics. Now that there's complete data on the human genome on the Web, they think they'll soon be able to eliminate disease and create supermen. That's the upside.' Pete paused. Martin recognised his cue.

'What's the downside?'

'Knowing the abilities of the same research students to manage their credit card balances, I'd prefer human evolution to be left to nature.' Martin managed another smile at this. Pete was much more interesting than the average Dragon drinker.

'So your programmes - software, you said - will find associations between our genes to help develop better drugs?'

'You must be joking! – no; I'm sticking to *social* networking and my higher degree. If I thought there was even a faint hope of modelling human gene evolution, I'd start a university spin-out company and hope to clean up when Big Pharma bought us out.'

'Big Pharma?'

'The pharmaceutical industry – Glaxo Smith Kline and the rest.'

'And they would be interested?'

'Bite my hand off. Cheers Mart!' Pete raised his glass in mock celebration of a highly profitable corporate flotation on the stock market.

'So what about you? I've seen you in here before, drinking on your own. Don't the others at your place go for a drink after work? Some of the women that I noticed when I came to the Woodlands for treatment were gorgeous and super-fit looking.'

'I think most of our female staff go straight home for a hot bath or to cook a meal for their blokes, And the Centre management would take a dim view of me dating my clients.'

'Well you *won't* get lucky in The Dragon, the punters are mostly either undergrads and or in same sex relationships.

'You're probably right; but you and your girlfriend don't fit either category!'

'Serena? Not my girlfriend and she's certainly not gay, but I don't think she's with anybody. At least not that I've seen. She's pretty serious about her work, but I don't think she's had very happy time at Uni Doesn't get on with her Ph.D. supervisor. She comes in here occasionally when she needs some intelligent conversation. Likes to talk to scientists like us. Says that her psychology colleagues are all fruitcakes!' Martin nodded absently.

'I don't think I'm in the mood to be with anyone either right now – want another drink?'

'Have you ever known a student turn one down?' The Dragon stayed open late to service a student population that did not keep normal hours. Tonight though, to Martin's surprise, the bars had almost emptied out. He commented on this to Pete when he returned with their drinks.

'Its quiet tonight isn't it?'

'It'll fill up later. There's an evening lecture and reception at the Uni for a speaker from the Cambridge Sanger Centre – that's where Serena and the others went. I'd have gone too, but, frankly, I've had enough of campus today.'

'Sanger Centre?'

'Not heard of it? It's world famous for sequencing the human genome. It's named after Frederick Sanger; he won *two* Nobel prizes for medicine, you know! The last one was for what we were discussing earlier – genetics.'

'From what you've said Pete, that doesn't sound up your street at all.'

'Computer programmes and *scientific* networks connected researchers round the world and were absolutely key to the success of sequencing the human genome.'

'Oh, I see – but isn't your friend Serena doing research in psychology?'

'What interests her isn't so much the science, but rather the psychology of high achievers like Sanger!' Pete studied Martin intently for a moment, furrowing his eyebrows and concentrating as if trying to read his thoughts.

'You know you really won't pick up a date here in the Green Dragon. You should check out the Web. That's where you might meet someone you could *really* connect with. And you can find out lots about them without even buying them a drink. Everyone does Internet dating now.'

'Including you?' Pete frowned. 'Can't afford the distraction; my research consumes all my time and energy, curse it. I'm in the last chance saloon now with my funding. If I blow this, I'm stacking shelves in the local supermarket. IT jobs don't grow on trees these days and there are hundreds of applicants for each one.' Martin shook his head sympathetically.

'I'm not on the Internet at home now. Cancelled my broadband subscription when I split with Helena and my mobile's not on a pay monthly contract, so Internet access is expensive and inconvenient. I'm also not sure where I'd look. I certainly wouldn't join a social network. Seems to me it's a dangerous jungle out there; especially when it comes to personal relationships.' Hearing this confession, Pete's face registered a mixture of surprise and shock. Here was someone who was *not* connected. Given that Martin was a professional physiotherapist, it seemed barely credible.

'What? You don't even use email?'

'The Woodlands Centre has a website and email. That's all taken care of for me by the administrator. And *policed* by her as well. She's hardly likely to tolerate messages from dating websites.' Pete paused to digest this admission.

'You've got a degree or a diploma in sports science or medicine haven't you?'

'Physiotherapy.'

'Whatever. That'll get you a user name and password on our Uni network as an external user - you'll need a pass from them for that. I can give you the access code to our department computer room; several external workers use it. Look, if you'll give me some feedback about your experience using my programme and perhaps the occasional beer . .' Pete waved his glass for emphasis.

'. . .I'll give you an early taste of "InterconNet" - that's what I've called my research project. I'll also show you how to look for potential hot . .' Pete hesitated, catching Martin's expression

' . . . I mean potential life partners; if that's your thing.' Receiving no reply, Peter shrugged his shoulders.

'Well anyway, the offer stands should you be interested.' Pete stood up, a little unsteadily, retrieved a pen from his jacket and a card from his wallet and scribbled something.

'OK Mart, in the words of the song; here's my number; call me maybe.' After the student had left, Martin looked at the card Peter had thrust into his hand. At the top right was some sort of logo consisting of a spidery network of lines interconnecting small geometric shapes. The same device appeared, enlarged in grey, behind the simple text:

InterconNet
Peter Swales, B Sc.

Under this were Pete's mobile number and email address. *Did even students have business cards these days?*, he wondered. Martin idly turned the flimsy rectangle over. On the back was a short message: "I did notice you watching Serena. Her full name is Serena Diane Peddy, can u believe! Perhaps you might meet *her* on-line!! Call me if you're interested (in my offer). Pete."

* * *

****

Martin was late arriving at the Centre the next day. Woodlands receptionist Julie was on the 'phone so just gave him a dirty look as he signed in. After lunch break, with no clients booked that afternoon, Martin decided to walk to the local park for some fresh air. He passed a couple on one of the benches. They were so intent on each other they paid no attention to him. Further on a man and woman were deep in conversation while their dogs circled each other suspiciously. Already feeling low, seeing these ordinary social contacts added to his present feeling of isolation.

After returning to his room in the Centre, his mood darkened further when he noticed the memo that had appeared on his desktop during his absence. It was held in place with a clock-weather station freebie from a physiotherapy equipment supplier. Even without reading the text he recognised the neat hand of the Centre's administrator; Noura Munday. No chance of missing her memo, or claiming it must have blown off his desk. Its message was unambiguous: "Please see me before you leave today". Noura would already have checked at reception and seen he'd signed in very late that morning. As he passed the reception desk, Julie flashed him a sympathetic look, but said nothing. Her silence spoke volumes. He must be about to be shown the door. Walking to Noura's office he glared at the supposedly uplifting murals on the corridor walls. He knocked, trying to avoid feeling like an naughty schoolboy.

'Ah; there you are at last, Martin. Take a seat.' Noura didn't ask where he'd been that afternoon or why he'd been late arriving in the morning; her tone made her disapproval perfectly clear. Martin fidgeted in his chair, whilst she eyed him. Noura was a short dark-haired woman who'd decided, while still young, to compensate for a lack of stature by deliberately fostering very formal speech, a forbidding manner and a sharp tongue. Centre staff referred in private to her as "Black Monday".

In truth her confrontational attitude had never really been natural to her. The conscious effort required, made her physically tense and distinctly irritable by the end of the working day. It was nearly that now. The irony was that the very Centre she managed had the capacity to help her, but to Noura, seeking help would seem too much like an admission of weakness. The only person aware of her personal lack of ease was the Centre's owner and director, Michael Timles. The only person she had ever opened up to; he had been so supportive and made her feel valued when she'd had a crisis of confidence. But right now it was her problem with Martin, not herself, that Noura had shared with Dr. Timles.

'Martin. I'm aware that you, like all our staff, operate with a degree of autonomy and are not directly accountable to me for your particular practice.' Noura paused to select the most apt line of attack from her personal management styles archive.

'However, in the present circumstances—' She hesitated and frowned just sufficiently to indicate that this exchange was distasteful to her, but was nevertheless her duty to perform.

'- I have to draw certain matters to your attention.' Noura paused again to make sure that she did, indeed, have Martin' attention.

'There have been complaints that you have not been present or contactable during part of your advertised hours. Furthermore, some of our other therapists have been telling me that you appear to be - and these are their words not mine - "away with the fairies". Precise as always, Noura made sure that her quotation marks could be plainly heard.

'More seriously, I have recently received disturbing comments from one of your patients, with whom I happen to meet socially. On two sessions this month, I was told, you left the person concerned feeling more uncomfortable and tense than when they presented for treatment. My contact formed the strong impression that although you were physically present in your clinic, your mind had left the room.

Martin experienced a cold chill. Noura had left the quotation marks off that last comment. That might mean that this unknown patient's words were judged too strong to be repeated verbatim. It was also possible that the patient she was talking about had been a plant and Noura was being careful not to blow their cover. Either way, things were clearly very serious. Even taking into account that this was Black Monday talking on a Friday evening; the lowest point in her working week.

'I know that you're usually very well regarded for your work and that you came to the practice with very commendable references. But I have to remind you that The Woodlands prides itself upon its local and even, I may say, its regional reputation.' Noura paused again for effect, then fired her warning shot:

'I must tell you, Martin, that I regularly receive enquiries about possible openings at the Woodlands from other practitioners in your field.' Noura sat back and raised her head and eyebrows in invitation of an explanation of these lamentable lapses of protocol and service. Martin was by now mentally wearing shorts and a grubby cardigan on a low stool in the headmistress's office. He attempted to regain some stature.

'I don't suppose that you'd like to tell me who's complained about my treatment?' Noura's eyebrows lifted still higher in response.'

'I think we both know very well that all information we receive from patients is confidential.' Martin glanced at the wall clock and noticed the old clock had been replaced by a digital one, with a large display that included a readout of seconds. It was only 10 minutes to Noura's official 5pm going home time, which on a Friday was sacrosanct. He knew that a rapid confession of guilt was the only way to avoid a real black Monday after the coming weekend.

'All right, yes - I've not been myself lately. Personal problems; not medical ones. Perhaps I should see one of the other therapists here?' Martin ventured a weak smile and looked at Noura to try and judge whether this was the right sort of response. Apparently it was, as the neat eyebrows sank back into place.

'Hmmm.' Noura too glanced rapidly at her clock.

'I'm pleased that you have taken a professional approach to acknowledging this situation. Otherwise things could have become very difficult for both The Woodlands and yourself. I'd *not* think it appropriate for you to consult one of our other staff.' Her eyebrows indicated the likelihood of idle tongues beyond the Woodlands walls.

'I have taken the precaution of speaking with our director, Dr. Timles, and he has said that he is available next weekend if you'd like to have a word with him. Provided of course you do not wish to make arrangements to take independent advice elsewhere.' Noura paused briefly and getting no reply continued.

'Would two-thirty pm a week tomorrow be suitable for seeing Dr. Timles?' This question was phrased in such a way that the only response could be a nod. As Martin slowly left Noura's office, mentally cancelling his regular trip to the Green Dragon, he overheard the start of a brief telephone call. Turning round at the end of the corridor he glanced back to see Noura locking the office. It was 5pm precisely.

Martin went straight to the small staff common room and made an instant coffee, spooning an excessive amount of powder into his mug. There was only gone-off milk in the small 'fridge. He picked up several magazines and flicked through them, not really taking in any content. Whilst he sipped his bitter drink he stared out of the window. Overcast all day, it was already dark and rain was striking the window. The sound was somehow comforting. Perhaps, unlike the magazines, it offered a distraction he could focus on.

It was quite late when he let himself back into his room. Instead of reviewing the following day's case notes, he sat and tried to recall the tall woman research worker he'd seen in Green Dragon the previous evening. Something about her manner, fragments of information gleaned from that student - Pete - and the odd message on the back of Pete's business card had wedged itself in a corner of his brain. He was having difficulty focusing on the next simple tasks. The actions of standing up, locking his door, leaving the Centre and going home seemed too demanding right now.

Tina, the Centre's Reiki therapist, walked by, hesitated outside the open door of Martin's room and glanced in. Martin was sitting awkwardly at his desk, apparently lost in thought. She noted his tense jawline and hunched shoulders. Since he joined the Woodlands, Martin had been of considerable interest to her for both professional and personal reasons. But he'd failed to acknowledge her, apparently wrapped up in his own work.

'You're working late – client problems, or can't you face your cooking tonight?' Martin stared at the slim figure in his doorway and came out of his reverie. Despite his low mood, thoughts suddenly tumbled in his head: *Reiki! That's getting in touch the universal life force; whatever that is. Could Reiki help? Tina knows my scepticism about all things "alternative". She might love a chance to prove me wrong; that Reiki could sort me out. What about us swapping a session or two? Reiki in exchange for really effective exercise routines and or a posh dinner for two?* He glanced down at his watch.

'Oh Hi Tina, I hadn't realised it was so late.' He saw her studying his shoulders and was suddenly aware of the tension. He relaxed them and forced a smile:

'I don't think I've seen you at this time of the evening either.' Tina grinned and gave an apologetic shrug, hugging the clip files she was carrying closer to her chest.

'I was expecting a couple of old friends for dinner tonight and they've cried off at the last moment. Rescheduled amateur drama rehearsal apparently. Disappointment leaves you feeling a bit aimless, doesn't it?' Her voice trailed off and her explanation hung in the air, creating an empty space that invited a sympathetic response. The corridor was quite gloomy now.

Martin stared gloomily out of the window. Passing car head and tail lights were distorted by raindrops on the pane, intensifying the gloom outside. Tina was still hesitating in the doorway. She thought: *Its obvious he hasn't anywhere special to go – surely he'll suggest we go for a drink or even food at the Green Dragon where he usually winds up in the evening. I'd even talk about physiotherapy if he wanted, instead of Reiki!* She focused on that thought; visualising them cocooned together between those high-backed pub seats that gave a cosy intimacy to the punters. Martin turned away from the window the same instant.

'Actually, I'd like to talk to you about Reiki, Tina.'

It took Tina a moment to steer her mind away from her day dream to grapple with this totally unexpected response. A couple of cut-out magazine articles worked loose from the files she was holding and floated into Martin's room. Tina followed their fluttering descent, but her thoughts were elsewhere. Practising Reiki produced a calm state of mind, but it did not altogether eliminate shock. She thought: *Either he can mind read, this is deja vu or I really am still day dreaming.* She pinched herself behind the camouflage of her files, but everything stayed the same. *Well, I still want that drink and now I've been given an unexpected opportunity to ask for it.* She gave him her best open smile.

'OK, but it will cost you a glass of wine in the Green Dragon.'

The rear bar of the Green Dragon was busy as usual on Friday. But Martin found himself and Tina a table for two that was fighting for space in a corner cubbyhole.

'Bit tight. Is this OK?' She nodded approval.

'What can I get you?' Martin noticed she'd picked up a menu whilst they were hunting for seats.

'Er. Perhaps you'd like to look through the menu. I may be a while at the bar.'

'A large red wine, please.' She looked a little guiltily at her menu.

'You did mean to eat here, didn't you?' She'd only been offered a drink, and automatically picking up the Dragon's menu now seemed a bit presumptuous. Martin reassured her.

'It's OK, I'd nothing else planned for tonight.' *Ouch!* Tina puckered her brow ever so slightly. Not quite the kind of warm response she was hoping for. She decided that she could definitely help this attractive man; if he would let her. It might also lead to a *less* professional relationship, if that was possible. Once the meals had been ordered, Martin and Tina sat down with their drinks. Tina found that, squeezed into the cubbyhole, it was almost impossible to avoid direct physical contact with Martin. This pleased her, although Martin appeared not to notice at first, but then decided to check again:

'Are you really OK with this table; we don't to seem have much room here, do we?' Tina thought a smile or, better still, a cheeky grin, accompanying his question would have been nice, but Martin's expression was serious. He seemed to have something weighty on his mind and it wasn't their accidental contact. For Martin's sake, Tina looked quickly around the crowded bar. To her satisfaction she saw there were still no other seating options; indeed, several couples were propping up the bar walls. She smiled up at Martin:

'Really, I'm OK like this.' She felt she should remind him about his unexpected request. She asked as casually as she could:

'You wanted to ask me about Reiki.' Martin looked down at the tabletop and twisted his glass until the engraved pint marker faced him. The self-conscious winding action seemed to give him the energy or confidence to begin.

'Frankly Tina, I'd like your advice.' It was Martin who now quickly looked around the bar. The chatter from customers filled the space like a sort of sound fog; it was difficult to pick out individual conversations. No one was looking at them and there were no familiar faces. Friday wasn't one of his usual drinking nights at The Dragon. Rather too boisterous. Tina adopted an open expression which she hoped conveyed attention, encouragement and concern. It seemed to have the desired effect as Martin stopped playing nervously with his glass.

'Can I ask you to keep our chat to yourself?' Tina allowed a bit of her detached, professional expression to creep in.

'Of course, Martin. That's what I do! Unless you've done something illegal of course.' Tina mentally kicked herself. That qualifier just slipped out. It was part of the code of practice she always went through with a new client. But Martin wasn't her client. Not yet anyway. She quickly tried to recover by grinning impishly at him.

'Only joking of course.' But Martin was struggling too much with what he had to say to worry about such sensitivities. There was an uncomfortable silence. Tina decided to risk helping him out, even though she would be guessing.

'Would you like me to I say what I'm feeling about you; to get our chat started, Martin?' She sought and held full eye contact and gently mirrored his own rather tense posture, leaning forward, gripping her own glass as it rested on the table. Martin looked surprised, but finally relaxed his shoulders and sat back with a slightly relieved:

'OK.' Tina spoke cautiously:

'Since you split from your partner—' She knew, but didn't use Helena's name.

'—you appear to all your colleagues at the Centre to have lost your way a bit.' She recruited the other staff at Woodlands to her cause here. Martin was unlikely to check. He continued to look directly at her, but didn't comment. Tina was obliged to carry on talking in the hope that he would soon help *her* out. Fortunately, at that moment their food arrived, which gave her time to collect her thoughts. Once they had settled to eat she continued more confidently:

'Well, when you started working at Woodlands, you were lively; you always shared a joke with our receptionist. You usually had something interesting to say to the other staff and watched the sports channel in the common room at quiet times. Now you don't appear to speak to anyone, more than is necessary that is, and you seem to be spending a lot of your evenings here.'

Tina glanced around the bar as if seeking a reason for the place's attraction, then found his eyes again. Martin felt a bit deflated by Tina's painfully accurate assessment. Noura Munday had just taken him to task on this very subject. Was his depressed state of mind really so obvious to everyone at the Centre? On the way to the Dragon he had been turning over in his mind what he would tell Tina about his flagging enthusiasm for work. How he would ask her about her own work with clients and whether her own therapy might help with psychological as well as physical problems.

His tutors had always stressed how closely mind and body were connected and affected each other if either were out of balance. Really this should be a component of his own therapeutic approach. Whilst working with their bodies, he was supposed to be open to any underlying mental issues his patients had. Modern physiotherapy, especially for competitive sporting types, now aimed to reduce stress by re-orientating any negative thinking as well as correcting strained muscles or injured or dislocated joints.

He knew he should feel grateful. By coming straight to the issue, Tina had unexpectedly lowered the barrier for him to confide in her. This wasn't the moment to be defensive or dismiss his present state of mind as a passing phase.

'Well yes, Tina. I *have* been feeling low since Helena broke with me, but things were not going very well long before then. In fact my mood probably contributed to the break up. Look, on the way to the Dragon I was trying to work out what to tell you about myself, but you're obviously ahead of me.

So now you've spared me the painful confession that I'm depressed, do you think you could help? One of my occasional sports injury clients also comes to you and she never fails to say how impressed she is with your treatment. In fact she makes me feel a bit inadequate. I've often wondered why she bothers to book herself into my clinic at all.'

Tina reflected on this: *you really are depressed, aren't you? You're a very attractive man and don't even realise the effect you have on some of your young female patients. The woman you're talking about – Linda – has asked me several times about you, but I'm certainly not going to tell you about that. I don't generally touch my Reiki clients as you do your physiotherapy patients. But you miss all their signals; even the ones I'm giving you right now*. Tina adjusted her position on the narrow curved bench that they were sharing, moving her thigh gently against his.

Martin was impressed with Tina's encouragement and how easy she was making this embarrassing confession to a professional colleague. *There's more to Tina than I thought, perhaps after all she does have that special perception claimed by Reiki practitioners.* Tina continued:

'Back at the Centre, you said you wanted to ask me about my treatment and whether it might help you. That *is* right, isn't it?' Tina decided to refer to "treatment" rather than "Reiki" in deference to Martin's views about alternative therapies. But for his part, Martin was glad to pick up the lifeline that Tina was offering and for now at least, set aside some of his scepticism.

'I know I've been dismissive in the past about the work of other therapists at Woodlands, but I've given that a lot more thought recently. I have to admit that when I encouraged them to talk about themselves and their concerns, even *my* patient's inflamed tendons seemed to better more quickly. Trouble is, I haven't been in a positive enough mood these last months to give my patients a very sympathetic ear.' Tina thought: *You're not the only one who's aware of that. All the Centre staff know things have been going downhill.* Martin looked so worried that Tina risked covering Martin's hand gently.

'Most of the Woodlands therapists believe there's more to their work than just creating a therapeutic feel-good factor—' Tina paused, thinking hard about how to pull in the lifeline Martin had finally grasped, without his letting go.

'—but I agree that encouraging *belief* that our clients will get better is very important part of the therapy we *all* do.' She chose her words to be inclusive; conscious of Martin's "me and them" attitude.

'I don't just make "magic passes" over parts of my clients that hurt. Like you do, or perhaps as you just said, like you *used* to do, I get to know them and talk about their worries, their relationships and other things that matter to them. The things that they enjoy when life is going well'. Tina could see that Martin was still holding her virtual lifeline in spite of her deliberate reference to Reiki's alternative therapy through symbolism and touch. But also she thought that some more down to earth therapy might help him stay connected now. She removed her hand.

'Look, I know you feel your *mental* glass is half empty, but your *actual* glass is completely empty', she quipped. Then offered:

'Can I get you another beer? Martin looked down at their drinks in surprise.'

'Absolutely not, this is on me tonight. Same again?' Whilst Martin shouldered his way to the bar, Tina relaxed by meditating on the last word he had used: *tonight*. It meant there could be other nights sharing ideas, hopefully not all in the pub. A deep river of prejudice still separated them, but as long as she could keep him holding her verbal lifeline, she could bring him to her side. After a lengthy wait, Martin returned with the drinks and an apologetic grin.

'A University rugby team's here, so there's a scrum at the bar. Now Tina, tell me what it is you do.'

'Well, I'm definitely *not* a present day witch - yes Martin I did recognise that quote you pinched from the weird sisters in Shakespeare's *Macbeth*. Are you going to listen seriously to me or am I just going to feed your prejudices?' It was a rebuke for his cheek, but Tina was secretly pleased by his attempt at humour. His depression couldn't be too deep. Martin might yet find that just like Lady Macbeth, she too had high ambitions and a weak male certainly wasn't part of *her* plans either. She felt she had the power to strengthen this man mentally. From the little she had seen of his body so far, Martin made the grade physically already. Tina decided it was time to talk about Reiki.

'You really want to hear about my own therapy and how it might help you?'

'Yes Tina, but no text book stuff, please. I don't rate everything published even in my *own* field. There seems to be a gap between what academics recommend in theory and what works in practice. You know I *have* browsed alternative therapy books in the Centre library. They mostly start OK, but they soon get too mystical and I always put them back half read when they lose me. I just can't connect with what they're telling me.' Tina frowned.

'Connect?'

'Well, OK – I really mean *believe*. Just give me your own take on all of this. And please make your explanation *holistic* to help me suspend my disbelief.' Tina realised Martin was deliberately using that favourite term of alternative therapy practitioners. She was pleased he was gently teasing her, even though some of his improved spirit was probably down to the beer.

'So my explanation should deal with the physical aspects and play down the spiritual ones?' It was a bold shot on her part to use the term *spiritual* but this element was key in all alternative therapies as well as conventional medicine, even though many medical practitioners still didn't accept that. Tapping into a client's own spiritual "energy" was the main objective of her work, but right now Tina was more than happy to agree to his request and focus on the therapeutic benefit of sensual touch.

'Do you promise you'll hear me out and not put *me* down *half read* like those library books?' Tina smiled inwardly at the double meaning of her reply. At some stage Martin ought to pick up the signals she was feeding him about her personal interest. If he *did* agree to a session or two with her, she would leave him in no doubt of that. If not, well then that would be as much down to her as to him. And it would be time for her to give up and look elsewhere.

Meanwhile, until she found out more about his hopes and desires, she had to be careful to keep their conversation professional. She didn't want to lose her tenuous hold on this sceptical yet desirable man. This certainly meant she couldn't take him on as a Centre patient. Noura wouldn't look kindly on therapists who crossed the Rubicon of inappropriate behaviour with clients; even where the client was also a member of staff.

But working *outside* the Woodlands; that was different. It was strange though. Here she was in the relaxed atmosphere of a local pub, her thigh meeting his; on the verge of a very personal conversation. Yet Martin had neither sensed her interest in him, nor appeared to notice her present heightened arousal. That was *very* strange for an experienced physio. She doubted Martin would have sufficient faith that Reiki could help him, but even if he had, she didn't think Reiki was the kind of alternative therapy he needed right now. And right at that moment, Martin's attention appeared to have wandered completely. Tina followed his gaze.

In the corner voices and laughter suddenly rose above the general conversation. A black cat had crept into the bar and had been ceremoniously lifted onto a table occupied by a noisy group of drinkers. Martin turned round with a worried expression.

'Oh Christ, I'm so sorry Tina. Seeing that cat's reminded me I'd promised a week ago to look after my neighbour's cat; feed it and let it out.' My neighbour's on a course somewhere today and tomorrow. I wasn't coming here this evening; I don't normally come Fridays because it's so crowded. Look, can I take a rain check on our chat. I really *do* want to talk to you, but I'll have to go now - sorry Tina. Look - what about meeting up here after work on Monday? I'll walk back to the Centre car park with you.' Tina was disappointed. She nodded and picked up her coat. Was the neighbour's cat an excuse to end their conversation? Would Monday's meeting really happen - or had Martin let go of the lifeline by which she had been gently reeling him in? She would now have to wait and see.

Martin arrived early at the Woodlands on Monday and was even cheerful during Julie's routine teasing in reception as he signed in. When he straightened up she had some more serious information for him.

'Had a message on the Centre's voice mail this morning asking for a booking with you. Today if poss, Mart. You've a slot at 3pm on your calendar. Want me to accept that on your behalf?'

'Who is it, Julie?'

'Someone called Evan Jones; Welsh wouldn't you say?'

'Sounds like it. Couldn't you tell from his accent?'

'No; his secretary made the enquiry. She was calling from a company called Thera Ltd in Slough. Her boss's in Tamford for a board meeting.' Julie was impressed; Martin's client sounded like a senior manager, and from out of town too.

'Perhaps your star's on the rise, Mart.'

'Don't know about that Julie, but yes, make the appointment please.' Martin puzzled about this all morning and his first patients found him even more distant than usual. His regular sports injury client had spent a great deal of time on her appearance that morning and had agonised over the colour co-ordination of her sports bra and briefs. She was miffed by Martin's offhand greeting and lack lustre massage and couldn't resist commenting about this to Julie as she was on her way out. Julie didn't like this client, even though she was a regular. She was too well developed for Julie's taste and her clothes were far too bright and tight.

It was quite clear why she was a regular, even though Martin couldn't see it. Julie rather fancied Martin herself and would be happy if this client decided not to rebook. She was sometimes tempted to lean over her desk and remark confidentially: "Martin was originally *Martine* you know. I expect that surprises you; it certainly surprised us? Anyway, her sex change hormones often make her feel particularly low on Mondays". But Julie was very professional, in her workplace at least. So she bit her tongue and commiserated with the wretched woman.

'I'm sorry you feel like that. I think he's going through a difficult time at present.' The tall woman still looked disgruntled.

'Well he's *single* isn't he? He ought to find himself a partner. He needs someone to lift his mood.' Julie thought: *that's not all you'd like to lift*, but she simply shrugged and smiled sympathetically. The woman pulled a sour face, turned and left, striding for the car park with no sign of discomfort or joint problems. Julie took a deep breath, drew a crude picture on her scratch pad, scrawled an obscene cation that would have made even Noura blush, then fed it to the shredder. She felt better for that.

At 2:30 Martin got a buzz on the intercom from Julie. She spoke in a hushed tone.

'Your Mr. Jones has has arrived to see you. He knows he's a bit early. I've sent him along to sit outside your surgery. I should think he's your oldest client to date, but charming with it. He's very posh Martin; you'd better take a couple of minutes to tidy your consulting room desk and do your hair, then see him a bit earlier, eh?'

It wasn't often that Martin paid much attention to Julie's banter, but this time her tone got him on his feet. Shortly after shovelling unsorted papers and magazines into his desk drawers and checking himself in the mirror, he opened the door and smiled at his visitor. His client was of medium height, but slightly stooped, with a good head of wavy, greying hair. He wore a light sports jacket and grey linen trousers, but as Julie had told Martin, his clothes said "high class tailoring" loud and clear. The man grasped Martin's hand in a firm handshake.

'Evan Jones. Thank you for seeing me at short notice, but I'm only staying here until tomorrow, when I have an all day meeting.' Mr Jones's voice had a gentle Welsh lilt.

'One of the chaps I'm meeting tomorrow has spoken very highly of physiotherapy at the Woodlands, so I'm here by recommendation you see.' Seated in front of Martin's desk, Evan Jones explained his problem.

'Over the last three or four months, I've had this pain in my lower back. My GP calls it the lumbar region. Look now I've always been pretty active; walking and golf especially. I've had sharp back pain before, through twisting badly in a drive or heaving a golf bag into the car boot. But now when I have to walk very far my legs feel increasingly heavy. It's as if all the power is gradually being turned off.'

'What's your GP said about this?

'Doc said I had to expect mobility problems with advancing years. Mind you, I'm younger than he is and I see *him* on the golf course. Chap recommended rest and painkillers. Prescribed a course of anti-inflammatory pills. Now these worked while I was taking them, but as soon as I finished the course, all the problems came back.'

'And you went back to your GP?'

'Yes and he set me up with more pills and recommended I see a physio. Asked if I wanted a referral, but I said I'd like to get a private recommendation if possible.'

'OK, before I take a closer look, I'm afraid there's some routine questions to complete' Evan Jones looked quite annoyed.

'You mean even when I'm paying I still have to complete more bloody paperwork!' Martin was taken aback at his visitor's unexpected outburst, but before he could think of what to say, his guest burst into laughter.

'Don't worry, I'm only joking. I deal with damn forms every day of my life and one more isn't going to make any difference.' Evan was compliant in providing all the answers to the standard questionnaire before Martin's examination. After that was completed, Martin asked if his patient had pain now.

'No. Well you see now that's the odd thing. When I sit for a while or bend down to pick up a golf ball, the pain subsides and the strength in my legs returns. Until I start walking about again, that is. I can drive a car all day pain free. In fact that's mostly how I get about at the moment.'

'Do your legs feel less tired if you walk much more slowly?'

'No, I've tried doing that and the tiredness comes on just the same.' Martin showed his patient through to the surgery and did an examination of his lumbar spine and legs, pressing these in places and asking about discomfort. He made his patient sit for a while until pain free, then got him to walk up and down the corridor outside until the heaviness in his legs returned. Finally, Martin asked his patient to return to the consulting room.

'I'm virtually certain you have a condition known as lumbar stenosis.

As we age, the ligaments that hold the individual vertebrae together in our spine swell, particularly in the lower, lumbar region of our spine. This region takes a lot of punishment over the years. These thickened ligaments then press on the nerves controlling our leg muscles at the point where they exit the spinal column, between the vertebrae.

So what's happening is that the signals sent from the brain to move your legs are getting cut off. When you bend over or sit down, your lumbar spine curves and the spaces between the vertebrae open up more so that nerve signals can reach your legs again.' Martin fetched his model of the spine from its niche and bent it to illustrate his point. Evan nodded.

'Yes I can see that. Can anything be done about it?'

'I wouldn't advise to keep taking anti-inflammatory medicines. But, as you say, you should be able to get around by car and you'd even be able to cycle for miles without much difficulty, because you're also in a sitting position. You could consult physiotherapists or chiropractors near your home or work. That would be to book regular manipulation or massage treatment to try to improve movement and flexibility in the lumbar spine. For now I can give you some exercises you can do at home.'

'So a slow process to recovery then?'

'Afraid so, but knowing what the problem is should help you get specialised help.'

'I'm an impatient bugger. Anything you could advise me to do to get me walking without pain quicker - surgery?'

'I'd definitely not go that route!' Martin hesitated.

'There is something I can offer, but you probably won't like it?'

'Wheelchair?'

'Well actually you've got it in one, but you'd need to push it, not sit in it!'

'What?'

'Well, you've told me how bending over gives almost instant relief. Bending to push a wheelchair would get you round the golf course, give you somewhere to sit while waiting for your opponent to tee off and could be adapted to carry your clubs as well.' Evan didn't seem to see either the logic or the intended humour in Martin's suggestion.

'No way would I turn up at my club or anywhere else with a wheelchair. I'd rather steal a supermarket trolley and take that for walks!'

'Well you could buy a couple of those trendy mountain walking sticks and adjust them both to a low height setting!' Now Evan looked really indignant. For a moment Martin wondered if he was going to hit him. Then, just as before, his patient threw back his head and roared with laughter. This went on for so long that Martin started to smile and then chuckle a little in sympathy at the image of this smartly dressed company executive pushing a shopping trolley into a high powered meeting. Finally, with moist eyes, Evan Jones rose and offered his hand.

'You've been more helpful and certainly much more fun than all the docs and specialists I've seen in the last 3 months. Would you like me to pay you now or should I write a cheque for Michael Timles when the Woodlands board meets tomorrow?' The shock of this remark left Martin speechless. Evan looked a little reproachful.

'I guess from the look on your face, Martin, that you don't read your Centre's Annual Report. Well they're generally very boring documents so I don't blame you. Look you, I don't really mind that you don't recognise your board members, but I do care that you're a damn good physio.' Evan moved round the desk whilst still shaking Martin's hand and clapped him on the back.

'Keep up the good work!' Evan shuffled to the door bent double, opened it, turned round to Martin, grinned and waved then set off down the corridor. Moments later, Julie buzzed.

'What on earth did you do to your client Mart? He just left here bent right over!'

As arranged Friday, at 7pm Tina appeared in the Green Dragon. She was wearing a close fitting sleeveless black dress with a contrasting white panel running diagonally from her shoulder to her hip. Her dark brown, almost black hair swept down across half her forehead. As she scanned the bar for Martin, she received many appraising glances, some of which were from men. Spotting her before she saw him, Martin waved her over to the rear bar.

'Hi Tina - this time I've reserved a decent table.' When they were facing each other across the table in one of the Dragon's high backed dining cubicles, Martin asked:

'Where did we get to when I had to rush off so rudely?'

'You were saying you'd lost patience with books on complementary medicine and put them down half-read.' Martin grinned.

'Oh yes; and you said you didn't want to explain Reiki just for me to put *you* down half read too!'

Tina was pleased he had remembered her remark, but disappointed to see from his expression that he clearly hadn't picked up her double meaning. No comment about her new dress either. Here she was again on a date she had effectively engineered herself, yet Martin hadn't picked up her personal interest in him. It seemed any progress on that front would all be down to Reiki. If he ever agreed to try it.

'OK, Martin, I don't want to bore you with things that you may already know. So first I've two questions for *you*. What do *you* think Reiki is and why do you feel it might help you?' Martin wrinkled his forehead to let Tina see he was concentrating. Above all he wanted to show her he was prepared to listen, even if it meant suspending his disbelief in all things alternative.

Tina watched him carefully as he gathered his thoughts to reply. It gave her time to assemble her own explanation. She knew Martin had a scientific and medical background. Most people like him were well aware of reports that, to put it crudely, rubbished alternative therapies. Authoritative publications pointed to the many clinical trials that showed no significant effectiveness for any alternative therapy apart from herbal medicine. And in many instances herbal remedies were really just natural equivalents of prescription drugs of known efficacy such as aspirin from tree bark and many other examples.

But professional alternative therapists all knew that trials of complementary therapies were often difficult to carry out objectively. Serious funding for such investigations was difficult to obtain. The design of some published trials that had shown no benefits were deeply flawed. Alternative therapy was still the poor relation of pharmaceutical medicine and was likely so to remain. Of course, massively funded by a multinational drugs industry, some *conventional* drug trials also suffered from selective reporting, bias and even corrupt practice.

Although Tina could hold her own in this area, she didn't want to get into such technical matters tonight. How Martin answered her question would help her shape her own explanations. Martin might be physically close right now, but in spirit he was still far off and she very much wanted to close that gap. After an almost painfully long interval Martin replied. Wanting to give Tina the impression of recalling his previous college training, in fact he was just repeating what he had read in the local library the day before.

'I forget now where this came up in my studies, Tina, but I think Reiki is a therapeutic practice which originated in Japan in the nineteenth century. It seems to have been the brainchild of one man and subsequently developed by a small number of disciples. It remained a minority, rather mystical practice until some of its adherents took it to the US in the twentieth century.

Not sure whereabouts in the States, but given the speed with which Reiki circulated to the rest of the World from then on, I'd be surprised if it wasn't California. As far as I know, its practitioners work by connecting their clients or patients to some form of natural energy. Either that or they aim to correct badly adjusted personal energy.' Martin paused for a sip of beer. He was quite pleased with his monologue so far.

'I don't think drugs or incantations are involved in Reiki, just a laying on of hands and, presumably, a nice bedside manner. There was also a lot of stuff about Reiki symbols which have their own power or ability to conduct or concentrate some other power, but that's where I became confused, lost interest and stopped following it up.

Honestly, right now I can't see how this system could actually heal people, but its very persistence as a therapy; its growth even, must mean patients and obviously Reiki practitioners, have benefited from it.' Martin had been looking down at the table as he recited all this, but now he looked up at Tina for a reaction. He expected her to be more than a little bit impressed. But Tina didn't comment; she just waited for him to finish, with that half smile of hers hovering on her lips. *Dammit, he was going to be straight with this woman.*

'Look Tina, I'm a physio in healing Centre mostly given over to alternative medicine and I hardly know anything about the other therapies on offer. Worse, because of personal laziness or cynicism or both, I've never bothered to find out. I'm sure that if I was worried that I had an infection or some nagging abdominal pain, I'd go straight round to see my GP. But my present problem is that much of the time I feel disconnected and low. I've few friends at present and no relationship, nor do I feel motivated to look for either. All I'm likely to be prescribed by my GP is a course of antidepressants. I don't believe the NHS has a remedy for my condition and I don't think The Woodlands has one either.'

Up until then Tina felt she had made progress with Martin, but his answer to her two questions told her she had a long way to go. About Reiki; his use of the term "incantation" annoyed her. She felt that he'd said it deliberately to ridicule alternative therapy. And his admission of lack of knowledge about the work of the Woodlands Centre was frankly shocking.

To add insult to injury, he'd generalised his view that the Centre's therapies must be ineffective and by implication, her own work too. She was here at his own invitation; to help him with his problems and had made an exceptional effort that evening with her hair and choice of clothes. Surely it wasn't too much, even from Martin, to hear that she looked nice? After all, she had received appraising glances from others when she came in and unlike a lot of the customers in the Dragon, Martin was straight.

Fortunately at that moment their food arrived. By the time they'd sorted out sauces and cutlery, some of Tina's irritation with Martin had subsided and appetite was beginning to replace annoyance. When she returned to their earlier discussion, she was ready to defend her profession and take up the bigger challenge of enticing her companion. At least he was still listening.

'There's not much wrong with your very brief history of Reiki, but as with conventional medicine, alternative practice also changes to reflect advancing knowledge. The popular press and even many more serious publications tend to dust off and re-run past prejudices if editors feel that these will engage reader attention and increase sales. A few Luddites even distrust the *medical* profession; look at all the anti-vaccination crowd. Worse; the Green movement deliberately employ emotive labels like "Frankenfood" to attack novel nutritional products that have many real advantages. They attempt to win their dubious cases through spreading a toxic mixture of misinformation and hysteria. Sadly, they have been quite successful at holding back progress so far.'

Martin was taken aback. He'd been expecting Tina to discuss her work, but this sounded like the introduction to a seminar. He wondered if he should be taking notes. He was trying to work out where on earth this was leading and how it was relevant, but at the same time, totally impressed with

Tina's knowledge. He hoped she wasn't going on to imply he was a Luddite just because he was cynical about alternative medicine. But Tina was already starting a new thread.

'What do you know about tribal medicine?' Martin didn't know much, but he had various snippets of information; Voodoo, strange rituals and shamans capable of effecting miraculous cures or dire curses.

'You're not going to tell me Reiki is based on black magic are you?' Tina ignored this jibe.

'Tribal medicine is presently an intense field of study both by pharmaceutical companies, who are looking for new drug leads and clinical psychiatrists who want deeper understanding of the brain.' Tina paused to take a sip of her wine. She had quite deliberately been talking about subjects that, even if new to Martin, he would probably accept. Now she was going to challenge him a bit.

'What all mainstream therapists are coming to accept is the very strong connection between state of mind and health. Everyone agrees that in humans this connection evolved back in deep time.'

Tina sipped her wine again, but Martin had left his drink untouched. Tina had his full attention as she continued.

'Who knows what pathways exist in *our* unconscious minds or what they are linked to? And who can really deny that they might be tapped into through alternative practices?'

Martin was was suddenly conscious that his jaw had dropped and quickly shut it as she went on.

'The astonishing quality and location of cave paintings of prey animals suggests that early humans made an *association* between the physical and mental worlds. Didn't someone say "What thin partitions sense from thought divide?". The body, its actions and the environment would all have been thought of as *spiritual* back then. The primitive beliefs and rituals of early man would probably have had a much stronger effect on their health and well being than now.

Back then, the simplistic ways early man attempted to communicate these things seems like primitive magic to us now, but it would have been seen very differently then. It's a fact that in primitive societies shamans can bring about strong physical as well as psychological changes in their patients.'

Tina paused, looked pointedly at Martin and deliberately took a very deep breath.

'I believe that practises like Reiki, which critics dismiss as ineffective, or at best as giving rise to a "placebo" response, attempts to harmoniously reconnect the mind with the body and its environment. A major problem with their wide acceptance is that our terminology hasn't kept pace with present day understanding. Many of us are still using ancient names and symbols from the Far East when the understanding of physiology and physiology was primitive.

Sadly, alternative practitioners like to stick with these archaic names and ideas because they impress customers who have exhausted the therapies offered by conventional psychiatric clinics or GP surgeries. But it's time now for quite a lot of "alternative practice" to enter the medical mainstream!'

Tina took another sip of wine and waited for Martin to speak. She considered that she'd been pretty ingenious with her explanation. She had been fair to the *principles* of her alternative profession, but had avoided discussion of its *practice*. But she was already certain that what Martin was missing was the same thing as herself; a fulfilling and sensual connection with someone, leading ultimately to a satisfying long term relationship.

It was hardly rocket science: everyone needed a life companion with an open mind. One where there was the potential to develop a shared vision of the future. In her case she had a subtext; she needed a partner for her new business ideas. Whatever Martin's reservations about alternative medicine, she was confident *her* novel alternative therapy could address his *actual* needs. Anyway, she fancied him in spite of his present depression and negative outlook. That would make her efforts to help him rewarding for her as well.

Martin's brain was attempting to fit all Tina's revelations into a coherent picture. He couldn't find fault with much she'd said. Yet what she'd told him was completely outside his expectations. He felt a new respect for his previously ignored Centre colleague. It seemed that she was not only an attractive young woman, she was also a bright one and presented a compelling case for her practice, even though she hadn't actually told him what she did. He made up his mind. After all it was he that had asked if she could help him.

'Phew, I can't argue with any of that because it would take me a couple of days to get my head round it all. You're not an external lecturer at the Uni by any chance are you?'

Tina built her half smile into a whole one. That was probably the highest compliment she was likely to be paid that evening.

'You know Tina, I'd convinced myself that Reiki was all just spiritual stuff - forces that can't be explained by science.'

'There are more things in heaven and earth, Martin, than are dreamt of in your philosophy'

'That's from Shakespeare, Tina - apart from the Martin bit! You know that's so strange; his plays were one of my obsessions at school. I'm amazed that you chose *that* quote out of the blue'

'Would you consider it outrageous if I said I somehow *knew* that?'

'If you hadn't already begun to undermine my prejudices about alternative therapy, I'd say it was just coincidence.'

'And what do you think now?' Martin hesitated. To his surprise he was enjoying Tina's company and felt he should try to be a bit better company himself.

'I used to be uncertain, but now I'm not so sure!'

Tina smiled, at last she'd found a small breach in the curtain walls Martin had thrown up round his mental stronghold. Time to pop the question.

'So you're willing to agree to a course of therapy with me? Not at the Woodlands, obviously?'

'Yes Tina' he grinned at her. 'Your place or mine?' At least he'd tidied up his flat.

Tina grinned back with what she intended to be a cheeky smile. Her fish had finally landed on the riverbank. Hopefully it would soon be gasping for breath, when she would have to decide whether to keep it or throw it back.

'Mine of course.'

CHAPTER TWO

Timles

On the following Saturday, Martin was due to see the Woodland's owner; Michael Timles. As his boss lived near the Centre, he decided to walk and do some hard thinking about his situation. It might help calm his nerves. He passed the front of a recruitment agency specialising in professional and technical jobs. That made him feel even more uneasy. He had to keep working, but what was the point of being a physio at the Woodlands? In spite of Tina's surprising analysis of alternative therapy, Martin doubted he could trust either the processes or the practitioners. He told himself again it was a bad idea to have taken the contract. He ought to have tried for a post attached to one of the regional hospitals.

He went over his chat with Tina in the Green Dragon again. Her surprising insight had impressed him, but in the cold light of day, he was inclined to give up on the whole crazy notion. If alternative therapy depended mostly on belief, his scepticism would surely prevent it helping. He might be better off seeing an accredited psychotherapist. At least they worked in mainstream medicine.

Martin turned into Timles's road. On the front wall of the first house a large tabby cat was watching him. Although the animal appeared totally relaxed, the physiotherapist in Martin noted the tension in the cat's haunches. *Ready for fight or flight depending on what I do as I pass* Martin thought. *Could I ever be so apparently at ease and yet so watchful at every moment?*

Soon he reached a large modern house set well back from the road. The long front garden was filled with tall shrubs interspersed with paving and gravel. Number 94; Timles's place. Martin picked his way through the shrubbery and pressed the doorbell. Almost immediately there was an electrical buzz and the door opened a fraction. A voice called out:

'I've been expecting you. Come straight in - my room's on the left.' Martin entered, but hesitated at the open door at the end of the hall.

'Come on in.' a friendly voice called. The room was comfortably furnished with easy chairs and a desk in front of a wide patio window. A tall man with silver-grey hair stood up and came over to greet him and extended his hand.

'Hello Martin. Noura has told me all about you. Pleased to meet you at last. Take a pew.' He indicated one of the easy chairs and when Martin was seated, turned to leave the room.

'I'll join you in a moment. Coffee?' Martin nodded. Through the patio window behind the desk, the garden appeared to stretch away towards a line of trees above which were wooded hills. Martin blinked. This was a housing estate not far from the city centre. He decided it must be an illusion created by clever landscaping. Martin turned back to look at the empty easy chair in front of him. The Centre's owner seemed reassuringly friendly, Martin wondered how he should address him. Timles' voice came from somewhere close at hand. 'By the way, please call me Michael.' When his host returned and they were both settled either side of a small coffee table, Timles leaned back in his easy chair. He pressed his hands together so that the fingertips rested just under his chin. Like a steeple, Martin thought.

'Well Martin, I know a little bit about you, but I imagine you know rather less about me?' Timles waited for Martin's nod.

'I took over the Woodlands Centre 10 years ago to indulge an ambition concerning integrated medicine. I also wanted to take the opportunity to "run my own show".' Timles paused.

'You will know the feeling I guess?' Martin nodded uncertainly. Timles continued.

'Before that I was a senior manager in the pharmaceutical industry. I suppose I had some rather idealistic notions when the Woodlands opened for business. But it was tough at first; dealing with the minefield of new regulations and gaining sufficient business connections and contacts to secure the place's future.' Timles watched Martin whilst he sipped his coffee. Martin was struck by the unusual grey ring round his irises. It made his look seem particularly penetrating. Timles continued:

'As you know the day-to-day management and other administrative matters are handled by Noura. Very well too, I should add. She's quite a formidable lady don't you think?'

'Noura's pretty efficient.' Timles smiled at this.

'So what does the Woodlands represent today? I believe in most cases our role is to heal the mind. And having done that the mind gets on with doing whatever is necessary to repair or reinvigorate the body. We don't yet know what it is the mind does to make its owner better. When we do know I imagine the Woodlands Centre will look more like the sickbay on Starship Enterprise. Our therapists will be able to wave little widgets over your head and you will be firing on all cylinders within 24 hours.' Here Timles gave an ambiguous smile so that Martin was unsure whether the last remark was intended as a joke or contained an element of truth.

'Now we come to you and your physiotherapy practice at the Centre.' Timles hesitated for a moment. Martin thought: *OK, so now we finally get to the real purpose of this meeting.*

'Clearly Noura is nervous about your work at the centre and when Noura is nervous she usually calls me. So that is *how* you happen to be here, but that is not *why* you're here.' Here Timles paused again. Martin thought: *I bet he's had lots of practice at dealing with under-performing staff as a senior manager in Big Pharma.'*

'I know from the practice reports and a number of our patient's letters that you're good at what you do. I also know from various sources that you enjoy what you do, or at least did do when you first came to us.' Martin was now wondering what Noura had actually told the Woodlands owner. Timles seemed to be skirting round the real issues that Noura had criticised him for back at the Centre. But Timles finally got to the point.

'I'm guessing that you have concerns that are coming to Woodlands with you and are continuing to demand your attention during your working day instead of sitting patiently in the waiting area until you go home. These worries are interfering with your normally commendable practice. You don't share your worries with Noura or anyone else at the Centre, so although support might be available, you don't give your colleagues a chance to help you.

Probably because you don't believe there's any proof that the alternative therapies offered at the Woodlands actually work. Unless, as I've said, our patients believe wholeheartedly that they will. Now would that be a fair assessment of the situation? If so, then I hope we can discuss your problems in confidence and see what might be done.' Martin thought about this. His feelings were mixed.

On the one hand he was a bit indignant Timles was inviting him to talk about things he felt were personal and private. On the other hand he wanted to keep his post at the Woodlands. That worry had been uppermost in his mind on his way there. The great attraction of working as a self-employed therapist was freedom from the direct supervision most people laboured under during their working lives. But of course, he was still professionally accountable for his practice and he was also under contract to the Centre, though he didn't remember the exact provisions of that. But he couldn't disagree with Timles's assessment. Frankly speaking, he was more than a little concerned about his present mental state.

The demeanour of this man Timles was quite a surprise. Martin had expected more of an inquisition; even to get a warning about his work. But the Centre's owner seemed completely relaxed and at pains to put Martin at ease. He suspected the truth was that Timles's calm, affable front probably masked a quick mind and an ability to focus intensely upon issues and take effective action.

Something about the lack of any of the normal physical signs of tension in Timles's body made him think of concert pianists. They were individuals with fingers that flew with exquisite precision over the keys, yet whose minds were completely relaxed. Music flowed directly from its mysterious stores in their brains to their finger tips, with no conscious thought or nervous worry to interrupt the flow. Timles's voice broke into Martin's reverie.

'Perhaps your silence means I'm experiencing a little of what some of your patients have reported?' It was a mild rebuke, but Timles's eyes were smiling as well as quizzical. Martin was still thinking about this when Timles continued.

'Are you still wrestling with the concerns that brought you here or trying to work out why you're here anyway?' Timles paused, then;

'I'd like to understand your problems and offer help if I can.' Martin started. Timles seemed friendly enough and he was clearly very perceptive. But help? Probably he needed a shrink. But psychiatrists were expensive and if he lost his contract with the Woodlands Centre, he would be even less able to afford one. He gathered his thoughts with some difficulty. For now it would probably be best to go along with whatever this unusual business owner suggested.

'Sorry; yes of course you're right. I do have things worrying me and I admit that I've let my mind wander when I should have been focused on my clients' needs. I probably should see a counsellor or psychotherapist. Are you going to read me the riot act?'

'I'd prefer to try and help you. Would you like me to do that? And as for professional counselling, if I can help, we might save you money, keep your present difficulties "in house" and you can continue to work with us at the Centre.' Martin was sufficiently surprised by this offer that he tried to back away.

'You haven't heard what my difficulties are yet and anyway, suppose I did choose to see a specialist, then any problems I have would be kept confidential.'

'The confidentiality offered by registered practitioners only means them not talking to your friends and family which, sadly, in many cases would be one of the most helpful things they could do. They all talk quite freely to their professional colleagues and their spouses which probably doesn't help at all, as you probably know.'

'I don't have a spouse to talk to.'

'Nor do you talk to your colleagues at the Woodlands, as I'm well aware. So what's different about you?' Martin stopped himself responding negatively. This man was clearly not going to bawl him out for under performing and he was offering to help.

'Are you a professional councillor too?'

'I do have training and experience in that area, but it's no longer part of my working life.'

'I'm not sure where to begin.'

'I don't want you to begin now. I only wanted to see if you were prepared to talk to me. If you are, then you need to go away and do something relaxing and distracting over the rest of the weekend.' Timles turned and opened a small book from his desk and flicked through its pages.

'You should organise your thoughts so you know how to start describing your problems, then call me to arrange a visit. And don't leave it too long Martin.' Timles turned back and Martin nodded agreement.

'What's your email address?'

'I only use the Centre email.' Timles registered surprise.

'Well give me your mobile number in case I need to call before you visit. Mine's on this card.' Timles handed him a Woodlands business card.

'Oh, and as we aren't emailing each other, I've printed up a mentoring plan and some thoughts for you to take away and read. Timles handed Martin an envelope.

'Just do whatever you do this weekend and don't open this until Monday.'

'Any particular reason for the secrecy?'

'I want you to relax this weekend and not spend it trying to worry about our next meeting.' Timles paused.

'Listen, Why don't you ask our Tina for a Reiki session? For once just give one of our alternative therapies the benefit of your doubt instead of doubting their benefit.' Martin decided not to say anything about his recent conversation with Tina.

'Tina is unlikely to consider me a suitable case for treatment.'

'Because of your scepticism? You might be surprised. At least you'd be distracted from those negative thoughts of yours for a time. OK Martin, please give me a call early next week to fix up our meeting. You can see yourself out. Oh, before you go, do you like my view?' Martin stared at him before replying.

'Yes, very much. But having walked here through a maze of residential streets, I can't quite see how it can be real – is it clever landscaping?' Timles appeared pleased with Martin's answer and turned himself to look at his garden while he replied.

'An open viewpoint is very important to me, but you're right, it is an illusion. Remember, Martin, that things are not always as they seem. We can't change things that are outside our control, but we can change our perception of them.' Timles turned back to Martin.

'There's so much emphasis now on knowing and understanding other people or things. That's important, of course, but the secret of a full and satisfying life involves knowing and understanding *ourselves*. Few master this fully, but you will recognise such people when you meet them.' Timles looked sadly at Martin, who just looked blank. *What was the Centre's owner talking about?*

'Don't forget to call me next week to make an appointment.' Timles rose and extended his hand.

'Goodbye Martin.' Martin closed the front door. Outside the street was busy with cars and a group of men in high vis. jackets were clustered round a manhole. As Martin passed by the hole, he saw a rat's nest of cables; the networks that linked these homes to just about everywhere else on the planet.

Still puzzled by the rural view from Timles's window, he glanced between the properties and looked up a few side streets. In the distance between buildings he could only make out clusters of high-rise apartments. No woods and certainly no uplands were visible. Martin shook his head several times quickly and walked to the end of the street. The tabby cat was still in the same place on the garden wall. This time it watched him without any sign of tension. Martin found the sight somehow comforting.

Not wanting to go back to the silence of his flat, Martin walked to The Woodlands Clinic, intending to look for a book on Reiki in its small library. Next time he met Tina *forewarned is forearmed*, he thought. There was a single car in the Clinic's park; Tina's. Martin let himself in, locking the doors behind him. As he headed down the corridor to his own room, Tina's door was propped open and she was putting books and other items into a large cardboard box in the corridor. He walked down to her room.

'Hi Tina. I wasn't expecting to meet anyone here on Saturday. But I'm glad you're here. You know, I was thinking about you before I came in just now.'

'Really? Tell me more, I'm all ears.'

'Oh, it's nothing dramatic.' Martin eyed the huge box she was packing and made a decision. Look, if I cart your box wherever you're taking it, can we arrange that Reiki session we talked about in the pub?' Tina looked a bit shaken for a moment but soon recovered her usual mischievous grin.

'Well, this is a pleasant surprise. I wasn't really expecting to see you again - socially that is.' Martin looked uncomfortable.

'Well I did have second thoughts about Reiki this morning, but I visited the Centre's owner, Michael Timles, and he's recommended I see you for a session; a professional one.' Martin hesitated.

'To be honest Tina, I went to him certain I'd be kicked out, but he seemed to take an interest in me and wants to do some mentoring or other of his own.'

'Oh I see . . . Are you working in the Centre this afternoon, Martin?' Tina was hurriedly closing the flaps of the box as she spoke, giving Martin the feeling that she didn't want him to see its contents. He thought: *I bet she's been making copies of some of the magazine articles in the library.*

'No, I just came in to borrow a book. What about you?' When Tina didn't reply and looked uncomfortable he reckoned he'd guessed correctly.

'Look, if you're doing some "Reiki" on the Centre's photocopier, don't feel embarrassed. I've spent enough time here to know everyone uses it out of hours. I justify it to myself as a perk to offset the fees the Centre charges me.' Tina flashed him a grateful smile, but didn't confirm or deny his assumption. She nodded her head toward the floor.

'To answer your first question, yes, I'd really appreciate a lift to the car with my boxes.' Martin followed her gesture and saw three more boxes by her desk as large as the one Tina had been filling when he entered.

'Goodness, Tina. Are you leaving us?'

'Would you miss me if I was? I think the most we've ever spoken to each other over the last few years was on Monday night in the pub.'

'Of course I'd miss you. You're probably the sanest alternative practitioner in this place.'

'That's a back-handed compliment if I ever heard one. But to answer your other question; tell me, are you really serious about wanting a Reiki session?'

'Oh yes, really.'

'Well, you'd need a proper course, not just a single consultation. Just as you do with your own clients, we'd have a discussion, then I'd devise a number of treatment sessions based on our initial chat. You'd be unlikely to get any benefit otherwise. I don't think it would be a good idea for me to treat you at the Woodlands, though. Perhaps at my place after work or at the weekend. Are you up for that?' Martin shrugged.

'Timles thought it would help.'

'But *you* have your doubts. Did he give you his views on what really underpins the work of this Centre?'

'You mean "your faith will heal you" and all that?'

'Pretty much. So how am I supposed to help you Martin, let alone heal you, unless you have some degree of faith in what I do?' Martin just looked at her while he struggled to think of a reply to that. Tina saw he looked a bit crestfallen as well as being temporarily at a loss for words. She softened her approach:

'Look, give me a hand with this lot to my car first.' Martin was relieved she had backed off from challenging his cynicism. But Tina had made her point. If he was going to make any progress at the Woodlands, he had to curb his hostility towards alternative practice. Tina was being friendly and he was short of friends right now. When Martin had lifted the last box into her car boot, Tina sat in the car and passed him a card taken from the glove compartment. My address; are you free in the evening a week tomorrow for our first session, Mart? Martin nodded.

'All right. See you at my place then and please try to leave your prejudices at home.' She closed the window and drove out of the Woodlands car park. Martin looked down at the card in his hand. It was an extremely smart business card with a butterfly graphic.

IMARGO

Tina Elves

Martin recognised the address given under the business name was one of the most upmarket areas of Tamford. The strange name rang a bell in his mind. Still in range of the Woodlands WiFi, he looked it up on the Free Dictionary on his mobile:, one of the few Websites he used at the Centre.

Imargo: a sexually mature adult form produced after metamorphosis.

So Tina had a business apart from her work at the Woodlands. Slipping Tina's card into his wallet, he wondered just what sort of metamorphosis Tina was proposing to work on him.

CHAPTER THREE
Pete

At loose end Sunday, Martin attempted to tidy his flat. This mostly involved relocating abandoned books and magazines to shelves and cupboards. His justification for this was that it was taking too long to find things. But at the back of his mind there was the possibility that Tina might ask to visit his flat for one of her Reiki sessions. Bringing order to his cluttered quarters was going to be a long job, but now there was a motivation for making a start. Under some magazines he found the business card given to him a few days ago in the Dragon:

Peter Swales BSc.
InterconNet.

Here was an option more interesting than housework. On impulse Martin rang the mobile number given. After a delay so long Martin was about to drop the connection, a sleepy voice answered.

'Pete here; who's that?'

'Hi, it's Martin Wright. We met in the Green Dragon and talked about the Web? You gave me your card and said to call if I was interested in learning to use it effectively.'

'Oh yeah, that's right. Er..did you apply to the Uni library for an external user's card?'

'No, I haven't had an opportunity.' Well, to be honest, I've only just found your card under a pile of papers in my flat.'

'Are you interested in taking up my offer then?'

'Yes Peter, I'd like to do that.'

'It's *Pete*. And you're still intent on looking for hot sex, sorry, I mean lasting love on-line?'

'I'd like to learn to walk before I run, Pete.' There was a brief pause before Pete replied.

'OK Martin, I'll help. Look, I'd better level with you first. My research project is to develop a special networking app. I call it an AWA that's Associative Web App. That's what I going to show you how to use.' This meant nothing to Martin.

'OK . .'

'Right, so the price for my help will be to be kept in touch with your experience using my app. That and a couple of beers when we discuss your progress in the Green Dragon.'

'That's all right with me. Thanks Pete.'

'Would you like to make a start today?'

'Excuse me?'

'If you can get over to the Green Dragon for a quick pint at lunchtime, I can take you back to our lab to get you started. But you must promise to register as an external user as soon as possible otherwise you'll get me into trouble with the admin people. I suppose you still haven't got your own computer to connect to Internet?'

'Not at home, no.'

'Well sometime you should think seriously about that. I still can't believe I'm talking to a physiotherapist without a laptop or tablet.'

'Perhaps you can recommend something?'

'Sure, OK. Now do we have a deal?'

'Sorry?'

'Are we meeting up in the Dragon in an hour's time?'

'Oh yes. See you there Pete.'

'Ciao Martin.' After lasagne, a tuna jacket potato and two pints of Theakston's Best Bitter, Martin walked to the university campus with Peter and followed him through the security doors of one of the faculty buildings. Peter led him to a first floor room and pulled up a spare chair for him in front of an impressively wide computer monitor. Martin glanced round the relatively cramped space.

'Is this the computer lab Pete? It seems very small.'

'Oh no, it's where I mostly work though and another Ph.D. student - Steve - also uses this room. Although it's pretty quiet on Sunday, it's not a good idea for me to take you into the main computer centre terminal room while you aren't an official user. So you're just here today informally as my guest should anyone ask. Once we get you registered and up and running on-line you could access the facilities I'll show you from outside the University. But as I'd like to use your efforts as part of my research, I'd appreciate it if you access the Internet as much as possible in the Computer Centre lab or my office.

I'll clear that with the admin people once you're properly registered. You'd get the benefit of very fast connections and advice from me or our sysop and I'd be able to monitor some aspects of your on-line sessions - with your permission of course. If things became very hot, I mean rather personal, you'd be able to keep your communication completely private. To be honest, you could go to an Internet Café or get a cheap laptop or tablet at home to start dating, but you'd be spending a lot of fruitless time on-line. I can help you cut to the chase.' But Martin was still a few sentences behind Pete.

'Excuse me..*sysop*?' Martin felt a slight panic starting. He was beginning to like Peter a lot, but he didn't want to show his general ignorance of computers.

'Oh, sorry Mart, geek speak for *computer systems operator*. That's Tuula Pippi. Now she *is* one hot bit of stuff. Finnish girl, over here to read for a higher degree, hone her English and escape from her employers; Kosketecessa. I suspect the latter's the main reason. When you next visit the computing centre you won't be able to mistake her; very short with ash blond hair and hot lips. She can help you do anything on the 'net; that is if she has any interest in what you're trying to do and you can concentrate on what she's saying, when she's close at hand.' Peter winked suggestively at him. Martin was struck by Peter's extremely politically incorrect way of referring to the opposite sex. But despite disapproving, he found his curiosity aroused. He tried to steer the conversation onto safer ground.

'Will you get a post in the Computer Science department, like Tuula when you've got your Ph.D.?'

'What? Oh, I see - no; there's no openings for new lecturers. And neither would Tuula for that matter; she's paying her way here by covering for our permanent systems operator, whilst he's doing a sabbatical in industry. The Uni gets paid by her company and so can support a temporary sysop. Tuula's so good, she can easily do systems support as well as her own research.' Martin's curiosity now got the better of him.

'You know a lot about her; are you two an item?' Peter grinned widely.

'I should be so lucky. No. I'm focused on my research; no time for women and I don't think for a moment Tuula would have time for me. Not in that way, at least. Her research here is in the same field as mine - social networks. By the way, did you know how the most famous social network of all - Face Book - got started? Martin shook his head.

'Well it was a programme running on Uni networks for students to rate the attractiveness of other female students: now look at it. A business valued in the billions of dollars! Anyway, about Tuula. We kind of collaborate and compete at the same time; but that's as far as it goes. OK, now let's get you up and running on the 'Net. First off, we've got to give you a valid reason for coming into the Computer lab. The only one that's going to pass scrutiny by admin, should they bother to check, would be to act as one of my subjects for my social networks research. Next, we'll need an email address for you.' He looked at Martin and grinned.

'We'll definitely *not* be using your work email. Do you have a personal email, Mart?'

'I did have one when Helena and I were on broadband.'

'That will have gone when you cancelled your subscription. We'll pick you one up free. Would you like me to do that bit for you?'

'OK by me. I'd only hold things up.' Peter swung his chair round to his keyboard and opened a public email programme. After a few failed attempts to register **Martin.wright** and various alternatives, he turned back to Martin.

'How old are you Mart?'

'35.'

'**Martphysio35** OK for you - or would you like something sexier?' Peter looked round and moved his shoulders suggestively.

'Oh, no go ahead with that. I don't imagine it matters.'

'That's good, you see with all the junk mail that's around, people often make snap judgements about you based on your email address. Best to have a neutral one.' Peter continued to enter information.

'OK, that's done. Now it's over to you.' With a sinking feeling, Martin edged his office chair in front of the screen.

'What do you want me to do?' Peter brought his own chair back to

Martin's side and guided him to his new email box.

'OK, Mart. You can't log onto the university network yet. Not until you complete their application form - would you believe they still use *paper*?' Peter reached into a drawer as cluttered as the desktop and handed Martin an A4 sheet. Fill this in whilst you're here, I'll sign to say you're working with me and drop it into the library. But for now let's assume you've done that. You'll also need a photo to display on InterconNet.' Peter pulled out his mobile. 'Smile please.' Before Martin could protest his picture was taken. Peter looked at it briefly, then told Martin it would appear later on the network when he first used it.

'I suppose you'll also want me to get accounts set up on Face Book, Twitter and dating sites.' Martin adopted an exaggerated expression of disgust.

'I wouldn't waste your time hanging out in such places. We've moved on from the Internet's Stone Age. Here we're at the leading edge of the connected world. With quick movements on a second small keypad Peter, he brought up a computer window displaying the same graphic as on the business card Martin had been given in the Green Dragon.

Welcome to InterconNet

Peter gave his widest grin so far. 'OK Mart. Now, let's get you started!

Following Peter's advice, Martin presented himself at the Uni library reception desk the following Saturday morning; a time, Peter told him, when most students were sleeping off the effects of Friday night. The desk was always manned at that hour by a part time library assistant and not too many questions were likely to be asked about his registration.

Just as Peter suggested, very few people were present. The petite Chinese girl on reception was evidently unfamiliar with the required procedure for registering visitors. She searched though several pigeon holes, coming back after each hunt to restudy the business card Martin had placed tentatively in front of her. Eventually she returned with a numbered envelope and a library receipt.

Martin signed, paid the modest subscription fee, thanked her and walked over to sit in one of the study cubicles. Inside the envelope there was a booklet on the rules and requirements for external users of the library and university computer network, a couple of plastic membership cards and a short letter addressed to "Martine" Wright. Cursing mildly under his breath, Martin returned to the library counter. 'Look, there's been an error. These are in the wrong name I'm afraid.' He put down the letter on the counter and handed one of the cards to the assistant, who peered at it intently.

'You *not* Marteen White?'

'No, I mean yes: my name's *Martin* Wright.' The assistant's oriental eyes narrowed even further.

'You a *diffewent* Marteen White?' The Chinese girl returned the plastic card quizzically. Irritated, Martin stared at it. Above the "University of Tamford, External Library User" was his correct name.

'Ah, OK, its all right. Sorry; my name's spelt wrongly on the letter, that's all.' Feeling stupid, Martin picked up his letter from the counter and retreated. He could imagine the eyes of the library assistant following him all the way to the exit.

Rather nervous after his library experience, Martin crossed the campus to the Computer Science Department. But the outside and computer room doors yielded obediently to the key card Peter had given him. The room was empty apart from one workstation occupied by a skinny man with a ginger beard. The space around his computer monitor was cluttered with empty plastic sandwich containers and drink cans. From his dishevelled appearance he looked as if he had been there all night. Martin acknowledged him in a deliberately confident tone. The man responded: "Hi", but didn't look up from his computer screen.

Martin settled at one of the workstations. It was his first time on his own, confronted by unfamiliar hardware. He took a deep breath, anticipating abject failure. Peter had told him that InterconNet was pretty self-explanatory and shown him the basics. But part of Peter's deal with him was apparently to see how he got on with minimal coaching.

As Peter explained: "I need to make this programme as user friendly as possible. To do that I need other people's feedback. Email me your complaints, but don't put any comments on the Web. My programme is experimental and confidential!". Peter had said even Face Book with its hundreds of millions of users had become overly complex and many first time users struggled. And many appeared to be unaware that they were sometimes giving away very personal information to all and sundry.

The University network accepted him and Martin copied the procedure Peter had shown him to log on to InterconNet. A few moments later, a small window opened containing a grinning image of Peter Swales and the text message: *Hi Martin, glad you made it. Welcome aboard. Enjoy . .Pete.*

Martin grinned, uttered an involuntary "yes" and made a small air punch. Then he looked up self consciously to check whether the only other occupant of the room had heard him. Apparently not; Ginger Beard was still lost in intense contemplation of his own monitor. Relieved, he looked back at his own screen. Peter's welcome message had disappeared. Now a form was asking for further information. For what seemed like the rest of that morning Martin answered questions on every aspect of his background and personality.

This tedious exercise was relieved from time to time by the appearance of a cartoon character; Peter's grinning face coupled to a squat metal spring. Text appeared next to this apparition which announced:"I'm Slinky; if you have any questions, just ask and I'll try to help". Martin warmed to Peter's fun and typed: "Where does your name come from, Slinky?" Slinky replied: "Actually it was the name of a 60's children's toy, but it's also like the phrase 'social link'. Between you and me, Pete thinks using InterconNet is child's play. See what you think".

More intriguing was the diagram which was beginning to form at the top of the screen as Martin supplied more and more information. Graphic circles and squares were gradually appearing on the display. Martin soon recognised the pattern as the logo on Peter's business card. In its centre was a square labelled "Martin Wright". As Martin continued to answer questions about himself, the surrounding graphics altered in appearance. Discs and squares came and went. Although many of the shapes were connected by lines, no line coupled his own square into the developing network around him. Finally he clicked the form's DONE button. The screen cleared to an animation of an hour glass through which virtual sand was slowly falling. A few minutes later the InterconNet diagram reappeared, now with more graphics. Now his own square was linked to two nearby shapes; a square and a disc.

Martin clicked on his own square and the picture taken by Peter appeared above a column of text displaying the answers he had completed. He next clicked the square linked to his own. Peter Swales's grinning face appeared in a window above what seemed to be a short CV. Martin glanced briefly at this, then turned his attention to the other graphic linked to his own. There were only two types of graphics in the InterconNet map; squares and circles.

It was by now obvious that the squares represented males so the discs must be females. He moved the mouse pointer over the disc next to his square. A name appeared. It was is ex partner; Helena. Martin moved the pointer away without without clicking on it. He moved the pointer over other squares and discs. Names appeared that meant nothing to him. He clicked on some experimentally, but nothing happened. He typed "Why does nothing show when I click on other network users graphics?". Slinky replied: "You're new and InterconNet hasn't finished screening you yet. Try again later". Slinky produced a noise like Zebidee from *The Magic Roundabout*.

Martin hovered his pointer over the nearest unconnected graphic to his own; a grey disc. The name "Anne Eres" appeared. Martin clicked. This time a picture was displayed accompanied by a few lines of text. Martin stared at the image of a girl with short brown hair and a striking, rounded face. The picture was in soft focus. Something about her face was compelling and the physiotherapist in Martin tried to work out what it was.

After a moment he decided that it was unusually symmetrical. Normally people had slightly different tensions in their facial muscles so that left and right hand eyes, mouth, cheeks or neck were different. Anne's mouth was almost straight, yet her expression suggested gentle mirth. Martin covered the eyes. The remaining features became neutral. He covered the mouth. The eyes were clear and bright but expressionless. He lifted his hand away and the girl once again smiled mildly, but warmly out of the screen. 'La Gioconda' he muttered involuntarily, thinking of the enigmatic portrait by Leonardo Da Vinci.

'What was that?' Martin looked up. Ginger Beard was standing up clutching an untidy sheaf of papers and staring at him.

'Oh nothing - just muttering to myself.' Ginger Beard came closer.

'You're running Peter Swales's InterconNet programme, aren't you?'

Martin stared at him. Peter had told him his sessions would be confidential and secure.

'How do you know?'

'Peter's bored everyone rigid for weeks trying to sign people up to test his software. I was running it in a window on my workstation when you came in. The programme shows how many people are logged in. I was the only one logged in until you suddenly shouted "yes!"'

'I was talking to myself just now because I was rather taken by someone in his network.' Ginger beard nodded slowly.

'I've finished for today. Need some sleep. May I look?' Without waiting for an answer he came round to Martin's workstation and bent down to look at the screen.

'Fancy her do you?' he asked Martin. When Martin didn't reply he continued:

'An Avatar; don't get too serious about her!'

'Anne Ava Tarr?, so Eres not her real name then? Are all the names in this programme invented ones?'

'No, no; that image is an *avatar*. You're not looking at a real person, but a computer generated face - a pretty good one in this case. Could be *based* on an real individual, of course. And as far the names in Peter's InterconNet database go, some will be real, others pseudonyms; just like on the wider Web. Mind you, Peter's software makes a good stab at rejecting false IDs by a proprietary cross - referencing algorithm, data mining and interrogation of meta information.'

'Sorry?'

'His programme checks names and descriptions for consistency across the Internet.'

'Oh.'

'I haven't seen you in the Computer lab before. Are you registered for a degree?'

'No. Actually, I'm a physiotherapist working at the Woodlands Centre. Martin Wright. I'm registered as an external user. Pete Swales invited me to use his programme in return for monitoring my progress - I think he wants to follow what I do as part of his Ph.D. work.' Ginger Beard was quiet for a moment. He looked rather annoyed.

'OK, that figures. Look, I'm often in here weekends. If you want any help when Peter's not around just ask me - I'm Chris Johns, by the way. If you're here in the evening, ask Tuula for help. She's our sysop. There's not much she doesn't know about programming for the Internet and she's a *real girl*, if that interests you, not like Anne here! Incidentally, as you're an external user, I'm surprised you aren't using one of the library workstations. Normally this suite is for staff and registered students only.'

'Pete said logging in here means he can monitor what I'm doing with his programme. Apparently Pete's cleared it with his supervisor.' Chris grinned.

'I doubt whether either of those statements are true. But you're probably better off working down here. There's more support available and there's nearly always people hogging the terminals in the library. Why don't you log in at work or at home?'

'Web access at work is policed by a dragon called Noura and I haven't got Internet access at home.' Chris stared at Martin in evident surprise. Professionals with no Web access seemed to him to be a contradiction in terms.

'Well then, the Uni it has to be. Good to meet you Martin. Got to get some kip. Bye for now.' Martin turned his attention back to the monitor. He stared again at the attractive face of Anne Eres. After Chris's dismissive comment, his first impressions now made sense. Her face and possibly even her name too weren't real and he experienced a feeling of disappointment. Somewhere, he thought he had seen that face before. But that was probably because it might be, as Chris had suggested, a synthesis based on a real person.

He read the accompanying text. This was very short. It stated that Anne had joined InterconNet to offer psychotherapy services to members. Apparently she did not aim to meet her clients face to face, but worked with them entirely on-line but, in emergency circumstances, by 'phone. For a limited period she was working *pro bono* - charging no fee.

Martin was well aware from his own background what that meant. Anne or whatever her (or his?) real name was, had recently qualified and needed to build up a portfolio of practical experience before launching her business and charging the going rate to clients.

It struck Martin as a pretty good idea. Working on-line meant easy, possibly 24 hour access for clients and super low overheads with a reasonable degree of anonymity and security for the practitioner. Clearly that was why the system was not showing the extensive sort of personal information that appeared in his own InterconNet profile. He thought: *Pete's system is great for shrinks, but useless for physiotherapists.* They, by definition, had to be hands on with their clients from the start.

As he was reading, a message window opened with a series of tick boxes; those irritating squares that opted you in to receiving endless bumf in your mailbox unless you either ticked or unticked them. The message queried: **Do you want to connect with Anne Eres?** Martin hesitated. The face on the web page seemed very young for someone claiming to offer psychological support, but her eyes seem to catch and hold his own. He thought, *if this woman was really anything like her picture and I was consulting her, I'd not be able to take my eyes off hers*. He felt that he might want to return sometime to see if Anne had added anything to her profile.

Impulsively he clicked "YES". A thin grey line appeared joining his graphic to Anne's in the InterconNet map. Martin narrowed his eyes in irritation. He hadn't wanted to flag his interest in such a public way. Now he recalled all those ticked boxes in the message which had popped up, which he hadn't cancelled. He searched for some way to bring up the message box again, but failed to make it reappear. Peter didn't seem to have provided a "help" facility with his programme other than Slinky, who was either sulking or had knocked off work by Saturday lunchtime. In the end he shrugged and gave up. Peter, or Chris or perhaps this Tuula person might be able to help later.

Feeling tired but reasonably pleased with his first session using Peter's programme, he logged off. The concept Peter was chasing seemed very good. Martin had little recent experience of the Internet but wondered whether his friend's idea was really unique. As he understood it, there were a lot of social networks and many clever programmers and Internet businesses out there. Whether this approach could help remained to be seen. Still, he liked Peter a lot and was more than happy if his efforts would help with his research work. In any case it made a pleasant diversion from drinking in the Green Dragon or jogging round the Tamford suburbs on his own.

Before logging out of the Uni network, he remembered to check his new email. When he finally connected after a number of failed attempts he was surprised to find a lot of messages. Several were from the email service and three from Peter urging him to try out his programme. Two messages had arrived that morning. The first welcomed him to InterconNet and congratulated him for successfully completing his profile. A copy of this was attached with an encouragement to keep it updated.

****

Martin logged off the Uni Network. The Computer Department appeared deserted and there were few people walking on campus. The absence of activity after the lengthy session in the silent computer building was depressing and he needed company or at least a buzz of conversation. Across a grass quad he spotted students squatting and lying outside amongst assorted beer and wine glasses. As he walked over to the Student Union building the low beat of music reached him and he soon found himself in the Union Bar wrapped up in a perfect storm of conversation. He bought a pint of ale dispensed from a row of hand pumps with names of beer he didn't recognise. Despite its unpromising name "The Dog's Bollocks" was very well hopped and tasted great.

The bar also served filled rolls and Martin was soon on his third pint despite his routine advice to clients to reduce the demon drink. After his intense, but apparently successful session in the Computer Centre, the beer was making him feel unusually relaxed. He hadn't looked at the ABV rating on the hand pump, but it was probably high. As he was scanning the room in the vague hope of recognising someone to talk to, perhaps Peter Swales, Chris came by with a tray holding a beefburger and a drink can. As he passed, Martin called out.

'Hey Chris, I thought you were going to hit the sack.' Chris looked round, recognised Martin then lowered his tray onto the barrel which served as a bar table.

'Hi. Yeah, changed priorities. Hunger got the better of me. Dumped my stuff then came to reboot.' Martin noticed Chris tended to drop into computer speak in his conversation.

'Am I in the company of a geek?' Immediately after he said this he wished he hadn't. He had intended to be witty but it had sounded rather rude. Desperately he tried to show that it was meant as a joke; he grinned madly and made a mock bow. But Chris didn't seem to take offence.

Instead, he chuckled.

'No, but my grandmother came from Greece, so perhaps you aren't so far wide of the mark.' Martin decided to change the subject quickly.

'You said you know Peter Swales, do you do any work with him?'

'Oh no, but I have attended a seminar he gave on his work. He has good ideas, but between you and me he's a bit of a maverick.'

'How do you mean?' Chris paused.

'Well, he's very ambitious. Nothing wrong with that; but he's a young man in a hurry. He'd be better off in a commercial environment, but there he wouldn't be ploughing his own furrow like he can in academia. He'd have to be a "team player", at least until he got to senior management. So at present he is caught between trying to be a big fish in a small pond - that's Uni - which really hasn't got the means to support his ambition. Or finding himself a small fish in a big pond - that's the corporate world - where he would have to fight off the sharks to rise to the top.' Martin nodded sagely. He was suddenly conscious that he had taken on board too much Dogs Bollocks and was in danger of talking it too. But Chris was continuing his assessment of Peter's character.

'Peter has grand ideas but I don't think he's got the drive and persistence to carry them through. Otherwise, I'd say his best future direction would be to aim to form a Uni spin-out company. That happens all the time now you know and the Uni is dead keen on it. If a spin-out business is viable it can be a significant source of revenue. The Uni isn't set up for manufacturing things, but it can make a lot of money from licensing out technology invented here to start-ups or big companies. If a member of staff plays their cards right they can remain in their tenured post, sheltered from the personal risks of commerce, but growing wealthy from consultancy fees or shares in a spin-out business.' Martin looked intently at Chris whilst he was speaking. Although he could usually guess people's ages correctly to within a few years, Chris had him confused. He looked like a typical post grad. student, but his conversation belied that. Martin's embarrassment at hinting that Chris was a computer nerd was still pink on his cheeks, assisted, of course, by liberal quantities of Dogs Bollocks. It really *was* difficult to tell whether he was student or staff. But at Uni often only a few years separated the two, especially in the sciences. He decided he should ask Chris about InterconNet.

'You said back in the Computer Centre that you were using Pete's programme.'

'Well not really. My speciality is AI; artificial intelligence. The specifics are rather dry and—', Here Chris glanced at Martin's empty glasses,

'—trying to follow them after 3 pints would be guaranteed to cause unconsciousness. I'll just say that Peter's programme offers me a real world opportunity to test out my own ideas.'

'I thought you didn't work with him?'

'Well not directly. We network with each other at software level.' Chris paused to lubricate his explanation with beer. While he drank, Martin's mind drifted back to the enigmatic face of Anne on the InterconNet programme. *She looked like someone I'd like to network with at software level*. Chris broke into his reverie.

'Peter's InterconNet has the potential to score over all the other social media. Mainly these provide an amusing diversion and escapism for their millions of users. Their use doesn't translate to much value in the real world and several tend to have a negative impact, spreading misinformation, malicious rumour and even contagion amongst the young and impressionable.' With that last pronouncement, Chris established firm eye contact with Martin, making him feel as if that last comment was partly aimed at him. But Chris continued:

'I think you know which social media I'm talking about. By contrast, InterconNet aims to collect verifiable information on the individuals who've signed up. It then uses AI methods - similar to those I use in my own research work - to suggest useful connections. But then you'd know that from having read the programme's terms and conditions, wouldn't you?' When Martin looked blank Chris answered the question for him.

'You *haven't* read the terms and conditions. Well why would you? Few do; we're all guilty of impatiently clicking "yes" and just getting stuck in. Actually, the InterconNet ones are mercifully brief and I suggest you do take a look at them next time you log on. Anyway, InterconNet continually checks the information its users supply, by cross-referencing. It even has an option to use a voluntary panel of human moderators. Dubious information is highlighted and referred back to the network member for correction or removal. There's a lot more to it, but that should give you a feel for the basics. In essence, InterconNet is a hybrid between a conventional social network - like Linked In say - and a *Wiki* like Wikipedia.' When Martin still looked puzzled, Chris explained.

'Wiki's are databases of information that are open for anyone to contribute to or amend. Cyberspace is composed not only of well intentioned consumers and contributors, but also free loaders and cyber vandals. Fortunately the latter are outnumbered and most attempts to provide misinformation or sabotage data are rapidly corrected by other Wiki users angry at such attempts to damage public property. Wouldn't that altruism be great in the real world, eh Martin?' Martin nodded, more because he felt that was expected of him, than through understanding. Chris continued:

'In this way, Wiki's are largely self policing and the quality of the information tends to increase rather than deteriorate. In summary, Peter's initiative is great and if it ever got off the ground he would have many big companies biting his hand off to purchase the set-up.'

'So why shouldn't it get off the ground?'

'All the networks that make big money are valued mainly by the number of active users. Access to huge user communities is what big business is after. If you have millions of active participants in your database the big boys will want to buy in, even if the actual content is dross.'

'And InterconNet doesn't have many users?' Chris smiled and shook his head slowly.

'Well, Mart - may I call you that - it sounds less formal?' Martin nodded again.

'For InterconNet it's early days. Basically it's an approved research project and Peter's academic supervisor has rights over anything he comes up with. His immediate objective is to gain a Ph.D. Peter on the other hand, and who would really criticise him for it, sees his time at Uni as a springboard to launch a profitable business. He's already looking beyond a higher degree. But to achieve his ambitions he'd have to come to some kind of commercial agreement with his supervisor and the Uni, promote his programme, raise serious funding and offer real value to consumers. And right now he would have to compete for users with the likes of Face Book, which has seen off most of the competition.' Chris paused to lubricate his explanation with beer before continuing.

'Peter would have to start small of course, like all the other Internet entrepreneurs have done. Then if InterconNet really did cut the mustard for its early members, they'd tell their friends using their other social media and the word would spread round the world like a forest fire. If by then Peter was still hosting his network on the Uni servers, the demand would take down university Internet service and Bill Meagh - that's our IT manager - would have to shut Peter's programme down. Permanently.' Chris waved his empty glass.

'I think it's time for another drink - don't you? Hopefully you're walking home?' When Martin returned rather unsteadily with a pint of Dogs Bollocks for Chris and a half for himself, Chris asked whether he had found any potential dates using InterconNet. Martin was taken aback at first; wondering once more about the whole issue of confidentiality. Then he recalled his own remark to Chris when Anne Eres's page was displayed on InterconNet: *I was rather taken by one of the people on the network*. But Chris had a more straightforward explanation for his question.

'Peter's got most of his early users on board by suggesting that they might find their perfect partner. I have to hand that to him as an inspired form of marketing, even though InterconNet's primary purpose is certainly not matchmaking.' Looking at Martin's rather disappointed expression, Chris smiled.

'Don't worry Mart, there's already a growing number of users and I can reassure you the quality is good. Chris winked suggestively. If *you're* wanting to make contact with some nice members of the opposite sex - or the same sex for that matter - InterconNet is well worth a try. For one thing, most of its current members are local, which makes a big difference if you decide to meet up in the real world.' Chris stopped speaking and glanced at his watch.

'Look, sorry Mart, after three and a half pints my "geek speak", as you called it, has probably already caused you permanent brain damage. Speaking of which, I really do need to get some sleep.' Chris clutched the remains of his beer, stood up and waved his free hand.

'Thanks for the drink. Ciao. See you around.' No one serving at the bar seemed to mind glassware walking out of the bar and Martin recalled the debris around Chris's workstation. It had been an enlightening session, taking him into territory he had never previously explored. His mood had definitely lifted. It was altogether a much better Saturday than usual. He hoped he would bump into Chris again. He looked around the noisy assembly in the Union bar. It was very hot and humid after the air conditioned atmosphere of the Computer Centre and the windows and fire doors were thrown open so that the drinkers spilt out from the warm shade of the bar onto the grass outside. A number of the female students chatting in small groups appeared to be wearing even less than he remembered from his own years at Uni Now he had no-one else to distract him, it made disturbing viewing. He hadn't felt physical stirrings like this for a long while. He shook his head ruefully, drank up and left for home.

CHAPTER FOUR
Tina

As agreed, Sunday evening, Martin stood and stared up at Tina's block of flats. Large Georgian style windows overlooked a wide avenue. Elevated beds of evergreen shrubs and maples confined within neat railings bordered both sides of the road. Mutely, it all spoke of an expensive development. Concerned that he had misheard the address, he pressed the button for flat 21. Tina's disembodied voice came over the intercom.

'Hi Martin, come on up.' The street door release mechanism buzzed. Martin's surprise mounted as he crossed the smart ground floor vestibule to a lift opposite a real reception desk, presently unmanned. He emerged on the second floor in darkness before automatic lighting came on. A short walk along a highly polished ceramic floor brought him to the part-open door of flat 21. He knocked.

'Come on in Martin.' His growing sense of amazement was complete. Tina was reclining on a sofa; the type that seems to curl round and hug itself. The room was very large, bright and minimalist with dining, cooking and living areas defined by different floor levels or island units. Doors suggested access to a surprising number of other rooms or storage spaces. Behind Tina, tall windows overlooked an urban park. Outside lighting was beginning to come on along pathways winding between trees. Tina voiced his thoughts for him.

'I *know* what you're thinking Martin. How come a single, self-employed alternative therapist can afford to rent a place like this?' Martin reddened. He hadn't realised his astonishment was so obvious.

'Oh, don't worry Martin, all my client's reactions are the same. And I don't rent this flat; it's mine. I had an unexpected inheritance and was advised to invest in property. So I bought this place, though actually I rattle about on my own in all this accommodation.' Tina winced inwardly. In concentrating on giving Martin the two hints: *single woman* and *over housed* she had let slip that her *clients* didn't just come to the Woodlands Centre. She hadn't wanted him to know that - not just yet anyway.

'Ooops, sorry. Force of habit. I find myself calling everybody 'clients' these days. But then you're a sort of client Martin - I did hint at payment in kind. Not the Dragon next time though!' Tina relaxed. That should cover her for now. Later, depending upon how things developed, she would probably have to be more open with him about her life and work. But all Martin registered was the fact that she had no live-in partner. He was frankly overwhelmed by the elegance of Tina's home and more than grateful that their first session was being held here and not in his cramped and untidy bachelor pad. At her invitation he sat down on the sofa whilst she fetched some drinks. When she returned she handed him a bottle and straight-sided glass. It was his favourite ale.

'My presumption, Martin. I hope that's OK with you?' Martin gave a slightly wide-eyed nod.

'I'm beginning to think my surprises this evening have only just begun, Tina.'

You don't know how right you are she thought. Tina settled in the easy chair opposite him.

'I always start, as I'm sure you do; by finding out about as much as I can about a new client, but you're a colleague and I hope by now a friend. I know we've already had a bit of a chat in The Dragon, but let's start again at the beginning. So tell me about you; I mean Martin the *person*, not the Woodlands physiotherapist.' Martin sighed.

'The short answer, Tina, is that I seem to have lost my way. I'm not enjoying my life or my work and I can remember a time when both were very important to me. I even recall times when I was enthusiastic about what I was learning or doing and excited about future events.'

'When did you start feeling like this, Martin?'

'I suppose it started after I broke up with Helena.'

'Tell me about your relationship with her. Was it Helena that broke it off?' Martin hesitated before replying.

'We met originally at Uni I was in my second year and Helena was a final year student. We were both mature students. I had dropped out of a degree in biological sciences, but managed to get a placement to train as a physiotherapist. Helena had been working at a leisure centre and was then studying physical education. We both attended some of the same lectures and after chatting at coffee breaks, we started to partner each other at tennis. We were both keen on sports. I didn't know it then, but she already had the ambition to take her tennis as far as she could. For her, PE was just going to be a means to support an ultimate end; Wimbledon and Olympic glory.

Anyway, we seemed to have quite a bit in common and the chemistry was good. We moved into a flat together. After her degree, Helena went back to a leisure centre as a trainer/instructor specialising in tennis. That's where things went wrong. Helena was on familiar ground. When she wasn't working at the Leisure Centre or competing somewhere, she wanted to hit the night-life, socialise with friends and so on. Her life had become all outgoing and physical, while I was still studying for my degree and was either in the library at Uni or studying course books and notes in our flat.

After I qualified, I'd have been relatively free to enjoy a more active social life; even to support Helena using my sports medicine skills. But she wasn't prepared to wait for that. The arguments became more heated and frequent.' Martin was quiet for a moment and stared down at his hands as if surprised by the mobility of his fingers. Then he shook his head slightly and continued.

'Shortly after I took up my position at The Woodlands, she found someone else; through Face Book. He was already a successful tennis player; a rising star apparently. When she finally packed her things, she said she was going to stay with a girlfriend until she had found her own space, but I had my doubts about that.'

As he was speaking, he recalled a couple he had watched recently in the Green Dragon; a slim blond girl with a dominant manner; obviously a sporty type. She was clearly very annoyed with the anxious brunette, equally obviously her life partner. Just then the good-looking blond reminded him strongly of Helena. If her subordinate companion that night hadn't been a woman, it might well have been him! Tina interrupted his thoughts:

'You see quite a few women who are into competitive sports, don't you?' Martin looked up at her in surprise. Was this woman a mind reader? But Tina explained:

'I mean in your physiotherapy practice. You must find some of them physically attractive.'

'That's not professional, Tina!'

'Oh come on Martin, you're not at the Woodlands now. I'm trying to find out about Martin the man, not Martin the physio. Now be honest with me. The tall dark girl who started consulting you a few weeks ago. She was gorgeous. What did you think of her?'

'You mean the runner with the Achilles tendon injury?'

'I don't know what was wrong with her, Martin, just that the few other men at the Woodlands are still talking about her in the staff room. I'm certain that they're envious of you. So are a couple of the female therapists!' Tina thought that as a very handsome young single male, Martin appeared surprisingly unaffected by his good looking clients. That was a bit disconcerting. He obviously couldn't confess to such feelings at work, but they were not at the Woodlands now and she given him the opportunity to talk to her in confidence. And so far he didn't appear to have picked up the signals *she* had been giving him. Tina wondered if that was the result of his present listless state or whether he was actually sexually repressed. Was *that* the main reason Helena had broken off their live-in relationship?

She knew Martin was good at what he did. When he started at The Woodlands, he'd been liked in spite of his scepticism about the treatments on offer. At that time he'd appeared to enjoy his work very much. Now his mood was slowly eroding that promising beginning. Tina watched him twisting his hands in his lap. The prospect of awakening emotion and restoring vitality to this good looking and capable man was arousing, but she had to be patient. He had clearly been very impressed by her flat, but he had not yet shown any promising interest in *her*.

Martin felt uncomfortable. He wasn't being challenged yet on professional grounds or on personal ones, although Tina seemed to be heading that way. Her preliminary questions certainly weren't like those he asked his own new clients: "what illnesses have you / your parents had?" and so on. But Tina's therapeutic skills, whatever *they* may were, were the reason he was here. If she could really help him shake off this dead feeling, he would go through with whatever Tina had in mind.

'A few very personal questions Martin, but they will help me design some treatment for you, if that's still what you want me to do?'

'Huh, yes, OK Tina, I'm in your hands.' Tina smiled and nodded thoughtfully: *Good job he can't mind read.*

'Did you have many relationships before you lived with Helena?' That question was harmless enough although Martin couldn't see where Tina was going with it.

'I had a few girlfriends and, yes, some one night stands; nothing serious though.'

'All right, then tell me about your relationship with Helena. Was it a passionate one?' Now things were definitely getting uncomfortable.

'What do you mean, Tina? I found her attractive yes; otherwise We wouldn't have got together, would we?'

'But that chemistry between you wasn't strong enough for you reach a compromise in other important aspects of your life, was it?' Tina paused for a moment, but continued after there was no reply.

'You know Martin, mutually adapting to a *new* way of life is the essential basis of any lasting relationship. You told me you'd plenty of arguments about your and Helena's career and leisure activities. Did you ever discuss each other's *physical* desires and needs? Did you try to find out if these were being met? You must have *spoken* about your feelings for Helena, but did you share them with her in other ways – how did you *demonstrate* that you desired her?' This was painful. At the back of his mind, Martin was astonished at the way Tina was homing in on a difficult and repressed part of his psyche. At the same time he was impressed by her perceptiveness; maybe there was something in Reiki. But his immediate reaction was defensive.

'Not sure what all this has got to do with Reiki. I thought you were going to help me with my depression by channelling universal energies or something'

'Well, Martin when *you* have a new patient, don't you have to decide from their answers to your initial questions whether they can be helped by you or whether they should be referred for advice or therapy elsewhere?'

'OK, I get it now; you're trying to work out if it'd be better for me to see a GP or a personal counsellor.'

'I'm trying to do my best for Martin' Although he was embarrassed, her perfectly reasonable answer had its desired effect and he felt calmer. He wondered what she would ask him next. But Tina had already finished probing. *For now you've told me all I need to know and your most important responses were unspoken…*

'I don't think you'd have the patience to see a counsellor. They would want to take you back to childhood, look for problems and work forward from there. How many months have you got? In fact, as an Reiki practitioner, I probably feel the same way about personal counsellors that you do about alternative therapists.' Martin appeared about to speak, but Tina continued before he could protest that wasn't what he meant.

'In any case, I'm not certain conventional Reiki could help your problem either. But if you'd allow me, I could try something else out with you. It's still an alternative therapy, but you won't find it in the textbooks. Not yet, anyway. And it must be done here: It's not something I can do at the Woodlands or your own flat.' Martin stared at her. This girl was full of surprises.

'Oh don't look so disappointed, Martin. I *will* give you a little bit of Reiki to take home tonight.' Martin quickly attempted to adjust his expression. Why did confident females always make him feel emasculated? Perhaps he did need a counsellor after all.

'What I'd like you to try is to think about 5 Reiki principles when you wake up each morning, starting from tomorrow.' Martin attempted to recover some of the dignity he felt he'd lost earlier in their conversation. This whole thing hadn't worked out the way he hoped.

'And they are?' Tina thought that the tone with which he asked this sounded more like an bruised appeal than a sceptical question. *He does sound like a boy sometimes; even if he doesn't look like one.*

'Say these phrases out loud before you get out of bed tomorrow. I'm assuming of course there's no-one else in bed with you.'

Tina flashed him her cheeky grin, lifted her chin and widened her eyes perceptibly. Except for her smile, Martin was reminded of the reproving look of one of his personal tutors at Uni whilst they remonstrated with him for a poor piece of written work.

'At least for today:
Don't be angry;
Do not worry;
Be grateful;
Be kind;
Work diligently.

* * *

Some Reiki adepts would also include or substitute: Honour your relatives and those close to you' Tina held his eyes closely as she recited and although this seemed to be the sort of embarrassing doggerel he'd expected, he was unable even to glance elsewhere whilst she was speaking. For some reason he also felt compelled to mirror her expression and lift his own eyelids beyond their natural position. By the time she had finished her quotes he felt vaguely uneasy.

'So. Please repeat the principles for me.' Martin complied rather grumpily and Tina prompted his first faulty attempt until he had repeated them correctly.

'Now it's not good enough simply to repeat these principles parrot fashion. Think *really* hard about instances where you fell short in the past and about ways in which you'll do better now and in future. I'll give you some suggestions to work on from what I've already picked up from our meetings so far.' Martin mumbled something indistinct in acknowledgement. Tina's look had softened once more. She watched him silently for a moment before she spoke again.

'Just for today, don't be *angry* with me for embarrassing you – or perhaps further denting your ego. Don't *worry* that you will never get back the happiness you felt when you first met Helena. Be *grateful* that you thought of asking me for help.' Tina couldn't resist a little giggle at her inventive interpretation.

'Just for tomorrow, be especially *kind and considerate* to your *first* client at the Woodlands tomorrow – hold this intention in your mind whilst you travel into work. And when they do arrive in your consulting room, w*ork diligently* to identify their problem, think of good advice you can give them and above all, encourage them to believe they will get better.'

Martin nodded. He was grudgingly impressed. It wasn't hard to see how Tina's rapid interpretation fitted both her Reiki tenets and applied to him personally. He would probably fail to live up her challenges tomorrow, Tina thought, but she had already identified *his* problem and decided Reiki wasn't the way to go.

'And what about this other treatment that you think might help me, Tina?'

'We'll discuss that next time we meet. Look Martin, I can only help you if you're prepared to keep an open mind about my treatment, whatever and whenever I decide that is to be.'

'All right then, I promise to be a good patient' Even Martin's present low sense of curiosity was engaged.

'And you're prepared for a *course* of treatment if I decide that's needed?'

'Well . .'

'I doubt many of your own clients recover after only a single treatment, do they?'

'No. All right; so far you haven't told me when you'd like to start.'

'Can't see you next weekend. Are you free to come back here next Sunday week in the afternoon, Martin?' Martin thought for a moment for effect, but of course he would be free. He wasn't going anywhere, except perhaps the Dragon. That was the problem.

'I think so: will contact you if anything comes up?'

'I think we agreed you're paying for my services, for now at least, with your company over a meal. Saturday week OK?'

Martin nodded. He'd looked enviously at her well equipped and spotless kitchen area when she was fetching their drinks. It crossed his mind he would enjoy dining in her flat. *I bet she's a good cook.*

Tina tilted her head slightly on one side and looked at him with slightly narrowed eyes.

'But another time I might cook for us here.' She flashed him another of her cheeky smiles. *She **can** read minds*, he thought.

****

Despite his cynicism, as he travelled to work Monday morning Martin remembered Tina's Reiki principles. In her example she had applied them to his first patient of the day, but knowing who that was, it was highly unlikely that they would help. Nevertheless, he dutifully repeated them and they did at least relieve his own frustration with the traffic. Having been cautioned by Noura Munday, he appeared in the reception area of the Woodlands Centre, forty minutes before official opening time. Noura and the Centre's receptionist, Julie, were talking at the front desk and both turned and looked at him. Julie's face registered surprise; Noura just looked like Noura, with perhaps just a hint of satisfaction playing around her dark eyebrows and lips. She was the first to speak;

'Nice to see you in first thing, Martin.' It was hard to miss the sarcasm in her voice. As She clacked away down the corridor to her office, Julie smiled sympathetically at Martin. When the office door closed behind the Woodland's manager she leaned across the desk towards him:

'Never mind old Munday; it's a good job you made it in early this morning, Martin. You've a patient booked in at 8:30.'

'I don't think so Julie; my first booking is 10:30.' Julie was now grinning widely at him.

'Well an appointment request was made on the Centre's website Sunday evening and it's automatically been accepted. The system should have sent you a text. Martin looked blank.

'You haven't switched your phone on have you?' Julie gave him her knowing look and continued without waiting for an answer.

'A woman called Pixie Small, according to the booking list.' Julie peered at Martin with dramatically lowered eyebrows. But it was now a conspiratorial expression. She had given up trying out her stock of flirtatious looks on Martin.

'Sounds to me like someone who's changed her name so her boyfriend or husband doesn't know she's going to be seeing you. Or perhaps she's a pop star?' But Martin didn't respond as Julie hoped to her gentle teasing.

'More likely some idiot messing around with our Website.'

'Possibly, Martin, but you'd better go and warm up your couch in case you get . .' Julie was interrupted by the reception desk phone ringing. She was still speaking to the caller as Martin walked to his office. Somehow he couldn't stop himself completing Julie's parting quip in his head. *I'm not likely to "get lucky". That's something that happens to others.*

Martin closed his door and surveyed the disorder. The cleaners just concentrated on his treatment room, having long since given up on his small office area and especially his desk, with its stacks of mail shots and trade magazines. Martin picked up *Physiology Today* and flicked through the back pages. Ads with Web addresses, ignored before he met Peter Swales, now caught his attention.

An attractive and smartly dressed young couple were looking at each other. The clever composition communicated a simple message. The background behind the pair - some sort of clinical setting - was out of focus. The strap-line read: "Meeting of Minds - Introductions for busy professionals." Below this the ad. stated: "Visit *MeetingOfMinds.com* today; you know you owe it to that special someone in your life: yourself!" His thoughts were suddenly disrupted by the reception buzzer. Irritated, Martin activated the intercom.

'Yes . .' Julie's professional tone announced:

'Your 8:30 client's arrived in reception, Mr. Wright. Hold the connection for me just a moment please.' Over the hum of the open intercom connection, there was a faint buzz of conversation which Martin couldn't make out. Julie came back on with a hushed, confiding tone Martin was more used to hear when she was in one of her teasing moods.

'I've sent your client to wait outside your office. Martin; she apologises for being slightly early, but - ' Julie lowered her voice even more.

'- I think you should see her straight away.' Julie seemed to be enjoying herself at his expense. Martin replied dryly:

'So she really *is* a pixie then and I suppose I'll be whisked off to fairyland if I keep her waiting?'

'More like an *elf*, I'd say, but if you play your cards right, you might well get to fairyland.' Julie's musical giggle ended the intercom call. Almost immediately there was a knock on the partly open door. Martin shrugged, seated himself at his desk and called:

'Come in.' Tina Elves appeared in the doorway.

'Oh hi Tina, look I've got a patient waiting outside just now, can we meet at coffee break?' Tina smiled, stepped to one side and pushed the door wide open. No-one else was seated in the chair opposite his door.

'Pixie Small?' was all Martin could manage.

'Tina Elves' corrected Tina with a wicked grin, closing the door.

'What are you playing at, Tina?'

'I have an appointment with you, Mr. Wright..' Tina emphasised his surname with obvious glee.

'But you're staff. You didn't need to make a on-line appointment.'

'*Was* staff, Martin. You helped me carry those boxes to the car, remember? I was clearing my desk. I've resigned from the Woodlands.' Martin now noticed she wasn't wearing her white Centre tunic.

'But why, Tina, what's happened?'

'Let's just say for now that my independent practice is doing very well and I want to focus on that.' While Martin was taking in this unexpected development she explained:

'That's partly the reason why I'm here. In my new work I'm more "hands on" than "hands over" with my clients.' She hesitated for a moment, then continued:

'For several months now, I've started to notice persistent lower back pain and it's beginning to affect my work with clients. Obviously I can't afford to allow it to become serious; particularly since I've given up my position at the Woodlands. I'm confident you give me some advice and possibly some treatment! Oh, and I've been proactive about filling in your health and capacity questionnaire, so you can make a practical start with me straight away.' Tina handed him a completed patient questionnaire. Still trying to catch up with this new development, Martin glanced automatically at her answers on the questionnaire form.

'But you're a *Reiki therapist*, Tina . . .'

'I thought you dismissed such complementary therapies as ineffective, Martin. Anyway, in spite of trying, I've never benefited from the same results from self-healing Reiki that I achieve with my clients.' Tina looked askance at Martin.

'And don't you *dare* say that's because I don't really believe in it.' By now Martin was recovering some of his more usual professional composure.

'You said the back pain was *part* of the reason you're here?'

'Yes. We've agreed that I should try to help with *your* problems. I'd also like to see at first hand how you treat your own patients; especially your female ones.' Tina gave him a cheeky grin that was deliberately intended to be open to several interpretations. Martin just took it as a challenge to his ability. He raised the completed form.

'According to this you're in A1 health.'

'Then you won't have worry about recommending your most effective treatment for me.'

'I'll need to feel your back and manipulate it until you can indicate exactly where the discomfort is. Then we can discuss any treatment options and also the way you're working with your own clients.' Martin indicated the folding screen. 'There's a clean dressing gown behind there. Normally I ask my female clients if they'd like a chaperone; someone else from the centre or a friend or relative to sit in while I work with them.'

'And do many of them take up that option?'

'A few have; most don't want a chaperone.'

Tina smiled at him. *I bet they don't,* she thought.

'Well, I don't think that'll be necessary, Martin.' Ignoring the modesty cubicle, Tina pulled her dress up over her head. Martin saw that she was wearing a plain black sports bra and briefs. 'But I *will* use your disposable slippers.' She disappeared briefly to hang up the dress and change into the Centre's soft fabric slippers.

When she was lying on her front on the treatment couch, Martin was also able to see that Tina's body was similar to those of the slim athletic individuals who often presented in his consulting room. Her physique, like her features, was perfectly symmetrical, which spoke, apart from youth, of good genes and a physically active lifestyle.

It wasn't until he had asked her to tense different muscle groups and manipulated the area close to the base of her spine that he discovered the uneven development of the muscle tissue on the left and right sides of her body. He immediately palpated the muscle around her two shoulder blades. There it was again; a minor but definite asymmetry in the tension and size of the muscle groups. Selecting his target areas carefully, Martin applied pressure in various spots until Tina reported discomfort. Incorporating the areas he had identified, he went into a short massage routine.

'Are you OK so far with this, Tina?'

He received a soft 'Mmm' in assent. Without being instructed to do so, Tina squeezed her buttocks, then relaxed them slowly several times. The fabric of her briefs lifted rhythmically away from the hollow at the top of her bottom. Martin found himself sorely tempted to extend the firm strokes he was using and follow her spine down and into into the cleft emphasised by the breathing of the tightly stretched fabric. He pulled his hands away feeling annoyed with himself.

'Still OK?' he asked, as much to recover his normal clinical frame of mind as to check with his client.'

'Yes Martin, I was just then trying to help pin down the area which hurts. But you've found something already, haven't you?'

'I think so Tina. You can get dressed now and we'll talk about it.'

Tina raised herself from the massage bed and swung her legs over the edge. A thought occurred to Martin.

'Wait a moment Tina. Do you use a similar treatment couch to this in your other work?' Tina nodded.

'OK, Just imagine you've got one of your own clients on this treatment bed. Wait..let me adjust the height for you.' He lowered the bed several inches.

'All right, now show me how you'd massage your patient - assuming that's what you do?' Obediently, Tina moved to the treatment bed and moved her hands fairly firmly down up and down its central axis. To Martin's surprise her posture seemed stiff and her movements rather forced. As if aware of how this would strike Martin she apologised:

'Of course, this isn't really the same set up I use.'

'Yes, I'm taking that into account, but it will serve for our purpose right now - just keep moving please, Tina.' With his client now standing bent over the treatment bed, Martin moved up close behind her, feeling her calves, thighs, lower back and shoulders. It certainly wasn't normal practise, but this didn't strike him as odd - he was so pleased with his clear diagnosis. He desperately needed to recover some self esteem and this confident woman had so far done little to contribute to that. His palms and fingers were still interrogating her shoulder blades when she asked to be released:

'OK to pause a moment Martin? Your examination's very pleasant, but my back's beginning to complain.' Martin stood back quickly.

'Sorry Tina. I think we can wrap up this session anyway.' Tina silently added her own afterthought: *And me too; for now*. After Tina retrieved her dress and shoes from the small cubicle and sat by his desk Martin continued:

'We both know where this is going don't we Tina?' Tina smiled and thought: *I do, but you've obviously not caught on yet, Martin*.

'Evidently your bedside manner is producing problems in your back and shoulder muscles. Uneven muscle development - and untreated - weakness of one set of muscle groups, can lead to the opposing ones or even unrelated muscles taking over inappropriately. This invariably leads to pain.

'Yes Martin, that's what I was beginning to conclude for myself. But what should I do about it?'

'In your case the muscle imbalance is relatively mild, but if you don't deal with it now it might become serious enough to stop you working some days - as you already were worried about. Obviously this is something that I have to be very careful to avoid in my own work here. If you make sure you keep aware of what your body is doing during the day, you'll adapt your programme of work, posture and position appropriately.

Try and look at people in the street with physio's eyes as you leave the Centre. You'll see lop sided expressions and uneven gait. Individuals with shoulders at different heights and other distortions. Most of them will be experiencing muscle pain; particularly in their upper arms and backs. You have a wonderful body shape; its particularly symmetrical when you relax. You'll want to keep it like that for a long time, I'm sure, and with the right approach you should definitely be able to. Tina glowed inwardly at his appraisal of her - *a wonderful body shape* - even though this was Martin the physio. speaking.

'Your imbalance is likely to have been caused by your static twisting at the side of your client and one arm applying more pressure than the other. Swap sides when you're standing beside your massage table and try to make all your movements even, applying equal and balanced pressure with both arms. Do you walk much Tina - I mean on countryside or local walks?'

'Not really Martin; not a great idea for a single young female, you know.'

'Well there might be a group or club you could join.'

'I don't think ramblers would be my ideal companions, Martin. I did join a local group for a while, but their rambling was more vocal than physical.'

'Yes, well ideally you should be striding fast enough to raise your heart rate, breathing deeply, concentrating on an even gait; swinging both arms freely from your shoulders.'

'From what you've told me so far, you don't practice what you're preaching either.'

'I have in the past, but you're right. At the moment it's a case of do as I say rather than as I do.'

'Perhaps you'll take me for a walk sometime to demonstrate good technique?'

'Perhaps.' Tina looked at him expectantly.

'I hope you haven't forgotten that you've a lunch date Sunday week and an appointment with me afterwards?'

Martin hesitated. That had slipped his mind. Let's meet outside the Centre at 12am on Sunday and we'll go on from there.'

'Not to the Dragon, Mart. Do you have a loyalty card for that place?'

'No and No, Tina.'

'OK, I'll look forward to that.' Tina picked up her bag. At the door she turned round with what she hoped came across as a warm and grateful smile.

'I really appreciated your help today. I hope that I can return the favour next Sunday.'

She closed the door gently behind her, leaving Martin to his thoughts. It was obvious Tina had planned this visit whilst he was at her flat. *She* had planned to be the patient in her example of how to apply the Reiki principles. He recalled her words now and was surprised how well her clever invention had helped him remember them:

Don't be angry with me for embarrassing you – or perhaps further denting your ego today.

Don't worry that you will never get back the happiness you felt when you first met Helena.

Be grateful that you thought of asking me for help.

Be especially kind and considerate to your first client at the Woodlands tomorrow – hold this intention in your mind whilst you travel into work. And when they do arrive in your consulting room:

Work diligently to identify their problem, think of good advice you can give them and above all, encourage them to believe they will get better.

He wondered just how real her problem actually was. Probably not as bad as she had made out. But anyway, she was the first client he'd had in a long time who had significantly lifted his mood. That was partly due to her helping him to recover some self esteem. But he also couldn't discount the effect on him of her shapely form. He could still feel the perfect "S" curve of her enticing exposed back. The third Reiki principle surfaced unheralded in his mind. Be grateful. It made him wonder if her promised treatment of him had somehow already started.

Part Two

CONNECTED

Computers can figure out all kinds of problems; except the things in the world that just don't add up.

James Magary

Happiness makes up in height for what it lacks in length.

Robert Frost

CHAPTER FIVE
Tuula

When Martin opened his eyes the following Sunday, he was lying on his back amongst bed clothes resembling a choppy sea. Ridges in his sheet, thrown up by a restless night, were uncomfortable to lie on, but he didn't attempt to adjust them. That would mean getting out of bed, which would add a painful awareness of his disorganised surroundings to his moderate feeling of discomfort. In fact it was already too late; just that brief glimpse of the lonely chaos of his flat was enough: closing his eyes quickly didn't erase the scene from his mind's eye.

His bedroom alone was a minefield of decisions waiting for his attention. Clothes piled on chairs to be washed or put away. Books stacked up by the bed. The wardrobe door hanging on the top hinge only, because screws had worked loose from the lower one. The calendar clock announced SUNDAY AUG 8 which meant more decisions. This time on what to do and where to eat.

Just for today don't worry. The first and most often needed of the 5 Reiki principles popped into his thoughts. They were just words, dammit. It seemed irrational to Martin, but saying or thinking them seemed to help. He would have forgotten them completely if it hadn't been for Tina turning up in his clinic unexpectedly last Monday. She had been, quite literally, the embodiment of the five principles she had shared with him in her flat.

Outside, wind-blown summer rain drops were angrily strafing the windows. The metal railings of the ersatz balcony off his second floor living room howled mournfully as strong gusts caught them. One of his rare visitors, hearing the metal music, had commented:

'That's cool, the builders fitted aeolian harps outside your flat'. He'd had to look "aeolian" up in a dictionary to find that these were "musical instruments which sound when air passes over their strings". After this, in an uncharacteristic gesture, Martin had unbolted the noisy railing, leaning precariously over the drop to do so. He noticed that his own balcony railings appeared to be different from those adjacent; the hollow tubing of the metal rails had not been welded shut at each end. So in a high wind they emitted sounds, like organ pipes.

He dragged the railings inside and stuffed them behind his sofa. The resulting peace on windy days didn't last long. The block residents' management committee wrote him a letter instructing him to replace his balcony rails "forthwith both on aesthetic grounds and those of health and safety".

It was a particularly officious communication, which spoke of "vandalism and wilful destruction of communal property". Unless he put them back and had the reinstatement inspected, they would be replaced by contractors at his own expense. Martin reinstalled the railings and the "aesthetic" benefits returned whenever there was a strong westerly wind. This Sunday he just pulled a pillow over his head until lying in bed became more painful than picking his way to the bathroom through the minefield of his flat.

At least the contents of the 'fridge and larder cupboard eased his decisions about breakfast. By a process of elimination this boiled down to a fried egg and two slices of toast whose crust was decorated in a few places with blue patches. Martin's inner nutritionist reminded him that bread mould contained the antibiotic penicillin. A Reiki positive take on this would be: *be grateful; a little of what you didn't much like could sometimes do you good.*

There were 3 items of mail lying unopened from the day before. Martin turned them over, looking at the printing and postmarks. His delay in opening the post was one of the many things that had irritated his ex. *For God's sake Martin; don't you think you'll find out more easily who sent it and what it's about if you open it.*

After breakfast he opened the unstamped, hand written envelope first, having decided the other two were just marketing. Addressed "To Whom It May Consern", it had been sent from the flat above his. The new occupants of no. 34 were complaining about the screeching noise that they had identified as coming from his flat. Evidently they liked to keep their own living room balcony doors open to the elements and the noise that Martin from his balcony railings was "degrading their ameanity".

Martin glared in frustration around his untidy breakfast kitchenette. It occurred to him that the only entertainment on offer that wet Sunday might be to log onto Peter Swales's experimental social network in the Uni computer centre. Dumping his cup and plate in the sink, he collected his man bag and cagoule and left the flat. Entering the campus 20 minutes later he was indistinguishable from the few other figures in anoraks bent against the late summer wind and rain.

Once on campus he had a thought. Suppose the Computer Centre key card didn't work on Sundays? No-one else around here seemed to be working; even the Union bar appeared to be closed at this time of the morning. That would really consign to the bin a morning that had started badly and gradually become worse. But the Computer Centre door submitted without fuss to Martin's key card and he gained access to the terminal room in the same manner. This time there were quite a few people sitting at the workstations. No-one looked up as he entered. He had half expected to see Chris, but he didn't recognise anyone.

He sat at a vacant workstation next to an oriental male student with bottle lenses in his glasses. His neighbour appeared to be to be Googling lingerie websites. His face positioned just a few inches away from the monitor; he didn't look up. Well, at least his myopic companion would not be taking any interest in Martin's own on-line activities. He logged himself onto InterconNet. This time Peter Swales's cheery welcome window had a new message for him.

Hi Mart! Great that you've joined the InterconNet community. If it's OK with you I want to see how you get on with the programme without much more instruction! I know that might be a tad frustrating for you to start with, but it will help me make the software more user friendly i.e. carry on my research, which is our deal! OK, without making TOO big an assumption that you're reading this and not just skipping to the programme, I reckon you'll want to get into the swim without too much splashing about. So here's a couple of tips to get you started. The girls are represented by circles and the size, colour and position of these relative to your own square all have meaning! You'll soon catch on what these are!!

What you DO need to know is that the closer on the InterconNet map a female (or a male!) symbol is to your own, the more likely its owner could be compatible / friendly / relevant / helpful / some or all of the foregoing / to you. These graphics - we geeks call them icons ha ha - are positioned on the map by some clever software, sadly not written by me, using all that information you have already painfully given (for which heartfelt thanks!!).

As you use the programme, it learns more about you with each session and also takes notice of on-line comments (otherwise known as 'net chat), that other network members make about you. Please don't get the idea here that you've been lined up for special treatment here. The same rule - sorry - democracy, applies to all network members. So you'll see the map change a bit (sometimes a lot!) each time you use the programme. Right. Enough about that. Don't want to coach you. OK, you may already have found that you can invite other network members to connect with you (and they can of course invite you to connect to them).

All I'll say for now is that only "safe and appropriate" connections are possible in InterconNet and the number of connections anyone can make are capped! So you can connect to others without worry, unlike in the rest of the WWW (also known as the Weird and Wonderful Web ha ha!!). Connection, of course, requires mutual agreement. You manage your connection status using your right mouse button (or if you're left handed you can change that assignment ..sorry..sorry..slipping into geek speak). Fine. Now at the moment I'm away with relatives in Ireland for a couple of weeks - long story, so we'll touch base when I'm back. Meet in the Union Bar this time. Two week's fee due, so that'll be two pints of Bollocks then. Bye for now and happy hunting!!   Pete

Martin noticed that Peter typed messages much as he spoke. He'd also learnt something new about Peter; there was an Irish connection. He had to read Peter's welcome message twice before he sifted out the basics from the blarney. Muttering instructions to himself, he closed Peter's message window. His own small image — icon, Peter called it — appeared mid-screen. As he'd been told, there were many more icons representing additional users since last Saturday. Tentatively he clicked on his image. As he did so, his wrist slipped. His icon was dragged aside, glued to the cursor. To his astonishment, dozens of other icons were pulled onto the screen; some linked, others unconnected.

When the penny dropped that he was able to move the whole network around the display using the mouse, it soon became obvious that he was quite isolated; out on the periphery. Other users were located nearer the map's centre, some with many connections. But Peter Swales's icon was the furthest out of all. This morning it was connected to no-one else but his own and when Martin accidentally moved it off the screen, disappeared altogether.

Anne Eres's and Helena's icons were still the closest to his own. He saw the grey line representing the link request he'd accidentally made to Anne had turned black. A small version of the image that had so fascinated him on Saturday now replaced her previously anonymous grey circle. She had accepted his inadvertent request to connect. He assumed she had read his biography, but then, to his surprise, had not immediately declined his invitation. He clicked on her small image. A larger image of Anne's enigmatic face appeared and this time her accompanying biopic was much more detailed. It appeared a friend had made her aware of InterconNet. It had sounded a safe environment for a trial run as an on-line psychotherapist whilst she was still at Uni.

A degree of protection was afforded not only to her clients but to herself as well, as both client and therapist could communicate anonymously. Obviously potential clients had to be existing users or sign up to InterconNet to communicate with her. A more detailed description of her qualifications and personal experience followed. At the end of her profile she emphasised her objective was to gain further experience whilst helping other members of the network. She *hadn't* joined the InterconNet community for romantic opportunities, as many others claimed in their own profiles.

Martin looked at Anne's compelling - *what was it Chris had called it?* - avatar. It all made perfect sense now. A newbie psychotherapist, probably working from her Uni accommodation. He presumed she was an attractive young woman who would want the support of a secure on-line environment and the anonymity of an avatar to make contact with potential clients. Unlike Anne though, he doubted the effectiveness of such impersonal therapy.

Surely Anne would have to meet any serious client face to face eventually. Any type of psycho-person needed to read and respond to their patient's body language as well as what they said. That non-verbal communication would be lost over InterconNet. Martin wondered why Anne had chosen such a young looking avatar. Surely clients would want to unburden themselves to someone who looked as though they had all manner of life experience. It would be rare indeed for someone looking like Anne's chosen image to possess that.

But somehow he couldn't dismiss Anne's picture. In the end he decided that it was the eyes of her on-line image. Even when he closed his own he could still see them. He knew it was a sensation with no basis in reality, but they seemed to be looking deep into his soul. It was also clear why Peter's programme had placed her InterconNet icon close to his own. Her biopic ticked many of the same boxes as his own, except for that final sentence. Unlike him, Anne made it clear that she was not on InterconNet seeking romantic connections.

Martin felt a keen sense of disappointment. No point in wasting this woman's time with idle conversation and he already had a shrink lined up in the person of Michael Timles. He clicked the mouse's right button to disconnect. A list of disconnection options appeared including: "**Thanks for accepting my request to connect, but I'd like to take a rain check on this at the moment**". Despite himself, Martin grinned at Peter's quirky programming. Listening to the storm outside, today that message was certainly apt. On impulse he selected this option and clicked OK to close Anne's profile.

Just ahead of his workstation, the entrance door opened. A short girl dressed in an expensive looking brown leather coat and a matching fur-trimmed hat, matted with rain, whirled into the room. As she passed him he recognised the shock of almost white hair below that hat. It was the girl who had been sitting with her back to him in the Green Dragon. Without looking round she walked up to a door in the far wall, stabbed at a key pad and disappeared.

Out of curiosity he looked to see if her sudden entrance had caused any of the other occupants to drag their intense focus away from their computer screens. He was very surprised to see that every head in the room was turned towards the closing side office door. All that was, except his myopic neighbour whom he saw was minutely inspecting underwear sported by a tall bronzed Amazon retailed by an outfit calling themselves Chaste Clothing Co. No-one had paid Martin the least attention when he'd entered.

Martin turned his attention back to the InterconNet display. Like his own, Anne's icon was on the edge of the social network, assuming he could call it that. Now he had worked out how to do it, he dragged the tangle of interconnected personal icons across the screen and stopped at an area where the icons and lines were particularly dense. A large red disk was surrounded by smaller black icons, mainly squares. This woman was a long way from his own position in the network, but she was clearly very popular with males, judging from the clustering of squares; *like bees round a honey pot*, Martin thought.

Curious to see what this siren looked like, but forgetting that the default procedure for requesting a connection was a "double click" on a network member's icon, Martin moved his mouse over the red icon and pressed the button twice. A grey line immediately drew itself between his own icon, now on the very edge of the screen, and the mysterious female's. He hesitated, startled by the result, but as he was fumbling to correct his slip, the line turned black and a small picture replaced the anonymous graphic. Within a matter of seconds, this woman, whoever she was, had accepted his request for a connection.

Martin clicked the tiny image and the woman's biopic came up in a new window. A sultry, blue eyed, almond shaped face, in three quarters profile looked at him from under a fringe of ash blond hair. Unusually large, parted lips matched the colour of her InterconNet disc. Set against the fairness of her skin and hair, these were a shocking bright red. In complete contrast with the haunting innocence of Anne's virtual image this girl's picture oozed sexuality. There was absolutely no doubt it was a likeness, not an computer-generated avatar. He read her name with a jolt of recognition; Tuula Pipi.

Her InterconNet e-audited summary was terse. A Finnish IT worker, she was in her late twenties. She had graduated from the University of Helsinki. Then worked for a start-up company in Baltimore in the USA developing operating system software and applications for mobile devices like phones and tablets. Returning home she had been appointed to a project manager position in Kosketecessa; a mobile phone manufacturer. She could not expand upon her project details for reasons of commercial interest. As part of her career ambitions she had taken up an opportunity to study for a higher degree at Tamford on novel social networking applications. She had been allowed to retain her post in industry, but had to make up her degree funding by acting as an assistant systems operator in the Computer Science Faculty.

She had joined the InterconNet community to "expand her social circle in the UK and learn more about the potential of social networks." Her leisure interests were fashion, music, travel and meeting people. Well, Martin thought, to judge from the social network map, she had certainly managed to get connected locally. He wondered whether he should request to break the connection. This girl already had more than enough friends. However she was clearly on-line right now. It would seem odd, perhaps even voyeuristic, to creep away after reading about Tuula's life, giving no explanation or apology. As he prevaricated about what to do with *this* inadvertent connection, someone spoke directly behind him.

'Hallå *Martin.* Är du Svensk?' Martin turned round abruptly. Grinning broadly at him was the girl he was just reading about on InterconNet. Clearly she had been the person who had come in earlier, swathed in outdoor clothing. But now she was wearing a tight fitting red tee shirt and yellow varsity style shorts over dark stockings or tights.

'Sorry?' was all he could think to say.

'I was asking if you were Swedish. Which clearly you're not! But your picture looks like a typical Swedish guy, even though you call yourself Martin on InterconNet. And physiotherapy is a very popular career in Scandinavian countries. I'm Tuula Pipi.' Tuula extended her hand. As an overawed Martin accepted it she looked past him at the monitor.

'But of course, we've already been introduced.' Finally Martin found his voice.

'I do apologise. I'm still completely new to this programme and I'm finding my way around. I hadn't meant to ask for a connection. I was exploring the social network map.'

'Well, you have connected now! Also you might well hold the record for going from a virtual introduction on-line to a physical one.' Tuula tilted her head slightly, narrowed her eyes as she looked him up and down and slowly parted her very red lips.

'I was working with the network map when you asked for a connection. I liked what I saw and read about you and accepted.' She closed her mouth in a mischievous grin. But as I'm a systems operator here, I also knew that you were logged on at one of the public workstations and came to take a closer look.' Martin's head had stopped spinning. Recalling that Peter had mentioned Tuula and explained about "Sysops", the whirling pieces of the jigsaw were all dropping into place. Peter had teased him: *Now she **is** one hot bit of stuff*. As Tuula grabbed the chair from a vacant workstation and commanded him to make space for her to sit, he had to agree with Pete's assessment.

Tuula dragged the InterconNet map back so that Martin's icon was centred on the screen. Then she opened a small window and typed a stream of instructions which scrolled up and disappeared as the computer accepted them. After she closed the window, almost all the icons on the screen changed to small pictures of their owners or, presumably, of their virtual representatives; their avatars. She looked round archly at him.

'OK Martin, now your search will be a little more convenient.'
Tuula didn't wait for a reply, but looked back at the monitor, selected a blank area of the screen and dragged the mouse. As she did so, the map enlarged, the small images connected to Martin growing larger and easier to make out. Tuula indicated the grey link connecting him to Helena's smiling face.

'Attractive woman. Did this one not want to connect with you?'

Martin wondered where this was heading. Things were getting a little intrusive.

'No that's my ex - my former partner. She's not on InterconNet. I don't know why she's here. I tried to break the connection, but it's still there in this virtual world.'

'And is there still some connection in the real world?'

'No certainly not.'

'The link will have been picked out of other social networks. If you can't disconnect, it's a due to a bug in the programme.' Once again Tuula opened a small window, typed instructions and both the link and Helena's image disappeared. Tuula next clicked on Anne Eres's image and scanned her short biography.

'I can see why this one interests you, Martin. Shows that the programme is improving. I don't think that's her real image though.' Tuula seemed to lose interest and pushed her chair back, looking at her wrist.

'Look it's 1pm, let's go for a drink and I'll show you how to run this programme - at least as far as Pete has developed it.'

'But won't we need to use the computer here?' Tuula glanced disdainfully at the workstation.

'I prefer not to work with legacy hardware.'

'Sorry?'

'These workstations. They are practically museum pieces, Mart - may I call you Mart?'

'Everybody does. By the way, where did you learn English?'

'In school in Finland and in Baltimore in the States - why are you asking?'

'It's very good.'

Martin noted that although she used some American words, she didn't abbreviate her verbs. It sounded odd for a young person to use such formally correct English.

'I have the Yanks to thank for that. In my role at Kosketecessa, there is no chance of further promotion unless I am fluent in English.'

'Are you going back there after your work here is finished?'

'That is in my contract. Look while you log off, I will just fetch my coat.'

Tuula disappeared into her side office and emerged swaddling her slight figure with her overcoat. Martin followed her outside into a steady drizzle. Tuula pulled her collar up.

'This weather's shit. The one thing I looked forward to most of all was your English summer. Right now it's probably better in Finland.' Now outside the faculty buildings and walking with Martin on campus, she had curiously dropped into a more relaxed colloquial conversation.

'Is the Uni bar open, Tuula? It was closed when I last looked.' Tuula assumed her disparaging look once again.

'Probably, but the food's not good. I'd prefer to go to the Green Local.'. Martin was again taken aback. This woman was full of surprises.

'Green Dragon. What's Dragon in your language?'

'Lohikäärme.' Martin could see where her "Local" might have come from and in his case her choice of word was spot on.

'What you called it first was good, I sort of count that pub as *my* local. But I've never seen you there.'

'Pete Swales took me there for a working lunch on Thursday. The beer is good.'

'Pete mentioned that you work on social networks like him.'

'Yes but not on his project. He wanted some programming advice.' They were leaving the campus now and turning to walk back towards the suburbs.

'Isn't he concerned that his work might be copied by a big company like yours? It sounds just the sort of thing a giant mobile phone business would want.'

'That's a fair question, but my company is a hardware business. If it wants phone software or apps it contracts programmers or licences technology in. In any case, a key component of Pete and his supervisor's work is protected by patent. It's OK to use it in an academic environment, but if Pete or his boss want to take their programme to the market, *they're* the ones who will have to negotiate licence fees. That's what Pete wanted to ask me about. He is trying either to find way a round the patent or attempt to re-write that part of the programme.'

Martin was now not only trying to grasp the gist of Tuula's replies, he was also attempting to keep up a dignified pace beside her. This girl was so fast! He looked up from watching the uneven pavement to steal a quick glance at his companion. With her fur collar trim pulled high round her neck, fur hat beaded with moisture, shocking red lips and neat bob of ash blond hair, she looked much more like a fashion model than an IT guru. He thought: *this girl's clearly one sharp cookie.*

As they entered the pub, Tuula was already shedding her outer coat and the effect on the customers was dramatic. Several dozen pairs of eyes swivelled their way and followed them to the bar. The place was fairly full, but that was not unexpected on a wet Sunday lunch hour. When they reached the bar, most of the punters had returned to their former conversations, but a few drinkers were still looking curiously in their direction. And they were mostly women.

'What's it to be then Tuula?'

'Mine's a White Shield, Mart.'

Martin decided it was time to stop being surprised. He had only just met this girl, but he decided he should follow her lead and drop his attempts to be politely formal. In spite of himself he was enjoying the occasional envious glances of the Dragon's customers. After ordering and finding somewhere to perch with their drinks he asked:

'Did Pete mention that this place has become a gay venue?'

'Yes. Is that why you drink here?' Martin thought *Caught on the back foot again!*

'No It's because the food and drinks are good.'

'Do you dislike homosexuals?' Martin was becoming a little annoyed with this girl.

'Look, I'm OK with whatever sexual orientation other people have and this is the nearest watering hole to home and work.' Now it was Tuula's turn to be confused.

'Watering hole?'

'Colloquial term for a public house.'

'Oh, OK, well as long as they don't do it to the beer.' Tuula managed to turn around in the blind alley she had entered and make a little joke. Martin's irritation faded a little as they both raised their pints.

'Well, we'd better check just in case. Cheers.'

'Gesundheit.' Martin glanced up at her as he sipped his beer.

'What language is that - sounds more like German than Finnish?'

'Correct. It is what Germans say when you sneeze.' Martin laughed. This was going better; he was recovering some of his lost equilibrium now he was on more familiar ground.

'I wasn't sneezing, Tuula. "Cheers" is an English expression meaning "good health".'

'Well, that's also the English translation of gesundheit.' Martin could see they were in a circular argument.

'What's Finnish for cheers or ger-sund-height, then?'

'Kippis!' Martin lifted his glass. I'll drink to that. Keypees! Martin's roast beef arrived with a plate of sandwiches and a salad garnish for Tuula. He checked again.

'*Sure* you don't want to try the carvery. It's pretty good here.'

'I'm eating with friends tonight, but thank you anyway"

After Martin had finished, Tuula collected their glasses and offered:

'Same again?'

'Absolutely.' If she had asked *One for the road?* Martin would no longer have been surprised. She declined his proffered note.

'OK Tuula, thanks.' When she returned from the crowded bar she extracted a large tablet PC from her bag and moved her chair round next to his. That had happened before with Tina on their first meeting in the back bar, but on this occasion he was more than conscious of the occasional pressure of a stockinged thigh.

Tuula started her computer and for a few moments entered data with quick finger movements. A window headed VPN opened briefly. When there seemed to be a lengthy pause on the tablet display, she glared angrily round the ceiling, eventually, Martin noticed, staring and muttering impatiently at a white box with winking green and red lights. Finally the InterconNet splash screen appeared.

'I thought Pete said that his programme was only accessible on the Uni network.'

'I'm on the Uni network.' Tuula squeezed her fingers together on the tablet's display. The network collapsed in on itself. It appeared to extend outwards a long way. The icons became just dots connected by spidery lines.

'The solid colour icons or small images are people signed up to Pete's network. They're the ones easiest to connect with on-line or actually to meet.' She smiled archly at him.

'Like me or your Anne here.' She next pointed at the edges of the display.

'The white or tinted graphics you see - we call them nodes by the way - are on other social networks, like Face Book or Linked In. If you want to connect to them, you'll have to invite them to sign up. But they will have to accept your invitation and InterconNet would have to permit the link. Not guaranteed, but then Pete has grand ideas and his programme is set to look for good reasons why a prospective member should *not* join, rather than looking for reasons why they should.' Martin thought of all the connections to Tuula's image.

'Why don't we see Pete Swales highly connected to users? It's his programme; his creation.' Tuula looked at him as if this was a dumb question.

'You can see churches everywhere - yes?'

'Yes?'

'And Church users; they accept that God is always watching over them?'

'You mean church-goers, Tuula. Well, yes, but what's that to do with Pete?'

'Well then, the users or goers can't see *God* can they?' Martin had to think about for a moment before the penny dropped.

Now Tuula dragged a menu in from the edge of the screen. It was the long list of options that Martin had seen in his first stumbling efforts with the programme.

'Through this menu you can make the programme select what other members you see on the screen.'

Tuula selected and deselected options including the Social Network names Martin had noticed earlier. As she did so, areas of the InterconNet map came and went.

'What may interest *you* more are options based on the profile you filled in when you registered with InterconNet.'

Tuula brought up a second menu next to the first. Martin recognised several of the keywords in the list. Now Tuula spread her fingers apart on the display and the network expanded until the small images of the network members were easily recognisable. On the first menu, she selected "Females". All the male pictures or squares vanished instantly. Then as Tuula ticked various keywords on the list specific to his profile, the small images on the map slowly disappeared until there were just two faces left; Anne Eres and Tuula. She turned to him with raised eyebrows and a wicked smile playing on her lips.

'Looks like, right now, your choice of women is limited.' She watched his face for a moment, then laughed.

'OK, *I* cheated to get this result. But this girl Anne, whoever she really is, is the closest to you on InterconNet. I see she's accepted you, but you've not confirmed the connection. I think she's worth connecting with, but I'll leave that to you now you know more about using the programme. Don't forget that InterconNet is not designed just for on-line dating though. I think Pete will be rather disappointed if that's all you try out. You may be looking for a partner, but he has his Ph.D. to think about!'

Her words suddenly reminded Martin that Pete wanted him to work out how to use the programme unassisted. Tuula seemed to read his thoughts as she stood up.

'Don't worry Mart - I shan't tell I've been coaching you. Anyway, don't church goers say: "God moves in a mysterious way"?' You found out more quickly about InterconNet through exploring the programme yourself and contacting me. That's the whole idea of Pete's programme isn't it?' Tuula looked at her watch again, collected her tablet and stood up.

'Thanks for the meal, Mart. Look, I've got some work to catch up on before my shift on Monday morning.' She held out a firm hand.

'Let me know how you get on with the programme and don't forget that now we are connected.' She blew him an ironic kiss and left the bar. As she did so, a number of eyes turned to look at him. They were mostly men.

****

Eight thirty Monday morning at the Woodlands, Martin was picking up his messages from Julie at reception, when Noura walked in.

'Good Morning Martin. Your early starts are becoming a habit. A welcome one though. Can you spare me fifteen minutes before you begin whatever it is you do at this early time in the day?' Martin's initially upbeat mood faded. What was it about this woman that unnerved him so much? What did she want now?

'OK I'll just put my post in my office. Five minutes?'

'So long as it's not much longer - I'm meeting a rep at 9am sharp and they know I'm not a customer to be kept or keep others waiting.' *I bet they do* Martin thought. Once in his room, Martin dumped his mail - mostly the usual marketing brochures - headed up the corridor to Noura's lair and knocked on the teak veneer.

'Come in Martin.' Noura's baritone sounded through the wood.

Noura was seated at her immaculately tidy desk, backed by rows of ring binders neatly identified with proper printed labels; not masking tape hastily marked up with different coloured Biro like his own.

'Sit down Martin. Now you may already know that Michael Timles is planning to expand our physiotherapy offering at the Woodlands, although given the present take up, I'm not sure exactly why he wants to do this.' Noura raised her bushy eyebrows and shook her head slightly.

'As far as I understand at present this means another treatment room with similar equipment to that which you have now and even ..' Noura paused, apparently from disapproval of the notion.

'..another therapist, probably more junior than yourself. Ours not not reason why eh Martin?' She took a deep breath having got the distasteful part of their meeting out of the way.

'Now; I will be looking into the question of space here at the Centre — no small matter - and costing out the whole exercise. Some of your existing equipment may be due for replacing or upgrading within the time frame of the present proposal and I must look into potential cost savings by taking this into account.

Then there will be administrative costs, advertising costs, new signage, disposables, services and so on. What I cannot do, Martin, is to determine the nature and provenance of new equipment needed and, since time has moved on, what existing items you can identify for me that will need replacing. I'd also like a list of all the fittings, instruments and consumables you'd require in operating an expanded service, with recommended manufacturers and their addresses.' Here Noura glanced at her wall clock. It was 8:50 am. Precisely. Noura turned back to him.

'And —' she paused again clearly punctuating her disapproval,

'— Michael has informed me that the Woodlands board feels we should all enter the digital age. Computers with an Internet connection are to be installed in all our therapy rooms. The existing network and booking system presently only available in the meeting room, reception desk and my office is to be extended to all our permanent therapists. Naturally, I as Centre manager will retain existing administrator privileges.' Noura leaned forward at this point

'I will tell you in confidence I'm not prepared to accept the "dumb terminal solution" that our chosen supplier will try to foist upon us. I know from previous experience that I can obtain hardware at a fraction of the cost of any devices a "network solutions" business would supply.' Noura adopted an expression that was both grim and knowing.

'But I will need you to tell me what sort of computer best suits your own IT needs and experience. Also remember that it may have to serve an expansion of your present physiotherapy service. The most important limitations on choice being cost, obviously, and a Windows Operating System.' Noura exhaled audibly through her nose. This meeting had clearly been an effort, but it was nearly at a close.

'I'd greatly appreciate it, Martin, if you could let me have your outline suggestions by email with any attachments, by the end of this week. I apologise for the short notice, but my annual leave comes up the week after next and I wish to submit my report to the directors before I leave.

You will obviously need more time to research and prepare your list of physiotherapy equipment with full costings and supplier addresses. Please aim to have this ready for me when I return from vacation.' Noura glanced once more at the wall clock. It was 9am and her intercom was already buzzing to announce the arrival of the expected sales representative. Both Martin and Noura stood up. As Martin returned to his room he passed Noura's visitor. His attaché case announced **Networks *Un*limited.**

Clearly that element of Noura's new instructions from the Woodlands board was to be put in place quickly. It did not escape his mind that he now knew someone who could not only tell him how to rapidly assemble most of the information Noura wanted, but also how to connect securely and privately to InterconNet from the Woodlands Centre. At the back of his mind he also recalled that she was someone whose InterconNet profile, unlike Anne Eres's, didn't rule out "romantic interest".

Martin headed for the Centre's small staff room. He mentally crossed his fingers that the room would be unoccupied when he opened the door. He was relieved to see that the assorted easy chairs were empty and no-one was making themselves a herbal tea or re-heating vine-leafed wrapped rolls in the tiny kitchenette. The last user had carelessly not logged out from the Woodlands computer network. Muttering his disapproval, Martin opened the email app and rummaged quickly in his wallet for his email address and password. After a short moment of panic, he found the appropriate scrap of paper and successfully opened his email box.

He saw that in addition to the email welcome messages there was an old one from Peter Swales sent about a week ago. This was a lengthy text in typical Pete Speak, hoping he would make a start with InterconNet and apologising he would be away in Ireland for a while. He mentioned Tuula again as someone attached to the Centre staff who could help if he had problems. Thoughtfully, Peter had supplied Tuula's email address. There was also an attachment containing further information that he'd forgotten to pass on. Martin decided not to open this just yet. Remembering that Noura would probably read all email sent over the Centre's network, he copied Tuula's email address then opened the Woodlands own email programme. He began to type the message that had been forming in his mind as he left Noura's office:

> From: Martin Wright
> To: Tuula
> Subject: Advice sought!
> Hi Tuula
> It was great to meet you while I was on the Uni campus yesterday. It's

very forward of me to take up your kind offer of IT assistance so soon, but there is an urgent requirement at my work to install new computers to extend the existing network at the Woodlands Centre where I'm based. I'd be most grateful for your recommendation for a computer running the Windows Operating System which would be cost effective in a small therapy clinic.

Important, but slightly less urgent than the need for the new hardware, I need to set up a comprehensive on-line search for new physiology equipment that will seek out the best deals on specific items. From this I can prepare a short list so that our centre manager, Noura Munday, can obtain quotes. Noura is also our network administrator here and oversees the security of our network and Internet connection. We are located very close to the University campus and if you were able to assist at such short notice, I could collect you from campus and bring you over to the Woodlands Centre.

Yours sincerely

Martin Wright
Physiotherapy
The Woodlands Centre
Tamford

Martin sent the message, then forwarded a copy to Noura with a brief explanation that he had by co-incidence met one of the University Computing Centre staff who was interested in his work at the Woodlands Centre and had offered their expertise in exchange for completing an anonymous survey programme they were developing. He pointed out to Noura that this opportunity could help him get her the information quickly which otherwise he might struggle to complete within her deadline.

Martin thought that this was near enough to the truth to satisfy Noura and allay any suspicions she would naturally have about information or advice concerning the Woodlands that was not coming directly through her office. He assumed that a smart cookie like Tuula would read between the lines of his message and not drop him in it with a highly familiar reply. But he was also slightly excited that she might. At present he wasn't flavour of the month here, but he still wasn't wedded to the idea of working indefinitely at the Woodlands.

Moments later, all these open questions were resolved. First of all, Noura responded to his message:

From: Noura.Munday

To: Martin Wright
Subject: Re: Advice sought!

Martin
This sounds good. Well done for moving quickly on this and potentially obtaining up to the minute advice for free. But do watch out that University people don't recommend hardware well in excess of what you will need. Also re: any survey you complete for the University. Please keep the name of our Centre and the Woodlands email addresses off the record. Most surveys have an "anonymous" option. Please ensure that you select it.
Noura Munday
Centre Manager
The Woodlands Alternative Medicine Centre
Tamford

A few moments later there was a reply from Tuula. As Martin half expected she was spot on with her reply. A copy had also been sent to Noura. He could imagine Tuula chuckling as she composed it.

From: Tuula Pipi
To: Martin Wright
Subject: Advice offered!

Dear Mr Wright
Thank you for your recent email. Regarding a Windows computer, I'd be more than happy to assist you make a suitable choice within your budgetary requirements. In relation to your need to source suppliers for your therapeutic instruments and other equipment, may I suggest you use a search facility we have developed here at Tamford University for similar purposes. There would be no cost involved for your Centre. The best way to do this would be for you to assemble an inventory of items and, where possible, manufacturer and model names and come over to the Computer Centre here.

I have a slot free tomorrow afternoon. If you can gather the data you will need by then, I'll take a walk over to your Woodlands Centre to look at your computer needs. Then you can give me a lift back to the University and we can do your search. Assuming all goes well, then, if you still agree, you could complete our survey for us while you're still in our Computer Centre. That way we both get more "bangs for our bucks." So to speak.
Sincerely,
Tuula Pipi

Systems Operator
Computing Centre
University of Tamford

A few minutes later another message from Noura popped into Martin's mailbox.

From: Noura Munday
To: Martin Wright
Subject: Re: Advice offered!
Martin
The arrangement you've made sounds excellent. It's a 'go' as far as I'm concerned. If I can get a recommendation for your computer before Friday, I'd be most grateful.
By the way, what a strange name for an American woman. But then nothing about the Americans should surprise us.
P.S. No need to keep copying me in on this. I'll just wait for your wish list to arrive now. Good luck at the University.
Noura Munday
Centre Manager
The Woodlands Alternative Medicine Centre
Tamford

Martin smiled to himself. Tuula's language and composition were impeccable, until her American slang crept in at the end. But this girl was so extraordinary that if at the end of her message she had "killed two birds with one stone" instead, he would not have been surprised. He was now certain that, once Tuula had helped him, he would be able to use InterconNet and exchange email from his treatment rooms without resorting to similar subterfuge again.

****

Tuesday afternoon, Martin found it difficult to focus on the task in hand: producing a inventory of his equipment. Every 20 minutes or so he checked his watch. He had picked up the same carton of TENS pads for the second time when he realised he was starting the inventory over again. Finally he sat down and wrote a short list of more specialised items that he thought could be shared between two physiotherapists; assuming that was what really might happen. He drifted into musing what an assistant physiotherapist might be like. In his reverie, he saw a young woman in a short white clinical tunic opening a drawer in his treatment room. He half expected to see Tina or Tuula's face, when she turned round, but it was Anne Eres's InterconNet image that smiled warmly at him.

The reception buzzer sounded and a crackly announcement from Julie came over the intercom.

'Your visitor is in reception, Mr Wright' Martin started and almost ran for his surgery door, concerned that while dreaming he'd missed an earlier call from Julie. He stepped briskly down the corridor and found Tuula waiting. For a moment he was speechless. *Talk about power dressing*. Tuula wore a smart figure hugging grey and white three-piece pin stripe. This time her dark stockings complemented her short business skirt demurely. Tucked under her arm she carried a smart leather folio emblazoned with the logo *Kosketecessa*. She fitted the stereotypical sales representative's appearance to a tee. Martin glanced back at the reception desk as he led his visitor to his office. Julie had lost interest and was reading a magazine. He could just imagine her expression had Tuula arrived attired as he had first met her in the Computer Centre. This time, Julie would not be passing comment over the Woodlands grapevine.

Once Martin's office door closed, Tuula asked him if she had been sufficiently discreet in her contacts so far with the Centre. Even Martin felt that this was begging the question.

'You know very well your performance is first class.' Tuula didn't answer, but put down her leather case on his desk and slid out a mobile phone with a large screen. She tapped at it then presented it face on to Martin. He was looking at some kind of virtual POST-IT note. It asked:

'Is your surgery bugged?' Martin didn't know whether to look serious or laugh, but Tuula kept a straight face.

'No!' Tuula wiped the note away with her fingers and another appeared:

'Are you sure?'

'I have good reason to be certain.' Tuula smiled and tucked her phone away.

'Good, now if you don't mind I'll hang up this jacket; I'm stifling in this business suit.' She hung the jacket on the back of his door, worked her crossover neck tie free of the collar and released several buttons of her disturbingly sheer pleated blouse.

'May I take a look around?' Attempting to keep his eyes on her face, Martin waved his hand in invitation. He trailed behind her, fielding her questions as she inspected his treatment room, massage bed and the assorted equipment. She did a couple of circuits of his office, examined the screened-off changing area then returned to sit by his desk. Martin joined her. Tuula stared at its cluttered surface.

'You really *don't* have a computer or even a dumb terminal in here, do you?' She sounded incredulous.

'Martin bridled a little.'

'I'd have brought you here under false pretences if I had.'

'Wouldn't be the first time *that's* happened to me Mart.' Martin couldn't think of an appropriate response to that.

'OK Mart, shoot. What do you need on your PC?'

'Up to now I have really only used the computer in the staff room for business purposes: email, physiotherapy websites, manufacturers and accessing my accounts with various professional bodies.'

'No porn or movies then?' Martin was shocked.

'Certainly not. Even if she hasn't blocked access to such websites, Noura can check which sites have been visited from work.'

'So you do that kind of browsing at home then do you?'

'No! I haven't got a computer at home either.' Martin was becoming embarrassed and a little irritated. It wasn't only the power dressing act that was disturbing about this girl.

'OK, OK Martin, I'm teasing you.' Tuula gave him one of her tilted smiles. Martin wasn't entirely sure whether these were meant to be consoling or condescending.

'Look, I'll just run through some options and you tell me yes, no or maybe - is that a plan?'

'All right.' Martin felt a bit silly about his reactions. Perhaps he should attempt to recover some lost dignity'

'I'm Sorry Tuula. Look, my former partner used the Web extensively, especially social media like Face book. I didn't like what she was doing on those and we argued a lot about that as well as other things. That's what led in the end to her being unfaithful. When she took our laptop with her other things I didn't replace it.' Tuula nodded sympathetically and reached over the desk to cover his hand briefly. Martin was touched but interpreted this unexpected gesture to mean: *I understand, let's stop this line of conversation*. Tuula removed her hand and sat back.

'Right, to business. She twisted her head round to read the inventory Martin had placed in the centre of the desk. Is that what you're bringing over to the Uni to do some searches with?'

'Yes, but I don't want to make myself unwelcome by taking up too much of your time. Would I need a long session with you?'

Tuula smiled seductively.

'Depends how long you'd like it to be.' Martin was by now getting more used to this peculiar style of Tuula's; turning questions round or making a puzzling or embarrassing reply.

'I'm not sure I understand, but I'm certain you'll enlighten me.' Tuula grinned broadly as if he had made a good joke.

'We should make a start on your list and then decide how much time we need based on results.' Martin watched her with a slight frown, still trying to work out why this girl was being so helpful.

'Look Mart, if you're worried about owing me; don't. It's good to have a break from programming and students suffering from lost passwords or computer viruses.' As she spoke, he thought again about all those InterconNet links to her; mostly males. Was she as friendly and familiar with them all?

'Let's agree what you need your office PC for. Here goes: a database for equipment, service schedule, reminders, consumables, suppliers, contacts . . Am I on the right lines here?'

Martin's attention jerked back to the task in hand.

'Oh. Yes.' He was shamefully aware of his current paper notebooks, diary and post-it notes.

'Patient records, bookings . .?'

'No, those are kept up by our receptionist, Julie'

'But wouldn't you want to have this data synced to the computer on your desk?'

'Sinked?'

'A data base on your own computer would pick up your own patient records and bookings from the Centre's server - I assume they have one - at regular intervals so you've always got access. Protects your schedule, even if the Centre's network goes down. Happens regularly in most organisations.

You could also sync your bookings to your mobile so you don't have to come into the Centre to check. You can share key information with your staff that way when you're out of the Centre. Martin was about to say that he didn't have an assistant when he remembered that this was one of the possible changes at the Woodlands. He didn't need to emphasise the fact that the Woodlands was behind the times in matters other than IT.

'Yes that would be a considerable improvement. You must think we are living in the Stone Age here as far as information technology goes. You see many of the therapists are *very* alternative and a computer is an intrusive object in a room full of soft lighting and candles.' Tuula smiled grimly at that.

'I wouldn't go as far as to call you guys Neolithic; Bronze Age, perhaps.' She brought out her mobile again. She entered text as they spoke.

'Apart from a database, what sort of office software do you use?' Martin didn't reply immediately. Tuula glanced up at his face and smoothly modified her question.

'Might you use a word processor?'

'Oh, Yes.'

'Spreadsheet?'

'Probably.'

'DTP?'

'Sorry?'

'Desktop publishing - you know; for newsletters, brochures and so on.'

'No. Noura does all that.'

'Never mind, you'll probably get one bundled with your office stuff anyway. Would you use Power Point or similar; you know for making slides for seminars and presentations?'

'Not really.'

'Do you give your patients exercises or other information to take home with them?'

'Oh yes. I'll need a printer then.'

'Sure, but if you want to get this place out of the Bronze Age your clients would probably do better being emailed You Tube video links or installing your Centre's app on their mobiles.' Martin thought it better not to comment on this. Tuula glanced at her phone and replaced it in her leather attaché case.

'OK, your requirements are pretty minimal, but I think you're going to find a hybrid useful.' She didn't wait for Martin's question.

'With a hybrid, the top part detaches and you can use it as a tablet PC - like the one I brought with me to the Green Dragon pub.' Tuula used the correct name this time.

'The base part has a standard keyboard and can run a separate display and a printer. That can stay in your office, where your staff can access it at any time.' Martin was surprised at Tuula's reference to "staff". How could she know about Timles's idea of a future expansion of physiotherapy at the Woodlands? But then she worked for a big outfit where the notion of technical assistants was a given. It suddenly dawned on him that Tuula was still describing her recommended IT hardware and his attention quickly returned to his visitor.

'The tablet can be carried around your surgery, used to inform or illustrate treatments to your patients. And even—'

Tuula gave him one of her parted lips and lowered eyelids looks

'—used in your treatment room and at your massage bed to take photographs. You know: before and after ones to help your patient.'

She gave him what he interpreted as a Scandinavian dirty look.

'Both the tablet and docking keyboard PC connect with networks by WiFi and you can take the tablet out of your Centre here for use elsewhere.' Tuula waited a moment for all this to sink in before continuing.

'Now a hybrid PC is a bit more expensive than a net book or a laptop, but what you spend on the hardware, you'll save on the software. In fact, I can identify all that stuff for you. I can give you a fixed price for your administrator here. If you tell her the programmes can be obtained free or at cost through your university contact, I have a feeling that she'll agree to it.' Tuula suddenly looked bored.

'Look Mart, I waste large amounts of my life with much more challenging tasks. If this Noura person approves your request, I'll set the computer up for you. But you will need to turn up at my place with a bottle of wine to answer all the dumb questions these Windows computers ask before they do anything useful for you. Is that a deal?' Martin thought of all the weak or false platitudes he could produce along the lines of: *I couldn't possibly expect you to go to so much trouble.* But even in his current state of ennui he realised that such replies would be strangled at birth by Tuula.

'Thanks. I can't think of a better way to be reintroduced to computing.'

Tuula looked pleased with this flattery. Then she lent forward and lowered her voice, adopting a confiding tone:

'And I will also set it up so you can pick up InterconNet on-line from here or your home. So then you'll be able to do something useful with that connection you "inadvertently" made to me.' The spinning fragments of feelings and hanging questions that Martin had experienced throughout Tuula's visit finally crystallised into an explanation. One of the InterconNet members was now working *off line* to pick *him* up.. Tuula straightened up.

'OK then; about your supplier and equipment search. I'm afraid something's come up this afternoon and I can't give any time to that for a few days. But I've emailed a form for you to fill in. When you've finished, return it to me and I'll get your search started for you. That will give us a starting point. Then you can come over to the University and we'll refine your initial search. Right Mart, anything else I can help you with?' Martin suddenly wanted to ask this astonishing female something; *anything* she couldn't have a ready answer for.

'Yes. I'm in trouble with my new neighbours at my flat. I've a balcony that's noisy when the wind is up and it's annoying them and me. I really need the noise to Finnish.' Martin drew out the double "n" and grinned a little at his own pun. Tuula either didn't pick up or ignored his weak attempt at humour.

'Sound like an aeolian harp?' Martin's jaw dropped a little.

'Yes.'

'The railings are probably open tubes. Block both ends with wax or, better, putty. You've probably got some wax at this Centre of yours.' Before Martin could respond, Tuula was rising from her seat.

'Now, I'd appreciate that lift back to campus, if it's still on offer?' She collected her jacket, but she didn't bother to put it on or button up her blouse to restore her neat crossover tie. It wasn't really her style. As they passed the reception desk, Julie looked up at Martin's attractive young business visitor, smiled sympathetically and remarked on how *warm* the day had become. With her highly developed dress sense, Julie always noticed things like that.

CHAPTER SIX
Timles

The following day, with no appointments after lunch, Martin remembered he was due to contact the Centre's owner, Michael Timles, to arrange a mentoring session. It took fifteen minutes rummaging in his desk to find Timles's home phone number. He had no wish to ask Noura for it. He called the Centre's owner, getting a answer straight away.

'Sure Martin; if you've no bookings this afternoon, come round now and we'll make a start. Don't forget to tell Noura, though. If she knows you're coming here you'll get brownie points instead of black marks. Hmmmm; where does that expression "brownie points" come from? Another intimation of the potency of the female, eh, Martin?'

As he was leaving the Centre, Martin remembered that Timles had given him something he was supposed to read and think about before his next visit. He returned to his desk and fetched Timles's envelope. He decided to wait to catch the bus from the stop outside to give himself time to read it. Expecting a sterile counselling-type list of personal questions, what was there took him by surprise. Printed on a sheet of Woodlands stationery, it was headed "A Comedy of Errors" which he instantly recognised as the title of a Shakespeare play.

A Comedy of Errors
Shakespeare recognised our human lives as a comedy of errors. And in writing his plays, the Bard of Avon incorporated most of them. His extraordinarily gifted mind even created hundreds of new words to describe thoughts and emotions he wanted to communicate to others in his plays. He entertains us as his characters make as many bad decisions as good. He makes us cry, but mostly laugh because of his masterly use of irony; his hapless players don't realise or refuse to admit their poor judgement, but we, the audience, know their life choices will lead to disaster or bathos. Shakespeare's winners are

those whose deeds are not precipitate; they think deeply before they act, then laugh at themselves and the world, whatever the outcome. Take home message: Reflection and humour are the cures for most of life's challenges. Don't bother with those self-help manuals; read Shakespeare's plays instead!
When (if!) you read this before contacting me again you were probably thinking that it would contain standard counselling speak (values and goals etc..) or some other psycho-babble. I haven't found that academic approach helpful and you can (if you seriously take up my offer of mentoring) expect a different experience from any you may previously have enjoyed (endured?).

We are such stuff that dreams are made of
And our little lives are rounded by a sleep.
Michael

On the other side of the sheet was something more recognisably like a mentoring plan:

Suggested sessions

1. Closure on past issues
2. Who are we?
3. Where do we go from here?
4. Partners and prospects
5. Progress to date
6. Review

Martin thoughtfully replaced it in the envelope. What was his boss's intention? To establish that Timles was different from other counsellors or mentors? That was clear enough. To encourage Martin to take a long hard look at his own life? Hopefully he would be doing that, although he had needed a push to get started. To tell him lighten up? That was easier said than done. To read Shakespeare's plays for inspiration? But which ones? Was it co-incidence that Timles had chosen to refer to the Bard to make his points hit home with Martin. How could Timles have known his fascination at school with the famous playwright. It was a mystery.

Turning into Timles's road, Martin passed by the Georgian fronted house where the watchful tabby lived. This afternoon the wall where it usually perched was deserted. He felt an irrational sense of loss. When a still puzzled Martin walked into Timles's back room, the Woodlands' owner wasn't behind his wide work desk, but sat comfortably opposite an empty easy chair, in which he signalled his visitor to sit.

'Tea or coffee, Martin?'

'A coffee for me, Dr. Timles.'

'It's *Michael*. Good; coffee's ready; I remembered your choice from last time. We'll both have a large dose of caffeine to sharpen our thinking.'

When they were settled, Martin felt relaxed enough to ask Timles about his unusual surname. Timles smiled widely:

'You may not believe this; it shows what strange things happen when a couple who have tried so hard for a child are finally successful. My father was Timothy and mum was Lesley. So they changed their surname, combining both. Hence *Timles*. The only regret I have, apart from constantly having to correct my name on documents, is that they didn't go the whole hog and make me *Timeless*. Anyway let's get on with our chat. Last time we didn't exactly work out how you could benefit by coming here, did we?' Martin shook his head slightly, not really knowing how to answer.

'I doubt you have given much thought to the sheet I gave you?' That question was easier.

'Well, I have *read* it.'

'Good. What you have read may *mean* something to you as well as we talk together. Keep what I've said in mind. Now if we are both going to get anything useful out of this, we'd better discuss our objectives and my terms and conditions. I'm offering you the option of mentoring sessions. You did wonder last time you were here whether I was qualified to do that, so I should repeat that I have had training and occasionally still practise. Why do I want to do this? I consider that you're very good at your work; when you put your mind to it, that is. The Woodlands Centre benefits from being able to offer physiotherapy. As a branch of health care fully recognised by the medical establishment, it lends status—credibility if you like— to the Woodlands. It brings clients through our doors who would otherwise never visit us and so be far less likely to encounter our complementary therapy options.

Of course if you can't shake off your present distracted state of mind with my help, then you might be faced with looking for another counsellor or even another job. So, what do you say? Will you agree to let me try and help?' By contrast with the cryptic comments on the sheet Martin had been given, Timles's proposal was clear enough.

'I appreciate your offer, Dr..*Michael*, but I'm not sure I can afford to pay for counselling right now, even though I accept that I need some form of help.'

'I've no intention of asking you for payment, Martin. I have just threatened you with the potential termination of your contract with us. I'm not going to add insult to injury by asking you to pay me to let you continue with us.' Timles paused a moment.

'Of course, *I'd* accept your deciding to seek counselling or mentoring elsewhere and I could even consider making a contribution to the fees for that. However, I sincerely hope you will take up my offer of help. So what's it to be?' Martin hesitated. It would be nice to recover some of the face he felt he had lost. He was going to say yes, but really wanted a more significant way of saying it. His boss had suggested in his curious message, that he should try to use humour to ease his passage through life. He thought about Timles's Shakespearean quotation. It probably *was* true that the Bard had a word or phrase for just about any situation. Macbeth had been his favourite tragedy; the one his form had studied for their English GCSE. Finally he found an appropriate affirmative for his boss:

'Lay on McDuff. And cursed be he who first cries: Hold, Enough.'

Timles instantly recognised Macbeth's famous words at the start of his last desperate fight with Malcolm. He smiled and extended his hand to shake Martin's own.

'I'll take that as a yes, then! Hopefully the outcome of your own struggle will be better than it was for Macbeth. OK, here are the ground rules. We'll aim for six meetings, then review our progress on the fourth one. We don't want to set a date for our meetings in advance; no point in us talking unless there are new developments to discuss or we've passed some milestone we've agreed and need to consolidate our progress. That said, we don't want to let more than three weeks pass before we hold our next session.' Martin had already noticed Timles's curious use of "we" and "us" rather than "I" and "you" in the mentoring summary and here were those inclusive terms again. But Timles was now explaining:

'This will be a shared journey, partly because I aim to learn from all the mentoring I undertake and partly because I really want you to become an effective member of our family at the Woodlands. I want you to live up to the promise you showed us at first.' Martin nodded in acknowledgement. So far his boss had put him at ease, but surely it wasn't all going to be like that?

'You'll find my approach very different from many professionals. Too much of the counselling and mentoring profession is heavy on theory and overly prescriptive. If I remember, you've met some of that during your own training?' Martin nodded.

'Well you'll notice I've discarded much of the jargon counsellors and mentors use. That's handy shorthand when these professionals communicate with other specialists. But I don't think it adds anything to mentoring and more often than not mystifies clients. In some cases, blinding customers with science or non-science is quite intentional. It's something I'm particularly aware of at the Woodlands. If our therapists have to hide behind jargon words and obscure explanations, then the sort of clients I want to attract and keep simply won't come back.' Martin recalled Tina's surprisingly powerful and convincing defence of Reiki and, indeed, all alternative therapies when they talked in the Green Dragon. He thought: *I can guess where her inspiration for that came from*. Now Timles had his full attention.

'We'll give ourselves about an hour this afternoon. First I want us to agree a name or description for your present state of mind that we'll both be reasonably comfortable with. It's important to get this right, as it will be the basis for all our later work. Of course we *may* find that this changes in the course of our discussions, but at that stage it might indicate good progress toward some resolution. I already know quite a few things about you, Martin. But it's important I don't nudge you now in particular direction that reflects my own viewpoint, then only later turns out to be a false trail. So, over to you.' Martin focused hard on answering Timles's question; how would someone else describe his disconnected state of mind? To give himself more time to collect his thoughts he answered indirectly:

'Can I say first that I followed up your suggestion to arrange some therapy with Tina Elves.' He deliberately avoided using the term "Reiki".

'She's already asked about my problem and offered me some treatment. But I'm not sure now where I stand on that. She's told me she's now resigned from the Woodlands.' Timles didn't comment on Tina's employment status.

'All right. How did you answer her then?'

'That I was depressed after breaking off a relationship with my long term girlfriend, Helena, shortly after joining The Woodlands. We didn't hit it off living together and she went off with another man. Since then as you've already pointed out, my work at the Centre's suffered and I have become pretty isolated socially. As Tina herself reminded me: I don't talk to the other Centre staff except as necessary and I spend too much of my spare time drinking alone in the Green Dragon pub. I filled my time there people watching. But the irony is I hadn't even noticed that it was becoming a gay venue until someone I met there pointed it out to me.' Martin laughed bitterly at this.'

'OK, that's a good start, Martin. I'm pleased you took up my suggestion to contact Tina, I was sure she would be willing to help. So that she and I get the same picture, is there anything else, relevant to our discussion, that you told Tina?' Timles looked expectantly at him. Martin noticed that his grey irises were ringed with a dark grey at their extremities. He wondered if his mentor was wearing contacts or if the striking pigmentation reflected some uncommon medical condition. Whatever the explanation, the effect was slightly alarming. And as he had thought, their discussion was about to become more uncomfortable. But he realised that he would have to be open with Timles if he was going to move forward and more significantly; keep his job.

'Tina asked about my personal relationships generally and with Helena in particular. She seemed to focus in one on issue especially. Martin hesitated wondering how to express this. He looked down at his hands resting uneasily in his lap.

'She wanted to know whether the physical side of our time together was satisfactory; I mean whether I was able to talk to her about her sexual needs as well as my own.'

'And what did you tell her?'

'I didn't really give any details about that. I thought she was straying too far away from her Reiki therapy. So I asked if she was trying to find out if I needed to see a GP or a relationship councillor.'

'What was her reply?'

'She didn't reply to that directly. She seemed satisfied with the answers I'd already given.' Martin narrowed his eyes while he tried to recall

Tina's parting words.

'She said she thought that Reiki might not be appropriate in my case, but then she had another type of therapy that could help me.' Martin paused and studied the carpet for a moment. He had been thinking quite a bit about this.

'I think she might have some sort of psychotherapy in mind.' Martin glanced quickly up at Timles. Tina, didn't seem to fit his impressions of the other Centre therapists. It suddenly occurred to him that Tina's resignation from Woodlands might not have been entirely voluntary. But Timles gave no sign of disapproval.

'Well, if you do continue to see Tina - even if she wants to offer psychological support, you'd be benefiting from a female perspective which obviously I can't give you. And she's a very personable and intelligent young woman. Professional considerations aside, that ought to make consulting her an attractive prospect. Unless my own intuition about you is wrong of course.' Timles didn't clarify his last remark, but smiled broadly.

'So, now that I've caught up with information you've so far shared with another potential therapist, let's continue. I need to know if you can recall periods of depression early on - before you were with Helena?'

'None that I can remember - although I probably had all the ups and downs of being a teenager. I hope you're not going to be taking me back to childhood. Four sessions probably wouldn't be enough!' Timles shook his head slowly.

'Searching client's childhood years for trauma has long been the favourite approach of councillors and psychotherapists. There may be circumstances where that's helpful. But it's my belief that it mostly wastes the client's and therapist's time. Knowing how someone arrived in a particular mental state rarely provides the answers for how to release them from it. We should be investing the maximum of time and effort towards dealing with the client's *now* and their immediate future. I'll only be asking a few questions about your past although between our sessions, *you* could go over old ground yourself. Far more in fact than we'd have time to explore together.

Now, the way I hope to play this is that in future meetings, you'll do most of the talking. I hope you'll be telling me about the steps you've taken towards a more positive frame of mind and report your successes as well as any concerns.' Martin nodded. After all, in his own therapy sessions, at first he asked all the questions and did almost all the talking. That was to be expected. As he was speaking Timles was looking down at a copy of the same cryptic comments he had given Martin. He next spoke almost to himself.

'You know, as it suggests in my odd prescription here reflecting deeply on things can help us understand who we are. But don't overdo that. Seeing the humorous side of our lives lightens our mood, but don't let that make you shallow.' Timles broke off and looked up.

'In case you may be wondering, Noura at the Centre won't be told anything about our conversations. Your reason for making future visits here will be to discuss plans to develop our physiotherapy offering at the Woodlands and look at taking on a physiotherapy assistant.' Timles fixed Martin's eyes with his own curiously pigmented ones.

'And that isn't just a smokescreen, Martin. Noura will be starting the ball rolling for me on this and will be speaking to you about it soon. So. *There's* a concrete objective to aim for. Do you want to be a part of the Centre's future or just involved in setting up good facilities for someone else? Give that careful thought and keep it in your mind as secondary motive for a successful outcome to our talks about you and your future.' This time Timles didn't smile and Martin realised that his mentor, having described the stick he could use, was now dangling a carrot. After a pause to let this sink in, Timles returned to his mentoring role.

'Am I right that you're not on and have never taken drugs to treat anxiety or depression?'

'Yes, that's right.'

'And you haven't seen a GP or spoken to anyone else apart from myself and Tina about this?'

Still searching his memory for any instances of drug abuse, it was a moment before Martin registered that he'd been asked a second question.

'Oh, No - I've not seen a GP. In fact I'm not registered with a local surgery.'

Timles raised his eyebrows.

'Well Martin, you should. In fact it's a requirement in our standard Woodlands contract, so please do it before we next meet.' Timles steepled his hands again. Martin had noticed this was a mannerism which signalled that Timles was starting on a new train of thought.

'Right, issue number one. Your dark mood descended after your break up with Helena. You then had time on your hands socially. Usually that's where friends step in to fill the vacuum.'

'Sadly I've very few friends. I was rather drawn into Helena's social circle, but I didn't really gel with any of her friends and contacts and haven't kept in touch with any of them.'

'What about all the time you spend in the pub. Don't you talk to anyone there?' Martin hesitated a moment before answering. He could be verging on confidential or at least awkward territory here.

'I've met an interesting mature postgraduate student called Peter.'

'He's not a gay punter, presumably?'

'I very much doubt it.'

Somewhat to his surprise, Martin found that he was opening up to his boss in a way that he would never have thought likely. Somehow Timles had managed to put them on an equal social footing. It was as if they were talking in a place where the labels: owner, boss, employee, contractor, were no longer relevant. Timles was speaking again.

'OK. Let's wrap up this session. I'll summarise for us. You've been sent up in front of the beak - that's me - because clients have given less than glowing feedback about your treatments. We've all noticed that you have become more withdrawn. Our administrator was worried to the extent that she actually stayed behind at the Woodlands to talk to me after five thirty one evening.' Timles grinned and shook his head wonderingly at this.

'That's when I knew things *must* be serious! From our chat this afternoon, you've identified depression as being behind this. You consider that your persistent low mood was triggered by Helena going off with a rival, but the roots of your depression may go back to long standing relationship problems. Do you agree so far?' Martin nodded.

'But you had already taken some steps to improve the situation before today by talking to Tina about things. On the plus side you have even thought of flirting with an alternative therapy — Reiki; another first! Tina has had time to observe you at The Woodlands and after you opened up to her about relationship problems, decided that she may be able to tweak your empathy controls. We aren't quite sure how she intends to go about this.

You've also made contact with someone from the university who sounds lively and intelligent. That's potentially opening up both technical and social opportunities.' Timles paused to give Martin time to think about this. He had already noticed that Martin took time to digest what was being said. Like Noura had commented to Timles, Martin sometimes seemed to be a young person groping in a mental fog. Timles continued:

'My advice is as follows: Do pursue some therapy with Tina. I think she's very good on empathy. She has a very pragmatic approach to her work and I know she has helped people who are much more sceptical about complementary medicine than you. See if your contact at the pub can introduce you to anyone at the University.

I've been told by a little bird at the Woodlands that one or two of your recent clients from the Uni are extremely attractive. Don't quote me on this but you might just meet them on campus.' Martin raised his eyebrows slightly. Timles looked directly at him, his head slightly tilted as though he was trying to assess how carefully he was paying attention now they had nearly finished their session.

'I was serious about suggesting you read some of Shakespeare: his poetry as well as his plays. Take a close look at how he deals with men and women talking to each other; in casual meetings as well as lover's trysts. But remember his wise words on relationships Martin: *The course of true love never did run smooth*. No-one probably has handled human feelings and emotions better. And at the end of the day, feelings and emotion are what our lives are all about.'

Timles rose and extended his hand. As Martin stood to take it, he glanced through the wide patio window. The distant hills were still there, but they were different from his previous visit; they seemed to be more sparsely wooded. Martin blinked. Timles coughed politely and Martin looked round and grasped his hand.

'You know your way out, I look forward to your call to arrange our next meeting.' On his way back, Martin turned and stared between the houses, but no vantage point brought the wooded hills seen from Timles' lounge into view. The Tabby was back on its wall and stared at him as he was passing. Suddenly Martin stopped as it came to him what had been different about those distant uplands.

The cat tensed and arched its back ready for fight or flight as Martin halted abruptly opposite. In those high woods the leaves were gone. In Tamford it was summer, but up there it was autumn. What was it that his new mentor had said on his last visit? Something like: *We can't change things that are out of our control, but we can change our perception of them.* At face value that was probably quite true, but how could the Woodlands reclusive owner change *Martin's* perception of things? As he walked on, the cat leapt down from its perch and disappeared into the garden behind. Just what *it* perceived, no human would ever know.

CHAPTER SEVEN
Martin

At a loose end that evening, Martin found himself once again in the Green Dragon. After fetching his pint, he sat and reviewed his week so far. Following his session with Timles, he'd thrown himself into work at the Centre, hoping that would be a distraction from going over and over it in his head. There had been a welcome trickle of new bookings, some of which he hoped might sign up for a course of treatment. He had noticed that most of his regulars were women. He put this down to females in general taking better care of themselves. This was particularly noticeable in the case of those who were sportswomen. They were more competitive and demanding than his male clients.

Even so, he felt several of his female patients had improved so much whilst coming to him, that their continued attendance was not strictly necessary. He even gave some hints that this might in fact be the case. But these hints were only gentle; at present there were not so many clients on his books that he could afford to show them the door whilst they still wished to attend his clinic.

He put down his beer glass and began to work systematically through this evening's customers. The two women in the first dining bay certainly looked in good shape and had chosen outfits to emphasise that fact. The dark-haired girl wore a smart figure hugging sleeveless top with some kind of sports logo over one breast. Her well proportioned and tanned arms were relaxed and were spaced apart on the table, one hand clasping a half-pint glass. It was a masculine posture, emphasised by straight shoulders and a steady gaze as she spoke. Her blond companion had her back to him, but when she glanced sideways he realised with a start that it was his ex: Helena.

The dark girl sat back and upright against the oak seat, whilst Helena kept leaning forward to respond to her companion's questions. This occasioned much sweeping back of hair. Martin noticed that Helena used both hands each time to reposition wayward strands. There was a definite crimp part way down her hair. Martin guessed that hair clips or a band had recently gone away without leave.

He decided Helena's drinking companion was either a PE teacher or instructor. Perhaps at the local leisure centre. He wondered what their relationship was. Helena seemed ill at ease. Sports lady appeared to be getting concerned by her companion's anxious hair adjustments, as a reassuring hand suddenly moved across and covered Helena's fidgeting wrist. After a moment, the dark girl stood up and Martin could see that she was tall and with well muscled arms. She moved round the side of the table to Helena, turned up her face towards her and kissed her. Helena reached for her hand and squeezed it, then the tall stranger left the bar.

At first Martin just sat still, thoughts racing through his head. He was torn between drinking up and leaving before Helena noticed him and going over and asking her how she was. He reached for the fragment of Reiki Tina had given him.

Be kind. Honour your relatives and those close to you.

Well, Helena was certainly close right now and the least he could do was to be kind. Clutching his glass, he walked over to Helena's table. She looked up in surprise. Martin noticed that her eyes were red rimmed.

'Hello Helena.' He saw that she was holding an empty glass.

'Can I get you a drink?' Helena gave him a lopsided smile.

'Hello Martin.' She looked down at the empty glass still moving in nervous hands.

'Yes please. A white wine soda would be lovely.' Martin ordered Helena's drink and a further pint for himself. When he returned, Helena was hurriedly stuffing something away in her bag. Martin made a point of not noticing what it was. He put down her drink and asked:

'May I join you?' Helena nodded wordlessly and readjusted her position, even though Martin was sitting down opposite her. He broke the awkward silence:

'Been a long time. How are things?' Helena sniffed and swallowed, although she hadn't touched her drink.

'Been better Mart. How about yourself?'

'I'd say pretty much the same.' Martin hesitated.

'Probably spend too much time in here. It's the first time I've seen you here though, Helena.'

'I suppose you saw George - I mean Georgina?' More relaxed now, Martin took in that Helena was wearing an attractive low cut sun top and the wrist supporting her untouched wine sported a series of bangles. He had never seen her dressed like this. His courage growing, Martin asked gently:

'Is she your girlfriend?' He thought Helena was going to cry - also a first for Martin - and he reached out for her free hand. Helena didn't withdraw it.

'Would it help to share?' he asked. Helena looked at him and gave a much less lopsided smile.

'Do you mean tell you what's been going on since I left or, if you're still on your own, share you with George?'

'Martin too grinned. The tension appearing to have gone out of this chance meeting he relaxed further. He now wondered why he hadn't tried to meet up with Helena before and just worried endlessly about her rejection. George/Georgina could explain a lot.

'Hey, Helena, Let's lay some ghosts. Tell me about yourself - and Georgina too if you like - and I'll say what's been happening to me. There are bits that you might find hard to believe, but it looks like that might be the same with your story too. Shall we toss a coin for who goes first?' Martin lifted his glass and Helena finally picked up her own.

CHAPTER EIGHT
Tina

Checking his email on Friday, Martin found a message from Tuula. This worried him at first, but there was a geeky email footer which assured him emails would not sent to his Woodlands Centre email box; all future messages would be private to him. He couldn't read the greeting and last few lines, which were presumably in Finnish and he wondered what was hidden there.

Tuula mailed she wouldn't be able to deal with his physio. equipment search at present. She had to report on her research in Tamford for Kosketecessa. But a quote for his new computer was attached. If he could get Noura's approval for invoicing before she left for her vacation, Tuula would order it for him. Once again, as if she read his mind, she added that he could decrypt the Finnish sentences using one of the on-line translation apps - *if he wanted to!*

Most men would have gone straight onto Google translate or the like, but Martin opened the attached quote. He was surprised by the reasonable cost and noted that even the VAT would be recoverable by the Woodlands. He forwarded the quote to Noura considering that as she was even more preoccupied than normal, she would be likely to agree without further scrutiny. Sure enough, minutes later a purchase order popped into his email box, with the brief message that as this was well within budget he was to forward it to his contact. Equally promptly, his email authorising Tuula to go ahead to was acknowledged. Martin felt some of the excitement most would feel at the prospect of a new toy. Besides, he told himself, it was the first small step towards his promised improved status at the Centre.

As Martin had predicted, for all of the following week, Noura kept out of his hair. She even smiled at him when she passed him signing out at the reception desk on Friday. Martin half wondered about Noura's vacation.

Could there be someone else, waiting to join her on holiday? If there was, Martin had never seen any sign of a friend or partner, of either sex. As he drove home, he remembered he was meeting Tina outside the Woodlands on Sunday to take her for lunch. Then there was this proposed Reiki or some other mysterious treatment.

It was curious how after spending so many weekends alone watching couples socialising in the pub, two females had appeared in his life. An interesting development certainly, but he didn't feel any especially pleasant anticipation. He didn't really feel any different at all. Perhaps he was, like Noura seemed to be; living only for his work and driven simply by a sense of duty. Could Timles, Tina or even Tuula change that? Curious that all his new contact's names began with "T". Was that just co-incidence? Timles, Tuula and Tina; Time would Tell. Then he stopped himself playing with alliteration. He was beginning to smile and that wasn't like him.

Once he let himself into his flat he faced the decision whether to cook whatever he could discover in the flat or to get a takeaway. Contemplating the sparse contents of the 'fridge he remembered he should book for his meal with Tina on Sunday. Most places would be full of people like him now; also wanting to escape having to cook at home. But where to suggest? Another decision; and it probably would be a bad one, whatever he chose. In the end, he decided to book at The Brown Bear in Read. He recalled good reports about its old world atmosphere and excellent food. Being near the Thames, though, it would be popular and reservations essential. He hoped it hadn't recently been converted into a ghastly gastropub or bought up by one of the big chains and brought into conformity with their national brand.

His 'fridge didn't offer much prospect and the freezer even less. It was too late to defrost anything anyway. Instead of visiting the convenience store, he decided to investigate the Brown Bear for an evening meal. It wasn't that far to drive and the Green Dragon would be packed with students.

It was dusk when he parked in the Brown Bear's courtyard. He walked round to the rear of the half timbered building. A vine covered loggia ran along the back of the Inn and there were diners and drinkers at lantern lit tables. Beyond, the lawn sloped down to the dark water of the Thames. Inside it was large, busy but unspoilt by the obligatory ersatz rural accessories present in so many big enterprise inns. He bought a beer, ordered a steak and ale pie with chips and booked two for lunch on Sunday. Could he reserve an outside table? No, but if he arrived at noon, there would be spaces available.

Martin settled with his drink. The atmosphere was completely different from the Dragon's. Many tables seated six or more and there was a much wider spread of ages. Conversations were animated, but not as boisterous as the nonsense of the airheads and their cronies in the Dragon. A very young waitress in a black and white dress with a matching wrap-around apron brought his food. She gave him a genuinely warm smile and asked if there was anything else she could fetch for him

When he shook his head, she turned and left for the kitchen. As she departed, he looked at her bobbed hair and neat little figure and felt sad. He couldn't go on feeling isolated like this. He would try whatever his self-appointed mentors might to suggest. Through the unexpected encouragement he'd been given by Timles and Tina, and now Tuula, he had dipped his toe in the water. It was time to wade in.

****

Sunday dawned bright with early morning sun in a cloudless sky, just as the TV weather lady had promised. Tina drew up outside the Woodlands Centre at a quarter to twelve and Martin was pleased he'd arrived early. He'd still been thinking of their meeting today as a "consultation", but after his negative feelings in the Brown Bear on Friday and two lonely, reflective nights, it seemed more cheerful to call it a "date". That might explain not only why he was uncharacteristically early, but also the trouble he had taken to dig out and iron his best summer casuals. Tina too wore smart light clothes that were easy on his eye, in complete contrast to the way Tuula's attire knocked it out. But then, he realised, Tina was always dressed in a co-ordinated, relaxed style which reflected the season and the occasion. Why hadn't he really seen that before? Was his ennui beginning to lift?

'Hi Tina, you're looking a picture today.' It came out awkwardly, but at least he was making the effort.

'Hello Martin, thank you. you're looking good yourself. Seems as if we're going to be lucky with the weather. Can you tell me where we're going or is that a secret; a mystery tour perhaps?'

'Oh no; I've reserved a table at the Brown Bear in Read.' Martin decided not to admit his own recent visit, but to check whether Tina knew the pub first. The years living with Helena had taught him not to overdo the delights of wherever or whatever he had planned as a treat or surprise.

'Have you been there before, Tina? I only know it by reputation, but it sounds good.'

'The old riverside inn? No I've heard about it too, but haven't visited.'

'Yes. When I booked, they said if we arrive close to noon we're likely to be able to sit outside in the garden. As you probably know, it goes down to the Thames. Apparently you can't reserve those tables so it's first come first served.' He was pleased with himself. He actually thought the Inn was lovely, but it was better to hear superlatives from his companion.

'If you're happy to leave your car at the Centre, we can travel in mine.' At his rather grimy Ford, Martin clicked the key fob, but his gallant attempt to open the passenger door for Tina was marred by the door refusing to budge. It took several inelegant tugs to finally coax it free. It had been a long time since he'd opened the passenger side. Martin battled against the all too familiar feeling of the day heading towards farce. But Tina had a knack of calming tension:

'In *my* car, the boot sticks every time I shop. I know I should get it sorted, but it always gets forgotten.' She sat, sweeping up her summer dress to avoid the dirt accumulated in the door surround. Soothing nerves instinctively was part of her working life.

The rest of the journey was uneventful and they were rewarded with a table under the loggia just where the vine parted to allow a view down to the river. Unlike the dark water of the previous night, the Thames was blue-green. The surface sparkled as the nearest bank slowed the flow, sending miniature eddies swirling across the water. Tina put down her menu, took in the garden and water and breathed in deeply. She smiled and lifted her shoulders appreciatively.

'As you haven't been here either, it's a great choice Martin. If the food's as good as the surroundings, I'd definitely come again. Have you chosen? This one's on me by the way.' Martin protested, but Tina continued to smile and shake her head. When someone came to take their order, it was the little waitress of Friday evening. She recognised Martin and gave him a big smile, ignoring Tina.

'Hello there, Nice to see you again so soon. Are you ready to order sir?' Martin groaned inwardly. First the jammed car door, now this girl's lack of experience or training by the establishment were doing their best to ruin his day. Martin didn't acknowledge her friendly greeting. He looked deliberately at Tina.

'You order. I'm terrible at remembering.' When they had both ordered food, Tina asked for a bottle of wine she said was her favourite. Martin noted it was also one of the most expensive. His confusion must have been apparent because as soon as the pretty youngster had departed with their orders Tina reached out and lightly covered his hand. For a moment she just studied him and Martin sensed his cheeks burning slightly.

'That's very sweet of you; coming secretly to check the place out.' That sympathetic gesture again. Quite unlike Tuula's when he shared his feelings about his split with Helena. Tina's reassuring hand meant *don't worry, I understand. You're doing all right.* He realised that he was getting an object lesson in social skills. And the promised therapy, whatever *that* was, hadn't even started.

Chatting with Tina over lunch was much more relaxing than his recent conversations with Tuula, when he felt he had to run, mentally and even physically, to keep abreast. Previously he'd talked with Tina almost exclusively about himself; now, away from his usual haunt and the state of mind it engendered, he wanted to find out more about his companion.

'When you told me you'd resigned from the Woodlands to build up an independent practice, you didn't really say what it was. I'm guessing it has more to do with psychology than Reiki.

'I wasn't sure then whether you'd really take up my offer to help. Now you have, I can tell you more about it, but it does involve an element of surprise—a shock perhaps—that I can't reveal in advance. Certain aspects of my treatment may not be suitable for everyone and that can only emerge after a few sessions.' Martin looked puzzled. Tina smiled and her eyes seemed as reassuring as her recent touch.

'Oh Martin, don't look so worried. There's a very simple explanation. I'm a single woman running a personal treatment business from her own home. I don't want . . don't need to promote my work openly for reasons that you'll see in due course. Before I work with clients I need to know as much or more about them as *they* want to understand about me and my practice.

For that reason I'm really only accepting people I already know or have been introduced or referred by individuals I trust. That makes sense doesn't it? I don't have the relative protection or infrastructure of a Centre like the Woodlands.' What Tina was explaining did indeed make perfect sense, but he was still not being told much about what she actually *did*. The Woodland's owner had also seemed reticent to discuss Tina's present practice, even though he had encouraged Martin to take up her offer of help. Martin thought he might learn a bit more by asking about Timles's referral. He leaned towards her slightly and dropped his voice.

'After I asked you about Reiki, Michael Timles suggested I ask you for some sessions. When I next visited, I told him I had. But that was after I learnt you were leaving the Woodlands. He still seemed very pleased. I thought he'd disapprove of me going outside the Woodlands for therapy.' As Martin spoke, he remembered Timles had asked what he had told Tina in their initial meeting. He thought perhaps he should confess that before things went much further.

'Timles pumped me a bit about our conversation in your flat. I told him what we'd discussed, even though it was rather personal. But he explained that since I had started coming to you formally, he wanted to start *his* mentoring with the same picture.' Martin didn't know whether Timles would continue to ask him about his sessions with Tina, but he didn't want either Timles or Tina to feel that he was sharing confidential information about the two practises.

Tina smiled at Martin and he found her eyes warm and reassuring.

'Well thanks for letting me know, Martin. But there's no problem. Now I also have something to confess. Michael helped me set up my new therapeutic practice. Some of the new techniques I use are his own invention and he is in effect a private investor. But he couldn't accommodate me at the Woodlands. My work is outside the range of therapies offered there, even though both he and I see it falling into the broad category of complementary medicine. So you see I really don't mind you sharing information with him. It's up to you to decide what you want to tell him.'

Martin realised that the more he asked, the more mysterious Tina's work became. The only way to find out would be to put himself in her hands and see what happened. He sat back in his chair.

'Are you ready to go, Tina?' She nodded and got up to pay the bill, motioning him to stay seated as she stood up.

'No; I said I'll pay this time, but you can bring that bottle of wine with us; there's enough for a glass or two after we've driven back to my flat.'

****

When they arrived at the Woodlands Centre, Tina asked him if he would mind travelling in her own car.

'I think after our session it would be best for you not to drive. I'll give you a lift back to your own flat afterwards.' Martin was surprised by this, but having agreed to submit to his new therapist, he didn't protest or ask why. Back at the Woodlands, leaving Martin's vehicle in the area reserved for staff, they piled into Tina's Smart car. Martin did feel confident enough to comment that it was *a highly suitable choice for an alternative therapist*. Tina smiled and retorted:

'I expect you're thinking *this eco-minded girl is trying to save the planet*, but you'll change your mind when you see the spaces in our underground car park.' Martin laughed at this, but his opinion of Tina kept rising. How was it he had practically ignored her all the time she was working at the Centre?

They drove in silence through relatively light afternoon traffic, but the absence of conversation seemed appropriate. Martin was left to his own musings about what was about to happen. They arrived outside Tina's block of flats and she drove down a ramp and through a wireless-operated barrier. Lights came on automatically and Martin saw that Tina's small vehicle was indeed an advantage negotiating round the concrete supporting pillars. Soon he was back in her comfortable lounge.

'Before we start, I think we should finish this wine, don't you? It's never quite the same the next day.' Tina fetched glasses and some kind of crackers in a dish. Martin poured the remainder of the wine and took a cracker.

'These are more-ish, what are they?'

'Poppy seed.'

'Isn't that hallucinogenic?' Tina furrowed her brow and stared at her half eaten cracker.

'I don't think the seeds are from opium poppies. Anyway, you'd probably have to eat several packets at the same time to notice any effect.'

'Probably just give you wind, rather than a trip.' They both laughed at this witticism.

'I don't think I've ever seen you so relaxed, Martin.'

'Nice wine, good company. I know I have dark moods, but not today.'

'That's good because I really need you to be relaxed and positive right now.'

'And I promise to suspend my disbelief as they say in acting.'

'Do you remember those Reiki principles I told you when you were last here?'

'Now you're challenging me. Let's see. Just for today . . Don't worry. Er, Don't be angry..'

'Work diligently?'

'Oh yes . .Be generous.'

'Kind.'

'Right, then be grateful.'

'That's not bad recall for someone who never gave those ideas a second thought after they left here. You must have been in amateur dramatics.'

'Ouch, I confess you're right about that first comment, but wrong about the second.'

'OK, well keep those principles in mind this afternoon. In that order too.'

'Mysteriouser and mysteriouser.'

'As I suggested when you came last time, we aren't going to do Reiki today. We're going to do a visualisation. When I consulted you at the Woodlands about my back pain I was assessing whether what I can do for you might work. I mean work as well for you as what you were able to do for me.' Martin looked hard at her.

'Oh, the pain was genuine, by the way —' Martin interrupted her as he remembered what Tina had said afterwards.

'After you gave me those principles, you told me that I should apply them to my first client the next morning, knowing it would be yourself. Pretty smart that.'

'Thank you. And whether or not you had them in mind, you held to them perfectly. On the therapy side I saw that you were able to enter my body mentally to identify the problem and fix things. On the personal side, I wanted to use the opportunity build trust.'

'Trust?' Tina sought and held his eyes. Men, she realised, often looked away when they were discussing sensitive or potentially embarrassing issues.

'I'll be touching you in a very intimate way during this session. I *hope* you'll stay relaxed - I'll help you do this. I'm not aiming to stimulate you in the conventional sense, but to introduce you to an emotion that I think is absent or repressed. Do you think you'll be OK with that?' Martin sensed the intensity of her gaze. Her eyes were a very light grey, but he noticed that the edges of her pupils were a darker colour. This variation in pigmentation gave them a slightly hypnotic effect. He blinked hard. Some of the clouds obscuring Tina's work were dispersing. So she gave *that* sort of massage. His reply was thoughtful and drawn out.

'Ohhhh Kay, Sounds a bit clinical. I'd better drink up, then.' As he drained his glass he noted that Tina had left hers untouched.

'Good. I'm afraid I can't offer you a chaperone like you offered me when I came to your clinic.' Tina gave him a cheeky grin.

'So then, my treatment room is over here.' She rose, came over to his easy chair and took his hand, leading him through one of the doors off the lounge and shutting it behind them. They stood in a dimly lit short corridor with a further door ahead. Tina indicated curtains at either side and pointed to the ones on the right.

'You can change in there.' Puzzled, Martin entered and drew the curtain behind him. In the small space there was a mirror and wall hooks holding a towel and swimming trunks. Martin lifted up the costume and sniffed it dubiously. It had a faint freshly laundered smell. Shrugging his shoulders he stripped off and pulled the costume on. The fit was firm but OK - he couldn't recall when he last wore swimming trunks. He drew the curtain aside and a few moments later Tina emerged, also in swim wear. Her dark bikini made of three fabric triangles on laces made his own costume feel positively Victorian. They stood facing each other in the small corridor. Tina explained:

'This is a visualisation exercise. Please try to enter in to the spirit of this, Martin. What's about to happen you will find very strange; possibly even rather disturbing at first.' Tina paused to allow this to sink in, then continued:

'I want you to imagine you're on holiday with your girlfriend; that's me OK?' Tina's expression adopted that cheeky grin Martin was now finding familiar.

'It's summer and the weather is perfect. We've driven down to our hotel together today, checked out our bedroom and spent the remainder of the day exploring the resort before chilling in a really nice seafront bar.' Tina looked at Martin.

'Shut your eyes if that helps. You've had a few drinks - and that's a fact Martin: you won't have to work at that bit too hard! It's now late evening and the sun's setting. Neither of us want this day to end yet and I suggest we go down on the beach. The crowds have left and there's just the two of us, the cooling sand and the summer sea. It's a bit of a laugh so I'm in a playful mood.'

'And what sort of mood am I in?' Martin asked, still with his eyes closed. He opened them quickly when he felt a kiss, though.

'You will be whatever you will be.'

'Cryptic; you're very masterful you know—' Tina interrupted him quickly.

'I hope you weren't going to say "for a woman".'

'Well, *mistressful* then.'

'You don't know the half. But you're sparring with me and that's what I want at this moment.'

'So what do you want me to do next?'

'OK. Now I'd like you to close your eyes again and start working on conjuring up a sea shore beyond the door ahead. It will be pretty dark on the shore, so you don't *have* to have Tina Elves with you. It can be any other woman you know or fancy.' Martin shut his eyes obediently, but he was beginning to be concerned that this whole thing was an elaborate farce. It seemed a bit childish. The sort of play acting you grew out of in your teenage years. Then he recalled the Reiki principles.

Might as well give it a go now I've come this far. Principle No.1 Don't worry. That was certainly appropriate. Now Tina needed him to think of a woman to take to the beach. It seemed a bit odd to choose his therapist although obviously that would be the easiest thing to do. *Tuula? Not her bag at all. Julie from the Centre? She'd certainly be game for this sort of thing, but her giggles would be overpowering and kill any atmosphere Tina hoped to create. Anne Eres; his mysterious InterconNet lady? He'd never met her. As far as he knew she was virtual, so would be perfect for this visualisation game of Tina's. He focused on her image, or rather on her avatar. It was surprisingly easy, as it was hard to dismiss it from his mind anyway.*

'OK *Anne,* let's hit the beach.'

'Wow, who's Anne?'

'As far as I know, just a figment of my imagination.'

'Just as well, Martin otherwise I might get jealous and give you a hard time in there.'

Martin refrained from making the obvious reply to her threat. He remembered his next Reiki principle - he wouldn't be angry, or at least annoyed or irritated by whatever lay beyond the next door.

'Right, let's go.'

There wasn't an answer, but two hands found his shoulders and gently ushered him ahead. Half-heartedly, he tried to imagine a slightly tipsy Anne shoving him in the direction of the surf. But Anne's eyes seemed too serious for him to cast her as a giggly thirty something out for a bit of fun on a night time beach. Still keeping his eyes closed, he walked in front of Tina, hearing the door opening and then closing behind them. As they entered, the guiding hands moved up from his shoulders to cover his eyes. They moved in this fashion a little way into the room.

'Just imagine you're on a dark beach, the only light comes from a clouded moon.' Martin followed his instructions, but reality was starting to replace his mental image of a seashore. As soon as he'd entered the room, the atmosphere felt much cooler, but what was quite extraordinary was the feeling under his feet, the sounds, the smell and the taste on his lips. The floor was firm but felt quite gritty. Ahead he could hear the unmistakable surge and drag of surf. A sharp, fishy, weedy odour wrapped itself around him, arriving on small warmer puffs of air. A damp gust stirred his hair. Involuntarily he licked his lips. They tasted salty. Tina's hands were withdrawn from his face.

'You can open your eyes now if you want.' But they were already open; wide open. The room or space they were in was quite dark, but he sensed Tina standing beside him, now holding his hand. Looking ahead, high up, there was some lightness. As he tried to make it out, it changed. As his eyes slowly dark adapted in the gloom, he realised with shock that he was looking at dark clouds moving slowly across a just distinguishable moon in a starless sky. To each side of where they were standing was darkness deepening to black. The sensation of having stepped outside onto some unknown shore was absolutely compelling.

'How on earth?' Martin was lost for words. He was answered by a giggle.

'Let's paddle.' Tina's voice seemed different; a lower register. *No, not a lower register. The echoes had gone. They had moved from the narrow changing room corridor in her flat into a space where there was no reverberation; no sound was being reflected, just as it would be if they were really outside on a shore. It made no sense.*

His companion led him forward. He sensed a shelving ground then water washed over his feet and ankles.

'Not too far - we don't know if there are strong currents.' Once again that giggle and he felt his back splashed with water a few times. It was tepid, like the gusts of wind. What had she given him?

'Are you sure those poppy seed crackers were safe?' He was only half joking about having been given something hallucinogenic.

'I had more than you.'

'But you're in this dream too, Tina! I know! it was the wine - I didn't see you drink yours at all!'

'Don't forget I'm driving you home after this. And it sounds like your Anne has already left you. That's OK, you're probably safer with me as I'm a *real* girl, not a figment of your imagination.' Tina squeezed his hand.

'For now just accept what you see and hear.' Tina sounded pleased and amused rather than cross with his pathetic accusations of her doping him. Martin was momentarily irritated that this woman had a perfectly correct answer for everything.

Principle no. 2 Don't be irritated.

'OK Tina; so where are we and how did we get here?'

'In the sea and we travelled from Tamford.' Martin sighed *She's done it again. Never wrong, but still not telling me what I want to know.*

Principle No. 3 Work diligently: shut up Martin. Go along with whatever she's planned. Answers on a postcard later.

'I'm sorry Tina. It's just such a surprise. I was expecting to have to imagine all this, not for it to actually happen. Are we going to swim next?'

'I don't swim Martin. I just want to play in the surf instead. I know, let's exchange costumes. No-one can see us here.' That was not really what Martin felt like right now. He wanted to know how this woman had managed to create this illusion—for that's what it had to be—in a first floor Tamford flat, but there were no immediate answers to be had without spoiling Tina's game.

Work diligently. Play along to see what would happen. Tina was keeping things light but it sounded like they were getting to the intimate bit she warned him about. Well, he would damn well work diligently at enjoying this experience.

'OK Tina but I've no breasts. I know it's too dark to see or be seen, but I'll feel *stupid* in a bikini top.'

'Just the briefs, silly.'

'You mean trunks.'

'Whatever.' He reached to lower his trunks, but felt his hands smacked away gently.

'It's *my* job to do that.'

'He allowed her to pull the costume down and obligingly stepped out, lifting his feet high, steadied by Tina's free arm and the trunks were whisked away. He sensed her removing the briefs of her own costume, still holding his arm for balance, then splashing about in the water for a moment, presumably putting on his own costume.

'Your cossie's a bit big on me. I expect *I* look very funny.' She pressed up against him to demonstrate and he felt the wet fabric against his buttocks. It was a surprisingly pleasant sensation.

'Well you don't *feel* funny.'

'Now it's your turn.' He felt each foot lifted in turn, then the bikini laces being pulled up his calves and thighs. As Tina eased it up over his groin, it held him very firmly, not being designed for an anatomy like his. The material felt surprisingly warm.

'Now if you could see, *you'd* look pretty funny too.' He reached down to explore the briefs and make himself more comfortable. He encountered laces round his waist but in place of the triangle of fabric below; a pair of hands. The illusion of wearing Tina's bikini bottom vanished like a soap bubble bursting.

'Tina!'

'Good trick?'

'You're full of them. Now what?'

'Your girlfriend - me now I suppose, since I think Anne's left in disgust - doesn't want to make love. She wants a bit of fun with you. But she also wants to show you something new. You just have to give in to her whims this evening - OK?'

'OK.'

'That means hands off.'

'Hands off you?'

'No, off you. Well and me as well - just be mindful of what's happening.' Martin had come across that term before. It meant to just focus on whatever it was and let it happen. *What was the term the mindfulness practitioners used? Oh yes, if your thought wanders off, worrying about whether you did send off the tax return you just bring it back kindly. Be kind. The fourth Reiki principle.* But then his own thoughts were brought back to the present moment because Tina's hands were on the move. His "costume" unwrapped itself leaving him naked in the surf.

'But of course before we came down to the beach you gave me permission to touch *you*. He felt a wet slap on his buttocks.

'Nice bum.' Another slap landed, with more force after the first experimental one.

'Ouch.'

'Well, aren't you going to defend yourself Martin?'

'But I'm not allowed to touch *you.*'

'Just try.'

Martin spun round gauging the level of her own bottom, but his swinging arm met empty air, Tina's hands were on both his shoulders and he felt her pressing on them as she skipped behind him which ever way he twisted, judging his next movement expertly and delivering another smack each time he missed. She was certainly fast. He was breathing heavily now. The water, so easy to walk slowly into, now resisted his attempts at fast movement and was soaking both of them with spray.

For a moment, an image of himself from childhood popped into his head; he was chasing a friend in the sea whilst the water clutched at his legs forcing him to leap high out of the surf to be able to run without falling. That's what she was doing. Eventually, buttocks stinging a bit, he gave up.

'OK, You win.' Tina giggled and he felt her hands release his shoulders. Immediately he whipped round and finally connected with the swimming trunks Tina had taken from him.

'Ow, you cheated!'

'All's fair in love and war.'

'Let's call a truce then.' They both laughed. In spite of himself, Tina had managed to lift his mood considerably. He felt Tina's hands slide back on to his shoulders. She turned him gently round towards the hazy moonlight, until she was once again behind him. One of her arms wrapped around him, her fingers pressing gently into his waist. The other hand took up its earlier position as surrogate bikini brief. Her cheek pressed itself into his back.

Having set up this intimate embrace, she remained still and silent. At first Martin expected some movement; a stimulating massage perhaps, but when Tina didn't move or speak, he somehow understood he was expected to follow suit. To his surprise a growing feeling of warmth and arousal; mental not physical, began to spread through him from her hand in his groin. The warmth travelled up through her encircling arm until it reached his neck and cheeks.

A feeling of peace stole over him and he was just content to stand and let things take their course, whatever that might be. By keeping quiet and still, he became aware of the dull boom of some distant wave breaking. And later, the sighing sound and tingle of receding surf as it flowed over his feet, excavating the supporting shingle below them. Martin was gradually aware he could see occasional glimmers of light from the water at his feet and looked upwards.

Ragged cloud was now drifting across the moon's face. He realised that he didn't want the present moment to end. In this extraordinary place, it was a peculiar sensation to feel both relaxed and mentally alert at the same time. He shook his head then, half expecting to wake up from an alcohol induced dream. Although if he was dreaming, how did it all seem so real and connect absolutely with what had gone before? But of course it wasn't a dream.

Why was Tina doing all this? Was this a heightened sense of *being* that she was aiming to bring about in him? As if sensing and trying to calm his tumbling stream of thought, Tina spoke softly behind him. She still held him, although she moved her cheek away from his back.

'From what you've told me, you've been missing the best part of intimacy with Helena or whoever; Anne, if that's why she came into your mind a while ago. You should know very well, as someone with physiological training, all about the stereotypical male sexual experience. But I'm willing to bet that you, like many males, have not put much thought or effort to developing a sensual connection with your partner. Well that's what we're doing at the moment.'

Martin was astonished all over again. Tina seemed able to sense what was going on in his brain. Was it just co-incidence or could she really read his mind through her hands, he wondered? He shivered a bit at the thought of such a talent and mused about what it could do for his own patients. Tina was concerned:

'Are you cold?'

'Not really. I think someone just walked over my grave.'

'Oh? Is that where the old Martin is buried?'

Martin didn't reply to this. It struck him as so profound that he stopped trying to work things out and forced himself to concentrate on what was happening to him right *now*.

'Where are we really, Tina?'

'We've not left my flat. Michael Timles helped me design this treatment room; it's his invention.' Tina paused to let her patient digest this information then continued.

'It can simulate other places than the seaside you know.'

Tina released his groin, still standing close behind him and massaged his scalp and forehead, sensing his pulse and waiting for it to calm a little. Martin relaxed against her body, which seemed remarkably strong, and closed his eyes. Tina continued her explanations as her fingers ran through his hair.

'You feel those warm gusts of wind Martin? Well, when the breeze is an onshore one at night, it often feels much warmer than the static air on the beach. You might know that as the air travels over the sea in picks up maritime heat, whereas the land radiates its own heat very quickly; especially if it's a clear night.' Martin thought: *No wonder Timles told him he couldn't accommodate Tina at the Woodlands. This place is a long way from low lighting and candles.*

'But how on earth does there seem to be no ceiling in here so we're just looking up at a dark night sky? Is it - Oooo - that's nice - back projection?'

'It's some kind of LED wallpaper. Can display almost anything. The walls and ceiling are covered with it. You'll have to ask Michael if you're really interested.'

'This room must have been extremely - Ahhhh Do that again - expensive.'

'Does knowing about my treatment room spoil the illusion for you?' Tina fingers were working gently in his hair.

'No; it's quite rem - aaaa - kable.'

By now most of his body was warmly tingling and he seemed to have lost track of time. His eyes closed, he listened to the surf and lazily followed Tina's hands smoothing his skin. Tina recreated her "bikini bottom" over his groin. It felt warm and comforting instead of creating tension and a desire for release and relief.

'Have you ever previously experienced the feelings that you have now?'

'I don't remember feeling like this.'

'You mean you might have had the same feelings in the past?'

'No, physiologically speaking I mean I've never been *mentally* aroused to this extent for so long without reaching a *physical* climax and then everything being over with a feeling of *anti*climax.' Tina moved both arms up to encircle his waist.

'And did you miss that sensation of climax?'

'No, but like a powerful *sexual* experience, I'm still not actually sure at this moment which way up I am. It would help if you just held me calmly for a while so I can re-orient myself.' Neither patient nor therapist spoke for a while. They just listened to the surf. Eventually Tina spoke softly.

'Did you enjoy that?'

'Of course I did; you could sense that.'

'So do women.'

'What?'

'That's what they like—most of them—and its how they feel too, given the opportunity.'

'You mean they like to be able to give those feelings to their partners?'

'Well, that too, but if I have to spell it out, that's how they prefer to be loved and when they are, they experience very similar physical sensations and emotions to the ones that you have felt today. I've aimed to put you in touch with your feminine side if you like.' Tina was still holding him against herself and Martin didn't want her to move just yet.

'But you couldn't know what I felt.'

'That's where my Reiki training comes in. You might have noticed it was a hands on experience from the first moment to right now.'

'And did you enjoy it too?'

'I love my work.'

'Tina?'

'Yes?'

'If this is lesson one, What on earth happens in lesson two?'

'Well, I don't know if there will be a lesson two; you were pretty sure that Reiki couldn't help you.

'What you do has nothing to do with Reiki.'

'No? Well then how do you feel about what I *have* done for you?' Martin thought about Tina's message. *Sensuality is important in relationships. It was more enjoyable and clearly much more sustainable than the sexual frenzies pumped out by the mass media.*

'I feel grateful.' And as he said it he realised he had just completed all five Reiki principles that afternoon. Tina seemed to know this too.

'So that's your 5-a-day then. Take my arm, you've got wobbly legs and its time for me to take you home.'

She eased his trunks off the bikini bottom she was still wearing and put them into his hand.

'And cover yourself up before we leave this treatment room; you wouldn't want me to see your bits now, would you?'

****

On Monday, Martin was late in at the Centre having overslept. When Tina dropped him at his own flat, he had sat up late into the night turning the whole experience over and over in his brain. Half expecting some kind of mystic oriental mumbo jumbo, or at the most some reasonably effective head massage, what actually happened had blown him away. He didn't know where he was going from here. Was what he had experienced specially prepared for him? He couldn't decide whether Tina fancied him and seriously wanted a relationship or whether the Sunday session had just been all in a day's work for her. If she was working as some kind of high class erotic masseuse it would explain her present situation. Perhaps her evident prosperity didn't come from an inheritance as she had suggested, but from the proceeds of her new business. But then the Woodlands Centre owner was somehow in on it. She had said that he had invested in her business and, what had she said: *Michael Timles helped me design this treatment room?* He couldn't answer the questions in his head, but he knew someone who probably could and he was due to see him for another sort of consultation. It was time to phone Timles and book an appointment.

Martin walked up to the reception desk. He wasn't too worried about being late as the Centre's manager was away on vacation. Administrative tasks were covered by one of the long term members of Centre staff who deputised for Noura, but didn't concern himself with the comings and goings of his contemporaries. Julie looked with mock accusation at him as he signed in.

'What time do you call this Mr. Wright?' She caught Noura's voice and intonation to a tee.

'Don't give me away Julie, you know - when *she* returns.' Martin played along with her teasing; deliberately sounding frightened. Julie giggled. She looked at him with new interest. *This was more like the old Martin. Perhaps that attractive rep who had visited him last week had made a breakthrough. After her visit, Martin had had a high colour and his female visitor wasn't wearing her tie.*

'You'll have to make it worth my while to keep quiet. Noura thinks you've turned over a new leaf.'

Martin felt he was on safe ground here. Julie's husband would kill her if she really did anything more than flirt. He always collected her from the Centre. No-one was quite sure what sort of work he did, but the rumours were that he worked for a security firm. He certainly had the build for it.

'How about a nice full body massage - gratis of course?' Julie closed her eyes and gave a dramatic sigh.

'That would be wonderful, but I don't think George would appreciate it.'

'We needn't tell him.'

'Mmmm. A nice box of chocolates and I'll say you came in every morning before 9 if Noura asks.'

'It's a deal, Julie. Dark or milk?'

'Ooo, *dark* please.' Julie elaborately wrote "9 am" in the column next to his signature and blew him a kiss.

As soon as he reached his room, having checked his bookings for the next few days, Martin phoned the Centre's owner. This time there was a long delay, but just as Martin was replacing the handset he heard Timles's voice answer.

'Hello, Timles speaking. Oh, Martin. Yes, apologies for the delay getting to the 'phone, I was outside. Well if you're free I could see you this afternoon. Do we have things to talk about? Yes? OK, How about two thirty? Good, see you then.'

Having called his mentor, Martin now turned all the previous meetings with Tina over in his mind again. There was little else to distract him that morning. He slumped into his chair and for lack of anything more exciting to occupy his mind, mentally rearranged the items on his desk to make space for a computer. The intercom buzzed. Julie's professional voice addressed him. 'Mr Wright? I have a John Sanders here from Networks Unlimited. If you're available, he wants a few moments with you regarding the new Centre IT system. He says it will be very brief.'

'OK Julie, send him along please.' Mr Saunders was a very personable individual, rather older than Martin was expecting. He was clarity itself even with Martin for whom IT was still a topic which generated anxiety.

'Good morning Dr Wright. Thank you for sparing me some time just now. Please forgive me if I'm telling you things you already know.' Martin replied that he was largely ignorant of what was proposed. He didn't correct the engineer's error about his title. That sounded rather good.

'Right then. Your new network connection will be delivered by wireless - I'm sure you will know about WiFi.' Here Saunders smiled and nodded to indicate that he was already aware of the answer to that.

'Well, my first task is to check the strength of the signal in your room from the transmitter we have installed - it's a special type of router. You've probably got one at home which came with your broadband subscription.' Martin nodded, but he hadn't of course. He made a mental note to order broadband. Otherwise he wouldn't be able to use Tuula's detachable tablet in his flat. Saunders fetched out a black instrument from his attaché case. After a moment or two, red and green lights started winking on the device.

'No problem there. Now you haven't got a computer in your room have you?' Martin said that one was on order.

'No problem at all. When you get that set up it will search for the local wireless network. There's only one detectable here; that's the Centre's own. It will ask you for a password or a wireless key; the same thing for our purpose here.' Saunders handed him a neat plastic card with the Networks Unlimited logo, web address and phone number.

'On the other side you'll find your network password. Just enter that into your computer and you'll be connected. We aren't supplying your computers or terminals, so we can't assist the staff here with that. Once you're connected, you'll need to log onto your Centre network. Obviously, keep this in a safe place. Ms Munday says that at present all staff here use a terminal in the staff room. Well, you will be able to log on using your existing credentials, just as if you were using the facility in your staff room. You won't have to keep doing this. Your computer will remember the information after you've given it the first time. I'm sure you have enough passwords to remember for using the Internet already.' Once again Martin smiled and nodded as he was sure would be expected of him.

'Any problems, please contact your administrator; Ms Munday. Please don't call Networks Unlimited. If there are technical problems that need our support, she will get in touch. Do you have any questions right now?' Martin said he couldn't think of anything.

'Well I will be in the building for about another thirty minutes or so testing the WiFi signal in your colleagues rooms, so if you think of anything you'd like to ask me, just tell your receptionist. It's been a pleasure meeting you Dr. Wright.' Saunders extended his hand, collected his case and left.

No-one was booked in that afternoon and the remainder of the morning passed quickly with just one patient signing on for a course of treatment for lower back pain; one of the most frequent complaints his clients presented with. After eating a couple of cheese rolls purchased from a one woman business that called regularly at lunch times, he alerted Julie that he had an appointment with the Centre's owner.

'My bookings are up to date Julie, so if anyone else wants to see me you can make them an appointment in any of the next available slots, but I don't want to see anyone this afternoon.'

'OK Martin. Don't forget those chocolates.' As Martin passed the Job Centre on the way to Timles's place, out of curiosity, he crossed the road to see what jobs were on offer on the window display panels. Scanning the openings for painters and decorators, care workers and checkout staff he stopped at an position for 'A Massage Therapist to work in a local complementary medicine centre - must hold accreditations recognised by the Complementary and Natural Health care Council (CNHC) or equivalent body. Surely the post couldn't relate Timles's plans to expand physiotherapy at the Centre; the qualifications requested were not appropriate. The card didn't specify the employer, but Martin wondered if it had become available because of Tina's resignation from the Woodlands. If so, then Reiki was being replaced by a more mainstream therapy.

Walking by the mock Georgian fronted property, Martin looked out for the tabby cat. He spotted it indoors on one of the windowsills. As the animal's eyes connected with his own and stared in that cold way cats have, a strange thought occurred to him. He wondered just what the creature was actually seeing and whether, in it's animal brain, the Martin it beheld looked anything like the image of himself he saw each day in the mirror. *We place ourselves at the pinnacle of the tree of life, but one day the scientists will be able to show us what animals see and it may well be a humbling revelation.* When he passed by, the cat's intense expression, like the grin of the Cheshire cat in Lewis Carol's famous tale of Alice, remained as a sort of after image, all the way to Timles's place.

Now familiar with the entry routine, Martin soon joined Timles in his study lounge.

'Hello Martin.' Timles gestured towards the two armchairs facing each other close to the patio window and came over to occupy one once Martin had sat. As he did so he enquired about Martin's health and the option of coffee now or later on. Martin replied that he was fine and maybe have a drink later. He was now anxious to get some answers to what was troubling him.

'A lot has happened in the short time since I was here last. You recommended I have some sessions with Tina Elves. Well I have and it has left me confused and I'm hoping you will be able to throw some light on what happened and why.' But Timles was not to be rushed.

'All in good time Martin, but we agreed a programme for our talks together and I'd like to keep to that as far as possible. Once we have discussed whether you have dealt with some of the past issues you told me about in our first meeting, we'll have a break and you can ask me about anything that's troubling you right now. Is that a plan?' Martin took a deep breath. Until he had spoken to Timles, he hadn't fully appreciated how worked up he had become about his recent experiences.

'Yes, that's all right.' Timles steepled his hands and sat back in his easy chair. Martin wondered if he was aware of his characteristic mannerism.

'The agreement was that we'd try to get closure on past issues that were still unresolved. One of the biggest was your break with Helena. Have you given further thought to dealing with that?' Martin felt irritated by his mentor's question, after the unexpected meeting with her he felt that the case was closed and he thought he'd already put it out of his mind. It was if he *was* being interrogated about his earlier life; something Timles had assured him would not happen.

'Actually I think I've now moved on.' Martin was anxious to talk about more recent happenings in his life.

'Well that's good news, but can you tell me why you feel that?' Martin's feeling of impatience was growing, but he checked himself. Timles was giving up his time to mentor or counsel him and was not only giving him the chance to keep his contract at the Woodlands, but had held out the carrot of improved status and facilities there. He wondered how he would react if his own patients decided to dictate the nature and pace of their own physiotherapy treatment.

'I have to confess that I'd done nothing about arranging a meeting with Helena. I suppose I thought it unlikely she would agree to one. But I accidentally bumped into her in the pub recently.'

'What was your reaction?' Martin's irritation was evaporating. He was beginning to see the logic of Timles's questions. After all the man couldn't help him unless he was given a full picture of all the things that had been troubling Martin. Timles couldn't help him unless he was willing to help himself. Martin honoured Timles's simple question by taking some time to collect his thoughts.

'I was embarrassed when I first saw her and had to pluck up courage to attract her attention. I imagined that I was going to hear the same old criticisms all over again. But there was none of that. She was very friendly;

even seemed pleased to see me. All her anger was directed against the man she had left the previous year. She even apologised for never having sent a text for my last birthday. Then she went on at length describing how wonderful it was living with another woman. She felt that living with men had been a mistake, but that the experience had at least helped her discover her true sexual orientation. There had been a bit of an issue with her partner recently, but Helena thought that it would be sorted out. She even hinted about a civil partnership some time in the future and I'm invited if I want to attend. When we went our separate ways, I felt no anger or disappointment. I thought how fortunate it was that I had gone to the pub that evening.'

'Has meeting her helped you draw a line under that relationship?'

'I'd say yes. Yes, because it's reassured me that I wasn't to blame for the break. Clearly, whatever I had or hadn't done while we were together it couldn't of worked out because she didn't want to be with a man. And I can't lay too much blame at her door either because it seems that she really didn't recognise it at the time.'

'So would you say that your painful period spent with Helena has helped her be happier with her own life.'

'Well it looks like it. No doubt the chap she left me for also put in his two pence worth!'

'Do you still feel angry with him for having an affair with Helena while you were still together?'

'Not at all. It was probably Helena that went after him and then dumped him too.'

'OK it looks like we are nearly getting to the point where, as you told me initially, you've moved on, But I have one more important question. Has your experience with Helena — both her being with you and later leaving you — helped you be happier with your life?' Martin wasn't expecting this question because he felt that he'd closed the Helena chapter in his life.

'I think I can let go of any feelings of guilt or personal inadequacy about my failed relationship and that's good. I suppose that means I should have more confidence in my ability to enter another relationship and sustain it successfully.'

'OK Martin, the outcome of your unexpected meeting with Helena has shortened this session. I think that you've been pretty patient with me going over what is now probably old ground to you. Even though your meeting with Helena only happened recently, I don't doubt you've given a lot of time to turning it over in your mind. In your last answer you told me that you *thought* you could let go of feelings of blame for your break up and you *supposed* that meant you'd be more confident in establishing a new relationship next time. We're going to work towards you *knowing* you can let go of those negative feelings and being *certain* that you have a lot to offer in a new relationship. To do that we need to establish who you are and what you're looking for in a relationship. Are you happy to move on to that in our next meeting?'

'Yes that's fine with me.'

'Now we'll have our break - coffee for you as usual?'

'Thanks.' Timles soon returned with a tray.

'Now you have some questions for me about Tina.' After the distraction of Timles's probing of his relationship with Helena, Martin had to refocus to formulate his questions about his experiences with Tina. From what Tina had said, Timles was involved in her new activities in some way. He thought he'd best be cautious and see if he could get some clues about Timles's relationship with Tina by asking less emotive questions to start with.

'Tina gave me a Reiki session in her own flat on Sunday. I was astonished by the treatment room she has there, which she said you had helped her design.'

'Yes Martin. Tina wanted to make her therapy as effective as possible by providing appropriate environments depending on the needs of her clients. She knew I had installed a special technology here and asked if it was possible for her to have something similar.'

'Is that to do with creating the illusion of outside spaces in an ordinary room.'

'What sort of outside space did you experience?'

'It was a beach; a shore in fact, but very dark; difficult to see apart from clouds high up and bizarrely water underfoot. But the room appeared to have no walls or ceiling. I have to admit it was quite disturbing at first. I still have no idea how it was done.'

'Would you like a demonstration?' Timles sipped his tea, then picked up a small remote control from his desk and turned to the patio window. Martin too slid round in his chair and looked out through the glass. Today the trees at the end of the garden seemed much taller and the distant hills weren't visible. He assumed it was because he'd been standing last time he noticed the view. Then as he looked, a mist was coming down. Gradually it obscured the garden boundary, then the flower beds until the patio right outside the window disappeared in a thick fog. Then, slowly, the obscuring vapour began to thin out, receding from the window frame. But now instead of paving, water rippled immediately below the glass. The mist withdrew further and further and the garden had gone; replaced by sea, moving with white topped waves out to join the sky on the horizon. It was just as if the house was now right on the edge of the waterline. Martin's jaw dropped, but in the next moment something even more unsettling happened. The water began to rise up the glass. Martin gripped the arms of his chair. The impression of motion, of sinking into the sea was irresistible. The water now covered the glass completely, but the impression of downward motion continued as the water outside darkened and weed drifted upwards. Finally a sandy sea bed appeared outside, level with what had once been a paved patio. Fish were swimming up to the glass and across the windows, disappearing out of view.

'Good God.' was all Martin could find to say.

'This is a VHD display system. Rather expensive, but essential for photo realistic scenes like this. Tina's room is decorated with a type of LED wallpaper. Not up to rendering this sort of daylight quality, but a VHD system on all the walls and ceiling would be overkill for what she needs and far too costly.'

'But there were no echoes in her room, the floor felt sandy and we walked into real water. It was just as if we were on a beach.'

'I'm not sure I want to give all her secrets away, Martin. Is that all that was troubling you about your session with Tina?'

'No. What she did in this session certainly wasn't Reiki; not as I understand it anyway.'

'But you told me last time that Tina thought that a conventional course of Reiki was unlikely to help you with the problems you discussed with her.'

'Yes, but her treatment involved some very intimate stuff; it was way over the boundaries that conventional therapy would stop short at.'

'Did she tell you that would be involved.'

'Yes, but it was a still bit of a shock.'

'Did you agree to her intimate treatment?'

'Well yes.'

'Did it help?'

'Her explanation of what she was doing and why has made me think in a new way about relationships.'

'So far so positive, Martin.'

'Isn't she crossing some ethical boundaries? I'm also worried about her safety doing this on her own.'

'Complementary medicine isn't regulated and I think that Tina is able to look after herself. We all take a certain amount of risk in our business.' Martin decided it was time to be more direct.

'Can you tell me then, is she a Reiki practitioner or an erotic masseuse - I think that's the term?'

'You know I don't think sticking a label on a therapist is helpful. Look at the all the different badges worn by professionals whose core business is helping people with problems generally related to anxiety, failure to cope or poor self image: personal councillor, life coach, psychotherapist, psychologist, psychiatrist, complementary therapist. The list goes on. So what happens? A patient's relatives or friends push them into getting treatment. They usually say "you need see X or Y therapist".

The troubled individual asks another friend for their advice and they usually say something like "Oh no you shouldn't go to an X or Y therapist, you really need a Z therapist. I had your problem and had a course of Z therapy and I got better". Confused, they turn to the Internet for descriptions of the roles of all these therapists and read testimonials and are startled to discover even more types of therapy on offer for their problem. They are either turned off altogether or simply elect to visit the therapist recommended by the most significant of their contacts, as much to please their friend or relative as from making a fully informed choice.'

'Yes but you've got to call yourself something or you wouldn't get any clients would you?'

'Well let me try to answer your direct question about Tina Elves. Going back to a time when we didn't have any of these labels, people still had most of the same psychological problems we have now. Communities then were smaller, tighter and stronger and a troubled individual would be told by everyone to visit "the wise woman". In primitive tribal societies her equivalent was the shaman or witch doctor. The individuals concerned were charismatic with great empathy for their fellow men - or women. Generally they did have some skill or ability out of the ordinary, for which they gained great respect but certainly no magic, white or black. Their cures generally worked because those sent to them believed absolutely that they would. I'd say that Tina is a latter day wise woman who in addition to unusual empathy has great skill with her hands, both for reading people and delivering comfort.' Timles stopped his explanation and finished his tea, before continuing.

'As far as the need for some sort of practice nameplate on her door goes, she doesn't need one. The Woodlands Centre staff, and myself are now beginning to refer clients to her where we think they could benefit. She may also have similar arrangements elsewhere. Don't forget, Tina no longer reports to me or any of the other Woodlands directors. She is running an independent business. Yes, I have invested in her business because I think it's an avenue of complementary medicine that we need to explore further. Look; mainstream medicine: pharmaceuticals and clinical practice; is constantly evolving. New drugs and physical treatments emerge all the time. Older medicines and treatments are consigned to the history books. Complementary medicine has to do the same or it will lose, to put it in crude business terms, its market share.' Martin was beginning to think he had misjudged a lot of people at the Woodlands, Timles especially.

'But what sort of therapist or rather, councillor are you?'

'There, you see Martin. It's hard to get away from those labels isn't it? We have a need to categorise everyone, don't we? OK, by training I'm a mix of person-centred councillor and mentor. But I'd like to think of myself and the Woodlands as working towards promoting our clients belief in their self-worth. Of helping them work out who they really are and what they want to achieve in their lives. It's really a talking therapy based on asking "powerful questions". Think of it as me waking your inner therapist - prodding the healer within to start working on you to restore faith in your own worth and ability to make sound decisions.'

'So are the Woodlands staff really faith healers?'

'You're still hung up on those labels Martin. No, both faith healing and conventional medicine works by creating external dependencies; namely relying on omnipotent Gods, drugs or doctors. I want the Woodlands to excel in *self-belief* healing. That aims to create *independence*. Once that's been achieved with a client, they can drop their crutches; drugs, booze, people pleasing and all kinds of other self destructive behaviours. I want to harness the power of self belief for our clients and—' Timles caught Martin's eyes. '—our staff.'

'How do you go about that?'

'Well the person-centred idea aims to get the client to recognise why they are in difficulty and to come up with suggestions about how to solve this, without being prompted or told what they should do. The mentoring comes in when the client is just floundering or going round in circle. Even then I prefer to provide nudges in the direction that seems likely to help my client. In other words I might make an alternative suggestion as an option they may not have considered. They can still make a free choice how they want to go forward. But my nudge might be presented to my client as a default option.'

'What does that mean?'

'When you first came to see me, I warned you that your continued contract with us depended on improvements in the way you were working. The *default* option was my offer to help you with your depression, but I also said that I was quite open to your seeking counselling elsewhere. It was a fairly strong nudge to choose me as your mentor, but it didn't take away your choice of action. You could also have decided to resign your position. Knowing this, I tempted you with the prospect of improved facilities for your practice at the Woodlands. That prospect, by the way, remains a genuine one.'

'So how does Tina build people's sense of self worth?'

'On a case by case basis. Let's say she has a client with a morbid fear of something. This is an absolute classic anxiety situation which can often be overcome by gradual exposure of the client to what they are fearful of whilst giving support and reassurance. Let's take fear of heights. Well, with Tina's novel treatment room she could accompany her client and deliver appropriate reassurance, higher and higher up a mountainside in a completely controlled environment without leaving her flat. You found your experience there real enough to affect you emotionally didn't you?' Martin didn't answer. Timles gave him a moment then asked:

'What's really troubling you about your session with Tina?' Martin let out a long breath.

'Tina worked quite hard to persuade me to have some Reiki treatment with her, even though I had thought about the possibility and asked her about her treatment first. She has not asked for any payment, but said that I should take her out for meals instead.'

Martin hesitated. 'I found the experience she planned for me so intensely moving and sensual that I'm now confused where this is going. Is she treating me as she would any of her other clients or is she doing this because she wants to have a personal relationship with me? You see my confusion?' Timles smiled broadly.

'Would you like me to respond to that question like a person-centred councillor or as a mentor?'

'I might get a better insight from your "person-centred" approach?'

'I think we both would.'

'OK, give me the person-centred treatment.'

'Did you had much contact with Tina while she was working at the Centre?'

'I spoke to her sometimes in the staff coffee room and exchanged greetings with her occasionally.'

'Would you say she showed any sign of interest in you?'

'She did sometimes work late and stop by my surgery for a chat.'

'How did you feel about that?'

'I didn't really give it a lot of thought. I just thought that what she did — Reiki I mean—was taking her clients for a ride; that it was unlikely to be of any therapeutic value. I suppose it made me a bit angry with her.'

'But you finally decided to ask her for treatment.'

'I was at a particularly low point. Then I was hauled over the coals by Noura about my work. I was getting a bit desperate I suppose. I was, am still, highly sceptical, but when I questioned Tina about her work— we began to meet up in the Green Dragon pub—I became more and more impressed.

'With Reiki or with Tina?' Martin hesitated before answering. He thought that Timles might expect him to say Reiki, as he was the Centre's founder and was championing complementary therapy. Timles seemed to know the reason for his reticence.

'If our sessions are going to help, you must always be honest and not tell me what you think I want or need to hear.'

'OK then it was Tina the person, not the Reiki therapist that I was beginning to respect.'

'And feel attracted to?' Martin thought about this.

'I wasn't conscious of that at the time. Not until she visited me for one session of physiotherapy. She claimed to have lower back pain and I did find tension where she was twisting to massage clients.'

'And something else happened?' Again Martin hesitated.

'I can be totally honest with you?'

'I expect nothing less.' Timles sounded grave, but he was smiling too.

'Tina stripped off her clothes. She was wearing sports underwear. She had - has a wonderfully athletic body and for the first time in my practice, I experienced sexual arousal and ... temptation to massage more than the area strictly necessary.'

'Would Tina have been aware of that?'

'At the time I'd have said "no way" it would have been highly unprofessional. Now I have serious doubts. I think she can read people in a manner I cannot understand. As I was massaging her for quite a while, goodness knows what she was picking up from me.'

'When you talked with her in the pub and agreed to take up her offer of treatment, did she seemed pleased she had been able to win you over? Even though you never hid your scepticism of all complementary therapies at the Woodlands?' At this barbed question, Martin looked anxiously at Timles, but he was still smiling.

'Well, I suppose yes she did. Frankly she looked like the cat that got the cream.'

'Perhaps the cream was not so much convincing a sceptic, as landing a hard to catch fish.'

'That's the same thing isn't it?'

'Not the way I mean it. Can we say that you find her attractive and would not be adverse to exploring a relationship with her?'

'Yes yes, OK. But that's the source of my confusion. In her treatment, Tina gave me an insight into connectedness and intimacy such that I have never previously known. Talk about "boy meets girl" situations. This one went straight for my jugular. So now I know that I'm fascinated by her, but I don't really know what she feels about me.'

Martin breathed in heavily. He had had no intention of telling Timles so much when he had come today; in fact he had still left out most of the emotional and physical sensations, but what he had said had been more than enough. But where was he to go from here? He looked almost pleadingly at

Timles.

'As a personal counsellor, you've teased an admission out of me that I'm attracted to Tina, but left it to me to decide what to do about that. But you offered me two approaches. What would you tell me to do as a mentor? Does she want to be my guru or my girlfriend?' Timles smiled and shook his head slowly.

'Have you ruled out the possibility that *both* those thoughts about Tina might be true?' When Martin didn't answer Timles relented and gave his advice.

'I'm glad you asked me for the non-directive approach first. I can neither read Tina's mind nor change it! But I can suggest a course of action. Tell Tina what you think of her and ask whether she would like to go out somewhere with you on a date, not therapy.

It was a logical response to his question, but one still not giving him the reassurance about Tina that Martin sought. Timles was rising and smiling and Martin followed suit. This was a natural moment to break and reconvene when Martin had made further progress. But as he walked away he knew he wasn't yet ready to risk rejection by putting Timles's practical suggestion into action. Not yet, anyway.

CHAPTER NINE

Anne

The next day Julie greeted Martin cheerily as he signed in.

'Hi Mart. You had a visitor yesterday afternoon whilst you were visiting Dr. Timles.'

'Have you given them an appointment?'

'Oh no.' Julie gave him one of her knowing grins.

'It was Tina. She wanted to speak to you. When I told her where you were she asked for some stationery, then sat over there—' Julie waved at one of the reception area chairs.

'— and left you a note.'

'Is it in my room?' Martin asked uncomfortably.

'No I kept it at reception.' Julie opened a drawer and handed him an envelope. She must have seen something in his expression because she stopped grinning and reassured him.

'She said it was private; she's sealed it. Were you expecting it?' Martin didn't comment.

'Right, thanks Julie.' He wandered off clutching his envelope as if it was likely to explode. Julie lent over her desk and watched him walk slowly to his office. She bit her bottom lip as he disappeared into the office. Martin sat down heavily and opened his letter. Whatever he was expecting, the contents were certainly not that. He read:

Dear Martin

I wanted to talk to you in person, but have left you this message as you're seeing Michael. By the time you pick this up I will be at my sister's home in Sheffield. She had to go in for an operation on

Sunday and a neighbour is kindly looking after her children; she's a single parent (long story). She's also recently moved to her flat in Sheffield and doesn't have any other friends or contacts who can help. I don't know how long I'll be away, so we'll have to put our next meeting on hold.

I need to ask a big favour. I'm expecting an important package in the post. Could you check my post box on Wednesday. It should certainly be there by then. It will be marked sent from 'You Tree Ltd.' I'd be so grateful if you could forward it to me in Sheffield. There wasn't time to make other arrangements.

I hope I didn't shock you so much on Sunday that you won't want to see me again! I was so impressed by the way that you entered into the spirit of things. I want to build on that. I must confess I had my doubts about you, but more particularly about what I was springing on you. I was going to discuss this with you 'the morning after' but fate has intervened.

Please excuse the note: I've lost your mobile number. Will you let me have that again, please. You can use my Woodlands email address. Noura has arranged (reluctantly!!) to forward my messages for a time.

* * *

Yours affectionately,

Tina

On a card, Tina included her Sheffield address, mobile number and key code for the flat complex. Her mailbox key was fixed to this with adhesive tape. But Martin didn't time to think about Tina's closing remarks because his intercom was already announcing the arrival of his next patient. This one complained of pain and stiffness in the middle of his back. Once on the massage bed, tightness was evident in his erector muscles - an extensive muscle group responsible for keeping the spine upright. These are easy to feel in the back as they are relatively superficial.

'How long have you been sitting at your computer?'

'How did you know that?'

'You feel how the muscles here are tightly locked?'

'Ow! Yes what's the problem then?'

'I call this muscle group *sacrospinalis monitori*.'

'That's Latin isn't it? What's that in English?'

'Muscles used to hold your back rigid in front of a computer screen.'

'You're kidding me!'

'Only partly.'

'And that's the problem?'

'Unless you're also spending too many hours at a keyhole looking at what the butler saw.'

'Can you help?'

'I can massage those muscles now to stretch them and you can come back for another session next week, but the best thing of all will be to change your working practice. Get your chair and monitor positioning checked at work and go on-line for advice on this; there are good videos on You Tube. And don't sit glued to your monitor for longer than 20 minutes without getting up and doing some other movements. I'll give you a sheet of gentle bending and twisting exercises you can do at work and home.' The remainder of the day passed busily but uneventfully with some of his regular sports injury patients. The only appointment the following day had been cancelled. At a loose end, Martin decided to go over to the University Computer Centre and carry on where he'd left off on InterconNet. Whilst he'd been turning things over in his head, he remembered that Anne Eres, his shadowy InterconNet contact, was offering free consultations to other network members.

He would look at her profile again and perhaps complete the tentative connection he had accidentally set up. That was if he could get onto a workstation. He imagined that the computer room would be fairly busy during the week; but there was no harm in finding out. Besides, he could pick up a snack at the Student Union bar. However much Tuula disparaged the bar food, the beer was good. Tuula. He'd almost forgotten her after his disturbing session with Tina. Perhaps Tuula would be there and he could ask if his computer had been ordered. Then at least he could look forward to using it in private at home.

The Computer Centre was as full as he'd anticipated, but a student told him he'd finished and was only writing up notes. Martin logged on and centred Anne's picture as he'd been shown. He read her profile again. Strong background in psychology. Offering psychotherapy. He hesitated. *Why not try this woman out? Neither of his two other self appointed mentors were what you could call independent to the extent they might give disinterested advice. He had form with both of them.* He made up his mind. Opening Anne's connection options he removed the tick that put things on hold and clicked OK. He was wondering what he should do next when a new window opened with Anne's image at the top. Underneath her picture the text informed him:

Anne Eres is now on-line. Do you wish to send a message?

Martin was startled. He recalled Tuula's instant response. Did these people never leave their computers? He thought again about the man with back problem he had treated that morning. Too many static hours in front of his screen... Martin clicked "YES". A message box appeared.

Hello Mr Wright how can I help you?

Clearly a reply was needed. Martin started typing:

Hello Anne. Sorry I delayed connecting to you before; it was my first session on InterconNet, and I didn't really know what I was doing at the time.

Martin clicked "SEND" and waited.

That's OK, but do you want to talk to me now?

Oh, yes. I've had a bit more instruction since, although it's all still very new to me.

You're doing fine. Now how can I help?

It might be difficult to explain things, typing like this I mean. I'm not very fast with keyboards.

Let's make a start like this anyway. I don't mind if you type slowly. Don't worry about spelling and U can use abbreviations if U like!

You've seen that I work at a local complementary medicine centre?

Absolutely: I understand that I'm talking to another therapist! An established physiotherapist, no less!

Thanks! But I must say it would be impossible for me to work with my own clients this way. I have my doubts how this can work even for psychological problems without us meeting face to face.

Well it *is* novel—for both of us—so let's see how it goes if you'll accept talking to me like this for now. So tell me what's troubling you.

All right. I'd like to ask your advice about a number of problems. But first, can I say that one of these is my long standing doubt about the efficacy of complementary medicine. You can see that's an awkward one, working where I do! So I wonder if you can give me some confidence in the method you've chosen to help your own clients?

Wow, I'm being challenged here! OK. Like InterconNet itself, this online consultation is experimental and it's free. I don't imagine your own services are like that. I'm potentially available to clients—in this way I hasten to add!—any time a client needs me. I'm hoping this won't mean too many 3am calls! Now the benefits first: You're having to put your thoughts together carefully and be concise about what you say because you have to type it... Are you still with me?

Yes of course.

I asked that because generally my own messages have to be kept short. I'm very aware I should be reading and thinking about your replies and not typing too much myself!

Please type on, Anne, I'm all eyes.

You're obviously getting into the spirit of this! Right; more benefits. Now we've both typed a bit can you see that "scroll bars" (up and down pointing arrows) have appeared on the right of this message box?

Err. No. Oh, yes.

Click the lower one and tell me what happens.

Oh I see, everything we type to each other is still there in one long column

So we can both check back to see what's been said. Can't do that in face to face discussion! Plus you can save our conversations and read them later when you want to remember what's been said.

I'm getting the message

I can see that! The downside to this of course is that our highly regarded "body language" is lost. But the upside is there's no distractions. You aren't going to be irritated by some visual tic of mine that annoys you. And I don't have to wonder why you haven't shaved today. Oops - apologies if you've grown a beard since you uploaded your picture! :-{

Anne's typing stopped for a while, leaving a minus sign blinking where she left off. Martin thought that if Anne looked anything like her avatar image, the average male client would indeed suffer distraction in a face to face consultation. But Anne was typing again

Above all I want to talk to clients in a way that breaks out of the doctor / patient consulting mode. You know: doctor in executive chair behind desk holds all the power; patient on hard seat has very little. My method levels the playing field; for both of us!

But what about carpel tunnel syndrome?

I'm sorry?

Its a wrist condition caused by excessive typing

OK. I see the psychologist is going to learn a bit of physiology! Where are you?

In the Uni Computer Centre

Surrounded by students developing carpel tunnel syndrome?

You're right there. I treated one this morning - back, not wrist though. Why do you ask?

I don't normally tell clients this early on, but if we continue sessions together, we can *speak* to each other using this programme, but you'd have to be somewhere private and have access to InterconNet. Perhaps in the Halls of Residence here?

Would we get to see each other too?

Woah! Let's take this step by step shall we? Do you still wish to proceed, Mr. Wright?

It's Martin. You may abbreviate me to Mart. And yes let's proceed. I'm sorry to be so dubious when you have offered your help.
You're doing fine. Now how can I help?
- - - - -
Mart? Are you still with me?
Yes, Sorry, I just scrolled back and that last but one question was exactly what you asked me right at the beginning. I'm warming to this!
OK Mart, over to you, I'm all eyes, as you said.
I broke up with my partner about 6 months ago and since then have felt isolated and suffer fits of depression. Even though I've now closure on that issue, I suppose some days I wonder whether it's worth carrying on with what I do. It's certainly affected my work. My Centre's owner called me in to see him. I thought he was going to show me the door, but he offered to mentor me himself. He says he does something in between "person-centred counselling" and "mentoring", but I think he's pretty unconventional. A bit like the Centre he's running!
OK Mart, I have noted that. I have some questions now. First one; how did you find InterconNet?
I met Peter Swales in my local—the Green Dragon—and he told me about his research and introduced me to InterconNet.
And what do you hope to get out of it?
Well, he suggested that I might find a soul mate using his software. Actually that was Pete's take on my situation. I didn't tell him that was what I was looking for. He gave me access here at the Uni in return for feedback of some sort for his Ph.D. work.
And is looking for a soul mate—I assume a female—the main reason you're here now?
Not entirely. I like Peter; he's a fascinating individual. For some time now I really have had no other social contacts and I was grateful he was prepared to chat about things and extend the hand of friendship. At the same time he was honest with me about wanting people to use his network. So I'm also here to help him.
And what made you ask for a connection with me? Did it just happen because you were unfamiliar with Peter's programme?
Peter wanted me to find my way around as much as possible on my own. Part of his research I assume. But he did tell me that when InterconNet

members are very close together on his map it's because they have a lot in common. Your image—Peter tells me I should call it a node—was very close to mine.

And it was a female node.

Yes. So obviously I had a look and I discovered you were offering psychotherapy.

But not offering romance.

No.

And you're OK with that?

Oh yes. Understood. I have a second thorny issue to discuss with you that does concern romance though, well relationship at least.

Right. Now let's take this step by step. You told me your problems started after you broke up with your partner and you mentioned periods of depression. Are you happy to start there? I have a feeling that this might also help us discuss the first problem you mentioned; your ambivalence towards alternative therapies.

OK.

Unless what you have just said about a specific relationship issue is urgent.

No not really. The individual concerned has had to go away for a period. It's just something I'm wrestling with at the moment. Look, before we start on relationships, can I ask you one last personal question. Tell me to mind my own business if you want.

What do you want to know?

The image on my InterconNet profile is me. But your picture looks so young and, well, striking. I look at it now and think "supermodel or actress", rather than psychotherapist. I mean is it really you? Several other InterconNet users have told me that many people use a proxy image; an avatar. I don't even know if you're a woman or a man!

As the lady in a pop song asks; do you want the truth or something beautiful?

I have already seen something beautiful, so perhaps I'd better have the truth.

Thank you. Well, as a *woman*, I admit I have allowed myself a little *indulgence*. But the image started life as mine.

So would I recognise you if I saw you in real life?

Look Mart, you told me the question before that was the last personal one. Perhaps we should talk about your problems now: your psychological ones. Otherwise we'll both be getting carpal tunnel syndrome!

Sorry Anne - may call you Anne?

Please do. What led to your break up with…?

Helena. She wanted a very active social life at a time when I needed to study for my future career. She found someone else. on-line like this in fact. Had an affair with him, then left me to set up home with him.

What was your immediate reaction to the failure of your relationship with Helena? Was it anger with Helena; a feeling of rejection? What was the main emotion you felt?

I think I blamed myself. I was angry with myself for not being able to give her what she wanted.

You didn't think her demands were unreasonable?

Well we argued about that, but she always seemed to win the argument.

Did you suggest any social activities to her when you were free yourself?

Yes, but she always had or found commitments at those times. I suppose I should have planned my studies round her calendar more.

I'm getting the impression that you were expected to be available when Helena wanted, but she didn't reciprocate. Would that be a fair impression?

Well, I suppose…

Do you miss Helena, Mart? If she wanted to get back together with you, would you agree to that?

Actually, I bumped into her recently in a pub. She split up with the man she was seeing when she was with me.

And?

She said she was had found someone else - a woman - and she was now much happier.

Did you ask her about getting back together?

No. In fact the meeting gave me a sense of closure. I didn't want that either. Not with Helena

But you do want a relationship with someone else?

Martin hesitated. This question was a bit embarrassing in view of his admission this was one of his reasons for agreeing to join InterconNet. And especially after the personal remarks he'd made and questions he'd directed at Anne.

Yes, but I haven't considered a new relationship for quite a long time. Having been rejected once, I didn't feel like taking the risk of trying to find someone else

In case you were rejected again?

Yes. Bloody hell, this all sounds rather pathetic now I can see it written down. Oops sorry!

Don't be. I swear at times too. Remember, you said our InterconNet nodes are close! Peter's programme thinks we have things in common. Perhaps we do! All right, how does all this make you feel?

Annoyed with myself.

OK, now scroll back through our chat so far. Can you see that your feelings of anger and blame are always directed at yourself?

Martin did as he was directed. Seeing the personal questions he'd asked Anne deepened his feeling of embarrassment and irritation with himself. How intrusive! How rude! He scrolled back to their present conversation.

Yes I can! But I still want to apologise for the very personal things I saw I asked you.

This is a psychotherapy session. You have my permission to say and ask anything. I'm not obliged to answer you and if I feel offended I can always close this session. OK. So what does all this tell us about you? And let's hear Martin the *successful* therapist answer.

Poor self image?

Are you telling me or asking me Mart?

I'm telling you.

And I can tell you that it isn't justified. And if *your InterconNet* image is a recent one I can also reassure you that it's one most women would find attractive.

Right. Thanks for the compliment!

So will you give me permission to work on that poorly self image with you in our next session - if you want to continue, that is?

Yes and I do.

How are your carpal tunnels doing?

Still OK, thanks for asking!

Before we sign off would you like to tell me, perhaps briefly as we've both done lots of typing, about that issue related to relationships you're currently concerned about?
It's really rather personal. Is that likely to mean you won't want to continue talking to me.
Most of what I deal with with is private and personal. Are you worried about offending or embarrassing me?
Well yes
If it did, would you be angry with yourself and blame yourself for telling me, even when I said you could?
OK, you've made your point!
Go ahead
Well, although I'm highly sceptical of alternative therapies, one of my colleagues at the Woodlands Centre offered me a course of Reiki. For various reasons I agreed and kept an open mind about it. But this therapist, a female, had by then set up on her own. She too asked about my relationships with women, not just my ex. and concluded that Reiki was not the therapy I needed. In her second session with me, well...
Go on, you're -
Doing fine, I know. She has an amazing therapy room which can simulate different environments appropriate to whatever treatment she has decided will help. In my case she took me to the seaside at night—believe me, it was totally convincing—and acted the part of a girlfriend of my choosing; it was dark, I couldn't actually see her. She drew me, willingly I have to admit, into horseplay on her virtual shore and...
I'm reading, Mart.
And, naked, she held me in an strange state of being I have never previously experienced, for so long I lost track of time.

There was a long pause in Anne's dialogue box. The little minus sign seemed to blink interminably whilst Martin waited for her response. Eventually he typed again.

With this story coming after my rather intrusive questions and remarks earlier, you're probably thinking that I'm just some on-line pervert or time waster.
No Mart, I don't. And there's several reasons for that. But an important one is that Peter's programme validates and constantly

updates its user's profiles. You continue to see the information you've given InterconNet. But the programme does its own character assessment on each of us and that's what *I* see at when I look at your node. And amongst other things it tells me you're a very honest person. In fact this unique feature of InterconNet is one of the reasons I'm on it offering on-line psychotherapy. InterconNet does some of my work for me!

Now, let's get back to the rather surprising things you just told me—and well done to you for sharing such a personal experience. That was certainly not Reiki, Mart! What was your therapist's explanation for her treatment?

She said I needed to appreciate the potency of sensuality rather than sexuality. That's what she judged had been missing in my past affairs. She said I should be offering that in my future relationships. She told me it would generate powerful and sustainable pair bonding.

Wow, this is new therapeutic territory for me too! So what's the dilemma? I'm guessing there is one.

I'm now confused. Was this really treatment designed for me? Was this, to mangle the lyrics of one of Meat Loaf's songs: "I bet you do that to all the boys" or is this woman hinting that she wants a relationship with me?

If the latter, it would have been a pretty strong hint. I have to say that metaphorically and factually, since we're typing; I'm speechless. I'm afraid you'll have to pursue that question with your other therapist. But I can say that you urgently need to work on that self image we have agreed needs to grow. That's if you really want us to work together? I can't possibly compete with this Reiki lady you describe, by the way.

I want to keep our discussion going. In fact, I'm expecting to get a personal computer that I can use at home and at work so we could talk instead of type.

But would you still be able to access InterconNet?

Yes, Pete Swales has told me that's possible. While we're talking about names; your name, Eres. That's quite unusual. How do you pronounce it? For when we get to talk, I mean.

Say it like the surname Ayres. You know the poet Pam Ayres?

Got it now!
Until you next log on then.
Yes, goodbye and thanks.
Your Session with Anne Eres has ended.

****

Martin suddenly realised he was hungry and looked at his watch. It was 2:30pm and he supposed that the Union bar would have stopped serving food. Still, the beer was Bollocks and for once that didn't mean it was bad. He smiled at his own quip. Perhaps he was feeling better. Well, not so isolated anyway. The Union bar wasn't empty as he'd supposed, but then he remembered that students didn't conform to a normal working life routine. The bar person was bent double under the counter apparently cursing fittings beneath the hand pumps. Martin waited patiently. When the man straightened up Martin felt a shock of recognition: It was Peter Swales. Peter grinned broadly.

'Hi Mart. Are you going to say it first?'

'Say what?'

'What are you doing here?'

'You didn't let me know you'd come back from Ireland.'

'Only just got back. What's it to be?'

'Oh, Bollocks.'

'Granted I'm sure. A pint?'

'Yes. Is there anything left to eat?'

'Sorry Mart. The cook's gone home and all the rolls have been sold.'

'What are you doing running the bar? I thought you were a Computer Science post grad.'

'And a pretty skint one at present, as you can see.'

Martin took a deep swig of his drink. Whatever Peter had been doing didn't seem to have affected the beer.

'Cheers. And you can have one on me.'

'Not allowed whilst I'm serving old chap, but I'd like a progress report from you on your InterconNet experience. So how about buying me a couple of drinks at the Dragon tonight?' Martin hesitated. Perhaps it was time to break some habits that had got him nowhere.

'How do you fancy supper at The Bear in Read instead?'

'The Bare? It's not a strip joint is it?'

'The very opposite of.'

'Pity, but if you're buying the drinks I'm your man. Have they banned you from The Dragon because you're straight then?'

'I fancy a change. It's a bit of a hike from here though and I'll be walking.'

'That's how I usually get around, Mart.'

'Meet me outside the Woodlands Centre after work; 6 pm?'

'OK. Don't want to arrive at the pub too early. How about giving me a guided tour of your workplace. Would you be allowed to do that?'

'Yes. Are you really interested?'

'You're one of my InterconNet guinea pigs: it will be instructive to see where you work. OK, I admit I'm also curious about alternative therapies.'

'In what way?'

'How people make a lot of money out of them?'

'Physiotherapy doesn't interest you?'

'You can show me that too. I don't imagine I can stop you.'

'Thanks for the vote of confidence.'

'You know something Mart?'

'No, what?'

'You've changed whilst I've been away. I do believe you've had some of the alternative therapy you were so negative about when we first met.'

Martin put down his empty glass.

'Look Pete, I need to eat. See you at 6 this evening.' He headed out of the bar to look for a café. Peter watched him leave and switched off the voice recorder app on his mobile.

Martin didn't have long to wait outside the Woodlands that evening. Peter appeared, casually dressed as usual and hailed him. The last few staff on the premises were talking in the lobby and acknowledged them briefly. Martin took Peter past the empty reception desk and along the corridor to his clinic.

'We won't bump into your boss will we?'

'Noura? She's not really my boss; she's the Centre's administrator. No; Noura's on vacation, if you can call it that, the amount of Centre papers she takes with her.' Martin gestured dramatically round his room.

'This is my domain. We're in my office stroke consulting room now.' Peter surveyed the cluttered desk with approval.

'Never bought into the concept of "A tidy desk, a tidy mind", me. It makes me think of bank managers and solicitors. What isn't already in their heads is on the other end of their intercoms. I See you've got one of those, but no computer.'

'My real boss has decreed that we all have to have one.'

'Do you get to choose?'

'That sysop you told me about is sorting one out for me.'

'Tuula? When did you meet her?'

'When she responded to my connection request on InterconNet. Haven't you seen our link?'

'Haven't got back in harness yet; too busy in Ireland. But watch out that she doesn't recommend some turbocharged laptop with power you'll never need. She does work for Kosketecessa you know; a pretty hot smart phone manufacturer.'

'She's looked around and done a proper assessment of my needs'

'I bet she has. So she's been here already?'

'She has indeed' Peter picked up a CD jewel case from Martin's crowded desk and glanced at the title. He looked up at Martin with exaggerated concern.'

'You're someone who's really into early pop aren't you?'

'Fills a vacuum. Why?'

'Because you'll know the song with the line "Watch it boy, she'll eat you up!"'

'Why does everybody assume I'm a pushover for women?'

'You'll have to ask a shrink. Did you know there's one pretty close to you on my network?'

'You mean Anne Eres?'

'That's the lady.'

'She's treating me. Free of charge too.'

'Christ, it's you that's the fast worker. Look let's do this tour then we can talk on the way to your Bear Inn.' Martin led him into his treatment room and explained its various fixtures and fittings.

'Treatment bench aka massage bed, changing area, various visual aids for patients: plastic spine; model vertebrae; charts of bones and muscle groups, tens machine.'

'Is that for treating tens elbow?' Martin was about to explain, but Peter's boyish grin told him it was unnecessary.

'Your puns are almost as bad as mine.' Peter walked over to the massage bed.

'Do you do much actual massage then?'

'Its one of my major treatments.'

'And you get to massage gorgeous young women as well as hairy rugby players with sprained Achilles tendons?'

'Yes, but I don't massage inflamed tissues!'

'I wasn't thinking about the rugger blokes ankles. I'm in the wrong business Mart!'

'Look, I think we should continue the tour. We've still got a longish walk ahead.'

'Do you have keys to all the other rooms?'

'No but most of the other therapists don't bother to lock up.' Rather more cursorily, Martin showed Peter the accessible rooms. The herbal medicine surgery was locked, but most of the other doors opened up to very different spaces to Martin's clinical suite. He explained that they had moved from the physiological (his domain) to the spiritual (almost everyone else's). The Woodlands offered natural healing; homoeopathy, Reiki and Ayurveda; massage related treatments including aromatherapy and reflexology and taught de-stressing interventions like T'ai Chi, yoga and meditation. As they looked round, Martin apologised.

'I'm afraid I can't tell you much about the more complementary therapies being carried on here. In fact I've been taken to task for not showing sufficient interest in what my colleagues are actually doing. But I think our big boss explained it to me best of all when he said that the actual healing that goes on here comes from within the clients. The different treatments engage the power of belief; belief that the various conditions will get better or at least improve. And remarkably, to me at least, most really do.' At that moment, Martin had opened the door to Tina's Reiki treatment room. This was now empty; the only content being a display panel of photos and diagrams. Peter wandered over to look. Martin explained from the doorway:

'This was the Reiki room, but the therapist resigned recently.'

'This her photo?' Martin joined him at the display panel.

'Yes - Tina Elves - she's now set up her own practice.'

'She's quite a looker isn't she? Those striking eyes - if anyone could sell magic to me, this one could.' Peter turned round and grinned.

'I don't suppose you have her business card?' Martin didn't bother to reply. They returned to reception.

'Apart from that empty one, those other treatment rooms remind me of when my mum took me to see Santa.'

'As I said, we've moved on now from medicine to metaphysics Pete, and on that note, we'd better stride out for dinner.' As they walked north through the suburbs, Peter explained his sudden disappearance to Ireland.

'Had an urgent call from my older brother Simon. He left his post with one of the computer businesses near Dublin. It was all to do with the collapse of what they called the 'Celtic Tiger' the tax incentivised location of many high tech American and other businesses in the Emerald Isle. Well, to cut a long story short he's importing Korean made tablet computers and badging them with his own marque. His USP, sorry; that's unique selling point, is that customers can go to his website and not just choose the tablet version they want, but can set it all up before it arrives.'

'I suppose I should ask why they would want to do that?'

'Tablets sell like hot cakes, but many customers struggle to get them set up properly. There are all kinds of issues, even if you're experienced with using computers, which most people aren't. Because tablets are powerful and flexible pieces of kit, they're generally more fiddly even to get to do what their smart phone does straight out of the box. The only difference for many users between their tablet and their smart phone then, is just that their tablet screen's bigger.'

'So how does your brother propose to achieve this miracle?'

'That's the clever bit. On the company website, clients see an image of the tablet they've chosen. Basically the site allows them to drag the apps they want onto the image of the tablet. They can choose from a huge range of free apps already available, but they can also specify any other app that's commercially available—at extra cost of course—and add it instantly. Then they can personalise the tablet and enter all their data and options in the apps and test the resulting fully set up virtual device as much as they like, making any changes they want.

There's no time limit to this remote setting up and prospective purchasers get on-line demos to help them. The website offers full interactive guidance and indicates when choices are incompatible, suggesting alternatives. When they're happy, they flash their credit card and Bingo! they are proud possessors of a fully customised tablet computer. Two to five days later, depending where you happen to be in the world, your fully set up device arrives. There's more; a lot more, but I think you get the picture.'

'Well I'd certainly want to buy something like that. But why did your brother want you in Ireland?'

'He couldn't find a programmer that could create the complex Internet programme needed; one that he could trust and, more to the point, actually afford.'

'Oh I see. So are you leaving Tamford? I assume he's offered you the post.'

'Yes he has. But I've turned it down.'

'What? Why? You wanted to make a fortune on the Web. Isn't that why you're developing InterconNet.'

'I judge my brother won't succeed. I can't risk giving up what I'm doing to go crash and burn in Ireland.'

'Why do you think his business will fail?'

'The field's too hot. If he starts to take market share with an idea like that—which he hasn't patented—one of the big boys, like Microsoft or Apple will throw money at it and leave him in the dust. Mind you he's got balls. I'll give him that.'

'How do you mean?'

'You'll never guess what he's proposing to call his tablet.'

'Give up.'

'I'll need to write it down. Got a pen?'

'Sorry.'

'OK, I'll use my phone.'

Peter typed for a few seconds on his mobile's keypad, then handed it to Martin.

'The EyePad Eire! But that sounds like…'

'Exactly.'

'Could he get away with it?'

'He says he's checked with his legal contacts. But that's not really the issue.'

'Was he angry that you've said no.'

'He wasn't over the moon. He'd paid for my flight and hotel. But we've struck a compromise.'

'What's that?'

'While I was staying over there we went through all the details and I've agreed to start putting together a version of the website he needs so he can show off to his backers. Even that will be a significant challenge. In return he'll cover my fees here to finish my degree. If he gets the further funding he needs, he'll invest in InterconNet; I'll need to pay a licence fee for some of the software I'm using. He'll get first refusal to launch an InterconNet app on his "EyePad" - I still can't believe his brass neck! I think that's partly why I'm helping him. That and the dosh of course.'

'I'm no businessman but that sounds like a potential win-win situation for both of you.' Martin stopped at the driveway leading down to The Bear.

'Maybe. Is this the place, Martin? It looks posh. Do they serve students?'

'Only if they are accompanied by a grown up.'

'You wouldn't have said that when I first met you in the Dragon. What's happened while I've been away?'

'Let's order and I'll tell you.'

'I'm all ears.'

'Well, actually Pete, *I'm* all confused.' When they'd ordered food and collected their drinks and were seated conveniently close to the bar, Martin explained:

'Things are on the move at the Woodlands. It's owner - Michael Timles - has said I must pull my socks up at work. There have been complaints from clients, apparently. My scepticism about the other therapies on offer hasn't gone down well either.'

'Don't you keep that to yourself?'

'That would have been more sensible, wouldn't it?'

'Go on.'

'Michael Timles offered to mentor me instead of terminating my contract. He's keen to keep me at the Woodlands and even tempted me with the prospect of better facilities and an assistant.'

'That doesn't sound like a vote of no confidence to me.'

'Well he was quite open with me about his reasons; politics comes into it.'

'Tell me about it! But that's surely not the source of your confusion is it?'

'No; now we get to InterconNet.'

'And all your mysterious women. I thought we were never getting there.' At that moment, the young waitress who had served Martin on his last visit arrived with their drink order.

'Hello Martin. Nice to see you again. John will be bringing your meals in just a moment.' She glanced at Peter, gave Martin a very saucy smile and turned back to the kitchens. Her trainer had emphasised that engaging with customers was now a key driver of repeat business in the hospitality trade. All she needed to do going forward was to fine tune this. Peter's face was a picture.

'Not sure you actually need InterconNet to help you with introductions, Mart.'

'Right now, I'm not sure either, but I'm hoping *you* will help me there.'

'Fire away.'

'OK. Well, when you left me to find my own way about your network—'

'Sorry about that. I did send you more info by email'

'—which I didn't pick up until later. Anyway, left to my own devices, I accidentally connected to a member who turned out to be your sysop, Tuula.'

'But she's miles away from your node on the network.'

'I realise that. So tell me exactly what that means—'

Peter adopted that enthusiastic smile of his which preceded any enquiry about his work.

'—in words of one syllable, please.'

Peter looked hurt. That was a fundamental aspect of his programme and he'd hoped that the graphical separation between users was self-explanatory.

'The short answer is your personality profiles are miles apart.' Now it was Martin's turn to feel hurt.

'Who says?'

'You, Tuula and anyone or anything out there in cyberspace who knows either of you. Don't blame me. The software takes into account what it's been told and, as far as possible weighs up the information for reliability then locates your nodes accordingly'

'So why was it as soon as I'd connected to Tuula she's suddenly all over me?'

'Because you were born lucky?' Martin ignored this cheap jibe.

'I mean if our personalities are so different, why is she taking so much trouble to help me?'

'Opposites attract? Look, I never intended InterconNet to be a matchmaking programme. It's designed to evolve an on-line community which represents a valuable resource for its members. The nodes nearest to you're likely to be helpful to you in many endeavours: friendship; business; creative media; discovery and OK then, yes - even love.'

'There are very few female nodes near mine.'

'Well it's early days for the network. Give it a chance. More people are joining all the time. Why don't you recommend it to some of the other alternative therapists whose rooms you showed me earlier? They're mostly women and very attractive ones if your Reiki lady is anything to go by. I'm surprised you're not dating one of them. You don't have to believe in magic for a successful relationship to happen, you know.'

'So you signed me up under false pretences?'

'By hinting that you might find the girl of your dreams? Well in spite of your particular female space being so sparsely occupied—'

'You're losing me Pete'

'—there being not many girls in your part of InterconNet, you've already told me you've met two and the waitress here just gave you a very big smile.'

'Met one. The other—Anne, who looks fantastic—doesn't want a relationship, well a romantic one anyway.'

'But she *is* giving you psychological counselling gratis?'

'Well, yes.'

'So that's exactly the kind of helpful connection InterconNet was designed for. Look Mart, forgive me being a crude student type, but from what you're telling me, you've so far made two connections through InterconNet. One of these ladies will lay your fears to rest, the other possibly will lay you. Period. What's not to like?'

Peter was enjoying their exchange. He was already getting great feedback from this subject and things had barely started yet. Looking on the positive side of life, Martin's angst seemed completely groundless. But it was evident that Martin couldn't see things from this viewpoint. He was at base a really nice guy and interesting company. Peter could see exactly why women were attracted to him, even though Martin appeared blind to this.

'Would you let a poor student, with no relationship of his own, but some track record in problem solving give you some advice?'

'Will it cost me another round?'

'That's already in my contract.'

'OK, what's the advice?'

'One. Continue seeing your boss for his version of worldly wisdom; although I suspect you don't have a lot of option there. Two. Have some fun with Tuula, if that's what's on offer. She'll be the driver I can assure you. Three. In order to live with my present impecunious state I have to have faith in the ultimate success of my programme. So I firmly believe you should work with your Anne Eres on her terms, whatever the outcome, because your two nodes are so close on InterconNet. Four. In my humble opinion you should submit to one of your alternative therapies and stop knocking the concept. Whether it works or not, it's a great business model. And if it works please tell me so I can contact the therapist concerned. As far as I'm aware, we don't have any such individuals on the InterconNet - yet. Cheers Mart.'

Peter drained the last of his pint and handed Martin the empty glass. Martin took it wordlessly for a moment. Did everyone else but him have the ability to read minds?'

'You look as if someone just walked over your grave, Mart.'

'Do you mean me or the old Martin?'

'I don't follow.'

'Never mind, it's just something someone said that's stuck in my head like one of Kate Bush's old song lyrics. Same again?'

'Need you even ask. And about Kate Bush: you must be thinking of

The Man with a Child in His Eyes? Not bad eh, Mart? And her music wasn't even part of my era.'

Martin shot Peter another strange glance then headed for the bar.

PART THREE

SOCIAL NETWORKS

The danger of the past was that men became slaves. The danger of the future is that men may become robots [and to err may thus become inhuman]

Erich From

Is not this the true romantic feeling— not the desire to escape life, but to prevent life escaping you?

Thomas Clayton Wolfe

CHAPTER TEN
Tuula

Towards the end of that week, Martin had a call from Julie.

'Can you come to reception, Martin. There's a delivery to sign for.' When Martin reached the front desk an man in denim work wear emblazoned with the University of Tamford logo was waiting.

'Mr Wright?'

'Yes.'

'Package for you sir. If you'll kindly sign here.' The delivery man held out a small tablet for Martin to sign. Martin was handed a cardboard box sporting a large plastic documents pouch bearing his name and the Woodlands Centre address. The contents were immediately obvious as the sender identified herself at the foot of the address docket; Tuula Pippi, Computer Science Dept.

Martin returned to his room to unpack his new computer. Inside the box was the manufacturer's original packaging, which had clearly been opened and re-sealed. He was not surprised by this: Tuula would clearly have wanted to check the contents and presumably to start to set things up for him. *What had she told him? Oh yes, that he would need to come over to the Uni for her to steer him through personalising his new toy.* Sure enough, when he broke with custom and visited the staff coffee room for his morning coffee and checked his email, there was a message from Tuula:

> From: Tuula Pipi
> To: Mart (Physio)
> Subject: We need to finish setting up your computer
>
> Hi Mart!
> You should receive your new PC today. I've loaded a new operating system for you and made a couple of tweaks. Now you need to 'introduce' yourself as a user and we can install the programmes on

your list. It will take a while because PC software is so f****ing slow (pardon my Finnish). So we'll both need that bottle of wine you're going to bring over. If you can make it this evening after work, that would be best for me. Just email when you're free. I'm in Room C32, Earley Hall. Give me a call when you get to the Hall lodge. I know it doesn't sound like a fun evening, but I promise it won't be boring.
Tuula

Putting down his coffee mug, Martin emailed that he had the new machine and could make it that evening. The reply was almost immediate.

From: Tuula Pipi
To: Mart (Physio)
Subject: no subject

OK Mart, that's fine. Arrive after 6pm. I'll feed us. Any type of red, but not less than £6 a bottle (my cut-off)..
See you later.
Tuula

It didn't take a degree in life sciences (which was fortunate as Martin had quit that course) to work out that this was a date Tuula was setting up. Despite the familiar anxiety this brought on, he couldn't help feeling rather excited as well. The rest of the day dragged, but 5:30 found him searching the wines and spirits aisles of the local supermarket and walking to the checkouts with a rather extravagant French vintage red.

An hour later, after despairingly rummaging in his wardrobe, he presented himself, tolerably attired, outside Tuula's Hall of Residence. Whilst he waited nervously for her to let him in, he recalled Peter's recent advice. *Have some fun with Tuula, if that's what's on offer. She'll be the driver I can assure you.*

When she finally appeared, Martin realised he'd made a miscalculation in the dress department. Tuula was wearing varsity shorts and a rather baggy Uni tee shirt. The outfit made her look like a first year undergrad, rather than a company sponsored postgraduate fellowship holder. His ego was further deflated when she exclaimed:

'Christ, Mart. I didn't say come in formal dress. Let's get to my room before the block warden sees you and thinks I've phoned an escort agency.'

Feeling foolish, Martin followed her athletic figure up to the third floor to where the door to room 32 was standing half open. Tuula closed the door behind them with an exaggerated expression of relief, then burst out laughing.

'I'm sorry, Mart; your face. Really. I was only joking. Our warden, Sarah, is probably entertaining her boyfriend right now and would only notice anything amiss if the fire sprinkler system kicked in. Even then she'd probably assume it was a better than average orgasm. But seriously, the student residences here are overheated. Take that jacket off.' Tuula looked him up and down and added archly:

'For a start.' Martin put down the computer box and wine carrier. While he looked for somewhere to hang his jacket, Tuula slid the bottle out and squealed.

'Chateauneuf du Pape! That's way above the call of duty and must be rewarded later.' Martin only half heard Tuula's exclamation. Giving up on looking for a hanger, he put his jacket on the back of a chair and took in the rest of the room. There was no trace of the pictures or soft toys he anticipated in a female student bedroom. Instead, the few bookshelves were crammed with serious looking volumes and the pin boards with what he recognised as computer flow charts. The sole ornament seemed to be a photo frame on the study bedroom's desk of a young Scandinavian-looking male. Tuula watched him looking around.

'Pretty Spartan, I guess you're thinking. Well, it's just a temporary home and I really only use it to crash out in. I expect -'

She was interrupted by her mobile.

'Pipi here.'

Tuula looked up at Martin and nodded towards the door.

'Dinner's arrived. Excuse me a moment.' She reappeared with a couple of large pizza boxes.

'Sorry Mart, I didn't check with you earlier. Pepperoni or Quatro Formaggio?'

'You choose first, Tuula.'

'You're my guest, but I accept the courtesy. I'll have the cheesy one. Now put that wine near the radiator. It needs a bit of warmth.' Martin did as asked, whilst Tuula fetched two plates and opened the pizza boxes.

'This is a working meal, but we can still be a bit civilised.' She went over to a built-in wardrobe and extracted two expensive looking cut glass flutes. As she walked back to the low coffee table with the pizzas she looked at Martin and reassured him:

'Don't worry. I did say red, not champagne. I liberated these from the Uni senior common room when I celebrated my Kosketecessa deal with my supervisor.'

'I didn't know you had an academic staff position.'

'I haven't. I have some responsibility in the Computer Science department, but I'm formally a postgraduate student; registered for a higher degree. Like all students here, I have to report to a tenured member of staff, although mine doesn't interfere beyond signing forms and reports. He's only too happy to have some tie in with Kosketecessa. Let's get started shall we? Get out your PC whilst I pour.' Once the PC had started up, just as Tuula had warned him, typing details into the seemingly interminable windows which opened up seemed to take forever. By the time the system congratulated him for a successful set up, the pizzas had long since disappeared. Tuula stood.

'Well that's it Mart. You're all set up. Now we can relax and enjoy ourselves for the rest of the evening.' She fetched a bottle of red from her wardrobe.

'Not as great a vintage as yours, but we'll manage somehow. I think we'll take our time, though. We don't want to lose concentration for the next bit.' She filled their glasses and stood next to him, showing him how to separate the PC screen from the keyboard to use as a portable tablet. Picking her own tablet up from the desk, she jabbed at the screen. After a moment, Martin saw the InterconNet welcome screen appear.

'Now, if you can still remember your log on credentials, enter them on your own tablet.' Martin logged in. The InterconNet network appeared as before. This time there was no welcome message from Peter.

'Now navigate to my node.' He dragged Tuula's small picture to the centre of the display on the desk and enlarged it as he had been shown.'

'OK, now just wait a moment.' Tuula disappeared into the small en-suite shower room with her tablet. Martin waited, puzzled. After a couple of minutes when nothing was happening, he took a sip of Tuula's wine. It wasn't bad, but then he was pretty relaxed now the Chateauneuf had eased most of his earlier anxiety. Abruptly a new window opened on the display in front of him. At the top was Tuula's picture with the message:

Tuula Pipi is now on-line and requests a connection. Do you wish to

accept? Martin was startled and at first wondered if his hostess had left the building through the bathroom window and run to her office in the computer centre. Then he recalled that she had taken her tablet with her. He typed:
Yes

The familiar double paned window appeared ready to display their conversation

Hi Mart It's time for dessert! The penny dropped. Martin replied:
I take it you're using the tablet PC in your bathroom?
Sure am. I'm going to leave setting up all your other programmes to you. As they say here "as an exercise for the student". It's time for a bit of fun.
What do you have in mind?
We're going to kill two birds with a single stone tonight! Martin was entering into the spirit of this, helped by the classic French vintage. He thought he remembered this exchange with Tuula the other way round. What was it his boss had said? "Reflection and humour are the salves for most of life's challenges". Peter had warned this girl was a challenge.
Don't you mean get "more bangs for your buck"?
You might be more "on the ball" there than you realise Mart! Anyway, I have a couple of important questions first. Did you drive here?
Yes.
Well I don't want you to drive back tonight.
I'll walk of course
I didn't mean that, Martin. Martin wasn't used to such a direct hint although he realised she'd been making suggestive remarks since he arrived. Once again he recalled Peter Swales's words: *Have some fun with Tuula, if that's what's on offer. She'll be the driver I can assure you.* Well she certainly didn't want him to drive tonight.
I haven't any early bookings at the Woodlands tomorrow. You've got me connected, what other birds are you going to kill, Tuula?
Tuula Pipi is requesting voice contact. Will you accept? Martin clicked to confirm. Tuula's voice came through on the tablet's speaker

'The answer to your question is that I'm going to take you through some other features of InterconNet.'

'That's better. It seemed daft *typing* messages to you in the bathroom. Do you really want me to stay the night here?'

'If you would really like to stay.' Another small message appeared on Martin's screen

Tuula Pipi is asking for a two way video link. Will you accept? Martin clicked the Yes button. Immediately a full screen image of Tuula's face appeared on the monitor.

'Hi Mart. Now, as an experienced physiotherapist, tell me what you think.'

Tuula's head turned as she walked away from the tablet's camera. Her varsity shorts and shapeless Uni tee shirt had gone. When she appeared full length on Martin's display she did a slow end-of-catwalk turn for him.

'Well, what do you think?' Martin was temporarily lost for words. Eventually he pulled himself together to reply.

'As a physio, I'd have to say you're in great physical shape.' He paused searching for something less trite to add.

'I shouldn't think you maintain that figure by spending hours at a computer screen.'

'Well I do that, but I'm also rather younger than you and play a lot of squash.' She faced the camera, hands on hips, legs akimbo.

'Any other comments physio?' Completely out of his depth, yet feeling early stirrings of arousal Martin decided it was in his best interest to play along with this scary woman.

'I'd need to make a closer inspection to be able to come up with more detailed conclusions.'

'Be my guest.'

'You'll need to come out of the bathroom.'

'Jesus, Mart. The camera on your new tablet is HD. Enlarge me; go on - I won't feel a thing.'

'Sorry?'

'You can inspect magnified areas of my image using two fingers on the touch screen. You know; like that myopic oriental guy next to your workstation when we first met was inspecting the stitching detail on some lingerie ad?' After a few moments fumbling, Martin found that he could indeed enlarge portions of Tuula's image. He noted the rosy flush of her skin between her breasts and throat and the erect nipples. His own arousal was growing in sympathy. Tuula was speaking again.

'You must be aware that teenagers are doing this on their cell phones,

Mart. It's a concern. At present my company and the main telecoms networks are batting that issue backwards and forwards, along with all the other health and safety problems and security glitches.

Young males feel the need to prove masculinity. Sharing explicit images of women and especially their girlfriends with other boys. Shouting at girls; embracing a macho culture of aggression and even violent threatening behaviour. Not able to express a softer side for fear of ridicule by their peers. In short a gang mentality. In some cultures this is exploited by leaders to obtain similar actions from adult males. I don't need to spell that out further, Mart, I'm sure.'

'But sexting teens aren't in the same room. You hardly know me, Tuula. I can't pretend I'm not enjoying this game, but aren't you taking a personal risk?'

'Christ Mart, There's a lock on the bathroom door and one of those emergency pull cords in here. I've read your life story on InterconNet, visited your workplace and picked up the vibes of your colleagues there. Pete Swales says you're a great guy and you regularly treat one of my squash partners; a young female. By now I know more about you than I do about my last boyfriend. Before I let you do that physical inspection you asked for, tell me something else that I might learn from a physio.'

'Are you getting cold in there?' Martin asked anxiously.

'No dammit, I'm hot! Come on physio. Let's have a diagnosis.'

'OK, stand back a bit from your camera.'

'This all right?'

'Yes, now put your hands on your head.' On the tablet screen, Tuula complied.

'Now raise and lower yourself on your heels, at a jogging pace'

As he had been shown, Martin zoomed the display in on her upper chest.

'OK stop now.'

'What?'

'There's very little independent movement of your mammary gland tissue when you jog on the spot. You have a particularly firm combination of Coopers ligaments, dermis, interstitial matrix and pectoral muscles.'

'What's that in Finnish?'

'You've exceptional boobs.' Tuula grinned.

'Now we're getting somewhere.'

'But you should still invest in a sports bra if you're going to keep playing squash or plan to get pregnant at some stage. Look Tuula, I'm beginning to feel like a grubby voyeur, do you want me to take my own clothes off for you now?'

'No way. You unwrapped *your* present earlier. Now it's my turn. But I want to do my own video inspection first.'

'What do you mean?'

'Prop up your tablet and stand back a bit from the camera above your screen.' Martin obeyed.

'Now put both hands on top of your head, like you asked me to do and stretch your body upwards. Are you still looking at me on your screen?' Tuula was now needlessly supporting those exceptional parts of her body Martin had referred to.

'Yes.' Whilst he watched, Tuula performed some advanced self-massage, keeping her eyes on Martin as she did so. After he'd completely lost track of time, she commanded:

'Now turn so I can see your body in side profile.' Martin twisted a quarter turn, now almost painfully aware what Tuula was looking for.

'That OK?'

'Looks promising, but I'll need a physical inspection to confirm it.' There was a click as the en-suite door opened.

****

Martin woke up with cramp in his lower back. This, he soon worked out was due to having slept with his back pinned against the wall in Tuula's narrow student bed. He also realised that this extreme posture was no longer necessary as the other occupant of the bed was missing.

'Tuula?' There was no answer, but there was a note written with felt tip on the bedside table. He propped himself up painfully and stiffly to recover it. It was bright outside and the curtains had been thrown back. Squinting in the glare, he read:

Hi Mart

You didn't get much sleep so didn't (couldn't?) wake you. Had to go give a tutorial. Occupational hazard! Coffee in the 2nd floor lounge. Don't worry about being seen. There'll probably be a queue of blokes at the vending machine! My door is self locking when you leave.

Tuula

After the high of the previous night, Martin felt abandoned and bleak. As he gathered his scattered clothes, Tuula's impersonal room made his nakedness feel crude and heavy. Devoid of decoration apart from the now accusing glance of the Scandinavian male in the single photo frame, he might have been making love in an office. In fact the pain in his back felt like this had been performed on the study desk rather than the narrow mattress.

Now his temptress had flown, he felt like an intruder and just wanted to leave as soon as possible. He had nearly closed the room door behind him when he remembered his computer. Pushing it open quickly he collected the tablet and it's keyboard and stuffed them back in the packaging. Hesitating at the door a second time, he went back, turned over Tuula's note and wrote in felt tip:

Hi Tuula, thanks for the PC and the "tutorial"! Hope to see you soon. Email or text me when you're free. Mart.

Despite his attempt to be light hearted, he didn't feel it. As he pulled her door shut the noise seemed to echo down the deserted concrete corridor like a prison cell closing. A young woman passed him on the stairs and gave him a brief glance. Martin didn't return her smile. Suddenly he felt much older than his years. He didn't stop at the second floor to look for the vending machine, but hurried on downstairs. He opened the wired glass lobby door and walked to the car park below the characterless residential block, without glancing back.

****

Martin parked in the Woodlands forecourt at 10:30 and mentally prepared for Julie's bright banter: *Oh you've decided to grace us with your presence today after all Mr Wright.* He suddenly remembered the chocolates promised in return for her covering up his late arrival to the Centre's manager. At the time they were only joking around, but this morning, he needed her support, not her sarcasm. He left the Woodlands site and drove down a neighbouring street where there was a convenience store.

He hurried out moments later with an expensive half milk/half plain assortment, forgetting which type of chocolate would suit, but guessing that the brand name would speak for itself. Back at the Woodlands, Martin adopted a brave face, hoping that Noura's deputy wouldn't be in reception. Before Julie could speak, Martin waved the box at her.

'You'd never guess how far out of Tamford I had to go this morning to get these, but you're worth it!' His ruse appeared to have worked as Julie's eyes lit up.

'Ooo Martin! These cost a bomb. Are you sure?' When Martin nodded she shook her head to indicate "you shouldn't have" although she had no intention of parting with her prize.

'I'm keeping these at reception. The animals at home would eat the lot.' Martin gave her a weak smile and watched her open the desk drawer to secrete his gift. That reminded him of the favour Tina had requested in her note.

'No one wants me this morning do they Julie?'

'What's left of it Mart; no.' but she was still smiling broadly.

'I've just remembered Tina asked me to pick up a package from her flats and forward it. She's had to drop everything to help her sister in Sheffield.'

'I know; she told me. Her poor little nieces. Are you and Tina an item now?'

'Oh no. I've been going to her for some Reiki.' Martin immediately regretted his slip, which he wouldn't have made had he not been feeling low. From the look on Julie's face he could see that, chocolates or no chocolates, this would be all over the Woodlands grapevine in minutes. Before she could ask him anything else, he seized his opportunity and left.

Twenty minutes later he drew up outside the smart flats where Tina lived. As he fumbled in his wallet for her mailbox key, all the details of his odd experience there came back to him. He had a queer sensation of being a chessboard piece; of not being in control of events and being moved by others in a game he didn't yet understand. He shivered slightly, not knowing whether that thought was insight or imagination.

Tina's key code opened the external door and he easily located the mailboxes to the right of the entrance. Inside Tina's was a small amount of mail. Amongst the bills and unsolicited marketing, there were a couple of similar looking packages. As expected, the first package was addressed to Tina Elves at the Tamford address, with a tree logo and a company name: You Tree Ltd. Martin took the package, then examined the remaining one. To his astonishment it was to himself at the same address. For a full minute he stared at the address labels and the packaging trying to see if there was some mistake by the supplier.

Finally, he closed the mailbox door and slowly walked back to his vehicle. Placing the packages on the back seat, he headed for the Woodlands. As soon as he turned onto the trunk road he joined crawling traffic. Several times it stopped completely. But when he tried to twist against the restraint of his seat belt to fetch the packages from the back seat and open the one addressed to him, the car in front lurched forward and he had to grab the wheel. His sense of confusion grew even stronger.

****

Peter Swales picked up his supervisor's email as soon as he came in to his office. It wasn't very long or difficult to interpret; being the non-verbal equivalent of "my office, now"! Peter dumped a paperback by his workstation and did as commanded. It was obvious when he got there that Chris wasn't in a good mood.

'Ah there you are at last. Sit. This may take some time.' Peter did as he was told.

'I met someone you know, Peter. Martin Wright; a physiotherapist from the Woodlands Centre here.' Chris waited for a reaction from Peter. When there was none he continued:

I'm giving you fair warning, Peter! We agreed that you'd restrict InterconNet membership to students and academic staff. Next time you try anything like this without discussing it with me first, I'll inform the graduate studies office that I'm withdrawing as your supervisor. You may well be self-funded, but without my support for your studies here you'd be up shit creek without a paddle.' Peter finally found his voice.

'Sorry Chris. It was such a good opportunity. You know me; strike while the iron's hot and all that. I was going to tell you but then the Irish trip came up and the urgency of all that meant it slipped my mind. There's still a way to go with InterconNet, but I can already see my publication in…'

'*Our* publication Peter. If I hadn't have bumped into Martin using InterconNet in the Computer Centre, I wouldn't have known anything about it.'

'Of course you would. I got him to register properly as an external visitor and cleared him as a Uni Network user with Bill Meagh. Tuula has also been keeping an eye on his use of the Computer Centre facilities.'

'So I would have been the *last* to know.'

'Sorry Chris. It won't happen again.'

'It had better not. You did get this Martin to sign the confidentiality agreement, I hope?' Peter hadn't, not wanting to put his first external user off at the start, then forgetting about it later.

'I've explained everything to Martin, Chris. His access is restricted within the University network and obviously I'm monitoring his on-line activity. Besides, the Uni students using InterconNet and even academic staff themselves are hardly watertight subjects.'

'No Peter, but they are accountable to the establishment and covered under the university's insurance policies; Martin isn't.' Looking at Peter's unusually worried expression, a sixth sense warned Peter's supervisor not to pursue this any further, for now at least. Chris leaned back in his chair and nodded slowly, giving the impression of being mollified.'

'Well, please keep a close eye on him and keep me posted in future. Anyway, how did the Irish visit go? Has your brother offered you a position in his new company?'

'He wanted me to work for him, but I turned his offer down.'

'Because you're aiming for an academic post? If so, don't forget you'll absolutely need a first class reference from me, Peter.'

'Because I think his business model is flawed.'

'From what you've told me he's been pretty successful so far. You know what they say about entrepreneurs; if they've never failed, they haven't been trying hard enough. So what's the deal, Peter? Don't tell me you've walked away from Simon with nothing to show for it.' Peter hesitated. He had been going to discuss all this calmly with his academic supervisor over a beer or two, but now Chris had jumped the gun. In view of his failure to ask him about recruiting Martin into the project, this needed careful handling.

'Well, *technically* I think Simon's new business idea is a good one. It's a novel kind of on-line application directly linked to sales of an IT product. Of course, I can't be specific as I've signed *his* confidentiality document.' He risked a look at Chris to see if he could detect any sign of approval of this evidence of discretion, but Chris's expression was impassive. Peter continued:

'There could be high initial earning potential, but without patent protection—which I don't think would be feasible for what he proposes—the big IT boys could copy his business model and undercut him.' Peter was watching Chris carefully and it was clear that he wasn't impressed.

'Business is all about taking risks, Peter. The rewards are high, but the price of failure is high too. That's why you and I are here and not operating out of a small unit on the local industrial estate.' Peter had a barbed reply to this remark along the lines that it was Chris and not himself who spoke from the security of lifetime tenure, but he bit his tongue.

'I didn't want to break with Simon completely. As you say, he's built up a profitable small business from scratch. He needs a computer simulation of his new idea to impress investors. He has no-one in house able to do this and so he has to contract out the programming.' Peter chose his words very carefully now.

'I said I'd be willing to do this programming, in my own time obviously, in return for sponsorship of my research project.' He paused waiting for an eruption from his supervisor. It was not forthcoming. Peter continued:

'I then said that I could see my, I mean our, own work adding value to his idea if that goes ahead. I didn't give him details of course. He said he would be willing to look at any proposal from us, under a suitable confidentiality arrangement in due course. He would be willing to license our technology for use as an application on his product.'

'I'll need to know a lot more before agreeing to anything along those lines. And any licensing arrangements arising from research done here will have to go through the University intellectual property section. Look Peter, I think you'd better get back to your brother and tell him if he wants to use anything developed here, he needs to send me an outline of its intended use.

You had better add that an informal arrangement won't wash and it would have to be a full legal agreement with the University.' Chris hesitated here. Academic salaries were nothing to write home about.

'But informally you can tell him that I'm certainly interested to learn more.' Chris leaned forward in his chair.

'Now what's all this about sponsorship of your project in return for doing some programming to impress Simon's potential investors? I'm not sure that Ph.D. students *have* time for external work and I certainly don't believe you won't be using the department's facilities to do it.' Chris sighed and leaned back.

'Mind you, from what I've seen, few students, or staff for that matter, distinguish between research and personal work. I'm only too well aware that Face Book started life on Uni computers.' Peter took a deep breath.

'He's agreed to pay my course fees up until the award of my Ph.D.'

'The *potential* award of your degree. Well, I suppose that does remove a degree of uncertainty about our project. Also you'd be able to eat better. OK Peter, you have my blessing. You want to be an entrepreneur some day. Draft a confidentiality agreement covering our work here what with both our names on it and let me see it before doing or agreeing to anything else.' Chris drew the keyboard on his desk towards him; a sure indication that the interrogation was over. But as Peter was opening the office door, Chris had a parting shot.

'And Peter…'

Peter turned back to be greeted with one of Chris's trademark expressions; half threat, half humour.

'About Martin and InterconNet. Don't fuck it up.'

CHAPTER ELEVEN

Martin

At last Martin arrived back at the Woodlands Centre. In his room, he stared at Tina's packages. He ran through several different explanations for the one addressed to him, but none seemed to make sense. He decided to call Tina. He was answered by a voice mail announcement. Martin broke the connection without leaving a message. Finally, he opened the package addressed to him. As soon as the transit cardboard was torn back he saw it was a paperback.

Universal Therapy

Towards a fully integrated healthcare
Michael Timles and Christina Elves

The books authors were a surprise, but at least something was clearer. Tina's package had to contain the same book. But if she had intended to give him one of the copies, why did she have the copy intended for him sent to her flat? She didn't mention it when she asked him to collect and forward her copy. He couldn't work it out.

Martin flicked through the pages. The coverage was impressive and looked very clearly written. He wondered if it would be available on Amazon. Immediately he thought of Amazon, he knew what had happened. Tina must have ordered the two copies from this You Tree place on-line. Then, with the stress of making last minute arrangements to visit her sister, had entered her own address instead his at the Woodlands Centre. But this reasonable explanation still left many nagging questions unanswered. It was worrying.
Idly Martin turned to the Introduction, which was signed by both authors. He sat and read.

* * *

Introduction

In early times the efforts to restore damaged bodies and minds to health lay in the hands of a single healer, shaman or lay person of acknowledged skills; someone in more recent times We'd have called the 'wise woman' for they were often female and their role frequently passed down in their families.

These individuals had no formal training but had learnt their therapies by word of mouth and trial and error. Their qualifications for practice came from the "university of life"; their undoubted effectiveness in tackling many ills bolstered by their own belief in their healing power and the absolute belief in it by their patients.

Today medicine is divided into many specialities and continues to fragment as technology and life science places ever more tools and knowledge at our disposal. The present day equivalents of the shamans or wise women; GPs, are overwhelmed by the totality of medicine and their practice often comes down to a decision about to whom their anxious patient should be referred.

Health specialists jealously guard their own turf and this too often means that the "whole" patient is no longer being treated. Patients end up with a doctor, doubtless with excellent narrow skills, but who fails to recognise or deal with either the underlying problem or other problems his patient may have.

A simple example of this can be given from the experience of one of us. Presenting for treatment of a serious fracture within a joint, the clinician dealing with this failed to refer his patient for physiotherapy. Perhaps the specialist assumed that such after care was self-evident, the responsibility either of his patient or another member of staff in the hospital admission chain. Result: frozen shoulder taking many months from which to recover.

Things become very much more serious in the field of mental health. The hang-over from the distant past; from the time of

Descartes, no less, has been that mind and body are quite separate entities and can be treated as such. A plethora of specialists has arisen and continues to diversify almost on a yearly basis: counsellors, coaches, cognitive therapists, psychologists, psychotherapists; the list goes on and on. Apart from the field of psychiatric medicine, few if any of these therapists have medical training. The risk of failure to detect serious disorders unrelated to their specialities and even to make existing conditions worse is very real.

Lastly we have the so-called complementary and alternative therapists who are like all the others, let's face it, earning their living through offering improvements to physical health and human happiness. The alternative sector is "alive and well" in Western and particularly Eastern societies. Sadly, although gaining a little ground in recent years, its claimed success has come under attack from mainstream practitioners. Where successful, its considered at best "due to the placebo effect" (it's patients expect to get better and indeed do so) and at worst, just quackery.

What conclusion to draw from all this? It is clear to the authors of this book that modern medical practice, despite the glowing statistics and all its undeniable wonders, is and is likely to remain, dis-integrated with respect to helping many sick individuals. Paradoxically, as medical research surges forward, the holes in its net are getting larger. In truth, for many conditions where modern medicine has failed, "self-help" remains the only option for such individuals to regain physical and mental health. But patients face navigating a medical minefield. Hundreds of formal and informal sources of advice are out there: relatives, friends, the Internet and of course, all those alternative and complementary practices.

Re-integrating medicine as a whole; the authors freely acknowledge, would be an enormous undertaking. Just to set down what new approaches, systems, facilities and training that would be necessary is beyond the scope of this book. Here we aim to show, definitively and comprehensively, how we believe alternative therapies "work" and how they could be integrated into mainstream medicine. In so doing we anticipate making enemies both in the fields of complementary medicine (we will debunk certain practises) and in mainstream medicine (we will weaken the entrenched positions of some clinical fundamentalists). If we survive their anticipated attacks, we hope that a wider readership will be enlightened, excited and in some chapters, entertained by our work. Above all our aim is to contribute to improving human health and happiness. We hope that few of those who may decry this book will be able to argue with that.

    Michael and Tina
    Tamford, 2021

    Martin recognised quite a bit of this. He remembered being amazed when Tina had given him her take on alternative therapy that time in The Dragon. Of course he had yet to read the book, but having met both authors he knew it would be full of common sense. It was also likely to disturb him. He'd been content with his scepticism of complementary medicine and to read this work might be like letting go of the side of the swimming pool at the deep end for the first time.

    After these initial thoughts had raced through his head, he did truly start to feel as though he was floundering out of his depth in dark water. Up until recently he had walled himself off from the rest of the staff at the Woodlands, feeling superior to them as the only therapist offering treatments widely accepted as effective.

    Deliberately isolating himself, he'd paid scant attention to what was actually happening at the Centre. He'd made no significant effort to integrate his own skills in exactly the way that this introduction called for. As a result he felt he had achieved little in his time there. In contrast, as now revealed, people like Tina and the Centre's owner were clearly using their time and talents to "push the frontiers" of medicine. It could have been someone like him instead of Tina, who might have collaborated with the Centre's owner to make a difference in healthcare.

    Thoughts of Tuula, which had been uppermost in his mind that morning were pushed aside as he mentally reassessed Tina. Here was a very attractive woman, kind to her relatives, self-evidently talented and ambitious. One who had taken an interest in him and demonstrated her concept of couple togetherness in the most unexpected and intimate manner. What was he to make of her? He still didn't know. But he was sure that he didn't deserve whatever it was she was doing for him; what she might do further to surprise him and, yes, delight him as well.

After a moment's thought, he tried her mobile again. This time after a while there was a curt network message announcing that the mobile being called was unavailable. He slowly put his phone back in his jacket and stared morosely at the clutter on his desk. He needed to make changes in his life and not put things off any longer. The screen of his new computer stared blankly up at him. InterconNet. If Tuula was right, he could now access it from his office. Powering it up he connected to the Centre's new WiFi following the simple instructions left by the network solutions engineer. He clicked on the small graphic image of Peter's network.

After a moment, the University splash screen invited him to log in. Soon he had Peter's programme up and running. It was a little slower than when he accessed it in the Computer Science building, but everything seemed to be working as before. He opened Tuula's network node. Her contact window announced: **Tuula Pipi is off line. Do you wish to send a message?** Martin hesitated. She hadn't been in touch since he left the note in her room for her to contact him when she was free. He didn't know what to add to that right now; he wanted to talk to her. Finally he repeated his request and sent it.

****

There seemed to be no-one in the Centre that afternoon. The silence of the place was oppressive. He couldn't recall a time when that had worried him - he generally enjoyed his own company between seeing patients. He scrolled across the network display to the image of Anne Eres. Unlike Tuula's her contact window announced that that his mysterious psychotherapist was on-line. Martin typed that he wanted to connect and after a minute he was rewarded with a response:
Hello Martin, how are things today?
Hi Anne. I'm glad you're available. Can you spare me some time now?

Yes Martin, What would you like to discuss?

Bear with me a moment Anne

Martin called Julie on the Intercom.

'I'm going to talk with a patient on the phone for a while Julie, please don't contact me until I call you back.'

He turned on his "clinic engaged" sign and locked the door before returning to the computer.

Sorry Anne, I just hung up my do not disturb sign. Can we talk instead of typing?

Where are you Martin?

In my clinic at the Woodlands Centre and I'm in my private office. Safe to speak here

A new window opened just as it had done in Tuula's room and asked if he accepted speech communication. He did. A pleasant female voice greeted him:

'Hello again Martin. Can you hear me OK?'

'Yes Anne. Your voice is very clear.'

'Thank you. I have to confess, Martin, that it's not quite me. Pete's clever programme changes it a bit; part of my privacy! Now are you sure this is a good moment for you?'

'My typed conversations with you felt less intrusive; like sending email, but this is very different.'

'Would you prefer to go back to typed messages?'

'Absolutely not. I want to continue like this, please.'

'Good; I'm sure we'll make faster progress this way. And our carpal tunnels will get a rest.'

'That's a condition I can often treat successfully, Anne.'

'I'll bear that in mind. You know I recalled the name of that wrist condition from looking a the record of our last discussion. But this way there won't be written record of our discussion, although there's an option to record what we say; if you'd like that?'

'I've just seen that. So it's OK with you to turn it on?'

'Please do, Martin. Last time we were talking about relationships. Do you want to carry on with that?'

'Yes, I'd like to.'

'Before we start Martin, there's an important new element in our session apart from the obvious freedom to communicate naturally. We can now hear the emotion behind what we say and our pauses mean we're reacting or thinking, not just trying to find "q" on the keyboard. Are you with me?'

'In spirit if not in person, Anne.'

'So I want us to work hard to imagine we're in the same room; your room at your Woodlands workplace. You can look at my InterconNet picture if that helps. Or perhaps better; you can close your eyes and try to visualise me sitting opposite you; perhaps on the other side of your desk - if that's where you are?'

'I am.'

'And I want you to talk openly and honestly; don't try to hide your feelings at all. If you're angry with me, let me hear your irritation. If you're pleased with our exchange, help me notice this in your voice. And, a big ask I know, if you get sad or upset don't hide this from me by masking your feelings when we talk. In return, Martin, I promise to do the same.' The voice coming through the speakers on his computer was calm. But it also sounded warm and engaging. He shut his eyes to blot out his impersonal clinical surroundings and attempted to visualise his mysterious mentor and himself sitting in Tina's old treatment room, which had been the most restful space in the Woodlands. He replied, making a big effort to sound enthusiastic.'

'Yes Anne; I'd really like to do that.'

'Good, but don't overdo it though; I will be able to sense if what you're saying is at odds with how you say it!' Anne's caution was firm but friendly.'

'Sorry.'

'Don't be. Just be Martin.'

'This is part of the treatment isn't it?'

'What do you mean?'

'Getting me to be more aware of the emotion in our voices.'

'Well, I hadn't intentionally set out to do that; that's emerged from our discussion. I haven't planned anything for us other than to go with the flow wherever it takes us. Would you say you're conscious of a need to pay more attention to other people's emotions?'

'That's probably an area where I'm weak. Look Anne, as a physio, I have had some pretty basic training in counselling - although this is focused mostly on helping clients change their lifestyle where necessary. In your profile you describe yourself as a psychotherapist. I understand enough about that to know the name covers all kinds of different specialists. Do you have your own speciality within this field? I mean you've told me that you're just starting out to do this…'

'Will me answering that question help?' Anne sounded a little miffed, as though he was questioning her credentials.

'This is still confidential, even though we're speaking now instead of typing?'

'Oh yes. As in your own career, patient confidentiality is paramount. If anything emerges from our sessions that I'd like to use—in a publication for example—I will always ask your permission.'

'OK. Let me explain. I've had a surprise today; well a big surprise actually. I've just found out that… a colleague of mine and our Centre's owner have published a book in which they are critical of the fragmentation of mental and physical medicine into many specialities.

Basically, they argue that if patients get sent down the wrong specialist pathway, they could be unable to cross over to another, possibly nearby, therapeutic route that would have been better able to diagnose and treat their problems. They're calling for better integration of medicine: physical, mental and complementary.'

Anne paused for a noticeable time before replying.

'Phew. You're also full of surprises for *me*, Martin. OK, I did urge openness and honesty, didn't I? Well as a fairly recent psychology graduate, I have been impressed with so-called cognitive approaches. In words of one or two syllables that means working with people's thinking more than their emotions.

Thoughts usually precede emotions and thinking is much easier for clients to describe, discuss and eventually control. Emotions, once they've been aroused, are very difficult or even impossible to control. Also most people have great difficulty describing and discussing them. So when the old school psychotherapists ask their distressed patients questions like "so how do you feel about your dad hitting your mum"? Or these days possibly the other way round, it probably isn't going to immediately improve their mental health.'

'So you're a cognitive therapist?'

'So unlike the two authors you just told me about, *you're* in favour of keeping we therapists in neatly labelled compartments?' This time it was Martin's turn for a reflective pause. He felt hurt that he had been misinterpreted, but it was his own fault.

'I thought if I knew what methods you use I might be a better patient and get better marks for any homework you set me.'

'It's all right Martin, I'm not offended.' Martin's attention on the tone of their discussion had wandered. He hadn't realised that his reply had sounded humble and contrite. He was going to try to smooth things over, but Anne continued:

'I too must be careful not to fall into a superior role as the "therapist" in my relationship with clients. I must always bear in mind that my clients can borrow books or go on-line to learn all about psychotherapy and read as many case histories as they wish.'

'I'm sorry I always seem to open our sessions by interrogating you, Anne.'

'We've only had one full session so far and anyway I don't want to jump straight into this one without some small talk first to relax us both and bring us up to date.'

'I'm not very good at small talk and I'm afraid what I opened our discussion with was more like heavy talk.'

'Martin, in our sessions, I'm not going to be judgemental or tell you what you should do. But I do want you to stop apologising. You'll know if you listen carefully if you have offended me and if you say sorry one more time, I might just take offence!'

'Ooops!'

'That's better. Now what's brought you to my cybersurgery? I have a feeling there's something other than your colleagues's book on your mind.'

'There's a new development, yes, but if we're to be honest with each other, I was feeling pretty down. I was trying to contact someone else on the network, but they were unavailable.' Martin thought that Anne must know of Tuula as she appeared to be one of the most highly connected individuals on the network. But he decided for now to keep her name out of the discussion. Anne commented:

'But *I* was available.'

'Yes; you're not offended are you?'

'Martin!'

'Only joking. You're cheering me up already.'

'Is the new development a relationship issue?'

'Oh, definitely.'

'Same woman as last time?'

'Err, well no.'

'All right, let's recap. You're actively looking for a new relationship?'

'Yes I think that's what's missing in my life.'

'What were you looking for in your earlier relationships; before you settled down with Helena?'

'All the girls I dated were good looking, lively, keen on sports.'

'What were you *looking* for?'

'Sex. Well and fun and friendship as well.'

'Nothing wrong with lust. Problem for many, if not most, is keeping that emotion alive. So with Helena, you decided to deepen the relationship. Was it the sex, fun or friendship that made you decide she was the one?' Martin paused for thought here. Anne took advantage of his hesitation to prompt him:

'Please don't tell me what you think I'd like to hear, unless it's also the truth.' She had a fantastic body. And she was ambitious. I was impressed that she seemed to know exactly where her career would take her.'

'Before you committed to setting up home together, did you meet her friends or family?'

'Not her mum and dad, but there was a small group of her mates we socialised with.'

'How did you find them?'

'I didn't like them much: loud and loose, I'd say.'

'Did you have any of your own friends who socialised with you and also knew Helena?'

'No; why?'

'When we meet someone we fancy a lot, that generally leads us to overlook or perhaps *not* to look for personality problems like selfishness or existing problems like debt. These things don't stop you having a great time as a couple, but can become serious issues in a long term relationship. Your friends and even their friends and family can sound warning bells - or at least give you a friendly nudge. That's what family or true friends try to do.'

'Not really something I worried about in the past.'

'But you do worry about now?'

'Well, obviously after what happened with Helena; once bitten and all that.'

'In our last session, you told me that Helena's character and behaviour really didn't change when you entered a long term relationship; yet she expected you to make big changes in your life.'

'I know now that was unfair. I never want that to happen again.'

'Most couples quickly identify things they don't like about each other. These disagreements lead to arguments and positions soon become entrenched.'

'And it's the men who generally back down for a quiet life rather than face female hysteria.'

'Whatever the truth of that generalisation, Martin, it represents failure by both parties. But let's get back to discussing partner choice. Apart from desire and social pressure to have a partner, what else could qualify a potential soul mate?'

'GSOH?'

'Good salary, own home! Come on Martin; we're not looking through the lonely hearts ads!' Anne deliberately adopted a mock tone of annoyance, but waited patiently for some sensible suggestions.

'Common interests.'

'And what was the shared interest with Helena?'

'Sport and other physical activity.'

'And your own sporting activities gave way when you started on your career path as a physiotherapist.'

'While parties and clubbing became increasingly important to Helena.'

'Any other things to look for in your girlfriend?'

'Shared opinions; common vision of the future; projects that you both get excited by?'

'So we've established that apart from talking to common friends and family, that small talk we mentioned earlier really does have a lot of work to do! OK. Is there anything else you'd want to see in your partner. How about intelligence?'

'Oh yes, she would have to have that. I couldn't cope with just discussing the latest activities of celebs or seeing her eyes glaze over at the very mention of my work. Helena was really into partying; but she was also very bright.'

'That covers a fair number of positive attributes, Martin. All right. Now you're referring to Helena quite a bit. Are you sure that you're ready to let go of her yet?'

'I met her by accident recently and we talked, not argued. I do feel we've both got closure on our relationship.'

'All right then. Here's a narrative. You've met the next girl of your dreams. At last you've got a great relationship. You make the decision to set up home together.'

'Sounds like end of story.'

'When in fact the challenges are just beginning. You worked hard to win fair lady. Now you're going to have to work even harder to keep her. We humans aren't good at sustaining relationships. We've already mentioned the inevitable arguments. We'll come back to those. What's the biggest problem that usually leads to those spats?' Martin had to think back to his only long term relationship.

'Being there for each other I suppose.'

'Certainly is. Any relationship can only be sustained through some kind of contact. Business, leisure, social activities, absorbing hobbies and even separate holidays easily lead to resentment. And then there are all those occasions when you really don't want to be present; parents evenings, time spent with relatives or friends of your partner you don't get on with. Long list, but being there for him or her then is important.'

'Grudgingly accepted, but it will still depress me when it happens!'

'So the arguments begin.'

'What are you going to do to calm things down when it happens?'

'Log in and ask Agony Auntie Eres?'

'I'm going to give you a bonus point for that remark! Keeping your sense of humour will help enormously. How about doing what we're both doing right now?'

'Listening carefully.'

'Yes; and waiting for each other to finish what they have to say.'

'And trying to see whatever it is from their point of view.'

'You're taking me to a works do. I'm not all that keen to go. I throw open my overstuffed wardrobe and complain: *But I haven't anything I can wear* You say? Martin had been there and done that one.

'I love to see you when you're in that blue dress we bought at M&S for your last birthday.'

'Do you? OK then. I'm smiling Martin. And I mean that outside our little role play as well; right now I'm wearing blue and it was from M&S.'

'I'd love to see that.'

'Be a good boy and I might just let you.'

'Are you flirting with me Anne?'

'At the moment I'm just testing your small talk!'

'Any more advice about defusing arguments?'

'How does "You're always late home when I've cooked something special for us" sound to you?'

'An exaggeration of a single or occasional incident intended as a slap.'

'Will you challenge it then?'

'Not in this session - no.'

'What would you do then?'

'I've disappointed my partner on this particular occasion so I'll apologise. If I'm asked for a reason, I'd be truthful if I'd forgotten or I'd explain about the traffic jam or whatever.'

'You see you do know how to handle these things. If you do think a remark is particularly unfair and remember previous hurtful accusations you decided to let go, isn't it a good time to air your grievances?'

'Yes!'

'No! You should stick to the current issue if your aim is to de-escalate the argument. When they happened was the only good time to deal with those other historic slights. So you're now angry and emotion takes over from where thinking left off and cognition gives way to cudgels. You accuse your partner of being a liar or a shrew and you both reach a stage where the argument ends not with resolution, but with one of you storming out.'

'So what's the answer, Anne?'

'There may not be a easy answer. Some issues take time and patience to resolve, but it helps at the outset if you aim for a negotiated settlement at best or at worst a temporary armistice. But seriously, between any two people, lovers or otherwise, compromise is almost always necessary.'

'You make it sound like the battle of the sexes.'

'That's just what it is in far too many cases.'

'So that's why you feel there's a big market for what you do.'

'Just as you're making a living from the aches and pains of angry spouses.'

'Touché.'

'That's one advantage to me of on-line psychotherapy.'

'What's that.'

'If you either get too annoyed or amorous with me, you can't touch!'

'Does that happen to psychotherapists?'

'All the time, apparently. Doesn't it happen to physiotherapists?'

'Now I'm smiling, Anne. I'll give you 2 points for that one.'

'I think we've ended this session. Would it be presumptuous of me to say I feel your mood has lifted.'

'No I'll accept that observation too.'

'So has there mostly been agreement about what's been said, Martin?'

'Yes and I'd like to continue to see you.'

'To hear me. OK. Do you want to make a definite booking now or call in a crisis?'

'Both please, Anne..'

'OK so how about this time next week or in an emergency any time except 2-4am? I keep my connection permanently open.'

'That's great; thanks. May I ask one last thing?'

'I'm listening.'

'Carefully?'

'You're feeling better, aren't you?'

'Since the end of the relationship with Helena, until now I haven't had the courage or perhaps even the motivation to start another relationship.'

'I had the sense you were in some demand.'

'Well two women have shown considerable interest in me recently. One you already know about from our last session. I'll be frank. In different ways they've initiated a physical relationship with me. Both these women are exceptional in just about all the attributes we've discussed. But they've confused me. I don't know what their real interest is.'

'Even though you've asked them?'

'I haven't asked them.'

'Are you afraid of rejection?'

'Partly, but it's more complicated than that. Until I'm more certain that their interest in me is romantic, I'm wary of going there.'

'So more small talk with your ladies and phone-a-friend may be needed first?'

'And even asking Auntie Anne.'

'If you keep calling me Auntie, you may notice a more offended tone creeping into this conversation!'

'Ooops! Yes, I will do what we've agreed.'

'We've really come full circle back to our last session haven't we?'

'Poor self image?'

'Let's tackle that in earnest next week. Is that OK with you?'

'Yes, Anne and thank you.'

'Martin.'

'Yes?'

'I don't know about the ladies you've mentioned, but I'm not surprised that you've attracted attention. You appear to have all the attributes yourself that you've told me are desirable in women. Works both ways, Martin. Talk to you soon.'

Anne Eres has terminated the connection.

CHAPTER TWELVE

Timles

Chris looked up from his tablet PC, clearly a bit relieved and gave Timles a thumbs up.
'I think we're finally going to get a connection to the University network.'
Both men stared at the screen whilst the various devices in the Internet chain between Timles's lounge and the University sent each other little messages. To fill the awkward silence whilst he waited, Chris tried to get his head round another chain of events. The one that had brought him to this modest house in the suburbs.

'I have to admit, Michael, I'm still hazy about how I happen to be here. We've not yet published any results from the artificial intelligence supported social network project we're developing. The first I knew about your interest was your phone call to the department.' Chris shook his head wonderingly.

'You said our computer manager, Meagh, referred you to me? That's most irregular.'

'Long story short. Heard good things about Tamford Computer Sciences and contacted the Innovation people at the University. They wanted to put me through to without success to your head of department, but apparently he's currently basking on sabbatical in sunny California. Even his usual secretary is on maternity leave and I ended up talking to a locum. Anyway this bright young lady immediately put me in touch with your computer manager; Mr Meagh. Where she usually works, people called "manager" rather than "professor" generally run the show. As it turned out, that was exactly the right contact because Meagh knows everything that goes on in your department and gave me your telephone number.' Chris nodded as watched his tablet display.

'Aha. We're connected!' Timles leaned back in his padded office chair with his hands steepled under his chin and relaxed. He watched, fascinated, as Chris, seated comfortably next to him, tapped at the tablet computer. Before them, linked by wireless to Chris's tablet, Timles's virtual patio window displayed not his garden, but dozens of small images and interconnecting lines - the links and nodes of tInterconNet. Chris effortlessly moved into lecturing mode:

'I'll start this demo with a caveat. I find it's always best to begin with the downside.' Chris looked expectantly at Timles and was acknowledged by a slow nod and raised eyebrows.

'You'll know about social networks, of course. They have, on the time scale of the Internet at least, a long history; perhaps as much as 30 years! There's been winners and losers just as species come and go, but evolution on the 'Net is fast and getting faster. Whatever computer scientists like myself do today will be quickly superseded tomorrow. So what I'm showing you is a work in progress. It works now and there will be updates appearing regularly. But, like all computer software, there will be something better or perhaps I should say different, "coming to a computer near you soon".

OK. That's dealt with the downside. Here's where we are today.' Chris now turned to watch Timles's patio window display. The InterconNet network moved in sympathy with his finger movements across Chris's tablet's screen. Chris found he had to do this quite slowly, because small movements on his tablet were greatly amplified the huge virtual window display. Quick movements made for rather uncomfortable viewing. Chris continued his explanation:

'InterconNet is a social network. Like Face Book on the Web, people can sign themselves up, make contact with existing members and also recruit others. They can "update their status" which generally means exchanging personal news and images, but members can upload pretty much anything. However there the similarity ends. Presently, InterconNet membership is restricted to the academic community in Tamford, although there are a few exceptions. New members submit a personal profile through an on-line question and answer session.

But their published profiles as seen by others are *different*. Our programme displays its own interpretation of the information it's given, rather than a verbatim version of what's typed or spoken. Also this is subject to continual review and potential revision as I'll explain later. In short our system doesn't parrot the information supplied by its members; it actively selects, interprets and manages it.' Chris looked at Timles to see if he was following. Acknowledged by a nod, he continued:

'Now for a few definitions!' Timles turned his attention back to the giant image on his picture window as Chris explained

'The entire image you'll see next is called the *network map*.' Chris pinched his fingers together over the tablet on his lap and the image on Timles's window shrank in sympathy, to what looked like a cobweb spun by a spider high on something narcotic.

'InterconNet members are each represented a small image. We call these *network nodes*. These members or nodes don't have to be individuals. They can be groups, organisations, businesses or even—' Chris turned his attention to Timles to emphasise the significance of what he would say next.

'—things.' Timles looked puzzled.

'Things?' Chris explained:

'For example your answer phone. Well, in fact any digital equipment you could connect on-line. Even domestic appliances if you wanted to do that! But I'm just indicating the broad potential of this approach. Right now we're only signing up folk, not 'fridges!' Timles smiled dutifully at Chris's quip as his guest continued:

'Associations of some kind between members of the InterconNet community are indicated by the lines you can see connecting their nodes. We call these *links*. People find it easier to visualise the links and nodes as spokes and hubs respectively, because there are sometimes many links to a single node and these end up graphically looking like the centre of a bicycle wheel.' Here Chris slid his fingers across the tablet. On Timles's patio window display a small region of the network was greatly enlarged showing just a few nodes. Chris commented:

'Incidentally, although you never see any *public* social networks displayed like this, it doesn't mean that the programmers at Face Book, Google and the like don't have access to views like this behind the scenes. In fact I'd be staggered if they don't because they will be extracting all the information they can from their millions of subscribers. The value of their huge networks lies not so much in their *content* which is generally of interest to a relatively small number of users, but the nature and patterns of their *links*.'

'Explain please, Chris.'

'Extracting information for sponsors and targeting products and services to consumers is the business model of all the Internet social network companies. Interrogating their social network maps in various ways provides extremely valuable information to advertisers and other major customers.' Timles was fascinated. He felt he was grasping at a very exciting idea here.

'I know I'm interrupting your demonstration, but could you just give me an example of what sort of information we're talking about.' Chris reflected a moment. Chris held all the cards at present. He didn't know what his host actually wanted. All he knew was that he was speaking to a potential sponsor of his research programme and needed to hold the man's interest for as long as possible.

'Please interrupt at any time, Michael. Rather than give you a specific example, I'll tell you about the most exciting general feature of networks and perhaps you might be able to slot whatever it is you have in mind into that framework.'

'Thank you, that's perfect.'

'OK. Well your brain and mine are fashioned as networks; the nodes are *nerve cells* and the links are *nerve fibres*. The property that results from this *neural* network is something that you could neither deliberately set out to design or even fully understand, but is massively important.'

'Consciousness!'

'Precisely. We call this an *emergent* property, because it only emerges once the network has been created. Before that it doesn't exist; it is not present in any of the individual components of the network, but is a feature of the whole.' Both men were silent for a moment. Chris out of reverence, because his adrenaline level always shot up when he was talking about his research; Timles because his mind was working overtime with this powerful new concept. Finally Chris completed his answer to Timles's probing question.

'So some of the social network companies' biggest clients often *don't actually know* what's going to emerge from the networks, but they damn well want to have first refusal to that knowledge when it does!' Timles was nodding. So far this was easier to follow than he had feared and certainly far more exciting. Chris now turned to highlight the enlarged area of the network map.

'InterconNet is still at an early stage in its development and doesn't have the vast membership of a Face Book or Linked In. But you'll notice that there are now enough members that some have multiple links to others. On the public social networks, these would usually be links to *friends*. On InterconNet the *position* of members in this display has a special meaning. Members with many links to others appear nearer the centre of the map than members with few or no links. But more significant than that, members with similar characteristics; especially for the *potential to create a meaningful connection* are placed near each other by the programme. It's a key feature of InterconNet and the magic is performed by an heuristic.' Chris glanced at Timles and checked himself.

'Sorry Michael, I'm slipping into jargon now. I mean a mathematical procedure. The one we use is very special. It actually learns and gets better as time goes on!' Timles frowned.

'Can I stop you there a moment Chris. What's to prevent members inputting false data? Won't that invalidate the whole system?'

'You're absolutely right to raise that point. Unlike most of the public social networks, InterconNet continually checks all its members' eligibility, identities and profiles for consistency using data mined from the entire Internet and government databases, where of course, as a public institution, we can gain privileged access.' Michael's steepled hands separated and moved to the arms of his chair; an indication of heightened interest.

'Including medical records?' Chris glanced back at him.

'I'd prefer not to discuss specific sources at the moment, Michael. We've still got to sign an agreement.'

'Yes yes, of course, please continue.' Chris turned back to the network map.

'Now we're getting closer to the power of this system. Unlike *public* social networks, where InterconNet determines that a connection is inappropriate, it will query this and *in extremis,* prevent it. Another big difference is that limits are set on the number of connections permitted and these are prioritised—' There was a polite cough from Timles and Chris glanced back at his host. He was going in too deep and realised he had to wrap things up. He changed tack smoothly:

'—but I think that it's time for you try for yourself and see InterconNet in action. I'll go first so you get the idea of how it can be queried. Let's take "boy meets girl" which is, unsurprisingly, one of the most popular activities of both our University student and even *staff* InterconNet users.' Chris turned briefly to Timles here.

'Of course, Michael, I do realise that "other gender relationships are available".' Timles nodded sagely.

'Evaluating female attractiveness was the objective of Face Book when it was also just a university based programme.'

Timles obligingly smiled at Chris's effort to provide a light hearted illustration as his guest entered instructions on his tablet.

'On the InterconNet map we do identify the sex of members; males are represented by a square, females by a disc. Generally, we don't show actual user images of the on the map, but where members permit, these can be seen by clicking on the shapes themselves.'

On the picture window display the network map changed. All the links disappeared and the nodes shuffled about, leaving only two near each other, linked by a red line. Chris explained that closeness of members' images indicated actual or potential *compatibility*, but making relationship *recommendations* was not the role of InterconNet.

It was up to members finding others located close to them to explore that for themselves. He clicked on the male node of the linked pair. The description that appeared was rather like a well-constructed *curriculum vitae* with a good personal profile section. Timles noted that the individual Chris had chosen to reveal to him was a Tamford lecturer in Computer Science by the name of Chris Johns. Timles was impressed with his candour.

'Sensitively done, Chris. I presume the lady you are linked with is your partner'.

'Was my wife, but we have since split up.'

'So InterconNet can be wrong sometimes on compatibility, Chris?'

'It was InterconNet that caused the separation, Michael! Well actually I was me; I spent far too many hours in Computer Sciences department working on this programme. It would be wrong of me to blame the programme, when the guilty party was the programmer! Sadly in this case her node remains there for test purposes.' Both men were quiet for a moment, before Chris broke the silence and invited Timles to query InterconNet himself. Timles thought for a moment.

'What I'd like to search for are therapists or perhaps people with some formal medical or psychological background if "therapists" is too narrow a search term. Would that be possible?'

'Lets try searching for therapists first, shall we?' Chris shrank the network map once more to bring most of the member community onto the display, then set up the search. The network map cleared instantly leaving only a few nodes visible. Chris selected an area and enlarged the display. Another square and circle close together appeared; male and female members. Chris clicked on both shapes and images appeared. Looking at the male image Timles experienced a jolt of recognition.

'Well, your system's right on one count at least. The man's Martin Wright; a physiotherapist who's a member of my Woodlands team. What's he doing on your network? I knew he had one or two contacts at the University, but didn't know he was studying at Tamford.' Chris swore inwardly. He'd completely forgotten that Martin was on the network and cursed his bad luck that Timles had requested him to search InterconNet for therapists, out of all the possible queries he could have chosen.

'No Michael; as far as I know he's not studying anything at Tamford, but he *is* registered as an external user of a number of Uni facilities and has to log onto our academic network for access to this system. He's presently one of the very few external members of InterconNet.

I should explain that although InterconNet is a research project of mine; most of the work being carried out at present by a postgraduate student called Peter Swales. An important part of Peter's Ph.D. study is to monitor how members use InterconNet. Peter recruited Martin having met him in a local pub, where I gather he spends a lot of time. At this stage of the project we'd agreed to restrict membership to registered University staff and students only, so I've censured Peter over this. Peter's been pressing me to widen the membership for some months now and I think his enthusiasm to get a local physiotherapist on board for his studies got the better of him. I apologise on Peter's behalf and hope no harm's been done.' Timles looked at Martin's image.

'Can you show me his InterconNet profile, Chris?' Chris opened up Martin's computer-edited biopic and Timles took a few moments to read it, with Chris scrolling the text when needed. As he read, Timles asked if the programme had really generated Martin's description from his own answers and information recovered elsewhere. He sounded very surprised.

'Yes; I can show you what questions the system asks when people sign up if you like.' Timles waved aside this offer and continued reading. Finally he leaned back and nodded.

'OK Chris. Thanks. Now about Martin's involvement. I don't foresee any difficulties from my point of view. Provided we reach an understanding over our potential use of your system, I'd be signing a comprehensive working agreement with you which would also cover all our Centre's contract staff.' Timles paused, looking in silence for a moment at the network display occupying the entire end wall of his lounge. Then he turned back to Chris.

'Having read the computer-generated personality summary on Martin, Chris, I don't think you could have shown me a more persuasive piece of evidence supporting the power of your system. But I'm intrigued about this other network member very close to Martin's image. Clearly she's a therapist of some description. Can you show me her profile, Chris?'

'Yes of course.' Moments later Timles was reading Anne Eres' biopic.

'An on-line psychotherapist reading for a Ph.D. at Tamford, indeed! Interesting idea, but surely that's not her real picture, Chris; does your system allow that?'

'Not in principle, but where there are good reasons, members may use an avatar; that's a proxy image, if you're not familiar with the term?' Timles nodded yes; he did know that. Chris continued his explanation:

'I don't know this individual, Michael, but she's evidently a postgraduate student working with clients during her studies here. So she doesn't have the security of an organisation like yours. At this stage in her career, I'd say she's wise to have opted for a degree of anonymity. She's certainly enthusiastic: see - she's even making herself available on-line to clients 24/7!.'

'Meaning?'

'Meaning it's almost certainly a big component of her research; perhaps it *is* her research project.'

'Would that be allowed—ethically I mean—without declaring it on your network. And wouldn't that be something InterconNet itself might pick up?'

'Well she's been given special privileges by the programme already;

she's using an avatar instead of her own photo as the majority of users are required to do. My guess is she's made a special arrangement with Peter Swales or Tuula Pippi.'

'Tuula Pippi?'

'Our Finnish Computer Systems Operator.' Timles nodded.

'Well, after reading both profiles, I can understand why your system has placed them close together, Chris. In a relationship they'd make a remarkable couple, don't you think?' Timles turned back to his guest.

'Can you turn on the *links* between members again for me Chris?'

Chris tapped on the tablet and the nodes became linked once more. Now a black line appeared between Martin and Anne's nodes.' Timles nodded then shook his head slowly either in acknowledgement or disbelief or possibly both.

'Martin's not shown much interest in his colleagues at the Woodlands who are mostly attractive young women, but if this therapist looked anything like her avatar, I feel she could make a breakthrough! Sadly for Martin in her biopic she clearly rules out that "boy meets girl" relationship you showed me first of all! So the link probably means he's currently one of her clients. Perhaps I'll get to hear more about that. OK Chris, I've seen enough for now and I like what I've seen. Let's get down to business.'

Chris logged off and Timles's picture window displayed his rear garden once more; this time with the addition of distant snow-covered peaks.

'I never thought I'd be so taken by a patio window, Michael; but I'm madly in love with yours. Sadly I'd never be able to afford one.'

'If we can reach an agreement to license your system and apply it in the way I have in mind, that situation might change one day, Chris. So let's drink to that possibility.' Timles rose and motioned his guest to the easy chairs round a small coffee table with vacuum jugs of tea and coffee.

'Tea or coffee, or perhaps you'd prefer something stronger?'

'I would, but I'm driving so I'll have coffee.' The two men sat comfortably opposite each other.

'Please. Help yourself, as you like it.' Chris filled his cup and sipped appreciatively.

'Can you give me a hint about how you might use our system Michael?' Timles returned Chris' gaze levelly

'You accept that what I'm going to tell you is covered by our informal confidentiality agreement?'

'Of course.' Timles paused again as Chris raised his coffee cup.

'I'm proposing to restructure the provision of UK health care.' Chris over sipped and spluttered his coffee.

'Oh gosh, I'm sorry. I wasn't expecting that!'

'I'm not surprised. That's the endgame. First I have a relatively lowly and certainly more achievable objective in mind.' For a while the two men drank in silence, each lost in their own thoughts. Eventually Timles put down his cup.

'Is this a good moment to sign the confidentiality agreements we've exchanged?'

'OK with me. The Uni innovation team have gone over yours with a fine tooth comb. If you're happy with ours, let's do it.' Timles picked up another of his remote controls and looked upwards. Chris also glanced up at the security camera.

'So this historic moment will be captured on video?'

'Yes.'

A red light appeared on the camera. Chris shook his head wonderingly.

'This is a new one on me, Michael. Blows the old fashioned notion of independent witnesses out of the water.'

'Yes and if very starchy lawyers insist on witness signatures on paper, I have plenty of contacts who will sign for me when I show them the video. Really Chris, this is overkill at this stage, but I like to make my security system work for its money; it was very expensive at the time it was installed.' The two men bent to their work in silence.

'Now it's my turn to give a presentation, Chris. This time to my staff at the Woodlands. But first can I ask how long it would take for you to set up a demonstration like you've shown me here at the Woodlands Centre?' Chris was clearly taken aback by this request.

'I'm not sure that we could allow general viewing of the data on this network, Michael. It's restricted to the University. We have agreed confidentiality here, but...'

'I accept that. What I'm asking for is a simple outline of how InterconNet works. Martin clearly knows how to operate the programme. I will ask him to input some of our own data. I don't imagine we'll need a lot of data just to give the audience an idea of how this can work. I'd like you to bring your postgraduate student, Peter, with you to The Woodlands as soon as possible for a meeting. It will be with myself, our Centre Manager, Noura and a couple of our Board members.' Timles noticed that Chris looked a little doubtful. He explained his suggestion.

'Martin and Peter clearly have a head start on both of us, Chris, and I feel it would be best to bring them in on our proposals now. That way we will hopefully be networking with each other physically rather than virtually. Are you OK with that?' Chris was irritated by this request to involve Peter in the business discussions, but on reflection, Peter was a bit of a loose cannon and Timles was perhaps right to bring him in now rather that have him discover what was going on somewhere down the line.

'Agreed.' Timles was rising to his feet, so Chris mirrored his action.

'My administrator at the Woodlands, Noura Munday, keeps my diary and you can get your own secretary to liaise with her.' Chris restrained himself from commenting that he didn't enjoy such a luxury.

'Right.' Timles reached into an attaché case beside his chair and withdrew a couple of books.

'I know there are many demands on your time, but if possible, before we next meet, could you scan this recent publication of mine. It will help as background to our discussions. Perhaps you'll give the other copy to Peter. Lastly, here's the Woodlands brochure which will give you a picture of our little enterprise. Look forward to our next meeting. Chris.' Chris reached out to shake the proffered hand.

'Until then, Michael.' Michael accompanied him to the front door. Chris had no idea how much he was being honoured by this action as he left.

CHAPTER THIRTEEN
Tuula

Martin's weekend had crawled by; heavy rain discouraged him from leaving the flat, even to visit his new watering hole; The Bear Inn at Read. He tried to distract himself from thinking about Tina and Tuula by tackling some much needed cleaning and tidying. On those infrequent occasions when he vacuumed, he was careful to do it on Saturday mornings when the woman with hypersensitive hearing in the adjacent flat was shopping and couldn't bang on the wall to express her annoyance. Depressing his mood still further, heavy metal music percolated through the ceiling from the flat above. Recalling the anger of its occupants at the vibration of his balcony railings, Martin reflected that wherever there seemed to be injustice in this block of flats, he always seemed to be on the receiving end.

It was almost a relief to get back to work on Monday. Julie greeted him with the news that the Centre's owner expected all staff to attend a meeting about the future of the Woodlands on Wednesday. She handed him a memo. He immediately worried this unusual event signalled serious news about the Centre and therefore his job. But the memo reassured him; Timles would be describing plans for changes that he already knew Noura was working on. The memo ended with the cryptic statement that The Woodlands would be taking a regional lead in a significant development of healthcare and well being. The rest of the day was quiet with only two patients booked in.

As he worked, Martin wondered how Timles was hoping to make an expanded Centre pay. They were under subscribed even as they were now. The following day, after his second client had left—persistent pain at a pinned tibia fracture site—Martin opened the email app on his new computer. It had pinged loudly announcing the arrival of messages whilst he was examining the patient. Hearing that, his patient had worried that the titanium rod in his leg bone was moving, before Martin realised what it was and reassured him.

Both of them had laughed about it afterwards; a good sign. There were 3 new messages. From Tina Elves, Tuula Pipi and someone called Ludmilla he didn't recognise. He opened Ludmilla's first. The subject was "Meeting up" which sounded strange, but the message just said—in effect— that this Russian lady could give him a good time and that further details were available by following the link to her website. Wisely he didn't and deleted it instead. Next he opened Tina's message. Up until now he'd not had any email contact and her mobile, on the few times he'd called it, had been unavailable.

To: Martin
From: Tina Elves
Subject: Update

Hi Mart
I know you've being trying to get in touch, but things have been hectic and I'm afraid I have kept putting off replying until now. When I'm in my sister's place with some free time, the network signal is weak or absent altogether. Sandra - my sister - lives in a small village in the Peak District National Park. Very nice environment, but not very practical under the present circumstances. Sandra's out of hospital now, but is under strict orders to rest. I'm organising the school run, shopping and catering etc. All very inefficient as there's lots of travelling involved and the area's completely new to me. Trouble is, it's almost as new to Sandra too, as she'd only just moved here when the problem arose and she had to go into Sheffield for her operation.

I wanted to thank you for forwarding the book of which, by now, you will also hopefully have received a copy. I expect the authors, if not the content, came as a bit of a surprise to you. In view of our joint therapeutic interests I sincerely hope you will read at least some of it. If you do, some of the questions which I'm sure you must have, may be partly answered. I do want to provide more complete answers when I next see you, Martin and hope we can carry on meeting as planned. Right now I haven't a firm date for returning to Tamford, but we can probably keep in touch by email in the meantime.
Affectionately,
Tina

Martin read Tina's email twice to extract as much meaning from its simple content as possible. He felt a sense of relief, even though his personal and professional relationship with her remained as ambiguous as ever. Trying to explain this feeling to himself, he could only come up with the warmth of Tina's short message and her expressed wish to see him again. Lack of that sort of social contact, he was beginning to understand, was one of the reasons for his depression.

Tuula's interest in him was less ambiguous, although just as puzzling. He couldn't think what this feisty woman could see in him. She was very easy on the eye, disturbingly athletic and apparently a rising star in IT, which had seemed to him to be one of the few remaining fields of male dominance. Her message was in his own email box, bypassing the Woodlands mail system as promised.

>
> From: Tuula
> To: Mart (Physio)
> Subject: R U up for an excursion?
>
> Hi Mart
> Hope your back's OK after a night spent propped up against my study bedroom wall! Didn't get back to you before as I was expecting to fly to Helsinki to present my annual report at Kosketecessa, which has now been postponed because the big boss has opted for a vacation. And thinking about holidays, if you've recovered feeling in your spine, how about a trip to the coast this weekend? The weather forecasts are good and I'm desperate to get out of town for some sun, sea and s**. Where I live, much of the year the sea is frozen and even in summer your bikini has to be fur lined.
> If U R up for an excursion, then here's the deal. You book us somewhere great near the sea for Friday and Saturday nights (I'll trust your choice after the Chateauneuf!) and provide transport. But make sure that the sleeping arrangements are king size! I'm paying - although you can buy me an ice cream and a couple of bottles of wine to take to the beach.
> What's it to be? Computer Centre or Coastal Commute?
> Tuula ;-)

Martin thought yes: *nothing ambiguous about Tuula*. Several key words in her text; beach, bikini and bed already had an uplifting effect on his mood. Being with someone like Tuula was exciting in every sense of the word. There was a big question about where she was taking him, but he distracted himself from trying to think of an answer by replying to Tuula's email. No point in sending a long response when this girl was so direct herself.

> From: Mart (Physio)
> To: Tuula
> Subject: Affirmative!
> Hi Tuula
> Seaside. Tell me where and when to pick you up Friday.
> Martin
> xxx

After he had sent this, the question he had deliberately suppressed resurfaced, triggered by the kisses at the end of his reply. Where was this going? Thinking logically about it, those email kisses were more like correcting typographic errors than sending endearments. Tina's email message had ended "affectionately". Well, *that* relationship also raised many questions. Under the present circumstances, her way of signing off the email seemed hardly more appropriate than Tuula's. His musing was interrupted by Tuula's emailed reply. He was to meet her 17:30 in her Hall of Residence car park.

Now all he needed to do was decide where they were going to go. It didn't seem so very long ago that he had nothing special to do after work. Nowhere to go but the Green Dragon and watch others living lives that he was certain were more rewarding than his own. Now, suddenly his life was being filled with challenge. But the curious thing was that he couldn't put his finger on what was happening to him. He was certainly caught up in a strong current, but he would have to wait to see where it was taking him. For now he had to keep himself afloat.

He looked at Tina's message again. She was telling him her book would help him understand a bit more about what was happening. It had certainly been a surprise, but on the other hand Tina had already mentioned she was working closely with Michael Timles. There was over an hour before his next client was due, so he pulled her book from under a pile of advertising fliers and turned the pages to the chapter on Reiki.

The next instant the intercom was buzzing with Julie announcing the arrival of his client. Irritated that his patient had arrived before time, he checked his watch and was astonished to see that an hour had indeed passed since he started reading. All through the following session, his mind was only just about connecting with the needs of his patient. He had read to the end of Tina's Reiki chapter and kept on going like a bus that had missed its scheduled stop.

He hadn't expected the science references and evidence based assertions in a book like this. In the last hour many of his prejudices against alternative therapy had been demonstrated to have little real foundation. His worship of a single deity named mainstream medicine had been shown to be a biased rather than a balanced belief. Among many other things, Timles and Tina had re-named and explained the placebo effect. They had harnessed belief and turned it into therapy.

After his patient had left, apparently satisfied with his treatment, Martin sat at his desk and went through his experience with Tina. Yes, she had been working on his whole being all right; mind and body. In her treatment room the formerly distinct specialisations of the psychologist and physician merged. She had already started practising from this book she had written with Timles.

He shivered a little. Tina had suggested in her email that her book provided only a partial explanation. She said that she would complete the picture herself. He wondered whether that would involve discussion or demonstration. If the latter, what on earth would that prove to be? Martin looked at his watch. He needed a drink. The Dragon was closer than The Bear and open now. Putting the new book and his tablet computer into his battered briefcase, he locked his room and left the Centre.

****

Martin drew up in the University Hall of Residence car park on Friday evening and sat in his car. It had been a bright day and the sun was still showing in a cloudless sky. The perennial plantings tried hard to enhance the utilitarian space despite random decoration by paper coffee cups, old magazines and a faded university scarf. At 17:30 precisely, Tuula appeared on the path between housing blocks. Despite her casual appearance, Martin suspected her clothes were rather expensive. He was relieved to see that, unlike what she had been wearing when he first met her, her present dress wouldn't attract undue attention. But he was rather surprised by the tiny holdall she was carrying. In his limited experience, even for a weekend trip, women usually packed a large amount of clothes. Either the largest size of wheeled trolley case or a 60 litre framed rucksack, depending on the nature of the girl and the trip. He clambered out quickly and waved. Tuula waved back and strolled over.

'Hi Mart. Weather's promising. See; I'm really getting into the English vernacular here. Shall I put this in the boot?' She held up the diminutive holdall.

'Or on the back seat if you like.' Martin held a rear door open for her luggage.

'Right I'm all yours. Take me away from all this.' Tuula swept her arm disdainfully around the scruffy parking area and climbed in next to him. She was quiet, relaxing as they drove; first through the centre then the suburbs. Martin appreciated that. He was grateful for peace to watch the commuter traffic and collect his thoughts about their trip. When he first drove his date somewhere he would have found such silence uncomfortable. After he turned onto the A33, Tuula stretched both her arms up; as a cat would flex both front legs after lying still for a while. She gave a sound which could have been something in Finnish or just a yawn. Either way it sounded satisfied and neatly punctuated the short interval of silence.

'So where *are* you taking us, Mart?'

'We're going to stay at a place called Studland on the South Coast. The area around is called The Isle of Purbeck, but it's really a peninsular, not an island. We're staying in a privately owned bungalow with the sea at the foot of the garden. Incredibly, I managed to hire it from the owner just for 2 nights as there was a last minute cancellation.'

'Take a lot of finding, Mart?' Martin smiled to himself

'I put out a general query on InterconNet a few days back, then forgot about it whilst I searched for accommodation on the Web. It was quite a surprise when a lecturer from the Uni got in touch to offer his holiday home for up to a week from tonight. He didn't mind us staying only for a couple of nights, if we brought our own linen. Said I could stay on if I liked as it would be unoccupied all that week.'

'The second lucky find you've made so far on InterconNet, then.' Martin knew he had to try to keep up with Tuula. At the moment he had the edge; for once it was he not Tuula who was in the driving seat.

'Yes, the first lucky find was a Finnish lady.'

'Right answer! You're not just a handsome guy, Mart.' Martin with his eyes on the road didn't see her expression, but he did hear her compliment. One day, he told himself, he might even let himself believe it. Martin thought about Tina and Anne Eres: *actually there had been three lucky finds so far*, but he kept this thought to himself.

'Have you been to this place Studland before, Mart?'

'I've visited Swanage which is nearby. The whole area's very attractive. There's the National Trust Heritage Coastline which is conserved coast and countryside. But it's also very popular with visitors. There'll be swarms of tourists at this time of year, I expect.'

'Well, we're tourists too, aren't we? How far is it to this place?'

'It's almost the nearest bit of coastline to Tamford, driving due south. Trouble is it's Friday evening and the roads will be busy, so it's hard to say how long it will take. A couple of hours at least, I'd guess. Would you like to chat or listen to some music? There are CDs in the glove compartment.' Tuula looked through the small music collection and frowned.

'How about something Scandinavian, Mart? It didn't all stop after Abba.'

'I can't help us there.'

'But I can.' Tuula removed a smart phone and lead from her bag and plugged it into the auxiliary socket on the transmission tunnel. Martin glanced down quickly.

'I never noticed that.' Soon some calming mood music was playing. Once again Martin was surprised. He'd been anticipating having to blot out some head banging stuff whilst trying to concentrate on the route and traffic ahead. Tuula fumbled for the rake adjustment on her seat and lowered the backrest.

'Tell me when we're getting near the sea, Mart. I'd like to chill for a bit now.' She lay back and closed her eyes, but her hand connected with Martin's thigh as a token of appreciation of her driver. This caused Martin to wobble slightly and Tuula to relocate her hand to a less sensitive region of his leg. Around 8 pm Martin reached across and patted Tuula's shoulder.

'Tuula; we're on the Isle of Purbeck now.' She yawned, repeated the stretching movement he'd seen earlier, wound the passenger seat back up and began to take in the countryside. A short time later, Martin turned down a long, sandy cul de sac and parked in the drive of a detached bungalow at the far end. On either side, strips of rough pasture separated the property from a few others in similar dead end roads which stopped just short of the beach.

All the homes seemed to hunker down amongst coarse grasses, with wide open views of the coast. Tuula positively hurtled out of the vehicle and disappeared round the side of the property. Martin decided to let her go and busied himself shifting Tuula's small holdall and his own more substantial bags of clothes, bed linen and boxes of basic provisions for the two days stay. When Tuula finally reappeared she was beaming.

'This is perfect; there's a small gate at the end of the garden and the sea is just the other side of a footpath through some sand dunes.' Martin was pleased with her response. In truth he'd started worrying about their accommodation as soon as they'd left Tamford. Would he have difficulty finding the place at night? Would the key be where the owner had said? Would Tuula like the place? Now that it seemed she did and the other concerns had been sorted, he began to relax and focus on immediate practical matters.

'Do you want to find a pub for food or would you like to stay here and see what we can make with the shopping I've brought?' Tuula rummaged in the bag-for-life carriers and the cardboard box Martin had dumped on the kitchen table.

'You've done all the work so far. I'll make a large plate of open sandwiches and we'll take them down to the beach. There's no wind tonight and I want to spend as much time by the sea as possible.'

Twenty minutes later, dressed in track suits; Martin's distinctly baggy, Tuula's predictably figure hugging, they carried provisions down to the beach. Martin spread a borrowed blanket in a small depression where the dunes gave way to open beach. Off to the West, the sun, now an enlarged dull orange, was slipping rapidly towards broken clouds sitting on the horizon. They ate, talking quietly, taking in the view and watching the surf as it piled up small bands of sand and shingle across the beach. Then every sixth or seventh wave the tiny sand bars were wiped away again. When the bread and beer were finished, Martin stood to collect the remains of their picnic. Tuula quickly got to her feet.

'Don't let's go in yet. Let's wait until the sun's gone right down.' She caught his hand and tugged him down the beach to the edge of the now inky surf. She cast off her sandals and rolled up the bottoms of both their joggers.

She straightened up with an expression of disgust and told him to take off his battered trainers.

'I'm not touching those, Mart!' When their ankles were washing in the slow surf, Tuula came up behind him, hugging his waist and turning him to face the setting sun. Her grip tightened and loosened rhythmically as the tide dragged sand from beneath their feet, forcing them to adjust their balance. The tickling of sand gains and shingle on the soles of his feet caused Martin to remember a similar dark shoreline in Tina's treatment room in Tamford. A virtual one. As they watched, the last solar fireworks died on the horizon, as if the sea itself had extinguished the light. But an afterglow remained in the sky where the sun had set and began fading almost imperceptibly as they watched.

In the gloom, Martin now felt he was reliving the experience, part real, part simulated, that he'd experienced in Tina's flat. The girl holding him from behind, the deepening darkness and moving surf triggered an emotional response in him just as it had on that other unexpected evening. But this time it was accompanied by a physical one as well. A cool breeze sprang up and Tuula thrust her hands for warmth into the large pockets of his joggers. She discovered his arousal immediately and, being the girl she was, made the most of it and once again, he had no inclination to resist.

'You know, Mart, I can't think why Pete's programme located our nodes so far apart. We've really got lots of things in common.' Martin couldn't resist the obvious response.

'But those areas where we're completely different feel nice too.' Tuula giggled.

'Hold onto that thought, Mart.' Once again he found himself dragged across the sand back into the shelter of the dunes.

'Sit down and I'll dry your feet.' Within the small depression in the dunes, the sand and coarse marram grass still retained some of the day's heat. Tuula knelt down and wiped away the coating of sand on his feet. Then standing up on the blanket, she put her hands on his shoulders to steady herself, lifted her own feet and commanded him to do the same for her. When next he was pushed firmly down on the blanket, he realised he had been skilfully set up. He didn't fight her removing his joggers or her deft fitting of a sheath from her beach bag.

'Finnish Sultan condoms; the best.' Naked from the waist down she straddled him. Martin made a gallant effort to contribute to the proceedings, but Tuula caught his hands and pushed them back.

'It's OK Mart, she reassured him rather jerkily, I'm orgasmic already. Just lie still and chill; but not too much.' She underlined this request by placing both feet on his upper arms, pinning them against the fabric.

'Not too heavy for you?' Martin didn't reply. He was busy holding out against her rocking and squeezing. The pressure on his hips helped delay matters, but eventually, as is well known, whatever goes up must eventually come down. Back in the neat bungalow, after a few more drinks, a similar process was repeated in the shower cubicle; this time vertically allowing Martin more freedom of movement. Afterwards Tuula became very inventive with the towels. The woman seemed to have endless stamina.

The following morning Martin could neither recall climbing into bed nor even being accompanied there. But at that moment the double bed was only occupied by him. The other pillow was dented, but his bedfellow was absent. Martin got up, slowly retrieved his clothes from various parts of the room and dressed. Later, wearing her trademark varsity shorts and tee shirt, Tuula appeared, pinkly explaining that she had run some miles along the coast path.

'Where I stopped to turn back a old guy out with his dog told me that the path was over 600 miles long and runs all round the South West peninsular. I guess that's about 1000 kilometres in my language. He asked if I was running it all! He said the place where I met him was called "Old Harry Rocks". But there was no sign of Old Harry or his band!' She grinned mischievously.

The two day excursion went by quickly. Although she had never been to Studland, or even visited the UK coastline, she appeared to have an intuitive grasp of its people, places and way of life. She joked about her knowledge:

'You know Mart, this isn't so different from parts of my country; apart from the people, food, climate and vegetation of course.' Her ability to bypass the superficial and uncover what lay beneath led to their brief stay being full of surprise encounters and discoveries away from the usual tourist haunts. Tuula seemed particularly taken with the location of the holiday home.

'If I wanted to book a place like this sometime, how much would it cost?', she wanted to know.

'Holiday home rental varies a lot. Summer's the most expensive time. This 2 bed place is £60 a day, Tuula' Martin was strongly attracted by this turbulent personality, but something was missing from their sudden intimate relationship. On their second night, in the King size bed, Tuula curled herself into a foetal position, facing away from him and seemed to fall asleep instantly. Martin lay awake a long time into the night, still too aroused to sleep, needing reassurance about where this was going, but not confident enough to ask her outright. His insomnia gave him time to muse. It was dawning on him that this was an affair that could not end happily for him.

He had been given an object lesson all those weeks ago by Tina yet had ignored it, seduced by Tuula's larger than life personality and sex. He realised that was really missing from this precipitate relationship was a loving touch. Tuula had made it perfectly clear what she wanted. But he had not been brave enough to call a halt and tell Tuula about his own needs. History was repeating itself. Again.

Late on Sunday afternoon, Martin dropped her off in the Halls of Residence car park. She lent across the transmission tunnel, crooked one arm round his neck and kissed him. It was light and quick; completely different from her hard and hungry mouth in the bungalow at Studland.

'That was fantastic. Thank you so much. Now I can face the Computer Science department for a few weeks again.' Then she was gone, without having discussed any further dates for meeting up.

Walking away with her bag, she turned for a single backward glance and wave from the path before disappearing between the housing blocks. For a short time, Martin sat in the car and gloomily surveyed the paper cups and scraps of paper caught up in the thorny shrubs enclosing the parking spaces. It all looked the same as when he arrived here on Friday, but now with little prospect of excitement and nothing more to look forward to apart from the emptiness of his flat.

He glanced down. Lying in his lap where Tuula had propped herself to kiss him was a Manila envelope with his name on it. Opening it expecting a card or letter, he found a series of printed sheets. As he unfolded them, he saw it was the list of the physio. equipment he'd entered on the form Tuula had emailed to him earlier. Against each entry was a price, item code and the supplier's contact details. Tucked between the sheets were six £20 notes; the rental of the holiday bungalow. There was no message enclosed, but none was really necessary. All their transactions had evidently been completed. Tuula had logged out. Now really feeling lonely and abandoned, he drove out of the deserted car park and headed home.

CHAPTER FOURTEEN

Timles

On Monday afternoon, Martin walked to Timles's place. Timles's voice welcomed him on the threshold.

'Martin! Come on in.' Once again, Martin sat in the easy chair opposite his boss. Timles skipped the small talk.

'As I recall, we ended our last mentoring session trying to identify past issues which remain unresolved. You told me you had closure over your relationship with Helena. Presumably that's still the case?'

'Yes it is. I'm not worrying about that any longer now.'

'So are there other things from the past on your mind?' Martin was silent a moment. There was the disastrous relationship with his father, but nothing could be done about *that*. Having waited patiently for a reply, Timles prompted:

'What about your parents, Martin? Are they still with us?' Yet again Martin was taken by surprise by Timles's uncanny ability to tease out the real issues. He decided it might be best to skirt around the sorry details of this one.

'My father's alive. He's in a flat in an assisted living complex which has a warden on site. One step short of a residential care home, I suppose you'd have to say. But his accommodation's pretty up market'

'In Tamford?'

'No; Beaconsfield. Did you know that it's one of the most expensive residential areas in the country? There's no way I could ever afford to live there.' Timles brought Martin back to the subject under discussion.

'And you feel guilty about not visiting him?'

This time Martin was really staggered. Had Timles been doing some detective work?

'How...? However could you know that?' Timles smiled, but the gentle nodding which accompanied his expression, conveyed sympathy rather than smugness.

'You wear your heart on your sleeve Martin. One of the things I like about you. That's another quote attributed to Shakespeare, by the way.' Timles now looked more serious.

'Sadly some of your patients can read you like a book too, but that's partly why we're having these talks, of course.' Martin sighed heavily. There was apparently no way he could hide from the forensic perception of his boss.

'Dad worked in the Diplomatic Service. It was on one of his tours of duty that he met mum; she was born in Oslo. I owe my hair and eye colour to her. But most of my life I've lived in the UK. Dad was very ambitious, but didn't make it to the top ambassadorial level. That always rankled with him. My own career went adrift too, as he saw it, after I moved in with Helena and dropped out of University. When I visited him after college terms ended and later when I was studying for my degree in physiotherapy, we used to have long arguments about my failure to focus on my own advancement. He had a vision of me climbing to the top of a life sciences career ladder. Perhaps compensating for his failure to do likewise in his own career.

I think the ethos of the Diplomatic Service was, in his time, intensely competitive. Senior staff thought themselves above ordinary citizens and almost above the common law. You know; 007 and all that. After mum died, things got worse. A moderating influence had been removed. Her loss didn't do his mental health any good and our rows got worse. In the end we virtually disowned each other and denied the other's existence.' After this confession, both men were quiet for a moment then Timles reached over and held his physiotherapist's arm gently. Martin recalled that both Tuula and Tina had made that gesture. He felt slightly ashamed they all recognised that he needed that kind of reassurance. Having thought of Tina he also remembered: *Be grateful.* When after a moment, Timles caught Martin's eyes, which were moist, he spoke quietly.

'So I don't think we have closure on *that* issue, do we? But I do understand why you needed a prompt from me to bring it up. You may have buried it in the past. But even interred somewhere in your subconscious, that bad relationship is another burden you're carrying right now. And if your father dies without you making peace with each other, you'll go on carrying it into the future too. Believe me on that one!' Martin was thoughtful for a moment.

'What do you think I should do about Dad?'

'When did you last see him?'

Martin looked embarrassed.

'I can't exactly remember. I know he's still alive as I'm registered next of kin with the company that runs the place where he lives. So I get occasional letters from them. I suppose it's several years now. I send him Christmas cards and I receive one each year from the Warden on Dad's behalf.

'What would you like to see happen? And what would be the best outcome, even if you now feel it would be unlikely?'

Martin concentrated on being objective. *Honour your relatives.* Reiki again. Now that Tina's simple principles had taken root in his brain, they popped up regularly, triggered by relevant situations and emotions. Perhaps their power lay in their very simplicity.

'I ought to write to the Warden and ask about my father's health. That way I'd get a personal reply. Then I could say to the Warden that I wanted to see him; that I had good news about my career, perhaps?'

Martin looked expectantly at Timles and was rewarded by a nod of assent. Encouraged, he continued:

'Initially I could try to open correspondence with Dad by writing. Send him letters via the Warden initially. That would be less confrontational for both of us. Then I could work up to a visit in person.' Timles was nodding as Martin spoke.

'That's a fine plan, but are you willing to do all that? Would you really *want* to do it? Or are you just assembling a scenario that you think I'd like to hear?' Martin thought hard. Timles was right of course. He *was* being coldly logical under questioning. He couldn't actually tell right now whether the falling out with his parent was contributing to his present ennui. But if he could put things right between them it couldn't deepen his dis-ease any further and might provide a lift to his present mood. His own emotions apart, what would be the practical benefits? Bringing some peace of mind to an elderly man? Achieving a small success through his own efforts? Going some way to assure an otherwise doubtful inheritance?

'I'll write to the warden of my dad's flats after we finish this meeting.'

Timles waited a moment, but Martin didn't add anything further.

'Good. Clearly, closure on that issue will take some time. But like the proposals for the Woodlands future, we do need to move ahead on several fronts at the same time. OK, next we were scheduled to discuss who we think we are. I say *we* not to be diplomatic because I really mean *you;* I'm going to say who I think I'm as well.

Asking you to bare your soul without giving anything of myself is too one-sided for my style. We'll collaborate on that in the next session! But I think we'll fix a date for that when you've some good news on the parent front.' Timles was working quite hard to restrict the emotional atmosphere of the session to a sharing of confidences between equals; not an interrogation by the headmaster. Martin was relieved Timles wasn't going to search for more skeletons in his mental cupboard today. God knows what else he was capable of disinterring with his forensic probing. But Timles was already changing the subject.

'Have you made any further appointments with Tina?'

A completely different topic and Martin was caught on the back foot with this question too. He was all at sea about his relationship with Tina and felt inhibited about discussing the whole issue. Martin decided the safest option was to stall for time.

'No. She asked me to forward her copy of your jointly authored book, but I felt she was too involved with her commitments at her sister's to bother her further about me.' Timles must have sensed Martin's discomfort, because he responded by gently gripping Martin's upper arm once again.

'Tina has a very high opinion of your abilities. And you're perhaps not as aware as you should be how well your work is respected by other staff at the Woodlands.' Timles released Martin's arm and lent back in his chair.

'I've also had a glowing report from one of our board members whom you helped; Evan Jones. He told me you weren't even aware he was connected with the Woodlands.' Martin looked even more embarrassed at this last comment.

'I'm afraid I don't read the annual report.'

'I take it as a positive that you didn't recognise Evan. It means he received the same attention from you as would any new client; the important point is that you were able to reassure and help him when his GP—or "NHS gatekeeper" as Evan would call him—had failed to help.' Timles paused to see whether this affirmation would lift Martin's mood a fraction. Receiving nothing more than a nod of acknowledgement, Timles stood and offered his hand. He summarised the outcome of their talk.

'Before we next meet, have a discussion with Tina about personal values. She'll know what to say. Don't forget to send that letter to enquire about your father. And Martin -'

Timles paused for Martin's acknowledgement

'Yes?'

'Do finish reading our book!'

CHAPTER FIFTEEN

Martin

It was mid afternoon the following Tuesday and for lack of bookings, Martin had decided to collect his thoughts over a pint. It was already lively in the Green Dragon. At this hour, the punters were largely students, although a few old regulars were already in place, propped up against the bar with their feet taking firm possession of the bar rail. Those that had not yet found another local, that was, as the Dragon's clientèle had gradually become younger and ever more gay. The previous landlord had had quite a sense of humour. At one time he'd engraved a few small brass plaques with the names of perennial old soaks and screwed them to the bar top in the spots they used to monopolise. Many of those plaques were now memorials.

Martin ordered a pint of Old Peculiar and headed for the rear bar. At least the large number of student drinkers ensured the Dragon offered a good choice of real ales. Much had happened to lift his spirits since he was last here, but as he eyed one of the high backed dining pews and smelt the fusty odour of the rear bar, his familiar sense of isolation returned.

As he looked around for some distraction, Peter Swales entered the pub with a tall man Martin hadn't seen before. The stranger sat at one of the small free-standing tables, whilst Peter headed for the bar. Clearly older than Peter and very smartly dressed, Martin guessed that he wasn't a student; not even a mature one. Peter returned with two glasses of beer.

Martin had never witnessed Peter actually parting with his cash, so his guest had to be very important. He looked nothing like Peter so probably wasn't a sibling and was too young to be his father. Even though it looked like Peter was with some kind of business contact, Martin hadn't exactly tried to keep out of sight, half hoping that he might be noticed and invited to join them. Martin's guessing game was brought to an abrupt end as Peter glanced up the room and spotted him.

'Mart! Come and join us.'

He got up and came over to their table.

'Mart, this is Jim Overbeck. Jim runs a small business in one of the Cambridge science parks. Jim, this is my friend and drinking companion Martin Wright. Mart's a physiotherapist who works in a Centre near here.'

While Jim and Martin shook hands, Peter, temporarily out of direct view of his guest, briefly pointed at Martin and then rapidly placed his index finger over his lips and just as quickly lowed it to point at himself. The message was clear: *Careful what you say; leave it to me to lead*. But it was Jim who took over the conversation:

'Pleased to meet you Mart, I've not spoken with a physio before. Always managed to keep out of their clutches; although some of the other rowing blues at Cambridge were always seeing someone for back or shoulder problems. Same problems with my staff; sitting too long without movement at their workstations.'

Jim positively oozed confidence. People suffering from depression are always hypersensitive to others showing buoyant optimism and Martin was no exception. He noted, and couldn't help admiring the man's hubris. In an indirect, but effective way, in just two sentences, Jim conveyed entrepreneurial acumen, exceptional physical prowess and his affiliation with one of the world's most elite Universities. Having communicated his worldly success, Jim moved seamlessly from physiotherapy to his own enterprise.

'As someone with a scientific background, Mart, you'll know there's never time today to do more than keep on top of your own field. So when I meet someone from another discipline, like yours for instance, I always ask them what's the latest thing in their neck of the woods. That way I get to know what's breaking news in as many different fields as possible. Of course, there's probably someone back in my company working their way up the physiotherapy learning curve right now, but I don't need to know all the details; my role is to *listen, learn* and *lead* and all my team know I insist on *life long learning*. That's why I've called my business ThreeLs Ltd; pronounced "Thrills" of course. Actually—funny story here—I asked our legal guy if we could register at Companies House as "ThreeLs *un*limited", but I knew immediately I saw his expression that he didn't appreciate my little joke.'

Still out of sight of Jim, Peter was rolling his eyes at this point. But, as though Jim had eyes in the back of his head, he suddenly snapped into serious mode.

'Sorry Mart, throwing all that stuff at you. I always relax in a pub. What I'm really interested in is where your sort of therapy stands today. I imagine that your centre offers complementary medicine which has got *elements* of what you chaps do—like massage for instance—but a lot of other stuff that's off the wall to most of us. Where do you guys actually stand on all this? Which camp are you in; the physician's or the faith healer's? Or are you actually working at some interface between the two - a sort of way station between medicine and mysticism?'

Jim was smiling a lot; evidently he was highly satisfied by his alliterative skill. Peter, unnoticed at the side of Jim, had his eyes closed and was rocking his head slowly backwards and forwards, perhaps invoking some IT deity to intervene in the conversation.

Martin's dislike of Jim was growing and irritation was dispelling the ennui that had brought him back to his old watering hole. Not long ago he would have been overawed by a personality like Jim's. Even where he disagreed, he would probably just have nodded for the sake of avoiding argument. But he had recently finished reading Timles and Tina's book; Universal Therapy and it had made a deep impression on him. He recalled how Tina had surprised him in the Dragon with her scientific defence of alternative therapy. He suddenly realised he'd been given a clear vision of the future of alternative therapy. Whereas Jim claimed to be able to squeeze that sort of knowledge from chance encounters.

'Well, Jim, rather than discussing breaking news, I think we're on the verge of a breakthrough in medicine. You see, back in the past when your only option for healing was to visit your local *shaman* or *wise woman*, these individuals knew all there was to know. They dispensed a mixture of natural pharmaceuticals and hope. These, combined with the absolute faith of their patients, meant that very many people were cured. Today, medicine is continually broken up into separate disciplines. By and large, the important *positive belief* component of therapy - and that's belief both by patient and therapist - has been overtaken by technology and impersonal information leaflets.'

Jim was now listening intently and nodding. He looked a bit startled. This was unexpected. Peter had opened his eyes wide as Martin warmed to his theme.

'There are now hundreds of different types of medicine men and women and, as you have already mentioned about yourself Jim, they haven't the time or capacity to keep abreast of what their colleagues are actually doing. Worse, funding, competition for promotion and even professional secrecy means that communication between the different types of specialist is getting worse as scientific medicine gets more complex. That's the bad news.'

Martin was now enjoying himself and paused a moment for effect. Neither Jim nor Peter spoke.

'OK Jim, here's what's new. Some grass roots practitioners working at the interface between the mainstream and the mystic, or alternative therapy as I prefer to call it, have found a new way to start giving us back joined up medicine.'

Martin stopped talking and raised his glass.

'Cheers!'

Peter's jaw had dropped. Jim was still nodding thoughtfully.

'What's the take on this new approach then Mart?'

'I suggest you get a copy of *Universa Therapy* by Timles and Elves. It's just appeared on the market published by You Tree.'

Jim stared at Martin, then suddenly looked down at his watch.

'Jesus, is that the time? Look guys, I've got to back to Cambridge before the M25 grinds to a halt.'

He rose and reached out for Martin's hand. When Martin took it back a business card had mystically appeared in it.

'Really great talking to you Mart. That was *very* useful.'

Jim seemed distracted and muttered "very useful" once again under his breath. He waved briefly at Peter.

'Ciao Pete; keep in touch and give my best to your boss.'

With that parting shot he was gone. Peter visibly relaxed in his chair.

'You're full of surprises Mart. You really shook that smarmy git. I could see where he was going with his supposed interest in physiotherapy.'

'Where's that?'

'Basically he's an insecure person who has to establish that he knows more than anyone else. He'd probably got some smart Alec cracks about physiotherapy he'd hoped to trot out. He's really a businessman rather than the scientist he pretends to be. His company's intellectual property has been creamed off from Cambridge academics through agreements of questionable quality.'

'So my answer cut the ground from under his feet?'

'And mine, Mart, and mine. What's been happening to you? You seem to be a completely different character these days?'

'InterconNet.'

'What?'

'Your network. That's what's been happening to me. That and developments at work which I don't yet understand.'

Peter grinned. Music to my ears, Mart. You'll have to bring me up to date on that later. Now Jim's hoofed it, I've got something important to tell you. Basically I got a right bollocking from my Ph.D. supervisor, Chris, whom I gather you've already met.'

'Chris from the Computer Science Department? Your supervisor? He seemed pretty smart, but I thought he was a post grad student.'

'No, he's a reader in the department; quite a senior academic post, but unlike old Jim, a fashion icon he's not.'

'But he talked a lot about you and never once said you were his research student.'

'That's not surprising. The InterconNet project isn't popular with our Prof and Chris has got into the habit of distancing himself from it in departmental discussions. He's also got another reason for being cagey about it.'

'What's the problem?'

'You, Mart. I didn't get his permission to sign you up on my InterconNet network. Well, formally it's Chris's intellectual property and only my Ph.D. project. He frequently reminds me of that.'

'So when Jim referred to your boss, he meant Chris.'

'That's a fact.'

'So where does Jim fit into this?'

'He's currently the fly in the ointment. His company, ThreeLs - can you *believe* that name - owns the patent on the artificial intelligence software we use in InterconNet. ThreeLs allows us to use this without charge for research purposes, but we'd have to pay a licence fee for any commercial or external application of InterconNet. Jim was here today to discuss this with Chris. He keeps a close eye on what we're doing with their software and he's just waiting for the time when we try to sell or licence any programme which uses it. As Chris would say, he's got us by the short and curlies.'

'Can't you get round it by writing your own routines?'

Martin had been reading a "Computers for Dummies" book of late and had picked up some jargon.

'We've been trying. Trouble is, they've sewn up the essential approach so thoroughly. Anyway, look, please keep all mention of InterconNet under your hat or I'll be toast. Chris wanted me to get you to sign a confidentiality agreement, but when I asked him for a suitable form of words recently he seemed to have cooled down about the issue and just asked me to tell you to keep what you're doing to yourself.'

'No trouble with that, Pete. Time for another jar?'

'Too right. Is that Old Peculiar? I'll have the same. When you come back, let's drink to traffic jams on the M25, then you can fill me in on what's been happening while you've been using InterconNet. Oh, there's something you ought to know. My office is right next to Chris's and I overheard him talking to someone he called Dr. Timles. Pretty unusual name that; so I thought it's got to be the owner of your Woodlands Centre. As far as I could make out from a one-sided conversation, your boss was asking Chris about the possibility of setting up some type of medical database. Chris sounded pretty interested and helpful. I imagine that your boss might have mentioned money. That would have kept Chris on the phone, even though building a database would bore him rigid.' Martin paused looking at Martin's expression.

'You did give your boss some sort of cover story about your visits to the Uni, Mart, didn't you?'

****

The following morning, on Martin's hallway floor was a hand addressed letter. A rare find amongst the weekly promotional mailings, utility bills and bank statements. He carried it to the kitchen and opened it whilst the kettle boiled. It was from the warden of his father's sheltered accommodation in Beaconsfield. It seemed lengthy for a reply to Martin's short enquiry about his father. With mounting apprehension, Martin read on. It appeared that his enquiry had arrived at an opportune moment and this reply conveyed a sense of relief that a family member had been in touch.

The warden—"Bill"—explained that his father had fallen a month ago, had been admitted to hospital with a fracture and had been kept on a ward for a week on account of his age and absence of anyone in his flat to provide immediate 24 hour care. Bill reassured Martin that his father was now back in his accommodation with some care arranged by social services. The warden had spent some time with his father and had been concerned that contact had been lost with any direct relatives; indeed Mr Wright couldn't remember if or where he had addresses or telephone numbers.

Bill indicated that his father remained a fiercely independent individual, but that after his accident, he had accepted his increasing vulnerability and the absolute need for the support that had been arranged for him up to now. When Bill told his father about Martin's enquiry, Mr Wright had asked to see the letter. Bill didn't go into details about his father's response, but suggested that a visit by Martin would not only be accepted, it would be welcomed. Bill pointed out that, clearly, there were decisions to be made about his father's future. In his opinion the recent trauma had brought home to "the old gentleman" his isolation and produced this "change of heart" regarding his son.

From the wording of the letter, Martin guessed that during the extra time the warden had had to spend with his father there must have been a full and frank exchange of words. He could imagine Bill, encouraged by Martin's contact at a difficult time, giving reassurance and thoughtful advice to the cantankerous old man.

Bill appeared to be a very sensitive and sensible individual. The occupants of his father's sheltered accommodation were probably very lucky to have him. Martin re-boiled his kettle, which had by this time cooled below tea making temperature and made himself a large mug of green tea. While this was infusing, he picked up the phone and called the number on the warden's letter. After a few rings, an answer phone message cut in. Martin left a message thanking the man for his letter and help, indicating his willingness to pay a visit and leaving his mobile phone number.

'I'm very grateful for what you're doing for my father and I will, in any case, call you again tomorrow.'

Martin carried his tea into the lounge, swept books and papers off the sofa and sat down. Trying to find a formula to make himself feel more positive about a possible meeting with his father, he remembered Tina's Reiki principles. Running mutely through the list he picked out three: *Just for now, don't worry*; *Just for now be grateful; Just for now, honour your relatives and those close to you.* Yes; all these were certainly relevant and should surely block out negative thoughts. He closed his eyes and tried to think positively about a visit, to feel gratitude for the care of warden Bill and concern for his father's health. But all he could see and sense, was Tina herself.

CHAPTER SIXTEEN

Timles

Julie greeted Martin cheerily as he entered the Woodlands.
'Dr. Timles is here and he'd like to meet you in Tina's old room. You've no-one booked in between 10 and 11am.' Just before 10 Martin knocked on the door of Tina's former treatment room. The Centre hadn't appointed anyone, Reiki therapist or otherwise, to replace Tina; Timles had evidently commandeered her office. Martin had rarely seen him at the Centre and wondered a little apprehensively what had brought him there today.

'Come in Martin.' The Centre's owner was seated in an easy chair holding a tablet PC. He'd reorganised the layout of Tina's room to mirror his lounge at home. The wall behind him, bizarrely, showed his back garden. Timles easily read Martin's thoughts.

'Yes; now you know how you saw those distant hills from my patio window when you visited. I operate best in my own environment, Martin. The large wall display will be useful whilst I'm here and required for therapeutic use at a later stage.' Martin nodded, without really understanding what his boss meant as he sat in one of the two easy chairs. He privately wondered whether his boss was enlightened or eccentric. Probably both. As Martin sat, Timles resumed typing on the tablet. Timles's back garden abruptly disappeared from the wall display and was replaced by the InterconNet network. Martin's eyes were wide as he tried to work out what was going on.

'InterconNet!' was all he could think of to say at that moment. The next instant, with a rush of adrenaline, he realised he'd revealed his own knowledge of it. The Centre's owner smiled at Martin, following his astonished gaze. Far from appearing annoyed, Timles appeared to be enjoying himself.

'Yes, it *is* surprising how quickly it's up and running here. A Ph.D.

student called Peter Swales and a Finnish girl from the University came in briefly to set it up and demonstrate it. Peter said he's met you. A frozen shoulder - one of your satisfied patients apparently?' Martin nodded uncertainly. Timles paused then delivered his bombshell.

'Also, Martin, I see you're a registered user of InterconNet. And hedging your bets on whatever help Tina and I might offer, you've connected with an on-line psychotherapist. Someone calling herself Anne Eres.' Martin was silent with shock. Was Timles clairvoyant? But then he remembered Peter saying he'd overheard his supervisor talking to Timles about arranging to meet.

'You saw that on InterconNet?'

'Yes. I asked Peter's supervisor, Chris Johns to visit my home to demonstrate this programme. He invited me to test it, so I asked him to search for therapists. Both you and this freelance psychotherapist, Anne, came up in his search with a link between you. Chris had forgotten his research assistant had recruited you and was discomforted that I had chosen the very search that would reveal your presence.' Martin floundered a bit trying to apologise.

'I'm sorry that I haven't mentioned any of this to you. I'm more than a little embarrassed about consulting Anne when you're already giving me support. As well as Tina.' Timles smiled.

'Well I'm impressed by your initiative and from what I read of Anne's profile - I'd say that you've a made a happy chance find there.'

Timles's phrase struck Martin as distinctly odd. First Pete, then Tuula and Chris and now his boss had all had commented positively about his anonymous on-line therapist. He wondered if one or more of them *knew* who she really was. Tuula was the most likely to know as she obviously had privileged access to InterconNet. But the others? He decided to risk probing his boss a little.

'She has such a unusual name. Do you think it can be real?'

Timles smiled. It was a perfect opportunity for a Shakespeare quote.

'What's in a name? A rose by any name would smell as sweet.' You know Martin, I'd like to see you take advantage of the chance contact with your on-line therapist, before our next chat; will you do that?'

Martin grinned ruefully. If his boss did know who she was, he wasn't saying. Timles interrupted his thoughts:

'Whoever she is, for a former critic of complementary medicine, you're at serious risk of conversion. You now have not one but three alternative therapists!'

'But Anne's offering psychotherapy.'

'Well Martin, Anne's work is certainly "alternative" to my help and Tina's but doesn't sound like mainstream psychology to me. Another thing; I'm offering you mentoring with no cost to you. Tina's applying her version of Reiki *gratis* and Anne's work with you is *pro bono*. I'd say all our offerings are complimentary as well as complementary!' Timles grinned at his play on words before continuing:

'The network you're looking at now is just a basic one Peter and this Finnish girl put together to test the set-up here. It's up to us to do all the hard work inputting data. Peter and his colleague have adapted the programme so that we will be able to enter not just individuals - therapists and patients - but also treatments and external organisations. Essentially anything or anyone that you could "interconnect" with. As information is entered, so the programme will suggest useful associations and learn as it goes along.' Martin was still nodding; from agreement, but mostly from surprise; his thoughts whirling.

So Timles intended to use InterconNet for some purpose at the Woodlands. No point now in hiding his working knowledge of it from his boss.

Even with his limited experience of computers, Martin was amazed by the speed with which Peter and Tuula had got this working in the Centre. Timles was watching Martin's puzzled expression.

'You're no doubt wondering how I got to learn about all this?'

'I expect you found out I gave Peter Swales a tour of the Woodlands.'

'No; I didn't know that. I contacted the Computer Sciences Department looking for someone to set up a Centre database for us and was put in touch with Peter's supervisor. Chris gave me a demonstration of InterconNet at my home. He told me that the power of InterconNet was that it *learnt* as people used it. It essentially continually improves what it can do. I had no idea how far artificial intelligence—AI—had progressed.' Timles looked at Martin with slightly narrowed eyes.

'He also revealed that you're not only on InterconNet, you're helping Peter with his research. Actually Chris was very angry about that. Peter wasn't supposed to canvas people outside the University, and certainly not without his supervisor's knowledge.' Martin's expression changed from puzzlement to concern.

'Don't look so worried, Martin. I saw what Peter and Chris's programme had independently worked out about *you*. And in such a short time! I think InterconNet could prove extremely powerful as a tool for healthcare and well being!' Timles gave Martin an appraising look then continued:

'I've signed a licence agreement with the University's innovation unit. I've also agreed with Chris and Peter to work with the Woodlands to adapt their programme for therapeutic applications.' Martin felt a mixture of surprise and relief at his boss's explanation and reassurance. Above all he was grateful he finally had the opportunity at be open about his involvement at the University.

'Well, *I'm* impressed that something experimental running on the University computers could be transferred to us so quickly.'

'That's the clever thing about it, Martin. It *isn't* running here. *Or* at the University for that matter. The Finn.. I can't keep calling her that. Do you know her name?'

'Tuula Pipi.' Martin saw Timles give him an odd glance and realised he'd replied rather too quickly.

'OK then, *Toolah* recommended we run it at Amazon.' Martin blinked hard at this.

'The on-line retailer?'

'Yes Toolah explained that Amazon has one of the biggest Internet server set-ups in the world. They're called server "farms" apparently, partly because they're set up in huge steel sheds out in the countryside. Amazon offers something called the "Elastic Compute Cloud". It's pay-as-you-go computing and will run exactly what they have at the University, but completely under client's own control. Now, the really clever bit is that the service is totally expandable. As much capacity as you need. If what we're doing here really takes off, neither a computer at the Woodlands or even at the university would be able to service the demand. But Amazon's Cloud service can. They have even supported international web services like Twitter.' Martin's mind swam at these revelations, but Timles was clearly in his element.

'Peter also shared his vision of the future of the Web with me. Fascinating.'

Martin recalled Pete's words when he first visited his office in Computer Sciences. At that time what he *had* understood of Pete's description, he'd assumed was simply exaggerated student idealism.

'Would that be "Web4"?'

Timles looked a little disappointed

'You know all about *that* as well, I suppose?'

'Actually no; Pete didn't really explain at the time he mentioned it. Not in sentences I could understand, anyway.' Timles leaned back and steepled his hands. Martin recognised the gesture; another explanation was coming.

'Chris gave me a pretty clear picture of the state of play of the World Wide Web. I was amazed, Martin, and I had to go and read up a bit; using the Web itself, of course!'

When we started the Woodlands, one of our director's children put our first Centre brochure on-line. All people could do with it was look at a series of static Web pages. At the time, many businesses didn't have anything much better.

That was the "Web1" era. Not long after that we went to a web design business, who gave us a *functional* Website. Potential clients could book an appointment on-line. We also had an area for clients to post feedback on their experience. Of course, we had to have Noura police that to remove inappropriate comment! That was "Web2" and that's where we are right now.

Martin nodded patiently. He was up to speed with all that. Timles watched his reactions.

'But I'm probably teaching you to suck eggs, Martin?' After the revelations about his involvement with Peter, Martin was careful to be diplomatic in his replies:

'I'm sure the best is yet to come.' Timles nodded and continued.

'"Web3 or the *semantic* Web" isn't quite with us yet. It's the vision of the inventor of the World Wide Web: Tim Berners Lee. Instead of a Web of linked *pages*, He and others envisage a web of linked *data*. I'll give you an example. Say Tina was working on some new Reiki therapy. She chooses a few search words she thinks relevant and types them into Google. In Web2 mode Google replies with links to half a million web *pages* listed in the order *Google* thinks best. People generally lose patience and give up after fifty links. Not very helpful is it?

Now in Web 3 mode, she would get a *single* document to read. AI would *extract* data from those half million or so sites to build a report that no human would have the time or capacity to achieve themselves. By reading that single report, Tina could rapidly refine her search to locate, providing it existed at all, exactly what she was looking for.' Martin nodded, but Timles's example gave him a strange feeling that Tina was also involved in all of this. He made a mental note to look for her on InterconNet. But Timles was continuing:

'Apparently Web3 programming is what Peter's supervisor at Tamford has been working on in his own AI research. Although computers are great at at finding and comparing stuff, they have no idea of the *meaning* of it. For example, given the phrase "the cow jumped over the moon" the present day Web could fetch you the complete text for that nursery rhyme, but it wouldn't have a clue that it was fantasy, or at least highly improbable! But Web3 aims to *interpret* the information stored on the Web.

Martin was now concentrating hard to follow his boss. Chris and Peter had evidently made a big impression on him. But then Timles was someone clearly excited by technology.

'And Web4?' Timles laughed at Martin's prompting.

'That's really Peter being cheeky. Research students are desperate to make original discoveries and christen them. "Web4" is supposed to have all the functions of Webs 1 to 3, but adds the ability to make *associations* between information on the web. It tries to do what we humans do: recognising patterns, learning from experience, making inferences and so on. InterconNet aims to enlighten its human users by creating meaningful associations between people, facts or things. Whether you want to say that InterconNet will eventually *understand* things would be the concern of the philosophers, not us. Here Timles paused a moment.

'You've already had a glimpse of that power.' Timles looked meaningfully at Martin, who blinked hard, wondering just how much his boss actually knew about his activities on InterconNet. Timles continued his explanation.

'As far as the Woodlands is concerned, Chris and Peter's

InterconNet could allow our website to have a *dialogue* with our clients 24/7; finding out about their progress, responding to concerns, updating them about appropriate developments in medicine, providing links to help groups and forums. For our therapists it could provide continuing education, continually sifting through the chaff represented by the vast amount of medical information on the Web, for the grains of wheat out there.'

Timles paused, contemplating the large display on the wall behind him. He seemed transported by his thoughts to some other place for a few moments. Then he returned to his explanation once more.

'Neither Peter nor his supervisor can say right now how powerful their programme might someday become. But if a similar programme, aimed at supporting health care, was running on the Web it could "creatively disrupt" our current medical practice.' Timles paused to find the right words, then:

'You could say that we are at the beginning here of creating a universal kind of therapy.'

He seemed to have moved onto another plane as he expounded this. Martin didn't know if he should speak. When Timles didn't add anything further he ventured:

'Is this what you're telling us about tomorrow?' Timles let out a long breath and seemed to relax.

'I think what I just told you was a bit over the top for general consumption don't you? No, I'll have to tone it down a lot. But you still need to come to the meeting! Now, about entering data onto our own version of InterconNet. I don't want to pull Centre staff off their duties and I've noticed, well, that you're not so busy at present, so I'm asking you to co-ordinate this with Noura.' Timles read Martin's face and grinned.

'Don't worry, entering information and checking things is right up Noura's street and she will be a first rate assistant. Besides, a bit of role reversal will be good for both of you.'

'What are we entering?'

Martin thought about the lengthy questionnaire he completed on-line when he signed up with InterconNet. Timles explained:

'Apparently this Toolah is working for a Ph.D. like Peter on social networks. She has programmes that could be used to extract information from all kinds of different sources given instructions about what to look for.

They can automatically gather the relevant data from CVs, patient records, reports, research papers, case histories and so on, both on and off line. Peter has produced a programme that can transfer all this into our version of InterconNet. Then InterconNet goes to work cross-checking and verifying the information and builds the network up, learning as it goes.'

'So we don't have to sit all day typing?'

'No; there will of course be material we'll have to input manually, but you'd never have the time to populate the programme with enough data to make it useful.'

'So want do you want Noura and I to do?'

'You and I have to set out the initial instructions for this data gathering programme. We are the brains that have to kick start the network and monitor what's happening until it eventually becomes cleverer than us! You will feed these instructions to Noura who is being taught how to run the data gathering bit. You will then check that InterconNet is working OK and show our staff here how to use it. They will maintain their own accounts on InterconNet and correct any errors relating to their own fields.'

'And it will have physiotherapy information as well as covering alternative medicine?'

'Absolutely, Martin. As I've said once before, your practice here will be the bridge between us and them; the "magicians" and the medics. When your material, together with that of our herbal medicine man is on our network, we'll have firm links to mainstream physiology and pharmacology. The more challenging area for us will be when we attempt to integrate our other more alternative therapies with mainstream psychology and psychiatric practice. If we succeed, it will mark the beginning of our eventual goal of joined up medicine.'

Martin wondered if Timles was including him in that reference to "our" eventual goal. But Timles was once again in full flight.

'There won't be any more treating something trivial with serious therapies or something serious with trivial ones. And at long last the true value of *belief* in maintaining human health may emerge. Of course, we both know now that *faith* in the ability of some of our therapists to cure is the basis of the healing or improvement achieved in many of our patient's conditions. Mainstream medicine is failing to provide the right conditions or to train their practitioners to deliver this important aspect of patient care.

At present I believe my ideas to provide optimum access to therapies for *every* sort of patient and practitioner will be revolutionary. But at the moment I'm juggling pieces of a health care jigsaw. I haven't prized the lid off the box where they're kept, so I can't see the final picture. Chris taught me that, you know. He pointed out that we can't predict the properties of complex systems from looking at the component parts. The whole is *greater* than the sum of the parts. It *emerges* for the first time when you put everything together. I gave you the example of a jigsaw. A more relevant example for us is *consciousness.* This only *emerged* when nature put in place billions of *unconscious* nerve cells and connected then up. That's exactly what I believe will happen if we build a medical version of InterconNet. It will somehow reveal the best available route to therapy. And there's another factor that Chris told me about emergence. Even though we all carry the "consciousness software" in our heads, even our brightest scientists can't explain how it actually operates. In a similar way we may not be able to understand how our final healthcare version of InterconNet works when its full power eventually emerges.'

Martin thought he had finally "got it" after Timles finished his long explanation. But then he'd now read some of Timles's and Tina's book. He wondered what the medical establishment and the specialist media would make of it. But he decided to keep these thoughts to himself. For now. But Timles hadn't yet wrapped up their discussion.

'I don't know what Chris and Peter are planning to do with their own version of InterconNet, but we don't want to use the name they've coined. We need our own label and it's important that it "says exactly what it does on the tin".' Timles laughed at his own joke, but didn't wait for Martin's response.

'You're the only person in the Woodlands who's used the programme. Have you any thoughts about what name we might call it?' Martin leant his elbow on his chair's armrest and raised his hand to his temple in thought. Rather than fishing for a name, most of his thoughts were about what had happen to him in such a short time. Especially the lifelines Tina and now Anne were offering him. Timles studied his face and continued:

'Of course we don't have to decide now. Think about it. Oh, and I've made time for our next and hopefully last mentoring session at my place if that's OK. Can you reserve a hour Thursday week at around 11am?'

Martin nodded and then looked again at the InterconNet image on Timles's wall mounted display. The key feature of the programme was making associations and creating valuable links between its nodes. Of course in Timles's vision of it these nodes wouldn't just be people. They would represent patients, practitioners, treatments, medicines or any other aspect of health care, disease or mental dis-ease. He considered these important connections carefully; lines that represented potential health giving or life affirming links.

'What about *LIFELINES*?' Timles looked transfixed for a moment. Then he smiled and stood up, offering Martin his hand.

'That's a great idea, Martin. I like that. Very much. I'll run it past my daughter and see what she thinks.' Martin was pleased, but also surprised.

'I didn't know you had a daughter. Is she involved in some aspect of health care too?'

'Oh yes. After her divorce several years ago, she went full time into alternative practice. But you know her very well. She's the co-author of my book. Her name's Christina, but you know her as Tina; Tina Elves.' It would be hard to exaggerate the shock this revelation gave Martin. Her eyes - the curious pigmentation - just like Timles's. Timles's apparent second sight about him. His lack of surprise about anything Tina said or did. Two therapists with a common vision: father and daughter. Between these two he'd laid his soul bare. He'd have to leave the Centre. But Timles hadn't finished:

'After my talk to staff tomorrow, I'd like to arrange a meeting with you to discuss the new direction the Centre will be taking and your role in it. I don't need to ask you about your progress with this exciting new network approach. You're clearly in advance of all of us.' Timles looked hard at Martin who found he had to connect with eyes that seemed to look into whatever counted as his soul.

'As I've already suggested, when we get our own version of InterconNet—*LIFELINES*—running well, I want you to be involved in training our staff to use it.'

Timles stood and offered his hand.

'Before we next meet, have a discussion with your Anne about personal values. She'll know what to say. Don't forget to send that letter to enquire about your father. And Martin…' Timles paused for Martin's acknowledgement.

'Yes?'

'If it takes off as I hope, *LIFELINES* could change your life too. Factor that thought into any decisions you make over the coming days and months.'

****

At 9:30 the next day, Woodlands staff and guests assembled in the Woodlands Centre reception. Julie, noticeably dressed in a smart two-piece and pin-striped blouse, was ticking off names as people arrived. Noura, smartly attired as ever, operated a selective version of meet and greet by the reception desk. Invited guests collecting their name badges, but not Centre staff, got Noura's welcoming smile and handshake.

There was a palpable buzz of excitement amongst the Centre's therapists, who had gathered at one side of the reception area. Opposite them were two well dressed men in their late fifties or early sixties, talking amiably with Timles himself. Against the area's picture wall, on a long refectory style table acquired at the eleventh hour by Noura, were plates of biscuits and vacuum jugs. In front of that, within easy reach of the refreshments, stood Chris and Peter from the University Computer Sciences Department. Having helped themselves to coffee as soon as they had registered, they were deep in conversation. Last through the Centre entrance door came Martin, looking rather pink from running. The Centre car park was full and he'd had to find on-street parking.

After Julie had ticked him off, both on her list and under her breath, he quickly scanned the assembly to identify with whom he was most comfortable to talk. Having collected coffee and a bourbon biscuit, Martin found himself talking to Chris; Peter having disappeared in search of the Centre's toilets.

'If my boss hadn't explained things yesterday, Chris, you and Peter would have been the last people I expected to find here this morning.' Martin glanced anxiously in the direction of the Centre's owner.

'InterconNet continually updates its information and connections, doesn't it Chris?'

'That's what it's programmed to do; yes.'

'So Timles would have seen an updated version of my profile ; one I haven't seen yet, when you demonstrated the programme to him?' Chris grinned at him.

'That's exactly why we're here, Mart.' Martin looked so shocked Chris stopped grinning and quickly tried to reassure him.

'What would be in your profile that might worry you, Mart?'

'I really hope it doesn't say what I've been thinking about the therapists at this Centre.'

'Michael finding your profile when I demonstrated InterconNet to him, was a co-incidence, Mart. Your boss knew nothing about InterconNet before I met him. But what he read about you seemed to make a big impression. I guess what he saw chimed with his own thoughts about you and I'd say they were pretty positive. It was InterconNet's take on you, not what you might have said or not said about yourself, that was one of the main factors that made him sign an agreement with us. He now wants to use our InterconNet software and we're here this morning to learn what he proposes to do with it.'

Martin's relief was evident, but he changed the subject and decided to talk about his physiotherapy work with the briefest mention of the other therapies. Chris listened patiently giving an occasional nod. Having read the Centre's brochure and skimmed Timles's book, he was up to speed with what was happening here. He glanced round to see if Peter was on his way to join them. Peter had been commandeered by Timles and was explaining something to the men with him, whilst they listened attentively. Knowing his research student only too well, Chris immediately wanted to join them and introduce himself. But he turned to Martin first.

'Who are the men with your boss, Martin?'

'I haven't met them, but I'm pretty sure they'll be members of the Woodlands board.' Hearing this, Chris decided to leave Peter to answer their questions on his own. If it later got back to him that Peter had said anything contentious, he could always pull rank and play it down it as student enthusiasm. But seeing Peter in full verbal flight reminded Martin about their last meeting in the Dragon with Jim Overbeck of ThreeLs. Now Chris had told him his unauthorised use of InterconNet had helped Chris and Peter get some kind of deal with the Woodlands, he risked asking a question that was troubling him.

'Pete told me an important part of InterconNet used the intellectual property of a Cambridge firm called ThreeLs Ltd. He said any commercial application of InterconNet would mean paying licence fees or royalties, even though you're the ones actually coming up with the ideas and developing the applications. I can't programme computers, but I learnt during my time at Uni that there is usually more than one way to do the same thing.' This remark came as a shock to Chris. It made him even more uneasy about what was being said by Peter to the small group on the other side of the room, but he contained his urge to butt in on that discussion. Instead he turned his back to them and focused on dealing with the very thorny issue Martin had raised.

'You did science at Uni didn't you?'

'Life sciences, yes; but I didn't complete the course.'

'Any maths or physics in that?'

'Some; the first year had all kinds of different modules. I did physics ones in both of those.'

'OK. What makes InterconNet such a powerful network application is a part of the programme which identifies connections between its members and assesses how significant these connections are.'

'Is that assessment made on the answers we give during signing up?'

'Partly, but as you've probably already heard, also on all the other data on a member that InterconNet can get its digital fingers on. To make a very long and mindbogglingly complex story short, we don't exactly know how the programme does this.'

'But you and Pete wrote the programme!'

'Most of it, yes, but the really clever part; the part we don't - actually can't - understand, is written by the programme itself.'

'How is that possible?'

'You'd say our brains are clever?'

'There are days I doubt you'd describe mine like that. But I'd say yours and Pete's have engineering by Ferrari.'

Chris smiled at Martin's analogy.

'I'd prefer *Lotus* technology myself, but thanks for the compliment! Anyway, neither Peter, me or even your good self know how our *brains* do what they do. Not in detail anyway. But two of the things they do best, and they do these because evolution has worked on the brain programme for at least 100 million years, are recognising patterns and assigning significance. That's because those two things are foremost among the reasons species like ours survived.'

'Yes, I think I can see that, but what's the link with InterconNet?'

'The pattern of InterconNet member connections and their significance is calculated by the kernel of our programme which emulates our brains - we call it a neural network. Each time the programme is run, this part of it changes slightly, which makes life pretty difficult if you want to keep track of what's happening. But even without that complication it's still too contorted for we mere computer scientists to fathom out how it works.'

'Why do you call that bit a kernel?'

'Because it's the core of a programme written by nuts! Sorry, Martin; my little attempt to lighten this conversation. By the way, this is great coffee isn't it? Ours comes out of a machine with an attitude problem. Anyway, as I was saying the part of our programme that generates and dynamically updates the neural network core or kernel is patent protected and that patent is owned by ThreeLs Ltd.'

'Can't you write another programme to do this instead?'

'No; the ThreeLs patent is based on a completely innovative and unfortunately for us, general idea. A Cambridge physicist saw how he could apply it to networks. Anyway, somehow ThreeLs got wind of this and offered to fund his research and provide any royalties from applications for him. In return, he gave up his rights if they were able to patent it. The University will be livid if and when the first applications come to the market. But by then ThreeLs will probably offer the academic concerned employment at 5 times his academic salary!' Martin assumed a very thoughtful expression.

'I see.' But he didn't. Peter suddenly spoke up from behind them where he had been listening to his supervisor's explanation.

'Think yourself lucky Chris spared you his mathematical description of the so called *personality space* that we use in InterconNet! Mart, can you excuse me for a moment while I have a private word with my boss.' Martin moved away and missed the look Chris gave his student. Circulating, Martin found himself exchanging pleasantries with a patrician looking gentleman, who introduced himself as Simon Black. Simon volunteered that his interest in this meeting was as an investor and non-executive director of the Woodlands Centre.

'Of course, Martin, you've possibly not met all the members of Centre's board before. I'm non-exec for the Woodlands and CEO of a small pharmaceutical business. At least, I am until my board starts to get even more uncomfortable about my external commercial responsibilities. Philip Gray - that's the other director here this afternoon - is the really important presence. He's financial controller of the Woodlands. Phil Gray founded a very successful fitness centre chain and then sold the business on. My firm is based in Surrey, although the board keeps raising the prospect of a move overseas for economic reasons. If that happens and the Woodlands could use my services full time, you might see more of me.' Martin had to step back a moment as Noura bustled past with a refilled jug of milk. Simon acknowledged her briefly. Then he turned back to Martin.

'So you're our physiotherapist. I hear good things about your work for us. We all want to see your activities at the Centre expand. At present it looks like the Centre is entering a particularly exciting period in its development. You will have read Timles's new book, of course?' Martin nodded. Simon continued: 'So I expect you've already put two and two together there?' Martin looked a bit sheepish.

'Actually, I've only recently picked up a copy and I'm still reading. I'm rather ashamed to admit that it has overturned my previous attitude to a number of alternative therapies the Woodlands offers.'

'Nothing to be ashamed of there. It's going to bring about a revolution in several quarters. Not overnight of course, but Michael and most of our board want the Woodlands to lead the field.' Simon sipped his coffee and smiled inclusively at Martin. This director seemed to be in a very good mood and Martin thought it might be a good opportunity to discover a bit more about the Centre's enigmatic owner.

'Have you known Michael Timles long?'

'Oh yes. You probably know that his background was also pharmaceuticals. We worked together as managers at Neukemie in Basle. Michael became more interested in developing his people than in products and profits. As a senior insider he was also aware of the many downsides of pharmaceuticals. What really fascinated him was the power of mind rather than medicine. At that time we began to see things rather differently. I remember we had quite bitter arguments about personalised medicine for example. you're aware of that dispute, which is still raging?'

'Tailoring drugs to the individual instead of just to the condition?'

'Essentially, yes. Take beta-blockers for instance; drugs which reduce blood pressure.'

'My father takes those.'

'Yes many millions of people are taking them, post diagnosis, for the remainder of their lives. Anyway, you will see on the enclosed information leaflets literally dozens of potential side effects listed, from quite common to very rare. A number of these side effects are even life-threatening, but of course this is justified because for many people *not* taking the drug carries even greater risk. People's biochemistry and genetics vary - often quite widely - and this affects not only potential for side effects, but even the efficacy of the drug itself.' Martin expressed his surprise.

'Obviously I knew about drug side effects, but I had no idea that some people didn't get the benefit either.'

'Oh yes, Martin, although GPs can be reasonably sure a drug will work, they cannot know whether their patient will react beneficially or adversely to the medicine being prescribed until they start taking it. But of course it's then up to the GP whether they recognise that any problems they experience might be caused by their medicine. Today there's no denying that individually tailored drug development would by itself represent a revolution in medicine. With the tremendous advances in biochemistry and genetics we can even see *how* one might produce personalised medicines. Unfortunately, the way drugs are currently developed rules this out for economic reasons. Companies must make profits to survive, so the over-riding influence of development costs on medicines shouldn't be so surprising should it? '

'So a given drug is licensed because it improves the condition of a *population* with a given ailment, but not necessarily the health of an *individual* with that condition?'

'Couldn't have put it better myself, Martin. I can see why Michael is keen to give you greater clout at our centre. Yes; better to have a new drug that helps many, but not everyone, rather than no drug at all. The UK Commission on Safety of Medicines licences a drug based on the *statistics* reported to them of its safety and efficacy; not its effect, good or bad, on, for example, Simon Black, Martin Wright or even our own super fit money man Phil Gray here. Simon paused a moment, but Martin didn't speak as he could see his director was working on something.

'So Martin, the decision whether a company develops a new drug isn't a "Black or Wright" issue, it's a "Gray" one!' Simon chuckled at his own joke and Martin laughed at this witticism as naturally as he could. Now

Simon looked serious.

'But we digressed, didn't we?' Martin nodded dutifully, but wondered how as a pure listener, he had also been held responsible for Simon's digression. However, that, he thought, was the difference between senior management and mere contract staff like himself. Simon continued:

'Returning to Michael's career: Michael realised complementary medicine is the polar opposite to the General Practice approach of prescribing pharmaceuticals. Alternative therapy is entirely focused on the *individual* patient and tailored to that patient's mental or physical ill health. That's the case, whether it's some form of psychotherapy, massage therapy, Tai Chi or even crystal ball gazing - though don't quote me on the latter.' Simon looked at Martin and smiled conspiratorially. After Martin had shaken his head, Simon continued.

'So he quit his job in Big Pharma and freelanced as a consultant for a number of years. Did some high powered courses in psychology and counselling as a sort of bridge to his present work. After that, by using an unexpected windfall and sweet talking investors like myself and our financial guru, Phil Gray, he set up the Woodlands. Now, I suspect we're about to witness another seismic shift in Michael's career.' Simon had clearly finished his brief commentary as he turned just then to look behind him. Martin looked down at the floor, wrapped in thought, Simon's explanations had supplied another piece of the Woodlands jigsaw puzzle. But his musing was interrupted by Simon gently holding his shoulder and indicating the meeting room door.

'I think we're being called to assemble for Michael's talk. I've probably pre-empted some of it, but I'm sure he'll put it better than I've done just now.' He offered Martin his hand.

'Have to leave promptly after this, so I'll say goodbye now. I look forward to hearing even better things about our physio department in future.' Simon moved away to say something to Philip Gray as everyone made their way into the Woodlands meeting room. After all had filed in and were seated, their different conversations gradually ceased and everyone turned to face Michael Timles. Behind him, occupying the entire wall, another high resolution display showed the front elevation of the Woodlands Centre. Timles welcomed his small audience and asked them to introduce themselves briefly. The most awkward introduction came, surprisingly, from Peter Swales.

Seated nearest the entrance, he was invited to speak first. But in the nature of these things, those present were rather more focused on what they themselves were going to say, than on listening critically to those speaking before them.

Timles, by contrast, was fluent and inspiring. In exactly 30 minutes he first gave an entertaining and thought-provoking survey of therapy, from tribal medicine men to the microbes and molecules of modern times. With some invisible sleight of hand, the images on the screen behind him changed in sympathy with the topics of his talk. He wound up this part of his presentation with a sequence from the iconic TV series, *Star Trek*. On the giant screen behind him, Spaceship Discovery's medico Scotty, waved a gizmo over a very sick patient. It bleeped and winked. Diagnosis! Another gadget was waved over the comatose patient. It bleeped and winked again. Cure! Timles and his small audience laughed. Timles explained:

'Since *Star Trek* was first broadcast, gadgets quite similar to that being used by Scotty in the TV series for diagnosing certain conditions are actually in use. Of course they aren't so easy to carry about in your white coat, but then look what's happened to the telephone! Sadly, the medicos themselves haven't changed as fast as the technology they use!' More laughter.

'Now before we get to the real business of this afternoon, I'm proposing a comfort break. We should reconvene here promptly in 20 minutes.' Timles looked enquiringly at his administrator. '

'Tea and coffee are still available I trust?' Most heads turned immediately to see Noura nodding assent. But she was looking at her boss and her expression communicated a second message intended only for Timles. There would be no way his audience would be a minute late returning to their places in the meeting room afterwards; Noura would see to that. Out in reception, Peter caught Martin's eye and came carefully over to him balancing a coffee and a handful of foil-wrapped biscuits.

'That was some talk, Mart! Wish I could hold an audience like that.'

'Yes; Timles never fails to inspire people. So the Woodlands could be the first real world application of your research project?'

'On the money, old chap. But I don't know the full story and I think Chris is still also largely in the dark, even though there's supposed to be an agreement in place for us to work with your boss.' As neither of them had anything further to add, their conversation moved on to a heated discussion about who was now going to buy the next round of drinks in The Dragon. But in the Woodlands drinking up time was already being called, as Noura started ushering the visitors back into the meeting room. Once all were seated, Timles welcomed them back.

'I must first apologise for all the recent secrecy. Apart from my fellow directors, most of you won't know what we are proposing. Now is the time to share our ideas with you all.' Timles paused dramatically and scanned his expectant audience. Every pair of eyes were fixed upon his; waiting. Timles lowered his eyebrows at this point and looked much more serious than during his opening talk.

'But on behalf of myself and the board, I do need you to keep what's said in here this afternoon strictly to yourselves. In taking you into our confidence, the board of the Woodlands Centre and myself are extending to you all a considerable measure of trust. We aren't yet ready to go public with these ideas. I hope that's clear to everyone?' There were nods of agreement from all the audience except Philip Gray. The only people he ever spoke to about *anything* to do with the Woodlands were the Inland Revenue. It was he who raised his hand before the next part of Timles's presentation began.

"I know that a number of those here will be very interested to explore the full implications of this, Michael. But can I express my opinion that we should restrict our discussions today to your Phase I, which will directly affect the Centre and those present?' Timles looked faintly annoyed by this request, but nodded his assent.

'I accept your guidance, Phil. But as you're the custodian of our wealth, please indulge me for 30 minutes as custodian of our future health!' Philip Gray didn't comment, but Timles was acknowledged by a terse smile. Timles then spoke about his vision for a new, fully integrated health care system. He showed the statistics for the major problems of human health and how these were changing.

'Very grave organic illness is in fact thankfully well recognised and therapeutic interventions improve all the time. This is where specialised pharmaceuticals and surgery are absolutely needed. We've not long ago come through a pandemic, which has demonstrated to *everyone* just how powerful mainstream medicine has become. But, as some of you're already aware, front line approaches to therapy have become seriously fragmented;

divided as they are between the growing number of specialisms. Many GP surgeries are small, practitioners overall are ageing, isolated and disconnected from the ever advancing leading edge of medicine. I believe many improvements are possible through restructuring.

But some of these ideas are dealt with in our recent book and in deference to our financial controller's request, I'll not go into that any further this afternoon.' A few in the audience glanced quickly at Philip Gray, but he didn't acknowledge Timles's remark. The meeting room screen was presently displaying a close up of a copy of his boss's book; *Universal Therapy*. Martin was puzzled. He was still trying to work out who or what was controlling the changes in the displayed images and videos. Timles was now moving slowly around his audience as he spoke. It was a rather effective presentation technique that Martin hadn't seen before. No chance of anyone nodding off!

'Now, right up with those major problems of heart disease and cancer is - what?' Timles raised his eyebrows and swept his eyes round to engage with everyone present, like a teacher demanding the correct answer to an easy mental arithmetic problem from his class. Chris looked around for an indication that any of the Centre's staff or directors were about to speak, then when no-one moved, offered:

'Obesity.'

'It's right up there, Chris and I'll come to that indirectly in a moment, but that wasn't what I was after.' There was an uncomfortable silence, then Martin suggested:

'Depression?'

'Correct. Cancer and Heart Disease may be the ubiquitous ugly sisters, but mental health is the sad Cinderella of our National Health Service. Once again, I'm not really concerned here with serious organic disease such as schizophrenia and dementias. I'm talking about low self esteem, anxiety, phobias, worry and biggest of all; depression. To make matters even worse, although science has protected our population against the physical scourge of COVID, we are left to cope with a huge wake of resulting mental dis-ease.

Our excellent NHS is not structured to deal effectively with this area and GPs don't have the time or capacity to do so. Most of the counselling or psychotherapy services, therapists frequently of last resort, are poorly resourced. Worse, some are untrained, the area is currently unregulated and, most serious of all, it's poorly connected with the rest of medicine.' Timles paused to let his audience make a comment or ask a question. No one moved, although Simon Gray cleared his throat in the ensuing silence. Timles returned to the front of his audience.

'It's well known that mental dis - ease is a major factor underlying many chronic and debilitating conditions which plague us; obesity, substance abuse, alcoholism, stress, poor lifestyle choices, social isolation…' Timles glanced briefly at Martin, which made him feel uncomfortable, but there was no indication that the significance of his boss's glance was interpreted by anyone else present.

'Not an exhaustive list, I think. And it's also the case, still not universally accepted, that mental dis - ease is a major contributing factor to organic *disease*. Sadly, because the link still hasn't been properly established in mainstream medicine, no-one is seriously tackling this issue. In fact no-one has any really good ideas about *how* to tackle it and, needless to say, the funding isn't there. But in spite of our lack of preparation, like the twin 'time bombs' represented by ageing population and climate change, a public health crisis of dis-ease is inevitable, just simply delayed.' Timles paused again to allow any feedback from his audience, but no-one spoke. No-one wished to delay further the point in Timles's talk that would involve them.

'Improving the health of the nation doesn't require ever more funding for the NHS, more new drugs or even increasingly sophisticated interventions. A lot of that is fire-fighting; a policy of trying to shut the stable doors after the horses have escaped. What's actually needed is preventative measures. The removal of the stigma of mental dis-ease, more education and simple grass roots support for people with problems before the downward spiral of mental ill health sets in.' Timles paused to gather breath. Simon Black could no longer contain himself. Fearing that Timles would start to outline his 'end game'; his plan to take his vision national and even international, he risked a prompt;

'And that's where we come in, isn't it Michael?' Timles looked hard at him, but swallowed his colleague's precautionary medicine.

'Yes. Well, I'm going to start this part of my talk with the *downside* of my proposal. One of us present here taught me to do this and I have been following his advice ever since.' Only two people in the audience had any idea to whom Timles was referring and one of those now glanced knowingly at his supervisor. Timles continued:

'The downside is that by taking this path we *are* going to meet resistance and ridicule from both the medical establishment and other alternative practises. We won't be making many new friends amongst professionals, but may make some new enemies. That's the bad news. Now here's the good news. We *will* be markedly improving the health and happiness of our patients and there's a chance we could sow seeds for a new flowering of health care.' The audience was now absolutely silent and focused on the Centre's owner. His rare appearances alone were sufficient to generate interest. And now this! The two directors were also focused on Timles. Their colleague was presenting a suitably scaled down version of his vision of future health care; so far, so good. After a weighty pause, Timles launched into his carefully scripted explanation:

'Complementary medicine has a unique opportunity to tackle the growing mental dis-ease challenges in this country. As I hinted earlier, our opportunity lies in the warmth and empathy with which our practitioners engage their clients, the openness and non-judgemental way they listen to their patients' anxieties and the time we are able to give to each of them. Our consultations and therapies focus on the individual, not his or her condition.' Both the Woodlands directors, who had previously been slightly fidgety in their seats were now nodding approvingly. They knew Timles was finally on the home straight.

'But our staff are able to go significantly further than good counsellors or psychotherapists. Here we are able to offer more than simply helping our patients look within themselves for answers, as counsellors do. We offer hands on *treatment*. In fact, the endlessly debated issue whether alternative therapies do or do not directly affect our patients' physiology isn't really relevant. It's their *belief* that they do, together with the *conviction* of our therapists, that is curative in so many instances. It's that all important mind-body link that I was about to describe before my two colleagues here quite correctly nudged me back on track.' Timles smiled at Simon and Philip, who looked slightly uncomfortable.

'The implications for the Woodlands Centre are that we need to be getting our message of hope over not just to the sick, but now also to the worried well. I'd like us as a team to work on educational material we can take out to local schools, the University and other statutory and voluntary organisations. We do need to engage everyone who has an interest in maintaining health. So I see gyms and fitness centres as especially important here and I'm sure Phil can provide valuable input.' Timles looked at Philip and received a rare nod of assent. But Noura, previously impassive, now seemed to be joining the ranks of the worried well.

'Will this mean budget implications; for new brochures, website and business cards?' Phil Gray answered that one.

'Yes Noura; we have already been reviewing the whole Centre's annual spending. We'll table a meeting with you soon to go through the marketing budget.' Noura looked pleased and relaxed visibly. Timles continued his explanations.

'Now, there are also important implications for our staff. The responsibility for the health and well-being of our patients is to become a collective matter; no longer just the concern of our individual therapists. We are going to enter a new phase of communicating with each other.' This time, Timles looked quite hard at Martin and the pointed stare did not go unnoticed by someone else who knew what it meant. Martin felt his hand, just then gripping the side of his seat, gently covered.

Startled, he looked round. Unnoticed by him, Tina Elves had crept into the meeting room after the presentation had started and was sitting directly behind him. Martin checked his neighbours quickly, but their eyes were on Timles. Tina's reassuring gesture made him think of the very personal treatment he had received in her flat. Combined with her warmth and empathy towards him, her striking role play had been a powerful force in penetrating his closed world. He forced his attention back to Timles's presentation.

'We intend that all our new clients will first see a Centre coordinator, who will get details from them and recommend an individual therapist or even several therapists. The details of this are to be worked out, but the directors and I would like to see everyone having an assistant or second in command. We may, after some training, ask our established therapists to fulfil the role of coordinator in rotation, so to speak.' Timles looked around the room and could see that nearly all his staff wanted to ask questions about that one.

'Obviously that is something we can't deal with this afternoon, but you will all have the chance to contribute to the discussion of this over the coming weeks.' Timles paused again. He was about to reveal something else that would now involve everyone present at his meeting.

'My aim; the aim of this Centre, is to *integrate* the work we do here not only with each other, but with mainstream medical practice. But whatever claims we'd like to make about our key role in restoring or maintaining our client's health and happiness, we won't be taken seriously unless we *recognise* existing organic disease as well as claiming to be able to help or even prevent illness in the first place.' Simon Black now leaned forward and focused intently. This was the bit that most fascinated him. Philip Gray lent back in his seat; he was more interested in the power of computers to help with cost accounting and tracking financial trends. It was now the senior therapist who deputised for Noura as Centre manager who looked worried.

'How on earth are we going to do that without medical training?'

'We'll do that by knowing when and where to refer patients and whom refer them to. At this stage, I'd like to ask Chris to give us a brief introduction to the innovative network system he and his research assistant Peter Swales have developed. Chris?' Timles walked to sit in the front row. Chris got to his feet. His pulse was elevated and he was slightly flushed; not that anyone would notice this under his full beard. But his raised blood pressure was due to mounting excitement, not nervousness. Timles had already told him he would like him to make a presentation, but had not given an explanation. Now Chris could finally see where Timles was headed and it really lit his fire. He was determined to make his own presentation lead as seamlessly as possible into what he now realised would be the climax of Timles's talk.

Over the next 20 minutes, using the large display screen as he had done at Timles's home, Chris demonstrated InterconNet to a fascinated audience. But he was careful to emphasise the ability of his programme to objectively analyse and present the personality of members and its power to spot potentially valuable associations between them. Now, that working and confidentiality agreements were in place with the Centre, he listed some of the sources of data to which the present version of the programme had access. Amongst these were feeds from NHS and private medical centre patient records - made suitably anonymous, naturally.

This revelation caused an audible gasp from some of the Centre staff. Chris gave some examples of the results of particular searches as he had done for Timles, but he was careful to avoid Martin's node appearing on the meeting room display. Concluding his talk with an upbeat: "Thanks for listening and I'm sure Dr. Timles will tell us what this all means for the work of your Centre'", he returned to his seat. Timles stood up, thanked Chris and addressed his expectant audience:

'I'd also like to thank all of you; you have been very patient. You obviously are aware we have beefed up the Centre's IT system and all of you, I know some more reluctant than others, now have access to our own network and the wider Internet in all your rooms or clinics. We are going to install a version of the programme you have just seen, here at the Woodlands. You have seen its power to join people, organisations and, Chris tells me, even *things* and *ideas* together. It can carry out powerful searches and allow rich communication between members wherever they are; in our Centre, in this country or the wider world. We are going to populate our version of InterconNet first with our own therapists, then gradually draw in others; from complimentary medicine, mental health and mainstream medicine. And I am talking not just about medical professionals, but patients as well.' Timles paused with a serious expression as he scanned his audience.

'I'm going to shock you. In the USA in sport, official bodies for many years took ethnicity into account when assessing the amount of legal compensation for head injuries. I won't need to spell out for you the discriminating thinking behind this. This injustice has been rectified. But shamefully it still exists in diagnoses in mainstream medicine - and I'm not talking about differences arising from genetics. In the networked medicine system I'm proposing, this and many other types of injustice could not survive.' Now on a lighter and, you will be relieved to hear, final benefit of the system I'm proposing. Our own patients will simply and securely be able to identify others with similar conditions or concerns. They will discover extended advice, support and, let's say it, friendship or even love.'

Both the listening Centre directors looked uneasy. There was no denying they had witnessed a powerful and compelling presentation. But Timles had, in spite of their prompting earlier, revealed more of the vision he'd shared with the board than had been agreed. Philip Gray was frowning and raised a point here in a hopeful attempt to put the brakes on.

'Aren't there major security issues here Timles? Think of all the bad stuff that goes on in the social networks.'

'A good point, Phil. Obviously we must never be complacent about such matters. But recall from Chris's presentation how InterconNet is built around security and continual validation of every member. And we don't propose to offer this to the public like Face Book or Twitter. Access will initially only be for therapists, then their patients and ultimately for a verifiable community of registered users.' Simon Black also raised a point that worried him.

'I know that you hope one day this system developed by Chris and Peter here will create the "joined up medicine" of your vision, but all the grand schemes to introduce on-line patient medical records and health care networks for the NHS have cost millions of tax payer's money and failed their potential users. The latest bold NHS Health care Web attempt closed down last year.'

'You're quite right, Simon. But all those have been attempts to introduce IT systems from the *top down*. As CEO of a Pharmaceutical company, you'll know how hard it is to impose ideas that seem great at board level, but don't fit the needs of those who will be working with them every day. No; our idea is to grow own health care network from the *bottom up*. That's exactly how the world's most successful social network started.' There was now an excited exchange of conversation in the room and Timles decided it was the moment to bring the meeting to a close. He raised his arms and the audience quickly quietened down.

'I think it's time to conclude our meeting. I'm aware I will have stimulated more questions than there's time to answer. We will be holding a series of meetings over the coming weeks to go through all this in much more detail. We are closed to patients today, so I do encourage those of you who can stay to use this room, the reception area and the staff coffee room to carry on talking. I'm expected elsewhere for a meeting now, but Simon, who knows as much as I do about our proposals has told me he will be staying on. So finally I'd like to thank our invited guests as well as our Centre staff for abandoning their clients for today and listening patiently this afternoon. Thank you all.' Timles moved to say a few words to the other directors, then walked over to Chris and Peter who were hovering uncertainly by the door. Shaking both their hands vigorously, he made an arrangement for a further visit for the pair to assess progress with the Centre's version of InterconNet. He dropped his voice safely below the level of excited conversation around them.

'Don't worry that my presentation just now probably seems wildly ambitious to you. That has more to do with politics than pragmatism. I'm a realist who appreciates that all this will take a considerable length of time to achieve, but I will have to carry people with widely differing interests with me during that time. It wouldn't have served my purpose today to flag up all the ifs and buts.' Timles glanced behind him towards Philip Gray, who was talking earnestly with Noura.

'I realise it will often be difficult to keep everyone on board; investors especially. What I need my staff and backers to maintain over the coming months and probably years is just what I have been talking about; *belief.* Faith that there will be a positive outcome and that the struggle will prove worthwhile!' Timles gave them both a look that was intended to say something like "trust me; I'm a doctor" and grasped Chris's upper arms in affirmation. Finally he moved towards Martin, who was still looking a little shell shocked.

'Martin. I think it would be a good idea to meet tomorrow - at my place please. When you've checked your bookings, just tell Noura if you're available.'

On the way out Timles called at Noura's office. No one answered and the door was locked. Timles consulted his watch. He immediately understood the reason. It was 17:31.

****

The following day, Martin walked to Timles's place to give himself time to collect his thoughts about all that had happened since they last met. Deep in thought he didn't even notice the tabby, sunning itself in its usual spot.

Everything he'd told Timles about his experiences with Tina was hugely embarrassing now he knew she was his daughter. But Timles had pointed him quite definitely in her direction and neither he nor Tina had made any secret of their collaboration. And now he was expected to work with one or even both of them in this startling new initiative to elevate the credibility of complementary medicine and perhaps beyond that to health care as a whole. Timles's front door was ajar and he let himself in, still deep in thought.

'Come on in Martin.'

Timles voice broke into his thoughts. As usual, Timles was seated in one of his easy chairs; deliberately not interposing the barrier of a consultants desk between his client and himself. That in itself was interesting. His own GP had repositioned *his* desk so that this authoritarian furniture item didn't separate him from his patient. An indication perhaps that established practice was moving towards bridging the gulf between patient and practitioner?

Once Martin was seated, Timles indicated an agenda on the coffee table. Martin recognised it from his visits to Timles's home, although he'd lost his own copy

Suggested Sessions

1. Closure on past issues
2. Who are we?
3. Where do we go from here?
4. Partners and prospects
5. Progress to date
6. Review

'Where do you think we have got to on this Martin?'

Martin read the items and considered for a moment, trying to recall their last session. Eventually he marshalled his thoughts.

'I've been in touch with the warden at dad's sheltered accommodation and it was quickly arranged for me to visit. In fact Dad really wanted to see me. He's quite come to terms with his past anger with me. He now wants to discuss his future rather than criticise my past. He's becoming too frail to stay in the warden assisted flats and a residential care home has been found for him. I will be visiting him from now on and we found so much to talk about after being out of touch for so long. I'm hoping to be able to discuss developments here. Respecting confidentiality of course. Martin looked enquiringly at Timles.

'Yes Martin, of course. That's excellent! Now I believe you have some on-line psychotherapist dealing with item no.2. Shall we leave that in her capable hands?'

After his revelation about Tina, Martin was beginning to wonder if Anne was another of Timles's relatives. After all, Chris and Tuula had immediately commented that her image was an avatar - a graphic behind which a real person could hide. Or perhaps *shelter* might be a kinder way of putting it. Martin thought he should agree with his boss's suggestion:

'I think that would be best.'

'When you first visited me at home, you were depressed and your work here was suffering. You weren't finding satisfaction in your physiotherapy practice and you were socially isolated. I get the impression things have improved on all those fronts. Would I be right?'

'Partly.'

'Where does it still hurt?'

Timles grinned at his medical allusion.

'I'm still mixed up about relationships.'

'Ah. Well the Bard of Avon had it about right when he wrote: *The course of true love never did run smooth*. I think we've come naturally to item 4 on my small agenda?'

'I suppose so.'

'So are any potential relationships in prospect?'

'I've eliminated one.'

'You told me earlier you were attracted by my daughter Tina. Is she still in favour?'

Martin was surprised at her father's candour, but it helped him to be honest about his feelings.

'I've come to realise that I'm attractive to successful and ambitious young women; like your daughter in fact. But I'm not confident that I have much I can offer them . .'

Timles interrupted quickly.

'Shouldn't they be the judge of that?'

Martin hesitated and thought hard about this before he replied. When he finally did, he felt happier continuing to answer Timles's earlier question.

'..and I'm also concerned that worldly success and ambition make uncomfortable bedfellows in a long term relationship.'

'You're thinking about Helena now aren't you?'

'Not just her.'

Timles looked levelly at him and spoke carefully.

'Tina and I are very close; for a modern father and daughter, that is. We share the same passion for restoring the health and happiness of our fellow men. We've had many long conversations while we compiled our book. She's confided in me that she wants to build another relationship following a long gap since the breakup of her marriage. In her opinion she married too young and her husband did not support her original ambitions; in fact he was openly hostile as she became successful in was she was then doing. That hurt has changed her attitude towards an emotional partner and will accompany her into any future relationship.' Martin was puzzled by this.

'But isn't the essence of any relationship a compromise between what you each might do if you weren't together?'

'Yes, but instead of each of you having to accept that your personal ambition has to be restricted by the relationship, you can formulate a *joint* ambition. Compromise is recast as co-operation. If you can do this, there's a big potential gain, instead of the negative feeling of losing something.'

'I see that, but wouldn't it be very hard for a couple to combine very different careers and outlook on life to arrive at something better than they both had as individuals?'

'Perhaps, but why choose the toughest situation as proof that co-operation isn't possible. I'm not saying it *is* always possible. I'm saying that both people thinking about a relationship should give working on a joint project—a dream if you like—serious thought. After all, look at the relationship casualty rate nowadays; my own daughter for one.'

'How could two people know co-operation like that will work out?'

'They don't know how any joint venture will work out, personal or professional. But I can tell you now that what emerges from successful co-operation in a relationship is far more satisfying than the compromise option.'

'So what does this say about me?'

'You want a relationship. you're attracted by the idea of doing things together. Explore how far you can take that. The more things you can successfully see yourselves doing together, the more satisfying—and durable—your relationship will be.'

'Tina's my therapist; should she be more than that?'

'If you really need to hear me say yes to that before you talk to Tina, then my answer would have to be no!'

Martin flinched inwardly. That was a silly question and he got the response he deserved. What was clearly "emerging" from all these therapy sessions he was having, whether alternative or not, was an appreciation of his own lack of self esteem. But Timles was continuing his questioning.

'Anyone else on the horizon?'

'Only my mysterious psychotherapist, Anne.'

'Are you attracted by her?'

'In a way, yes, she seems to be a particularly warm and sympathetic woman, but she's made it clear on her InterconNet profile that she's offering counselling, not cuddles. Besides I don't even know her real name or what she looks like.'

'I wouldn't take anything a therapist says early on in a consultation as cast in stone, Martin. Did you know that a surprisingly high number of therapeutic relationships end up as personal ones. Sometimes the therapist initiates an affair, sometimes the patient, but quite often the nature of the relationship changes by unspoken agreement on both sides.'

'Are you hinting that I should seek a personal relationship with a therapist?'

'Anne and Tina are both therapists; you haven't mentioned anyone else.'

'Or are you counselling me to look elsewhere?' Martin didn't think it appropriate to mention Tuula.

'What do *you* think you should do now?'

Martin thought his question would be thrown back at him. But he saw that without telling him what to do, Timles had nudged him to this point but was not going to be drawn further. Even though one of the people they were talking about was his own daughter. Once again Martin found himself admiring the calm, analytical nature of the Woodlands owner. Shaking himself out of his reflections to speak he replied carefully:

'I have to make decisions about my own future here. I should decide what I want from my life and what I have to offer in a relationship.'

'And perhaps whether that could be professional as well as personal some day! Sounds like a plan. Now let's progress in your career at the Woodlands. Are you going to stay with us, whether our health network venture flies or flops? Tina likes your *LIFELINES* name for it, by the way.'

Martin had no difficulty with this question.

'Oh yes - I always worried that I might be shown the door!'

'Good. Now back to physiotherapy. I understand new physio gear is on order for you. We'll need new promotional material for your service. And also to prioritise appointment of an assistant physio - you're going to be busy with additional responsibilities as we discussed yesterday. Are you sure you're up for all this?'

Martin knew he needed to give a firm response.

'Absolutely.'

'Excellent. So our last session will be a review of your progress. As before, let's leave the date for that open.'

Timles was getting up to move on to his next task and held out his hand. From his parting expression, he had caught Martin's uncertainty.

'Build a bright present for yourself now and don't waste too much energy constructing a dark future. Remember what Shakespeare wrote in Hamlet? *We know what we are, but know not what we may be.* Good Luck Martin!'

CHAPTER SEVENTEEN
Martin

Martin intended to finish Timles's and Tina's book after he returned to his flat that evening. The more he read, the easier it was to see the potential of the proposed *LIFELINES* project. Pete's InterconNet programme discovered associations between people. *LIFELINES* would learn to link dis - ease, as he was now learning to call it, with appropriate therapies and, of course, therapists. Like InterconNet, the power of programme would continue to develop with use. Pete and Chris called this "deep learning". In principle, with enough users—patients and professionals—it might improve until it could outperform the most outstanding practitioners in every field of medicine. The idea of software becoming "super intelligent" was mind-blowing. Quite literally. He could scarcely believe that such revolutionary thinking had been taking place at the Centre.

He had dismissed the work of his fellow therapists as little better than magic. A week went by before Martin called at Noura's office. It was the holiday season and had been a very slack time for physio consultations. Noura had taken some rare leave. But at least he had used the opportunity to start the ball rolling with the warden at his father's sheltered accommodation. When he finally knocked on Noura's office, he had decided to raise the subject of a physiotherapy assistant appointment. But the afternoon was free of bookings and he wondered just what an extra pair of hands would be doing.

'I'm not very busy at the moment, Noura.' he began. Noura cut him short rather sharply.

'Well, any time *you* have free, Martin, I could certainly use some help myself.'

'I meant I'm not sure whether there would be enough work for a physiotherapy assistant at present.'

'Martin, by all accounts you will be kept busy explaining the boss's new schemes to the rest of us, equipping your new physiotherapy suite and training a successful applicant; if we can find one that is.'

'Is that likely to be a problem?'

'Well it has taken on average three months to find and induct other staff here. The short answer to your question is that until I see the specification for your assistant, I really couldn't say how long it might take. But the long answer is "indefinitely" unless we get moving with an advert.'

'Have you any recent examples of advertised Centre positions I could look at?' Martin was thinking about Tina's unfilled post at the Centre.

'Yes, but it would confuse more than help for you to look at them.'

'What about my own position here?'

'That advert's out of date now, but we do have a copy. Look, why don't you write down the key attributes you feel are essential for the position and I'll take it from there. I'll check with you first, of course, before we place it in the local paper and the specialist press. There's one important matter you should be aware of though. Your assistant here will not be under contract to the Centre. He or she will be sub contracted by *you*. That way I'm sure you will make certain who ever is appointed will earn their keep!' Martin managed somehow to combine a look of surprise and terror in a single expression. Noura half smiled at his evident discomfort, but then offered some reassurance.

'Don't worry, you'll be able to charge the expense against our new budget; although funds are not in place yet.' Noura's expression instantly became more serious at the thought of the looming annual accounts.

'So you will want to catch up on employer responsibilities.' She followed this remark by sliding a substantial booklet across the desk.

'Some bedtime reading for you.' Her half smile re-instated itself.

'Now just drop off your wish list for your physiotherapy assistant's skills and qualifications and I'll draft an advert. Do make it brief; advertising is expensive. Rambling descriptions actually make applicants wonder if their potential employer knows what it is they are looking for.' Noura's raised eyebrows signalled that their meeting was over. Martin nodded gloomily and got to his feet. After closing her door he moved thoughtfully to his own office. Tina had finally been in touch by email to make an arrangement to meet. Her message was short. She invited him to phone her when he was free at work. For a long moment he sat at his desk thinking, then he reached for his mobile, found Tina's number and called her.

'Hello?'

'It's me; I mean it's Martin. Sorry I was slow getting back to you. I had appointments with Timles. I'm still in the dark about why you never said he was your father. Especially when I was sharing so much about *myself* with him.'

'Well Martin, I didn't think it appropriate to admit our relationship when you were sharing quite a bit of *yourself* with me.' He was treated to an amused giggle. Martin moved the phone away from his head and took a deep breath.

'Would you like to meet up? I mean I'm free Saturday evening. How about dinner?'

'Social or psychological?'

'The dinner?'

'No, the meeting up.' The penny finally dropped for Martin. He didn't want a session that evening, Reiki or otherwise.

'Let's make it social on this occasion.'

'But we *can* discuss our work and worries if we want?'

'I think that's inevitable.'

'You've visited my place; what about me coming over to you. We can have a good chat in surroundings where perhaps you'll feel less threatened!'

'It's not very tidy!'

'I'm coming to see you, not buy your flat. Look if you don't feel up to cooking at short notice, get in some wine and I'll bring a takeaway. Does spicy food give you any problems?'

'No and the answer to the first question is yes.' Tina laughed again.

'Wait a moment while I work that reply out. OK got it. Now Martin where do you live and what time?' Martin gave Tina details how to reach his own flat and suggested they meet at 7pm on Saturday. He spent the rest of the afternoon in an odd frame of mind. Having someone for dinner at his flat was a first for him; well, for a long time at least. He decided to try not to worry about it; that certainly would be Tina's advice. After all that had passed between them, he should hardly be feeling as apprehensive as he was. But he couldn't say whether Tina wanted to be his girlfriend or his guru. To distract himself from thinking about what he was going to say to her, he logged onto his new computer and searched the Web for recommended wines to go with meals containing chilli. This was inconclusive. The most common recommendation was that the wine should be red. But even then only three quarters of reviewers agreed.

On impulse he switched from this frustrating search to looking for ads for physiotherapy assistant posts. This proved to be much more successful. From this he was able to make a list of must-have attributes and get an impression of pay levels. After a quick exercise of copying from websites and pasting text into his own summary, he emailed Noura, marvelling at his new facility with the computer. Having nothing else to do, he watched his wall clock. This was not a good move. It seemed to slow almost to a standstill. Eventually it limped to 5:30pm.

Martin locked his office and left to head for the nearby supermarket. Noura passed him in reception on her own way out and acknowledged his emailed job description. Julie was struggling with her short and rather tight fur-trimmed outdoor coat. She was astonished when Martin stopped and helped her settle it round her shoulders and gave her a chaste peck on the cheek.

'Have a good time this evening, Julie.' Wide-eyed with surprise, she thanked him, whilst anxiously scanning the entrance area for any sign of husband George. If he spotted them together, she *wouldn't* have a good time that evening or for the next few days either.

****

Late Saturday afternoon, Martin busied himself around his flat, trying to see the rooms from the viewpoint of a visitor and making what he thought were suitable adjustments. This mostly involved hiding clutter in cupboards and a wardrobe. The task had to be abandoned when it was nearly time for his guest to arrive. He collected glasses, plates and cutlery and opened a South African Pinotage. This was recommended by the assistant in the wine shop, without any recourse to the Web. The entrance intercom coughed into life and Martin released the street door. Minutes later, Tina was sitting with a glass of red wine leaving Martin to unpack a generous double Balti and accompanying side dishes in his small kitchen. When he joined her with his own drink he was only too aware of the difference in size and quality of their two flats. He anxiously followed her gaze as she took in the surroundings.

'Not as well appointed as your place, I'm afraid.'

'Don't be. What's that singing I can hear Martin?'

Martin hadn't been aware of any sound, but now Tina drew his attention to it, he realised that it was his musical balcony. A Westerly wind must have increased in strength above the threshold where the balcony gave voice. He recalled Tuula's suggestion that he could block the hollow railings with wax, which he'd failed to follow up. The singing railings were in some sense a fortunate opportunity. It gave him a story to tell. Irritating for him to recall, but amusing for his guest to hear. After explaining, Martin got up.

'Can't change the weather, but I can change the track.' Martin put a CD with a selection of New Age music on his player, reasoning that this would suit an alternative therapist. He turned the volume up to a comfortable level that masked the plaintive notes outside. Tina smiled then asked:

'If you can point me to some plates, I'll dish up.' Martin made to rise, then sat back down.

'OK. Thanks Tina. They're keeping warm in the oven.' They both ate in silence for a moment, enjoying the bite of the spiced meat. Then Tina put down her fork and sat back with a second glass of Pinotage.

'You must have been disappointed with me. Having worked hard to at least get you to connect with alternative therapy, what I do? I abandon you and fail to keep in touch.' Martin was anxious to reassure her and suddenly recalled Tina's first Reiki lesson - *Honour your relatives and those close to you*

'I'm not at all disappointed. I admire what you've being doing for your sister. How is she by the way?'

'Almost back to normal now. Although I haven't been in contact with you all these weeks, I do hear what's being going on at the Woodlands. My father has kept in touch with me.'

'About that. I had no idea my boss was your father! He never mentioned that, even when he encouraged me to see you. While seeing *him*, I've been pretty open about what you've been doing with me. Even though your father has never even seemed surprised, it was really embarrassing.'

'Only Noura at the Centre knew our relationship. We've kept it a secret for all kinds of reasons; until now that is.' Tina nodded at the book which Martin had left prominently on the coffee table. She hesitated a moment.

'From what I'm hearing and seeing, it appears that you've become more like the "old Martin" who joined the Woodlands shortly after it opened.'

'A lot's happened since that last session we had.'

'Yes; I imagine that must have left you pretty confused and I couldn't offer a follow up because of my going off to Sheffield.'

'I *was* confused; I'm still trying find an answer.'

'Well, here I am at last. Ask me.' Now it was Martin's turn to hesitate.

'Did you offer me all that emotional support and that very *sensual* experience because that's just what you do in your new work, or...' Tina prompted him gently when he hesitated again.

'Or what, Mart?' He had to say it, but the words were tricky to put together.

'Or was it because you'd like a relationship with me?'

'Couldn't it be a bit of both?'

'So you do like me?'

'Yes Martin, I had hoped that would be obvious by now. But there's still something missing from this exchange.'

'You mean do I like you? Yes, I do; very much. I never really paid much attention to you; or to any of the other alternative therapy staff at the Woodlands for that matter. As you know I was at a pretty low ebb and I wasn't really thinking about another relationship. Now things are changing and I think what you have done for me has contributed to that. But shortly after we started talking to each other, I became a patient and you my therapist. That's a different type of relationship. It's professional rather than personal.'

'Haven't you ever been tempted to seek a personal relationship with one of your patients? All those young sportswomen with ideal figures?' Martin reflected on this for a moment. The tension had eased now that he had finally said what he had been thinking and he felt more relaxed.

'I only once ever felt aroused whilst massaging a female patient. Mind you I only treated this patient once.'

'Who was that?'

'Pixie Small!' Tina smiled.

'Didn't you realise that I could sense that while you worked on me?'

'I'm embarrassed to hear you say it.' Tina looked serious again. But we've both had broken relationships. You've told me a lot about yours. After mine I felt rather the same as you. I rejected the idea of getting close to someone else; becoming vulnerable and dependent. Instead I focused on building my career and as you have seen and heard, that's going very well. And I'm really excited about the work I've done with my father and I desperately want to see his vision succeed. Although I don't think he accepts how much resistance his grand idea is going to meet. I know he'll continue to need my help and support.'

'So you're *not* looking for a relationship then?' Tina looked searchingly at Martin.

'I *know* what I want, but I don't know if it will prove possible. I work alone, from my flat. It's not an ideal arrangement and it's difficult to expand my business or even to be consistently available to my clients. I'd like a partner to come in with me. Another therapist; a male one. Learn some of the things I do; maybe teach me some of the things they do.'

'But what *do* you do Tina and how would someone working with you help?'

'Well. You've read my chapter in the book my father and I produced. What do you think?' The evening had already moved from the social to the psychological. All the same, Martin collected his thoughts to construct a sensible response.

'You offer an holistic approach: reuniting the mind and body which have been treated separately for too long. That's the deliberate or unconscious aim of many types of alternative medicine including Reiki. You deal with the *mind* in your future therapeutic business and so I imagine you might like to work with someone skilled in working with the body. Someone also with a strong belief in complementary medicine.' Tina looked very pleased with this analysis.

'That's me nicely summed up. There are many more people ill at ease with themselves or their bodies than there are people with back pain or tennis elbow. More women than men I find, but plenty of both sexes.' Martin needed to bring their conversation back from the general to the personal.

'When you offered to help me, you decided I needed to work on establishing a more emotional than sexual connection with women? That's why your treatment designed for me was so sensual?'

'If you want to find and keep a relationship that will be mutually satisfying for a very long time, yes. You were switched off to both patients and staff at work and that was my *own* experience of you. And *you* told me that your relationships were either fleeting or unsatisfactory. Sensuality creates a bond that outlasts lust. My treatment was aimed to highlight some sensual opportunities between a man and a woman.'

'Why all the elaborate audiovisual stuff in your treatment room?'

'Many people have difficulty forming mental pictures or are completely unable to visualise. Rather than hoping they have the image I want them to have in their heads, how much more effective for me to immerse them in an appropriate environment during treatment? In some cases, that might *be* the treatment. As Marshall McLuhan once said; the medium *is* the message.

'You enjoyed your trip to the seaside, didn't you?' Much more vivid than me saying "shut your eyes and imagine you're with a girl on a deserted private beach".' Tina gave him one of her wicked grins. Martin didn't have much difficulty visualising *that*. Her words triggered an image in his mind. But it wasn't Tina in the darkness of her treatment room; it was Tuula in the evening sand dunes at Studland. That was lust and no mistake and it was now absolutely clear *that* wasn't going to last. But he and Tina seemed to be talking in circles round each other without getting to the real point. He asked awkwardly:

'Would your potential life partner get involved in that sort of thing?'

'Oh yes. I think at least as many women as men have a worrying disconnect between their perceived and actual personal needs. Frequently that missing link is sensual or even sexual, I'm not really the right sex to help. You wouldn't have wanted to play that little scenario on my imaginary beach with a bloke now would you?'

'So where does your *emotional* partner choice come in, Tina?' She looked down at her hands resting on the table and slid her fingers apart slightly. There was no jewellery on either hand and her nails were similarly unadorned. Then she looked up seeking Martin's eyes with her own. Martin was struck once again by the curious ring of dark grey pigmentation surrounding her lighter irises. Tina interrupted his thoughts. She spoke quite slowly and thoughtfully, looking directly at him.

'I'd prefer a personal relationship to grow out of shared objectives rather than, as for most people, arising first of all out of lust or just a need not to live alone.' Tina hesitated a moment and, seeing his pained expression, caught Martin's hand. He was getting used to this gesture from his female contacts.

'But I'm certainly *capable* of feeling those things, Martin. And I was feeling all of them when I sent you that last text.' Martin remembered he had been very slow to reply to her.

'I'm so sorry that it took me so long to get back to you, Tina. My phone normally should have been on.'

'But you're here now.' Tina was still holding his hand. Martin hesitated. The normal "rules of life" stated that he should gather Tina up in his arms and, if that felt right look into her eyes at point blank range to see whether a passionate kiss would be appropriate. But Tina had thrown an oddly shaped spanner into the usual workings. She seemed to want a business partner first and a lover second. The spanner was an odd shape because most people started off with *one* of these kinds of partnership; the other one developing later. Or not. Tina was looking for the full deal up front. Martin decided that a hug was indicated, but not urgent oral contact. After that it was time for him to speak his own mind. Holding Tina gently and looking over her shoulder, he was quiet for a moment, then:

'Your father has made a very attractive proposal. He's already offered me more space at the Centre, an assistant and an enhanced profile as a physio. But he also wants me to contribute actively to this vision of a joined-up future for health care. He and of course you, Tina, have revolutionised my view of complementary medicine. Right now I can't see myself giving up my work at Woodlands. In a way I feel like it's only just starting. It's given me a purpose which you and just about everybody else I've talked with recently has told me I lacked. But I don't need to tell you that as a therapist I admire you and as a woman you affect me deeply.'

'Whatever you think I already know, I still need to hear from you, Martin.' Martin hesitated. He thought hard. *Why did this have to be so complicated?*

'I'd like to take you out. Do some fun stuff. See how we get on together doing ordinary everyday things. Our relationship at present is still therapist and patient. I need to spend some quality time with *Tina*. At work it's all change and I still have only a hazy idea how things will turn out there. Soon I may be able to see the "Woodlands from the trees".' He paused, not looking directly at her, but hoping that Tina was smiling at his little play on words.

'Does that sound like I'm dodging the question?' As he asked this, Martin looked anxious. He was still holding Tina and she easily sensed his anxiety. She gently pushed him away and kissed him lightly.

'Well if you are, you're an artful dodger. Maybe I *have* met my match!' Tina chose her words to try and shrink the distance created by those "patient and therapist" labels. Martin tried to follow her lead.

'Well, I do feel confident that I'm at least as good as you at fixing backs.' The tension had gone out of their conversation. Both of them concentrated hard on just being Martin and Tina; on being who they were rather than what they both did. This unstated arrangement worked well enough and the rest of the evening passed pleasantly. Martin talked about his efforts to make peace with his estranged father after their long and hostile silence. In this he found an opportunity to praise Tina's father.

'It all worked out very well. Your father was the catalyst. I don't think I'd ever have got in touch without his encouragement. The warden of his sheltered accommodation in Beaconsfield has been wonderful. He arranged everything for me and has recommended a great care home for dad. He even came along with me on my first visit there. Dad's become very frail these last months. That has been a big factor in easing our previous stand off. Once dad is settled in to his new home, we've agreed I'll visit him some weekends; Beaconsfield's not a bad run up the M4 from here.' Tina then spoke about her time in Sheffield.

'Being mum to two lively and very demanding children was a world away from my life here. I was hardly in contact with anyone back in Tamford because every minute of the day seemed to be occupied with writing lists, coping with an unfamiliar household, transporting children, shopping, catering, cleaning and hospital visits. If everyone had the opportunity to try *that* out before they were committed to it, the birth rate in this country would drop like a stone!' In that almost subconscious way people tick boxes when considering a relationship with someone, Martin was pleased to hear this. Right now he didn't relish the prospect of infants. Half the patients he saw on a regular basis gave unsolicited reports of the problems they faced with their offspring. These ranged from financial to physical, but the biggest issue appeared to be the strain it put on their personal relationships; where these had survived at all, that is.

'Are you back in Tamford permanently now, Tina?'

'Yes, but tomorrow I'm returning to Sheffield for a while. My sister is going back for her assessment and then we're going out for a small celebration at the weekend. Then I'm travelling to see mum in Mansfield before returning to try and pick up where I left off here.'

'So your parents are separated?'

'Divorced. That was a long time ago now, but we all keep in touch.' Eventually Tina made her apologies.

'Well I must go and pack for my trip tomorrow. Thanks for having me and listening to me going on alarmingly about my hopes and dreams. Now you'll be thinking what a complicated person I am. "Like father, like daughter"; that sort of thing.'

'I think I have the edge when it comes to talking about my problem life and loves, Tina. I'm grateful for your sympathetic ears.'

'Goodnight Martin.' She gave him a chaste kiss.

'I'll text you when I get back.'

CHAPTER EIGHTEEN
Everyone

It was a rare moment at the Royal British Pharmaceutical Society Soirée. All round the banqueting hall, the great and the good from the Pharmaceutical Industry and many representatives from small pharmaceutical and biotechnology companies were all on their feet to give their speaker a standing ovation. That was even more remarkable, considering the quantities of wine that had been consumed with the evening meal.

The convener, Sir James White of University College London, still beaming and applauding, took the speaker's place at the lectern and waited for the applause and scraping of dining chairs to settle down.

'I'm certain there will be many questions for our speaker. But in view of the lateness of the hour, I'm proposing we defer questions until after tomorrow's morning session. For those of you who have burning issues to discuss we have arranged a late bar in the Galton room which is open now. For those leaving tonight, if you haven't already purchased a copy of our speaker's book, you just need to mark the appropriate place on the attendance form available in reception on your way out. Or just place your order on-line direct with the distributors. The address is on your programmes. I can imagine some of you will be wanting multiple copies for other board members.'

At this remark there was a single burst of applause from the floor. Sir James turned to his guest speaker and beamed.

'You didn't tell me you had sneaked in your publisher this evening!'

There was good natured general laughter at this closing quip and many heads turned to locate the individual mentioned. Sir James took the opportunity of this upbeat moment to usher his guest off the speaker's platform and into the small room directly off the banqueting hall. There were various beverages and some nibbles on a table in front of an ornate fireplace.

Sir James closed the door behind them and turned to his guest.

'It's just us here Michael - no microphones either. Wanted a private word in your ear. Pharm. Soc. President asked to meet you after your talk, so I'm in trouble there, but we'll give him some time tomorrow.'

Sir James motioned his guest towards the refreshments.

'I'm sure you're in need of a drink after that marathon session, Michael. Please help yourself while we chat.'

Michael Timles raised both hands in a warding off gesture.

'Really, I'm fine Jim. I ate a late lunch in my hotel. I didn't want to talk on a full stomach in front of such illustrious company. I have to admit though, the fare at the Radisson didn't compare with the menu you laid on tonight. By the way, I haven't had time to thank you for giving me the opportunity to speak this evening.'

'For pity's sake dear chap. The only thanks due are mine! I had thought you'd disappeared off the map altogether, Michael. I've really missed your contributions at previous gatherings. Your ability to find a path through the social, ethical and legal swamps has been sorely missed ever since. But I see now that your time in the alternative wilderness, if you'll forgive that crude remark, has been far from wasted. Now here you're at the top of your game with something revolutionary.'

'You really think that?'

'No doubt at all, Michael. When I noticed your name in the *Med Pharm Reviews* I had a quick look for old times sake. I'd not have sent for the book had the reviewer, whom I respect highly, not been foaming at the mouth with praise for the work. I had a late cancellation from our scheduled speaker tonight, but that turned out to be a real blessing in disguise.'

'I think you're too kind. What Tina and I have published will make us some important enemies.'

'But many more friends than enemies, dear chap. Once this hits the popular press, Pharma will be selling more pills to the substantial alternative market and many more complementary practitioners will find good positions in the NHS and Biotech. What's not to like, as I believe we have to say nowadays.'

'But we've got our sights set on health care reform across the board, Jim.'

Sir James managed to smile, frown and shake his head slowly all at the same time.

'You know Michael, one of the things I like best about you is your idealism. But I'm sure they warned you that you'd never be wealthy holding on to ideals. Had to shed most of mine to get where I am today. Only good thing about that is that having got here, I can see where true progress lies and do my bit to nudge the capitalists and bean counters in that direction. Look, may I give you a bit of advice, Michael?'

'Could I stop you even if I wanted to?'

'Take it easy Michael. Don't go for the establishment jugular too soon. As you rightly say, you'll make enough enemies with just this first step. You've my backing, but I'm not big enough. Get some of the head honchos that were here to night batting for you and a handful of senior people in the Department of Health. Once the media have got their fangs into this, see if you can't get into No.10 to talk to the PM some time. Jamie Oliver has managed it on school meals.'

'Yes, and I suppose he's *also* in the business of keeping us healthy and happy, Jim.'

'Ha Ha. Well said. You see we need someone like yourself to lift us at our gatherings. At present it's all doom and gloom. Pharma pipelines running dry, orphan drugs going unfunded, medicine's future dependent on individually tailored drugs which are too expensive to develop; antibiotics Armageddon approaching. Come back to us, Michael. You know in the Bible, they forgave their prodigal son.'

'And killed the fatted calf for him? I'll bear that thought in mind. I expect you'll need to press the flesh in the Galton bar, Jim, and I need to rest up now. You've given the wolves 12 hours to think of objections to what I propose; I'll need a clear head for my question time tomorrow.'

'Goodnight Michael.'

' 'night Jim. And I won't forget your advice. Thanks for that.'

Peter

Steve, the graduate student who shared Peter Swales's office shut down his computer for the evening and stood up stiffly.

'Coming for a jar Pete?' he asked from the doorway. Peter looked up and shook his head. In addition to delayed Ph.D. thesis work he had a web demo to programme for his brother in Ireland.

'Not tonight; lots to catch up on.' Peter narrowed his eyes, his computer mouse still negotiating his desktop.

'You know Steve, you ought to see someone about that back of yours. I've a contact who could help.' Steve shook his head and turned into the corridor.

'Can't afford it mate.' Peter sat on as the dusk fell outside. He was programming the tablet website for his brother in Ireland; software that would help pay his course fees. The room was dimly lit by the computer monitor. Waiting for a download to complete, he stared moodily out of the window at a border of hardy shrubs swaying in gusts of wind. He tried to concentrate on coding, but his thoughts kept being distracted by a much tougher challenge. How could he keep InterconNet out of the clutches of Jim Overbeck of ThreeLs.

Outside, a couple were sitting together on a low wall; the male's face hidden by his girlfriend's long hair and gently flapping scarf. Others were walking past the window as the path lamps came on, throwing large, fuzzy shadows onto the wall behind him. The easy companionship of the passers-by and the couple's obvious signs of intimacy were unsettling. He'd so far avoided starting a relationship, although that would be relatively easy with so many young unattached people living and working together. As a postgraduate student, academic success here was too important to risk major distraction of that kind.

But he was none the less frustrated. Annoyed by his supervisor pulling rank although he was only a few years older than Peter. Angry about his keeping him in the dark about the exciting option to apply of his research work at Martin's Centre. Irritated that they were up against a seemingly impregnable wall called Jim Overbeck for the commercial application of his programme. Sexually frustrated because the women undergraduates or postgraduates here would, perhaps rightly, make demands on him he had neither the time nor the funds to afford. Bored with coding and creating the hundreds of Web graphics needed to simulate his brother's tablet, he decided to sort out his email. His in box had become bloated whilst he was away and he'd put off going back through older messages. There would be a lot of junk, but sometimes it was spicy junk and he could do with a laugh right now.

Deleting out-of-date departmental memos and unsolicited marketing he stopped suddenly at a message from Tuula Pipi. Intrigued, he opened it.

> From: Tuula Pipi
> To: Pete Swales
> Subject: We must talk about Social Media.
> Pete, A topic of mutual interest to you, me and my director at Kosketecessa has come up. Let me know as soon as you're free.
> Tuula

Peter thought: *Now there's a spicy email and no mistake* He replied:

> From: Pete Swales
> To: Tuula Pipi
> Subject: Re: We must talk about Social Media
> Hi Tuula. Sounds intriguing. Am available to talk to a fellow EU member at any time of the day - or night!
> Do you want to meet in the bar sometime or is this a confidential chat?
> Pete

Although her email was a week old, he received an almost immediate reply. Peter thought:

No doubt she carries a high-end Kosketecessa phone about her person 24/7

> From: Tuula Pipi
> To: Pete Swales
> Subject: Re: Re: We must talk about Social Media
> Pete! Where have you been? This is getting urgent. Can you come over right now? Room C32 Block C, Earley Hall. Door code 3178; but it's rarely locked. And bring a bottle; this could be a long session.
> Tuula

He replied he was on his way. It wasn't particularly hard to decide to suspend his work on Simon's website, with the prospect of such lively female company; one that was unlikely to make any emotional demands. Peter unlocked his file drawer, dragged the suspension file holders towards him and fished out his bottle of Laphroaig. It was half empty; the residue of a number of late nights in the Computer Centre. But a North Scandinavian was unlikely to object to that. It was a quality spirit. He pulled the office door shut, left the building and headed for the halls of residence.

Noura

Noura sat in the Italian restaurant at a table for two and studied the menu and wine list for the third time. She'd already decided what she wanted, but was now making further selections and ranking these in order of appeal. That way she could avoid delay if her preference happened to be unavailable. It would also allow her to change her mind if necessary to complement whatever her date chose. Except he hadn't turned up. He was now late even by normal considerations of unavoidable delay, let alone Noura Munday's meagre allowance for lack of punctuality. The glances of the passing waiters were becoming less discreet.

The restaurant was well regarded and was now full; *il patrone* was forced to turn away speculative diners and Noura had not missed his quick glance at her half empty table as he commiserated with a young couple at the door. She hailed one of the Italian staff and ordered a glass of Lambrusco. It arrived very promptly accompanied by a glass of bread sticks. The man gave her a sympathetic smile. He knew all about this situation where he came from. *Il suo amante non era arrivato.* Now that she had at least made a token order, the waiters stopped staring as they passed her table.

Noura had met her date on-line and they had been corresponding for a while now. On her recent holiday with a long term married girlfriend of hers, she had listened late into the evening to her friend waxing lyrical about on-line dating. Noura at first thought she was just repeating some editorial feature from one of *those* women's magazines. But her friend suddenly made this personal. By choosing an up market dating site, Jean said she had met some wonderfully romantic and considerate men.

Noura was astonished by this frank admission. She had no idea that her friend's marriage had failed, even though her last vacation had been with her and not her husband. Shocked at casual way her friend admitted dating other men, but also privately intrigued, Noura asked for more details. Hadn't Jean encountered some damaged individuals? Surely her success rate must have been low and her on-line dates burdened with all kinds of unfortunate baggage? Jean had just laughed.

'Oh they're all on their best behaviour you know. Of course if you want a bit of sex, you have to make that quite clear in advance; they're unlikely to take advantage of you. Most are happy with a warm cuddle after the theatre or a restaurant.'

Noura was incredulous. She told her friend that was not what *she* had heard about on-line dating. People had reported it was fraught with danger and that it was not even possible to be sure what age or even sex your date was until you met them. How could it be that her companion's dating experience was so consistent?

'Well my dear, all the men are *married* you see. So they're mostly well trained and know what pleases women and what turns them off.' Noura was astounded by this revelation.

'Surely the fact that they are blatantly having affairs means none of them can be trusted. Don't their wives know?'

'Oh yes, Noura, their wives *recommend* them. The men can't get listed on the site without the agreement of their spouses.'

Noura was rendered speechless, so her friend continued to explain.

'You see their wives are on the dating site as well; they have their own section.'

The penny dropped.

'So basically, it's a partner swapping site?'

'Exactly and it works brilliantly.'

'Except if you're single.'

Her companion suddenly looked sympathetic.

'Yes, that's the downside.'

She was quiet for a moment, then a thought occurred to her.

'If you're interested in the website Noura, you could always get married first.'

Noura didn't answer this. Her friend was good company on trips and outings, but not one of the brightest stars in the firmament.

Needless to say Noura didn't investigate her friend's website, but did sign up with an established site of impeccable repute. She had gone through all the preliminaries and exchanged messages with a most suitable sounding gentleman. This had progressed to an exchange of *real* letters and finally a phone call. The voice on the other end had not disappointed; it was neither female, nor too young or too old. They had agreed to meet for dinner. And now; nothing.

A continuous blanket of sound from the conversations and clatter of other diners wrapped around her. But as she stared at the empty place setting opposite, it seemed as if the restaurant was deserted apart from the waiters walking up and down. Waiting patiently. Like her. After she drained her Lambrusco and nibbled half-heartedly at a bread stick, she put a £10 note on the table, gathered her bag and coat and left. A few moments later, a well dressed, red-faced man, breathing heavily from some unknown exertion entered the restaurant alone. He looked wildly round, then appealed to one of the waiters. The waiter listened patiently, then shook his head, gave a sad smile, raised his shoulders and lifted both arms, palms facing upwards. The Italian waiter spoke English well, but no words were necessary, his gesture was eloquent in itself.

Peter & Tuula

The security lighting brightened as Peter headed along the 3rd floor corridor in residential block C. The door to Room 32 was ajar. He knocked tentatively and a muffled voice called out:

'Pete?' He confirmed that it was he.

'Come in; I'm in the bathroom. I'll be right with you.' The study bedroom was dark apart from a desk lamp and a blue-white glow from an open laptop. He closed the door and looked around curiously. The room was a carbon copy of his own except that it was depersonalised; no cosmetics, hunk posters or furry toys. Nothing to suggest female occupancy; the few items visible were strictly functional and logically arranged. Water stopped running in the small en suite and Tuula emerged. It was getting late and Peter half wondered if this disturbing Finn would appear in nightwear, but she was dressed in tired looking jeans and a university tee shirt. Of course, to Peter her casual dress was irrelevant. Her athletic figure, short, bobbed almost white hair, wide blue eyes and full red lips would inevitably make her a fantasy female to most young men.

'Pete. Glad you've come over at last. What kept you?' Glancing at the bottle he was carrying, she pulled out a pair of glasses from the wardrobe and a bottle of some kind of mineral water. She waved him to the single easy chair.

'Take a pew.' While Tuula poured the drinks, Peter wondered, not for the first time, whether her occasional old fashioned sayings were still taught in Finnish schools. When the drinks were installed on the coffee table, she turned her bucket desk chair round to face him. Peter reached for the whiskey but Tuula restrained his hand.

'Not yet - later. We need clear heads at the moment.' Intrigued the phrase "at the moment", Peter sat back in his chair.

'How can I help, Tuula?' Tuula studied him for a moment through half closed lids. The effect of this on Peter was probably neither what she intended nor what he expected; she suddenly reached into her desk draw and produced a pair of stapled A4 sheets.

'I'm going to fast track this discussion. I think the research you're doing could help me. And maybe I can help you in return.' Peter thought: *right now the only help I need is cash, but I'll accept kind for now if it happens to be offered.* Tuula tossed the printed sheets onto the coffee table.

'I'm going to take you into my, or rather my company's confidence. And I also need to ask you about your unpublished work. Please read through these agreements first. I'm hoping you can sign, if you agree, without involving Chris. Things would get complicated if we have to bring in academic staff, because then it would go through the Uni legal people and I don't want that.' Peter felt a pang of disappointment. Being called at night to bring a bottle of booze to Tuula's study bedroom had given him a premonition of cosy intimacy. It now sounded like a business meeting. He glanced at her single bed beside him. He was never very comfortable with formal occasions and this present juxtaposition of bed and business was unsettling. Oh well, if she wanted him to be formal, he could oblige.

'You *have* surprised me, Tuula. But then I've always found you a surprising woman.' was all he managed to say as he picked up his copy to read.

'Less of the "lady" Pete, just read the agreement.'

Timles

After finishing his complementary drink in the buffet car, Timles returned to his seat in first class. The train was rocking slightly around a steep bend in the track and he had to steady himself against the corridor as he walked. He glanced at the receipt still clutched in the hand pressed against the glass while the carriage swaying subsided. He wouldn't be charging The Woodlands Centre for this trip. Noura was already fretting about the new and greatly increased recurrent and capital costs. It was typical of the organisation that had invited his contribution to the recent conference that they didn't offer expenses. Big Pharma covered the costs of most of the other speakers and delegates; many of whom had their own accommodation in London anyway.

Still swaying slightly as he regained his seat, he looked out at the dark fields and occasional patches of light flashing by the carriage windows. Why, he wondered, was he starting this crusade to mend a fragmented medical establishment in his sixties? Although at the banquet the night before Sir James White had offered him encouragement, it was to join their talking shop, not to become an alternative activist or worse, a medical militant. Sir James's expression belied his advice. His face said: *Don't go down that path, Michael. It's stony and you could easily twist an ankle. You should be feathering your nest now for a comfortable retirement. Vent your spleen if necessary at the Association meetings and then we'll all make up over dinner and round off the evening with a distinguished port.*

He had languished too long in the wings, building his business and dealing with the minutiae of day to day tasks. Now he wanted to go on stage and face the public. He had a vision of how things could be so much better in the public health arena. As Sir James had warned, it was no use appealing to Big Pharma. Right now these hard headed businesses would see his ideas as speculative; unproven. And their core business was drugs not dreams.

But it was also no use, as Sir James had suggested, going to the top, to cabinet level to get this done. They had too much on their plate right now and would only put real money behind things that would clearly advance their political agenda. With a general election due within two years, his ideas would be seen as too dangerous at this stage in the political cycle. And unless ignoring a new development or idea would cause public outrage, it could safely be shelved. If it stood the test of time or could sway voting statistics; perhaps. Otherwise it could be safely buried under the weight of other more pressing legislation.

No, this had to be achieved working from the bottom up. His new book would cause a stir in the profession, get the academics talking and appear in the columns of the quality press. But it would only cause minor ripples on the surface of wider society, which would soon die away. *Social media* was the way to go now. He needed to get their own version of InterconNet up and running and he needed a new name. Names were important. Choose the right one and it would be on the tip of everyone's tongue. Look at Face Book, Google and Twitter.

He needed someone who wasn't so close to the project. Martin's suggestion of *LIFELINES* was inspired, but would it really catch on with its eventual user community? It was then that the solution presented itself, the book was published, the lectures given. His ideas were finally out in the public domain. He would ask the growing InterconNet community *itself* whether *LIFELINES* was the answer or could they suggest an even more compelling name. With that Eureka moment ringing in his brain, Timles set his phone alarm to ring just before the scheduled arrival in Tamford, gave way to tiredness and dozed in his seat.

Peter & Tuula

Peter reached the end of the document Tuula had given him. At the bottom both their names were printed with underlines for signatures. The agreement was short and to the point. It simply stated that the fact of the conversation they were presumably about to have would not be divulged to anyone else; that information that was not already in the public domain would not be communicated to anyone else without either parties' prior agreement.

'So all you want from me is an agreement that this is a private conversation?'

'And that any ideas which emerge from it are jointly owned. Neither of us can use them without the other's agreement.' Peter re-read the document.

'Shouldn't something like this be witnessed?'

'I'm recording our meeting.' Peter glanced up at the small camera built into her open laptop and shook his head.

'I think *I'm* going to need a drink, Tuula.'

'OK. Just a small one then.' Tuula opened the whiskey and poured him a finger's worth. He noted that she didn't fill her own glass. Martin read for a third time, then put down the agreement and shrugged.

'Can't see any problem with this.' Tuula gave him a pen and in silence they both signed and exchanged the documents for a counter signature. He noticed that Tuula gave her occupation as "Network security manager, Kosketecessa AG" It sounded very impressive. Martin sat back and sipped his spirit.

'OK, shoot. Tell me what this is all about.' Tuula leaned towards him as if this would make their exchange somehow even more confidential.

'You know my research here is in connection with social media.'

'Yes but that's about all I know.'

'Well with both phones and tablets it's now one of the major applications. A growing problem is the transmission of inappropriate content of all kinds. Everyone's aware of on-line paedophilia and fundamentalism but there's currently an increasing use by teenagers (and adults who should know better) to exchange compromising and even violent images or movies. There's also a growing number of video clips of crazy stunts uploaded to make money quickly from the the associated advertising. For the mobile manufacturers, networks and retailers this is a grey area. No one is sure whether to do something about this, what to do about it and who should be responsible. So what ends up being done is too little, too late. High level meetings go on with government and the CEOs of Google, Face book and the like, but the social network businesses don't really have an answer. Except to go *out* of business of course, and no-one wants that.

Kosketecessa wants to have in the wings an answer to all this. Things are bad right now, but at some stage there will be a succession of really terrible events, leading to a public outcry and then everyone in the business will start blaming each other. The network providers and even the device manufacturers won't be able to avoid their share of blame. It will suddenly prove very expensive indeed and my firm wants to avoid that and come out of any such crisis as the good guys.

I've worked under cover on this problem, while my research agreed with the University has been on new ways to mine social media data to improve the quality of Internet searches. As it happens, Pete, what I have *said* I'm doing here isn't so far away from what I'm *actually* doing, but I wouldn't want to spell out to the powers that be here, what I've just told you.' Peter was paying very close attention:

'Internet data mining. That's the area where I've always thought we were in competition.'

'Up to now Kosketecessa has outsourced all software development, but now they want to do this new work in house.'

'So where do I fit in?'

'Well, I have to say that my work on this problem hasn't gone very far. Obviously there's programmes out there which are pretty good at recognising stuff, but if you think of the huge variation of material which could be inappropriate for person A to send to person B, then the situation appears hopeless. A human censor could do this—they do have hundreds of such people in China—but computers are still poor at recognising patterns compared with people.' Peter's programming mind was engaged. He contributed:

'Poor, but I wouldn't say impossible. For example. it ought to be feasible to screen automatically for sexual content.' He looked hopefully for a lead from Tuula.

'Obviously InterconNet, as a special form of social network, has always interested me. I have to say I'm very impressed with its artificial intelligence capabilities and recently I have begun to think that within InterconNet there's something that could be used by the world wide networks to identify inappropriate content. Operated by them rather than built into mobile phones, of course. So I started to use InterconNet more often and got quite a few connections.'

'I wasn't surprised by that!' Tuula lowered her eyes and leaned forward a little towards Peter.

'You might be more surprised what many of these people here at the Uni wanted to exchange. Collected quite a lot of material for my research! But I had to go onto the conventional social networks in most cases to get this stuff. Your program is quite obviously learning as people sign up and use it and it's even now pretty good at inferring *appropriate* connections; Unlike the public social networks, the software is *finding* you suitable friends and even *blocking* unsuitable contacts. And each day it's getting much smarter.' Tuula paused before continuing

'I couldn't programme this and I suspect, neither can you. There has to be a shit hot neural network embedded in your programme.' She paused again, looking at Peter a little guiltily.

'Whilst you were in Ireland and your supervisor away at that conference in Sussex, I dumped out the working code from InterconNet onto my workstation. Then I made some new connections on InterconNet. Others were also using the programme and some new users signed up. After 24hours I dumped out the code again and compared the two dumps. Neither you nor Chris logged in when you were both away, but sections of the code had changed. Your software is re-writing itself, isn't it? That's why it's getting so good. Basically some part of your programme is out of your control. The neural network within InterconNet is being regularly re-written by some fiendishly clever code as people use the system. I think *that's* what I need as the basis for identifying and blocking inappropriate network content.

Tina

Tina's last client had left over two hours ago, but she felt physically and mentally drained. Stretched full length on one of her long leather sofas, she sipped her wine. She had had no idea how demanding managing two young children would be. The unfamiliar routines and responsibilities of that combined with anxiety for her sister had been exhausting. So much so that it had taken her a week before she felt able to see any of her existing clients and had had to turn down referrals from the Woodlands Centre. The experience had for now purged the occasional broody feeling she had when she watched mothers carrying or wheeling a newborn child in a pushchair.

When she returned to her flat and to her normal pattern of daily activities, the peace had been a blessing. Now she was finding the silence oppressive. All the previous week she had exulted in being free to choose, moment to moment, to do whatever she wanted. But the pleasure of this had since worn rather thin. She had all these skills to heal and help others, but was frustratingly poor at applying them to herself. She had worked intensively on developing her sensitivity to and perception of the emotional and physical needs of others. But this effort had somehow her weakened her ability to distract herself from negative thoughts or to take pleasure in what she had recently achieved; even her work with her father, Michael Timles. Their book was completed, but her life was a work in progress with some very important decisions pending.

She got up and moved over to the window and looked down at the communal garden. Partly in shadow, a couple were embracing not far from one of the garden lights. As she watched, the woman moved her head and smiled at her partner, her face suddenly entering the pool of light. Tina recognised the woman as a neighbour from an adjacent flat. She turned away abruptly, conscious that she was intruding on their privacy; the woman might notice her at the window at any moment. Apart from that, their intimacy emphasised her own sense of social isolation. Tina walked over to her kitchen to pour another glass of wine. She had to shake off this present feeling of ennui. Meditation would help, but right now, just as in her neighbours case, a man's company would be better. She sat with her wine, picked up her mobile and stared indecisively at Martin's number in the contacts list. Finally she put down her mobile. This was not the moment to call him. Tomorrow she was travelling up to her sister's in Sheffield. Planning and packing for her brief stay would take her mind off things for now.

Timles

The mobile in Timles's jacket pocket was ringing insistently. Timles started awake, sleepily expecting arrival in Tamford Central. But it was soon clear that it was a call, not the phone's alarm. The display showed Simon Black was calling.

'Hello Simon. What's up? I'm on the train to Tamford.' Timles looked through the carriage window. It was pitch black outside and the train was stationary.

'But at the moment it looks like I'm not going anywhere.'

'Sorry to call late. Can you talk now?' Timles looked around the first class carriage. One other passenger was slumped asleep against the padded headrest by the window.

'Yes it's all right at the moment. What's the problem?'

'Security, Michael. That's what's been keeping me awake at night. How the devil are you proposing to keep this *LIFELINES* system of yours secure? Even the big players like Face Book et. al. are getting hacked. Their CEO has said that there's not a great deal any Internet set up can do to keep everything under wraps, yet provide the global service users want. Chap said in effect it's an arms race against the bad guys, like everything else in life.' Timles looked at his sleeping companion wearily.

'You aren't the first and certainly won't be the last to cast rocks at this idea. Sir James White suggested that the establishment would make progress hard enough. He thought I should just come along to warm up the British Pharmaceutical Association meetings and enjoy a well aged glass of port.'

'Well Michael, I'm supporting your idea as you know, but you're going to have to come up with a very convincing proposal about making and keeping this network of yours safe and secure at our next meeting. That's going to be question *numerous duo* that the potential investors Philip and I will be bringing along will be asking.'

'Point well taken Simon, but what's question number one?'

'For God's sake Michael. You know very well. How is this going to provide an eventual return on investment. The people at the next board meeting will not *all* be benefactors. Even if this notion of yours proves its worth over the next year or so, taxpayer's cash is going to be very slow to come on stream, if ever. Too many failed public network systems!'

Look, if you want me to delay the meeting until we've all had more time to talk this through, I'll be only too happy to do it. These University chaps are bright, but they're ivory tower idealists at heart. Just get some real Internet security advice and think hard about the business model. I'll get someone from the investment banks to talk to us about security. You know what a fight they have on their hands!' Timles sighed. He was tired from his emotional investment in the recent London meetings and his interrupted doze. Simon seemed to pick that up and switched to a softer tone, just as the train lurched back into motion.

'Look Michael, we all support what you're doing. But let's just make sure we get a firm base to build on. I don't know what you've said in London, but I'm guessing that the pharmaceutical chaps will have forgotten most of it by lunchtime tomorrow. To many fires to fight when they get back to their companies. Keep this as an incubator project until we're sure we're really on the right track. We're going to need time Michael. Time to work out who the enemy will be. Time to get the funding and security right. Oh, and time to think about what to say, eventually, to the media. Our case will have to be made and watertight by then!' Timles thought for a moment and then replied.

'OK Mark Anthony. I hear you.'

'What are you talking about Michael?'

'*I come not to praise Caesar, but to bury him.*' Simon Black was silent a moment, then laughed at Timles's quote.

'All right, Michael. Goodnight and sweet dreams.'

Peter & Tuula

Seated on Tuula's bed, Peter looked down at the confidentiality agreement. So far it was Tuula who had taken him into his confidence. He was angry she'd been prying into his programme. But what she'd told him was quite compromising; she could be in trouble with her employer if her company's plans were leaked. So she was trusting him a lot, despite the paper exercise of confidentiality agreements. It obviously gave him "leverage" to use a term popular in business.

'I can see exactly where you're going with this scheme; especially to monitor image and video traffic. I'm excited by it and we could both benefit enormously from bringing something like that about. But there's a big problem. Since we're now exchanging confidences, here's mine. The coding in InterconNet you're referring to doesn't belong to Chris and I. It's owned by a Cambridge business called ThreeLs Ltd. Its avaricious founder and CEO bought the rights to use it from academics at Cambridge University. I'll bet any money the Cambridge scientists didn't realise what they were giving away!

But much more seriously for us, ThreeLs have patent protected the *concept* on which it's based. Anyone wanting to distribute software incorporating their idea has to purchase a licence from ThreeLs. If it was incorporated in mobile phones or tablets or run on phone company computers, under the terms of ThreeLs licence a fee's payable for *each* end user. ThreeLs owner, Jim Overbeck, would wet himself if he got wind that his software could be used in phone apps. He would be looking around for a small island in the Caribbean to purchase.'

'I've never heard of this ThreeLs, Pete.'

'Overbeck doesn't advertise on-line. Jim doesn't believe in paying third parties for things like that. We're a kind of test bed for applications. As academics, we don't pay licence fees for his software. But we're obliged to give him progress reports.' Tuula's initially excited expression faded. She now looked serious; focused.

'Do you have copies of the ThreeLs's patent and the licence agreement?'

'Yes and no; the patent is still pending while it's examined. That's normal, but I've got a copy you can look at.'

'OK, well there would be time to challenge the patent then.'

'Yes but I think that it will be granted. In my opinion it meets the usual criteria of novelty and usefulness.'

'What about the licence agreement?'

'I've a copy of that too; there are already a small number of ThreeLs's business clients using it; and paying the licence fees.'

'Can you show me a copy?' Peter asked to use Tuula's laptop. Tuula stood behind him as he logged into his Uni computer account and brought up the ThreeLs licence agreement. Both of them read through the lengthy terms and conditions. Tuula put her hands on Peter's shoulders.

'Look Pete, give me some time and I'll see what I can come up with.'

'Of course it means the Woodlands Centre will have to pay licence fees if they create a special public healthcare version of InterconNet.'

'Come again, Peter?' Peter suddenly realised he was giving away information that was supposed to be confidential. He quickly tried to cover himself.

'I meant if the Woodlands Centre ever wanted to take InterconNet public.' It was a very poor red herring, but Tuula was still pursuing her own line of thought and didn't question Peter further.

'I want to test this software of ThreeLs's with the programme I'm developing to see if it can improve independent recognition of inappropriate image and video material.'

'I can give you Jim Overbeck's email address.'

'I can't discuss what I'm doing with a business like that. It would have to be done by senior management at Kosketecessa. Right now it's just an idea. I couldn't even raise it yet with my boss at Kosketecessa. Can you give me a copy of their software for me to assess?'

'Our agreement with ThreeLs doesn't permit that. It's restricted for use with InterconNet.' Tuula thought:

'But if I did some work *myself* on InterconNet, I could get access, couldn't I? I have signed an agreement with you just now. Look, you have a fixed deadline for your Ph.D. submission don't you?'

'It's even closer than you might think. I'm funding myself right now.'

'Well you could use some help. Two heads are better than one. You thought we might be competing in our Ph.D. work on social networks. Let's collaborate instead.' Peter considered this completely unexpected suggestion. Tuula was a bright cookie; he had no doubt she could accelerate his progress. And *her* company had very deep pockets indeed. He was already moonlighting on his brother's tablet sales website for cash to continue his studies. InterconNet still needed improvements and he had to collect further data from its users for his thesis. Now Chris had involved him in yet another application of InterconNet for the Woodlands Centre, which would mean new programming, probably even more demanding than what had gone before.

It was a failing of all academics that as individuals, they set themselves goals and undertook tasks that, in commerce, would not be considered feasible without a large team. Sometimes individual academics were successful through working 24/7 and retaining control of the whole discovery process. But they were the minority that you read about. Peter didn't want to work in the shadows and leave Tamford University with letters after his name, but with debts and no job in prospect.

Martin

Back in his flat in the evening, Martin was unable to settle. There was nothing of interest on the TV. He'd watched all the films on the small stack of DVDs, which were in any case now acting as a makeshift bracket to support an overflow bookshelf. He was still waiting for his recently ordered broadband pack to arrive so he couldn't use his tablet to access the Internet. At other times he would have escaped his present ennui by immersing himself in the lively atmosphere of the Dragon. But now the thought of sitting there alone, even with a good ale in his hand, deepened his sense of isolation. Above him, the murmur of a TV programme suddenly increased in volume and descended in pitch to a steady drum beat. In the adjacent flat, a just audible conversation evolved into a shouting match. It sounded like something was thrown against the party wall. Exasperated, Martin fetched his jacket and left for the University Campus.

Peter & Tuula

Tuula's offer of collaboration was very attractive right now. And by reputation, more was on offer from her than just great programming.

'This agreement we've signed, Tuula, will it cover everything I tell you in confidence now?'

'Yes; if it's related to your work or mine.'

'I see from InterconNet that you know a Martin Wright from the Woodlands Complementary Centre.' Tuula started inwardly. The true answer to that was "intimately" but she gave a more restrained reply instead.

'Yes; met him in the Computer Centre and he asked for my help with using InterconNet and some IT support at his Woodlands therapy Centre. He's shown me round and I've helped him get a good deal on buying new physiotherapy stuff using the Uni equipment search facility.' Peter looked puzzled. 'And what do you get out of that connection?' Tuula paused a moment, wondering how best to answer that.

'In exchange he's given me some material I can use in my own research here.' Peter got the message. Martin was being used. In more ways than one, knowing Tuula. He decided not to pursue this tonight. There was likely to be more than one interesting outcome to their meeting this evening. He continued.

'OK so you have some background on the Woodlands already. Well, Chris was contacted by the Woodland's owner who also wanted some IT help. Neither knew the other or their work prior to that. The computer centre manager, Bill Meagh, put them in touch as Prof's away on Sabbatical. Anyway, it's been agreed to implement a new version of InterconNet at the Woodlands Centre.'

'Why wouldn't they just use the version you and I got up and running there?'

'Because they want to use it for a specialised purpose. The Centre's owner, Michael Timles, hopes to use it to build bridges between complementary and mainstream medicine. When Chris ran a demo for him he was struck by InterconNet's power to spot the potential of association between people. Timles wants to harness that power to include associations between conditions and treatment, patients and therapists. His company's board are backing this with substantial new investment. They're dead keen on the idea because they see it as enhancing the Woodlands's reputation and increasing revenue for their business.'

'And the Centre's owner shares that view?'

'He's the one who had the idea. He's more of an evangelist than a hard headed businessman. His grand design is the full integration of medicine across the board. He wants to restructure health care in the UK.'

'No shit? Well at least the guy has ambition. I like that in a man.' Peter didn't comment on Tuula's curious response. It was clear she had plenty of ambition herself to have got so far so young. Now she was offering to work with him. His answer, as many would say, was a "no-brainer". Or should that be a two-brainer? Martin offered his hand.

'Do we need a new agreement?' Tuula shook his hand firmly.

'No we need to start work.'

'I'll email you a copy of the programme.'

'I already have it.' Peter grinned. She was a sysop. Of course she had privileges at the Computer Centre even beyond his own.

'What do you suggest we do first?'

'Your new friends at the Woodland Centre will be in the same bind as you and Chris; coming up against the ThreeLs patent. Send me their instruction manual on incorporating and using their software and I'll see how we can pull it out of InterconNet so it works independently. I'll also run our idea, anonymously, through our legal department at Kosketecessa to see whether it stacks up as a way of avoiding the multi-user fees.'

'Will you try it out on your own application for detecting inappropriate mobile content?'

'You bet.'

'How are we going to work together?'

'I'll give you access to my file store as a common work area.'

'What about security. I suppose your company must fret about that?' Tuula suddenly smiled seductively.

'They do but all my sensitive stuff's on a hot disk.' It wasn't difficult for Peter to catch up with where the conversation was headed. It was obvious that success—even potential future success—was an aphrodisiac for Tuula. Their conversation had switched suddenly to become a word game. Tuula was leading as usual, but tonight he didn't care. He followed her lead, happy to give into his arousal:

'I'm not familiar with Sysop hardware. Can you explain?'

'A hot disk - like mine - has a quick release. You remove it and and insert a replacement back into the empty slot.' Peter laughed at her clever answer and wasn't slow to pick up its double meaning. Now that they had both exchanged confidences and realised how their future paths had converged, there was a highly charged atmosphere in the small study bedroom.

'I thought you'd be using some sophisticated techniques for data protection, Tuula?'

'Oh I picked up some exciting new techniques while I was speaking at a conference in Tokyo. One of the other speakers showed me some very interesting new data handling routines. Would you like to see them?'

'Is the Pope a catholic?'

'Shall we drink to our collaboration before we start?' Her expression, posture and meaning were unambiguous. He was in no hurry now to return to his room on the other side of Campus. Peter patted the narrow single bed.

'But you've only got one chair with arms and this bed isn't going to be very comfortable for working on.'

'You're right - we'll need a firmer surface than that.' Tuula opened her wardrobe and pulled a tight roll of material off the wide top shelf. It was a futon. Peter glanced at the Scandinavian-looking male framed on Tuula's coffee table as she unrolled the bed.

'The chap in your picture. Is he related?' Tuula pulled a sour face.

'He's there to remind me not to get emotionally involved with ambitious men.'

'But *you're* ambitious, Tuula.'

'Exactly Pete!' Peter nodded slowly and poured the drinks. He handed her a glass and raised his own.

'Cheers, Tuula!'

'Kippis Pete!'

Martin

Martin hadn't been on the University site at night before, but as he drew up in the Student Halls car park, the windows of the residential blocks cast plenty of light on the parking area and paths. It wasn't difficult to gain access to Tuula's block as the lobby door wasn't closed. Martin remembered from his own short time at Uni that students either ignored the exhortation to ensure access doors were secured or that the locks simply gave up with the volume of traffic. Outside Tuula's room he paused. The impulsiveness that had brought him this far was now fading. He hesitated before knocking; it was late and she probably wouldn't answer the door. He raised his arm tentatively. From behind the door there was a squeal. Then a male voice spoke. Tuula's distinctive voice called something. Laughter followed. Martin lowered his arm and backed away from the door. After a few seconds that seemed like an eternity, he turned and headed back to the car park, walking quickly. At least the Dragon was still open.

Chris

Chris Johns tore open the wrapper round the cheese and onion sandwiches. His back hurt and his eyes were dry from staring too long at the monitor. He should have packed it in hours ago, but he was still here in his office in the silent Computer Sciences building. It was by no means the first time he'd worked all night. That was partly why his wife had walked out of their marriage. A street survey conducted by the top journal *Nature* years ago asked people in the street what phrase would describe scientists (they included programmers). Their answers were instructive. Most people described them as "highly intelligent, but incomprehensible individuals". The smaller number of people who actually *knew* a scientist or IT worker personally simply said "A person who is unkind to their spouse". They were in love with their work and it didn't leave much room for human relationships.

These days there really wasn't any pressing reason for Chris to go from an empty faculty building to an empty flat. Anyway, by this time in the morning, he'd lost the impetus to back up his work, close down his computer, lock up and walk home. Even though that would have been far simpler than what he was trying to do now. Because, in a fog of exhaustion, stopping required uploading a new set of mental instructions to his brain. That was too much to contemplate. He hoped that the sandwiches would just keep him going until he'd finished; whenever *that* was likely to happen. Whilst controlling the computer mouse with one hand, he rubbed his chest with the other. That heartburn had returned again. Cheese sandwiches at 3 am certainly wouldn't help and he reached for his tube of indigestion tablets.

The software routine he was testing crashed again and a long column of error messages scrolled up the screen to fast to read until he terminated the display angrily. He leaned back, shut his eyes and waited for the pain to subside. There seemed to be nothing but problems ahead. While Prof was away he was nominal head of department, which meant all of Prof's admin responsibilities with none of the real head's status or any additional pay. He had once hoped for the head of department's position himself, but had not realised until now how many tedious faculty and senate meetings that would entail. Worse, with Prof's secretary away for months as well, he had to work with an agency woman who was completely unfamiliar with the way things were done.

Without re-directing a lot of her questions to Bill Meagh, his own research would have ground to a halt. The only bright spot on the horizon had been the opportunity to work with the Woodlands Centre. Quite apart from the exciting challenge of a real world application of his research, there was the prospect of serious funding for future work. Sadly, even this opportunity was tainted. Chris had no doubt they could deliver a system that would work as Timles hoped, but that would mean lining the pockets of Jim Overbeck at ThreeLs; the owners of the commercial rights to an indispensable component of InterconNet as it was now programmed. He had yet to reveal this hitch to Timles. That was why he was still here; another all night session. Trying to find a way round the problem. He would have to admit defeat again soon. The pain in his chest was worse despite the chalk tablets and his wrists were burning and tingling on the computer keys.

* * *

Martin

What was Tuula doing and who with? Martin's mind was in a whirl as he drove away from the University Halls of Residence. He was only aware of the red traffic light at the last minute as he was about to drive across a junction and had to brake hard, the front of his car screeching to a halt well over the line. While vehicles crossed the junction in front of him, he tried to make sense of why he would want to build a relationship with this tantalising Finn. She had picked him up in the Computing Centre and quickly researched his background. She had had an advantage over him from the first moment and had kept it. The relatively few times they had been together had been productive for his work; he was quickly up and running with his new computer. She had efficiently sourced the optimum suppliers of the new physio equipment he needed to pass on to Noura.

Their time together had been overtly sexual with Tuula very much in charge; when *he* wanted company she was difficult to get hold of. Was she merely toying with him, careless of whether or not he was forming an emotional attachment to her? Wouldn't she be returning to her company in Finland at some stage, where she seemed to be building a very promising career? What then? If they were just passing strangers enjoying an intimate tryst, what was the problem with that? Tuula had never placed any price tag on her sexual favours; she had made little or no demands on him, even meeting the cost of the weekend break she'd asked him to organise.

He recalled the single photo of a young Scandinavian male on the desk in her study bedroom. A partner? Her husband? It might even have been the person he had overheard, although the voice had sounded English. He couldn't ask Tuula. She would want to know why he'd been listening at her door. If he described his one sided affair to the few male friends he had, they would probably just tell him that Christmas had come early. But he could talk to his on-line muse; Anne. He had been quite explicit in describing his experience with Tina and had already hinted at another relationship. Anne had been non-judgemental and helpful. He would discuss it with her. Martin took the next turn, driving away from his flat, heading for the Woodlands Centre where he would have access to InterconNet.

***
Anne

Anne Eres was drinking a herbal infusion. It tasted like a rather stale chamomile tea, but could have been nettle and something, as the labels had dropped off the containers where she put the tea bags last term. She wanted to finish the chapter she was reading, but the authors' discussion was difficult to follow without constantly referring back, making progress slow and tiring. If it hadn't been so late she would have made a coffee to pep herself up a bit. The open laptop on her study bedroom desk lit up and a message window opened. Partly irritated at the interruption and partly grateful for a diversion, Anne put a beer mat marker into her book and read the on screen text.

Martin Wright is now on-line and requests a connection. Do you wish to accept?

Anne looked at her watch. Well, she had given him an open invitation to contact her and she was now struggling with the cognitive psychology she had been reading. She touched the "yes" button and the chat window opened. Martin's image and name headed the message box. She thought once again how Nordic his face appeared, yet in their conversations he was the antithesis of a Viking. Since they had agreed speech communication, she had been stuck by how gentle his voice was. Right now he seemed to be a bit of a lost soul, but at least he hadn't lost his sense of humour. On impulse she climbed onto the bed, wiggled the pillow into a comfortable position against her back and rested the computer on her lap. At the time she thought it was because she was tired, but later, she grew aware of the sensuality of her action. She ran her fingers quickly over the keys:

Hi Mart. Do you want to talk or type?

Talk please; I'm too tired to type and I'm sorry to call so late. I hope you hadn't gone to bed? Anne enabled voice contact.

'Well I'm resting comfortably at the moment, Mart and I did give you permission to get in touch any time you felt the need. What do you want to tell me?'

'I just need to talk with someone who'll listen sympathetically and tell me what to do.'

'And I'm that "someone" tonight?'

'You're the only one I can to talk to right now.' Anne pulled her laptop closer to her. Her automatic response was to get closer to the computer's microphone so she could lower her voice and not be overheard by the student in the neighbouring room. But it also seemed as if she was reaching out reassuringly for her client's hand. And the friction of the machine as she slid it over her waist felt surprisingly like a caress. She was suddenly conscious of being slightly aroused. But that meant admitting to herself that she had just such a need. She had to be very careful.

'That's a very big compliment; I'm not sure I deserve it. Of course I'll listen sympathetically, and I'll help *you* decide what to do.'

'You remember I'd decided my depression; well anyway, my feeling low and disconnected was all due to my split with Helena. Well I have managed to draw a line under that but that hasn't really helped. I now realise I want and am ready for another relationship. Two women had come into my life, but I wasn't sure whether it was me they were interested in or what I represented.'

'You'll have to help me out with that one, Mart. How do you think these women see you?'

'I think one of them is—was—simply looking for a short term sexual partner. To her I may represent a casual diversion from an intense working life. The other, I'm not sure about. She seems to connect with me on both a professional and personal level. She's quickly concluded that my difficulty in sustaining a satisfying relationship with women is down to my not understanding and responding to their emotional needs. I find her very deep and difficult to read, but as a therapist with a new approach, I think she also has things to prove, to herself and others.'

'And you happen to be a particularly interesting case for her?'

'Something like that.' There was a longish pause. Martin thought his psychotherapist was probably analysing his explanation. He wondered if he'd really been able to explain clearly enough what was troubling him. In reality, Anne was waiting for her mind to calm down before she spoke again. What he was telling her about this woman, whom she remembered he'd called Tina, was rather too close for comfort to the way she felt about him herself. Finally she gathered herself to reply.

'Let's go through what attracted you to these two women. I'd like to get a better picture of that.' Martin hesitated. But he recalled his agreement with Anne to be open and honest with her. There wasn't really any point to this if he tried to put a spin on things simply to avoid embarrassment.

'First off, these women both made themselves available. I'm afraid I wasn't really looking for a relationship before they both found me and awoke in me the realisation that I wanted one again.'

'And *I'm* awake to the fact that you're being very honest with me Martin. But once they had introduced themselves in their different ways, you were interested in them. So is what about them that you now find attractive?'

'They are both very good looking with almost athletic figures. Both are career women; very intelligent and ambitious.

'Good in bed? Like sports?'

'Yes; well one of them is very much into squash and the other one uses massage in her job.' There was another pause.

'Think about what you've just said. You've mentioned a number of superficial characteristics, but not any sort of emotional connection with these women. Whilst you were speaking, I remembered our second on-line conversation, Martin; when we were still typing to each other. Didn't your ex girlfriend, Helena, have all these characteristics?'

'You're saying I shouldn't be thinking about a relationship with either of the women I've described?'

'Not at all; I'm just remarking that you're consistent; that's the type of female that you find attractive. There's no reason why you shouldn't build a successful relationship with someone like that. Even if you met Helena for the first time tomorrow, things would probably be different from last time. Both your circumstances have changed; you've changed. Successful partnerships do exist between ambitious high flyers even if many fail. There's no reason why things wouldn't work out for you next time. You've given one of these ladies a name; Tina. Would it help us discussing this to name the other one?' Martin thought carefully. It was probable that Anne knew of Tuula; perhaps many staff and students did, as she was an acting systems operator in the Computer Science department. Well, he was being as open and honest as possible so…

'She's called Tuula Pipi.' There was an even longer pause. Finally Anne replied. There was a strained note in her voice.

'Well I'm going to break my rules here, Martin. You were absolutely right to comment that one of your women saw you as a short term sexual partner. That relationship won't work out. Not unless you want to share that woman's affections with a surprising number of Tamford Uni staff and students. You appear to have met some powerful females, Martin! For someone feeling isolated and concerned about holding your own in relationships, you need to be very careful!' Martin felt crushed. He had been wrong to name Tuula. It would have been better to have relied on his own instinct and backed off without bringing her into his consultation with Anne. What would she be thinking of him now? He wondered how he could recover some dignity from the situation.

'I'm sorry Anne. I now feel stupid to have been taken in by Tuula. I can see only too well now that she has been playing with me. In fact the reason I contacted you so late was that I think I discovered her "entertaining" someone else. The problem was that she appeared when I was feeling down and was very helpful with getting me up and running with InterconNet and sourcing equipment for our Centre. I can see now I have been a fly drawn into a spider's web.'

This outburst from Martin affected Anne deeply. She decided not to ask him about the circumstances of his "discovery". She could hear that he was mortified and embarrassed and she also realised she had made a mistake in reacting angrily to his admission he'd been having sex with this awful industrial Ph.D. student. There was no doubt that she was very attractive, but also highly promiscuous. Given that it was rumoured she had bestowed her favours on one very senior member of faculty, there was precious little likelihood of her being shown the door before her studies here were completed or unless her company called her back early.

'Martin. *I* should to apologise to *you*. I was being judgemental and I have hurt your feelings. It's a poor excuse in the circumstances, but all I can say is that it's late and I have taxed my poor head reading some especially dry cognitive therapy book. When I pick it up again I'm sure it will tell me exactly not to do what I have just done. Perhaps we should stop our session here and both sleep with our thoughts. You will contact me again Martin, won't you? I should be very distressed if you didn't. I really do think we have other things to discuss and I'm certain we can make progress.'

'Yes Anne. If you're prepared to keep me as your client, I'd like to keep talking. Goodnight now. And thank you for being so understanding.'

'Goodnight Martin.'

Anne Eres has terminated the connection.

CHAPTER NINETEEN

Chris

The following afternoon, Peter walked rather unsteadily through the entrance of Computer Science building. There was a slight ringing in his ears and his brain still felt like part had been removed and replaced with cotton wool. It had been a mentally and physically demanding session with Tuula the previous night. He wondered where she found the energy. She claimed to work 16 hour days. Yet this still left her with the ability to play aggressively competitive squash in addition to, well, other forms of demanding personal exercise.

Passing the unmanned reception area, he squinted painfully at several brightly lit mural posters celebrating successful Computer Science projects. The intention was to catch the attention of visiting industrialists, but Peter found them static and uninspiring. In his mind's eye he conjured up wall mounted interactive displays of InterconNet. Or even better active examples of the sort of images that Tuula's software was intended to detect and block. They would really get the attention of corporate suits.

In a dazed but buoyant mood, he headed for his shared office. The collaboration agreed last night with Tuula was perfect. With the sex thrown in, although he didn't rate his long term chances of that, it was a win/win situation. But as he passed Chris's office door, his mood darkened. The thorny problem of his status at Tamford and the power of his supervisor over his future had been pushed to the back of his mind. Once again he had acted impulsively without reference to his supervisor. Chris had not sanctioned him for getting Martin on board neither was Chris party to the deal just struck with Tuula. And he'd warned Peter in effect: "two strikes and you're out".

But Tuula might be his saviour here. He was sure the woman could programme her way out of any situation. She had spotted a way to *limit* the licence related fees to ThreeLs, which would make InterconNet commercially attractive. He told himself, not entirely convincingly, that she would find a way to let Chris know what was going on. Logging on to his account, Peter saw that there were unopened emails waiting for him; from Tuula, the Centre manager, Bill Meagh and Chris. Tuula's emails inviting him to meet were several days old, but obviously now redundant. Today's email from Tuula was a copy of the printed agreement he had signed in her room. Quickly he deleted it, annoyed that Tuula had used the insecure public email service.

Bill Meagh's message had been sent that morning. Peter read it with growing alarm. As a "courtesy", Bill informed him that his supervisor had been urgently looking for some patent information concerning a company called "ThreeLs". Apparently Chris's copy had been mislaid. He was aware that a copy was stored on Peter's personal computer. Peter not being contactable, Bill had granted Chris access privileges that morning to Peter's computer account. Peter's heart skipped a beat. That meant that his boss could have seen Tuula's *proforma* agreement. With a sinking feeling, Peter opened his supervisor's message. His worst fears were confirmed. The brief email just stated: "Please see me as soon as you get in". Now he fully expected to be asked to clear his desk that day.

His supervisor's door was slightly open. Peter knocked but there was no answer. Peter called his name and knocked harder. The door opened a fraction in response. After a moment, Peter finally pushed the door open and went in unbidden. Chris was slumped over his keyboard in front of his monitor. A number of lager cans decorated the work surface, together with a jumble of those plastic triangles which protect sandwiches in vending machines. Assuming his boss had fallen asleep at his desk—a not unknown occurrence—Peter called his name. Getting no response, he walked over to Chris and tentatively moved his shoulder. When Peter could still not rouse his boss, anxiety got the better of him and he lifted Chris's torso off the desk and back into his bucket seat. The man lolled limply.

Feeling out of his depth, Peter fumbled desperately to find a pulse in the neck and put his ear to the open mouth. He felt a moist breath and the suggestion of a pulse. Straining with the dead weight he pulled his boss from the chair and lowered him to the floor into the recovery position. Grabbing the 'phone he called 999, described the situation and their location and knelt beside his boss on the floor. Chris was now making a low moaning, which could have been an attempt to speak.

Peter returned to his own office and removed the car rug and dog-eared cushion that his room mate used to pad his chair. Armed with these accessories he made his boss as comfortable as he could and then rang Bill Meagh, explaining what had happened. In less than a minute, Bill appeared, rapidly assessed the situation, removed a supplier's freebie with a mirrored surface from the desk and held it over the prostrate lecturer's nose and mouth. The haze that formed confirmed that Chris was still breathing. Bill nodded and departed to lock back intervening fire and other doors in preparation for the arrival of paramedics.

The team that attended thought it was likely Chris had suffered a heart attack and after setting up oxygen and checking the desk for any medicines, rushed him from the building on a trolley. The next few hours would prove critical, they said. Bill Meagh accompanied the paramedics in the ambulance, assuring Peter that he would phone through with any news. He sent Peter to try and locate Chris's next of kin via the departmental office. The departmental secretary was still away on sabbatical and the startled locum couldn't give Peter much assistance. After a fruitless hour on the phone, Peter had only been able to leave a message on an answer phone at a number thought to belong to Chris's ex. Finally, he left all the details with the University Registry Office.

Peter trailed despondently back to Chris's office. He knew that Chris had long been risking health problems by his lifestyle. But he was deeply distressed at the thought that Chris's discovery of his, well *treachery* in setting up an independent deal with Tuula might have precipitated the attack. He always felt slightly uneasy in his supervisor's office. Now the empty room seemed to be accusing him. Standing there, wondering what to do next, he noticed that the indicator LEDs on Chris' computer were still alight. If his boss hadn't logged off, there might be a clue to what he had been doing before he collapsed. Peter sat and activated the monitor. Sure enough, Chris's account was still open. On screen was a cascade of windows containing documents. Peter was puzzled. Most of the documents were were in a script he didn't recognise.

He clicked back to the document that had been displayed on the monitor when he'd come in and scrolled through it. There was an English translation following the foreign script. It was a short communication from two academics in the mathematics faculty, Seoul University, South Korea.

There was a translator-added note indicating that the original text was "Hangul". Peter read, then re-read the paper with growing amazement.

The researchers described a novel method for dynamically constructing neural networks. Their approach was identical to the Cambridge researcher's; the concept for which ThreeLs Ltd had applied for a patent. Hurriedly, Peter scrolled back through the paper to search for the communication's date. It had been published in 2013, two years before the ThreeLs patent application. The patent examiners had missed the publication; it was not in a mainstream journal and was written in Korean. But Chris had found it somehow. *That* was why Chris had asked Bill Meagh for access to his account. He'd lost the ThreeLs patent and had been urgently looking for it that morning; to find the date. The Korean research paper constituted "prior art".

Armed with this bombshell, anyone would be able to mount a successful challenge; the ThreeLs patent and their licence agreements would then be declared void. Considering the significance of what Chris had found, his boss's stern command to come and see him was probably because of the Korean paper. Chris may not have looked at his email and seen Tuula's attachment before collapsing. If he was quick about it, Tuula could help him access the Uni system logs. She might be able to put his mind at rest, if not about his supervisor, then about his present feeling of guilt. There was nothing else he could do to help Chris and he left his office.

Five minutes later, he was sitting beside Tuula in the Computer Centre as she scrolled through reams of system data that was impenetrable even to him. Eventually she was able to announce that Chris had not accessed any of Peter's emails.

'Good job you thought to look, Pete. This mail server log file is set to clear once the user signs out. OK, now how about this Korean research paper?'

'It's still open in his account.'

'Good. Go back to his office and email us both copies of all the stuff that Chris has dug out. Oh, and you might want to ask Bill Meagh to give you temporary access privileges to your supervisor's account in the present circumstances.' Tuula reached out and squeezed his hand. Peter was surprised and touched. It was the first truly affectionate gesture he had ever seen her make. He squeezed back in acknowledgement.

'If you carry on like that Tuula, I'll start to think you're human and not a female android.' Tuula grinned and gave him a V-sign. When he returned she had already got the Korean researcher's paper open. She looked up at Peter.

'Well Pete, I don't think we need to worry about pulling the ThreeLs software out of InterconNet now. We can leave it where it is. It's effectively open source since the Koreans put their programme details into the public domain. All we need to do is acknowledge the original authors in our coding.'

'Do you think the Cambridge academics knew about the Korean researcher's work?'

'Best not to go there Pete. Cambridge and Oxford do top flight work but have been prone to doublethink about the sources of original ideas.' Peter stared at Tuula, who was concentrating on the screen. He followed her intense gaze. She was reading the original paper; not the translation. He was about to say that the English version was appended, but checked himself. Tuula wasn't English. To her, Korean was, after all, just another foreign language. He shook his head slowly, in amazement at this woman. Tuula reached the end of the paper and nodded.

'We need a plan of action. I have to confess I pulled out the core of your programme several months back. Just to test it out with my image recognition programme, you understand. It worked brilliantly.' At other times, Peter would have been incensed by this brazen admission of piracy. But these were not normal times. If Chris didn't recover, his whole future here would be in the balance.

'So that's why you went to the trouble of drafting that agreement between us?'

'Evidently.' He shrugged and grinned in spite of himself.

'OK so you're a software pirate. Now what's the plan?'

'Well most of the programme's yours so if Kosketecessa likes my work, then I need to have you on board.'

'Is that gratitude or because you still need some work doing on it?'

'That, plus I fancy you; for the moment, that is.' Peter thought: *Not only clever, but brazen with it!*

'I need examples to demonstrate the power of the system to block inappropriate on-line image and video content.'

'Surely you don't need to look further than the Internet for stuff like that!'

'Of course, but most of that stuff is tracked and we need to keep what we're doing under wraps until I can talk to Kosketecessa.'

'So where are you going to get your explicit content?' Tuula smiled at him with that seductive sideways inclination of her head and slowly raised her eyebrows.

'OK Tuula; I get the picture.'

'No Peter—*I"ll* get the pictures. That way we can demonstrate the cut-off between acceptable and inappropriate with the same two people.'

'OK, so long as you don't show our faces.' Tuula narrowed her eyes and Peter knew a barbed comment was on its way.

'Well that really wouldn't be a problem would it? I know from InterconNet that you're an expert with "graphic surgery". You can give us both new IDs. Useful and fun. What's not to like?' Peter was about to ask how she knew he'd given certain InterconNet members anonymity by changing their faces in this way when the phone rang in Tuula's room. Tuula listened then passed the phone to Peter.

'Its the Faculty Office. They've got Bill Meagh on the line.'

****

Peter took the handset from Tuula and listened. Tuula watched Peter's face. She could only hear an indistinct envelope of sound, but Peter's expression suggested that the news wasn't good. Peter mumbled an acknowledgement then slowly replaced the receiver. He sat down heavily.

'Chris died a few hours after arrival; a further attack and the medics weren't able to save him: too much damage to the heart by that time. Apparently the registry have been able to contact his ex wife. Someone answering from the number I found knew where she was.' Tuula reached out and covered his hand again; the second time she had made that expression of sympathy. For a moment neither of them said anything. Eventually Tuula patted the back of his hand a couple of times and pulled them into the present again.

'We were talking about making plans for the future. Now that's even more urgent, isn't it?' Peter nodded.

'Yes.' He looked at her hand covering his.

'Thanks, Tuula.' He reversed his palm and gave hers a squeeze in return.'

'From today I'm an orphan post grad. I'll have to talk to the Graduate Studies Office to find out what that means for me. I'm self-funded here so there's no public sector grant involved for my project. But the Uni subsidises the faculty facilities I use. I think I'll need another staff member as a nominal supervisor, even if they have no interest or stake in my research. Our head of department would normally get involved, but he's presently having a good time in Silicon Valley. Between you and me, I doubt he'll come back.'

'What about me? I have a recognised Uni post here.' This suggestion put a smile back on Peter's face.

'Chris was a tough supervisor in many ways, but I don't think I could cope with you being my boss, Tuula. Anyway, I doubt you'd be eligible, although I do appreciate the offer.'

'OK Pete, go talk to the Graduate Office, but here's the deal: we both know they'll be very sympathetic about your boss, but will still need funds for you to stay on. I need your programme to solve the inappropriate content filter Kosketecessa have tasked me to find. They will have to cover your costs.' Hearing this Peter's smile remained in place.

'That would be fantastic. But when I talk to the Graduate Office, I'll probably need an official letter of support from your sponsors, Tuula.'

'Kosketecessa already know I'm on to something here and my boss is happy to help; there's already a significant in house budget for this.'

'You know that Chris didn't mention the ThreeLs licence issue to the Woodlands Centre's owner. That could have been an obstacle for what they hoped to do with their version of InterconNet. That's no longer an issue but we should install a new version of the programme - one with modifications to the ThreeLs software, when we're happy with it.'

'Look Pete, why don't you ask the Woodland folk if you can adapt your original research project's aim, so that the objective is now this networked alternative medicine they all seem so fired up about? I wasn't ever optimistic about where you hoped to take what you've done so far. You were never going to compete with the front runners in social media.'

'It's the Woodlands *Centre* by the way, but I love your "Woodland Folk". That's straight out of "Wind in the Willows" you know. I think The Woodlands owner would be "Badger" and Martin would be "Moley".'

'And their administrator lady would definitely be "Ratty".' Peter was taken aback.

'Tuula, how do you *know* all these things? Peter shook his head. In the rush of unfolding events he'd almost forgotten to comment on the other thing that had amazed him. You were reading Korean just now, weren't you?'

'Mom and Dad thought I had a mind like absorbent tissue. *Eidetic* I think you call it. I guess I'm just fascinated by almost everything. But the Korean is because I have keep up with the technical competition there; after all, businesses like Samsung in South Korea are my company's major competitors. And The Wind in the Willows was a cult thing where I was studying in the States. So I'm not the polymath you're implying.' Peter nodded, but he wasn't convinced by Tuula's self deprecation. If they were going to work together, he'd have to watch his back.

'OK Chief, where do we go from here?' Peter asked.

'I think we both need some of that single malt of yours.' Tuula shook her head as Peter retrieved the bottle from the back of his desk filing system.

'I'm surprised you get any programming done.'

'My office mate keeps me sober; he's teetotal and makes sarcastic comments if I take this out whilst he's here. But his put-downs are usually funny as well so I humour him.' Tuula grinned.

'Do you want to talk about us?' Peter made a determined effort to be cheerful. Depression right now would serve no purpose and get him precisely nowhere.

'I didn't know you cared!'

'*No;* I mean about our collaboration. We will need to put on a good act for the decision makers in Kosketecessa' Peter had to agree with her. It would take his mind off his present situation. The irritating thing about Tuula was that she always seemed to be several steps ahead of everyone else. Probably that's how she had landed such a good position in Kosketecessa. He decided to challenge her big idea. The executives in her firm would be doing just that. He folded his arms and tried to look like a business "suit". This attempt was somewhat undermined by his rather scruffy Uni tee shirt and jeans.

'The Internet's open and unregulated. The sexy thing about it is that anyone can view, send or post anything they want at present. Even though there may be consequences for them later; right?'

'What's your point?'

'The Internet exploded world wide because it took away some of the power and monopolies appropriated for themselves by states, media moguls and telecom giants and gave it back to ordinary people. Convince me that by developing software that blocks "inappropriate content" being sent, uploaded or viewed on the Internet won't make Kosketecessa as hated as Big Brother in Orwell's classic *1984*. Surely information "wants to be free". If it isn't, progress is stifled for reasons of political control or corporate greed.'

Peter furrowed his eyebrows and did his best to fix Tuula's eyes with a sceptical expression. But challenging a girl with smouldering glamour model looks and a powerful analytical mind was a risky business. Tuula mirrored his own serious face, but didn't fold her arms. Instead she leaned towards him and like Peter's description of the 'net, her blouse temporarily became open and unregulated.

'The Internet's sexy and empowering in the West, Yes. But not if you happen to live in China, Iran or a surprisingly large number of other countries.' Peter frowned. He felt one of the supports of his platform weakening.

'New technology always introduces risks as well as rewards. Keeping the Internet completely open for the entertainment and empowering of individuals also risks creeping subversion by criminal gangs and the sexualisation and radicalisation of youth.' Peter was waiting to pounce on a point, but was silent.

'Kosketecessa estimates that within 5 years, practically all Internet communications will be via mobile phones or pretty similar hand-held devices. By then, in the West at least, public outrage at unacceptable, intrusive and downright tasteless content delivered by it will be at an all time high. Our senior management has been advised that a tipping point will have been reached where the voices of the advocates of freedom of speech and information will have been drowned by a Tsunami of public revulsion.' Peter's platform had lost a leg and was now wobbling. He said nothing.

'Kosketecessa manufactures phones. It doesn't operate networks; nor does it any longer produce the software that runs on its phones. But the shit will hit Kosketecessa's fan, or more relevantly, their shares, because their product is the obvious "point of presence" of the increasingly vilified public Internet.' Peter was no longer challenging her.

'So what are you saying?'

'Regulation of the Internet is inevitable, even in the West. To remain free and open, established businesses like Google and Face book will have to demonstrate they are capable of policing their content. Others would, by law, have to introduce controls to allow their user communities to police their content for them. It works for Wikipedia.'

'So the ultimate control of the Internet would be taken over by the State.'

'In most of Asia, it is now. It's just that in the West Civil Liberties and Human Rights spook democratic administrations and they don't clamp down on Internet traffic. As I said, that will change, sad as it may seem.'

'But what about key business, medical, military and scientific users of the 'Net?'

'Will all run on private networks. A lot of it does already. Well out of the reach or the pockets of mass users.' Tuula lent back. Her blouse closed once more. A previously inviting view became regulated. Peter's platform was in ruins. Tuula wound up her arguments and summarised:

'So Kosketecessa is funding research on methods for blocking inappropriate content. If successful, it will be kept on ice and supplied to all the relevant mobile phone networks when the board decides it's time to act.'

'It doesn't sound like we'll need to convince your company to keep funding your research.'

'No it's not that. My boss at Kosketecessa will have external consultants - specialists - as well as senior management listening to our presentation. We have to convince *them* that our approach will work.' Peter was silent in thought a moment

'And you trust me to do that?' Tuula's face lost its intense look.

'Yes; but if you fill my glass again it would help.'

****

Martin woke up feeling quite positive. He'd put the whole affair with Tuula behind him. What was it Peter had told him about Tuula? Something like "enjoy it while it lasts", he couldn't remember exactly. But he recalled only too well now the advice on relationships given by his two therapists; Tina and Anne. He was also beginning to respect the impartial discernment of compatibility by InterconNet. That programme had located Tuula's personal "node" a long way away from his. *There's none so blind as those that will not see.* He and Tuula were chalk and cheese. And he was most definitely the cheese.

There were more uplifting developments. Last night when he returned to his flat, he'd found a scruffy note saying that his neighbour had taken in a parcel for him. When he finally caught the neighbour at home it proved to be the long awaited broadband equipment. Setting it up proved surprisingly hassle-free. He did at least have Tuula to thank for that. Now he was now able to browse the Web at home. At the Woodlands, he was making good progress explaining the new *LIFELINES* network to the other Centre therapists. And there was a steady flow of data to pass to Noura. He was also looking forward to a fresh start with new physiotherapy equipment and, at some stage, an assistant. When Martin entered the Woodlands later, Julie signalled him to come quickly over to her desk.

'I'm *early* today Julie. What's the panic?'

Martin picked up the registration book to move it within reach of the pen Noura insisted was kept fixed to the desk by a cable. More waving from Julie.

'No, leave that for a moment Martin. There's a consignment for you. I wasn't able to sign it off and asked the couriers to wait outside until you or Noura arrived. They were very irritated with me and only agreed to wait 10 minutes.'

'Is that the TNT van parked outside?'

'Yes; you'd better hurry, they've been there 5 minutes already. Store room key.' Julie pressed a key into his hand. Martin walked out again to negotiate with the driver and his mate. A few minutes later a number of cardboard boxes were being stowed away in the storeroom off the reception area. Martin returned the key to Julie.

'Thanks Julie; you can let Noura know that I've checked off everything we ordered and it's all OK. It'll have to stay in storage until I learn from the powers that be what's happening about physiotherapy here. I'll take a look at the equipment later. I've got an unusually busy morning today.' Martin played nonchalant for Julie's benefit. But inside he was excited. It wasn't every day that thousands of pounds worth of the latest physiotherapy gear arrived on his doorstep. When everyone else had gone home this evening, it would be an early Christmas in the Centre's storeroom. Mid morning, Martin received a text from Peter.

"Hi Mart, I need to talk to you as soon as poss. Lunchtime in the Dragon?"

Martin sent a reply.

"Can do Pete, C U there 1pm."

Martin found Peter installed in the main bar of the Dragon with what remained of a pint in front of him. He got to his feet as Martin came over.

'No need to stand on ceremony, Pete.' Peter shook his head.

'I'm not. Can we go into the back where it's a bit more private?' Peter looked serious which stopped Martin making a joke about this.

'OK. I'll get a drink and meet you in there. Another for you?'

'Please - I'm Pedigree.' Martin didn't make a crack about this either. There were only a couple of drinkers at the rear of the Dragon. Peter was seated in one of the high backed "pews". Martin put down their drinks and sat opposite, mirroring Peter's serious mood with questioning eyebrows.

'Thanks for meeting me, Mart. Sorry I've been out of touch, but I've been working round the clock since we were last in touch.' Peter hadn't picked up his pint, which was quite uncharacteristic. He continued:

'Chris had a heart attack in his office a few days ago. I'd gone in expecting a bollocking from him. I found him slumped over his computer. He died in hospital the same day.' Martin put down his own glass in shock

'Christ, Pete. I mean I'm very sorry to hear that. Were you at the hospital with him?'

'No. Our computer centre manager, Bill Meagh, went in with the paramedics. I spent hours on the phone in the Uni Registry office trying to locate his family. Chris was separated, you know, and had no children. Eventually the Registry staff were able to contact his ex wife and a cousin. They're talking to the funeral people now. Bill's representing the University. Prof's still away in the States, but he's been told about it.' Martin was quiet, he'd begun to like Chris a lot after he'd got to know him better, but then another thought struck him.

'What will this mean for your Ph.D. work, Pete?'

'That's a very good question. I've had a word with the Graduate Studies Office to check where I stand. They were very sympathetic, but pointed out that graduates are what they call "overheads in cost centres". With my supervisor gone, revenue allocated to his lab will be frozen until Prof returns to decide whether there will be another appointment or not. That's only part of the problem. I must have at least a nominal supervisor on the permanent staff. The default choice for that would be the Head of Department. Trouble is that Chris and our Prof were at daggers drawn. Chris was turned down for the Head of Department's post. And with Prof away on sabbatical, he may have felt that Chris was a potential loose cannon in his department. Prof made no secret of the fact that he didn't approve of the InterconNet project. All of which means Prof probably won't put himself out to support any of Chris's research.'

'But you're self funded and your brother was going to cover expenses. Won't you be able to meet the University fees?'

'I haven't finished the bad news yet, Mart. You remember I said I'd agreed to work on a demonstration website for my brother Simon's tablet sales venture? We had a deal going. When Simon got the investment he was expecting, he said he would pay my course fees and even backdate payments to cover the whole time I've spent at Tamford. That would have dealt with my debts. Well, I completed his computer tablet demo web and Simon was over the moon about it. But first the venture capital company and then the banks have turned his business proposal down. I've been paid for the demo work, but there'll be no money to complete my course or clear my debts. Doing bar and other work, I could probably scrape by, but I won't be able to meet the Departmental overhead costs. So when Chris died, I was first gutted and then after hearing the bad news from Simon at "EyePad Eire" I was stuffed.' Martin stared at his friend.

'Is there *any* good news Pete?'

'Well, yes and no. As it happens Tuula Pipi; you know, that blond bombshell Kosketecessa industrial post grad, is very interested in part of my InterconNet programme. I told you she's also doing research on social media didn't I?' Martin didn't say anything, but just nodded.

'Well she's going to ask her boss if they'll provide a year's funding for me to work with her.'

'Why would they do that? I thought Kosketecessa weren't even paying all of Tuula's costs. Isn't that why she's a temporary systems operator?' Peter looked around covertly.

'Actually, Tuula had a brief from her firm to work on something that's become of increased interest to them. 'Fraid I've been sworn to silence on the details. Anyway, she says there's a good chance I could be supported by them to continue my research. I have to go to Finland to make a presentation. Tuula and I have had several discussions about it and she was very confident that the suits at Kosketecessa would play ball.' Martin was now wondering if it was Peter's voice he had heard that night when he hesitated outside Tuula's room in the halls of residence. *That* conversation had sounded as if it involved *another* type of software. But Peter was continuing.

'The main reason I asked to meet you is about InterconNet itself. We've installed a version for the Woodlands, but the problem is that a crucial part of the programme is commercial; you remember that creep Overbeck? I told you his company had applied for a patent on the method involved and are licensing its use in any and all applications. There would in effect be a cost per user. Not too bad for an individual, but bad news for a network system with millions of subscribers.' Peter waved his hand dismissively.

'But anyway, it looks like that may no longer be a problem after all. Before he died, Chris had discovered that the method ThreeLs are licensing had already been invented and published a couple of years before the Cambridge scientists came up with it. As it was already in the public domain, the method isn't patentable, well at least the patent can be successfully challenged.' Martin got lost somewhere near the end of this.

'So what does that mean for us?'

'It means we can shake off any need to pay fees to ThreeLs. If I modify the Woodlands version of InterconNet slightly. It will work just the same, but my edits will make everything above board.'

'Will that take a long time?' Martin was already thinking about the work ongoing with *LIFELINES* at the Woodlands

'About as long as removing this.' Peter held up a beer mat on which he'd scrawled:

#** *This module is the property of ThreeLs Ltd. And is subject to the licence terms and conditions available at www.ThreeLs.com* Peter flicked the cardboard disc back on the table and placed his pint on it with grim satisfaction.

'Well actually, there's some other stuff to do as well, but I won't bother you with that.' Martin was about to speak, but Peter was clearly building up to say something else important.

'Now Chris has gone I wonder if you could ask your boss whether he can put me onto the consultancy agreement with the Woodlands instead. I believe there was a fee negotiated too ...' Peter hesitated, hoping he wasn't going too far, too fast, but Martin waded in to reassure his friend.

'Say no more, Pete. Of course I'll take up your case with my boss. But perhaps you can write a summary of what you've said and email it to me. Oh, and you'd better include everyone who now has a stake in your programme. I've lost track of that myself. I want to be sure of my facts when I speak to Michael Timles.' Peter looked very relieved.

'Cheers Mart. It's been great drinking with you and it will be even better if I can also work with you at the Woodlands.' Peter picked up his pint, which he had not touched whilst he had been talking to Martin about the vital matter of funding. After a deep draft he changed the subject.

'Do you want to come to the funeral, Mart? I know you had some long conversations with Chris.' Martin thought about this. Of course he had become quite friendly with Chris in the short time he'd known him.

'Of course I'll come, Pete. But The Woodlands Centre should be represented officially, given the importance Timles attaches to InterconNet. Let me know as soon as you have a date. I'll speak to Timles about the InterconNet consultancy arrangements and ask him how he would like the Centre to acknowledge Chris'

'Mart; why do you always refer to your boss by his surname. Does he insist on formality like that?'

'I don't really know Pete. Apart from being my boss, he's a very unusual man and "Michael" just doesn't seem right. You know he once told me how he got his surname and hinted that he would have enjoyed being called "Timeless" but that was a step too far even for his doting parents! I have dropped the "Dr." bit though.'

'Well *I'm* looking forward to *that* "bit" Mart. Peter raised his glass and smiled.

'If this all does work out, Mart, the next round will be *definitely* be on me.'

CHAPTER TWENTY

Timles

When Martin returned to the Woodlands, Julie called him over to the reception desk.

'Dr. Timles is asking for you, Mart. He's in the meeting room.' Martin knocked and waited. He'd often wondered why an alternative centre needed such a large, infrequently used room, but perhaps Timles had already plans in mind when the Centre was being designed. Timles called for him to come in. He'd had the room rearranged with a desk replacing the speaker's lectern in front of the large wall mounted screen. A small horseshoe of chairs had been set up in front of it.

'Ah, Martin. Thanks for coming at short notice. Things are becoming increasingly busy and I wanted to get in our last mentoring session before other activities take up most of my time. But first, how is progress with implementing InterconNet? Or perhaps I should now call it *LIFELINES*?' Martin took a deep breath to give himself time to think and get his thoughts in order. Getting the Centre's version of Peter and Chris's networking programme up and running had slipped from the top of his agenda. His first priority now was to tell his boss about Chris's death and discuss how that would affect the agreement with the University in general and Peter in particular.

'I've just met Pete Swales in the Green Dragon. He wanted to see me urgently.' Martin hesitated a moment. His personal loss had only really just begun to sink in. He'd made so few friends in Tamford the last few years and now he'd lost Chris shortly after finding him.

'Chris Johns had a heart attack a few days ago and died later in hospital.'

'Good God. I'm shocked.' Timles was silent a moment, digesting this bombshell. Then he motioned Martin to the seat closest to his desk.

Timles closed the open screen of the laptop he was working with and gave Martin his full attention.

'Chris wasn't that much older than Pete, apparently?' Martin nodded.

'Pete told me Chris didn't look after his health. He said Chris had an appalling diet and spent too many hours in front of computer screens.'

'Did he have family?' Timles asked.

'Pete had difficulty contacting them. Eventually he got in touch with Chris's former partner and a cousin and they've taken over managing things with support from the University. Chris's boss—the Head of Computer Sciences—is on sabbatical in California. He's been told, of course.'

'Has a funeral been arranged?'

'Pete's going to let me know. Should the Woodlands be represented?'

'Yes of course. I think you and I should attend. Please pass on the details as soon as you learn more.' Timles paused, he steepled his hands and rubbed his thumbs together a moment. Watching him, Martin guessed what was now going through his boss's mind.

'Did Pete say where that would leave us with *LIFELINES*?' Martin thought hard. He would need to summarise the present delicate situation regarding Peter and InterconNet. It would be a disaster if Timles decided to go elsewhere at this late stage.

'That was the other thing Pete wanted to tell me. Now his supervisor's died the University has as good as told him that he has to wind up his research. All the capital funding and revenue relating to Chris's projects will be frozen until the Head of Department returns from the States to make decisions.'

'Surely his Prof can deal with this by phone and email!'

'That's another problem. Apparently the Department head doesn't like Chris's research. Pete said there were some personal issues involved as well..' Timles looked worried by this news, but made no comment. Martin continued:

'Pete has been supporting himself up to now and he may get some funding from elsewhere through programming work, but that's still uncertain. He's more than willing to continue to help us get *LIFELINES* up and running and support us.' Martin hesitated again.

'And there's another issue. Pete says he will in any case have to edit part of the programme we've got here. Apparently, as it stands now, that part could be subject to "per user" licence fees by a company called ThreeLs.' Timles face darkened further at this news so Martin hurried to reassure his boss.

'But before Chris had a heart attack, Pete said he'd discovered a Korean research paper which makes a patent ThreeLs owns invalid. Pete only has to make a few edits to escape paying any licence fees.' Timles still didn't reply, but from his expression he was thinking hard. Martin decided it was time to put Peter's request to his boss.

'Pete's asked if he can take over Chris's consultancy arrangement with you.' Timles considered this.

'It's a tough time for Pete right now I realise, but can you ask Pete, as soon as he can, to contact me and say exactly where he and everyone else with a stake in his programme now stands.'

'I've already asked him to produce a summary for you.'

'Good. But the University Innovation Department is also involved. They too have a licence agreement with us. I can't just rewrite that exchanging Pete's name for Chris's without referring back to them.' Timles was thoughtful for a while, then seemed to come to a decision.

'Of course if Pete's name does go on a new agreement, that could make a big difference to his future at the University. Look, I'll need to read the agreement again, then after the funeral, we need to get Pete in for a chat. When you contact him next, do say that in principle I'm keen to keep him on board. I just need to know what's involved.' Timles consulted his watch.

'Do you still feel like talking about yourself now or has all this broken the spirit of any mentoring session?'

'I'm happy to talk if you have time.'

'Do you mind if I summarise where I think we've got to? It will help take my mind off the news you've come to me with today.'

'OK.'

'Right. From what I have heard and seen, you've come a long way from that day Noura shared her concerns about you. Back then you were depressed and lacked motivation to engage with life. You had a stand off with your elderly parent and were still bitter about your ex; Helena. You weren't talking to colleagues or interested in finding ways you might work with them.

You were making little or no effort to socialise. You were spending too many lonely hours in the pub or at home. Am I painting too black a picture here?'

'No. You're probably holding back so as not to hurt my feelings.' Timles smiled at that one.

'OK. So taking that last reply for a start, you seem to have recovered your sense of humour. Your physiotherapy work, always good before your black dog came on, is now excellent. One of my co-directors can't speak highly enough of you. You've made at least one good friend: Peter Swales. Through him you're helping with this exciting complementary medicine network project. You've now talked to all our other therapists and assistants and have gone from little understanding of what we are trying to achieve here, to become one of our ambassadors; possibly eventually an evangelist for us. You seem to have seen the light regarding complementary medicine. You've settled your mind about Helena. You've made peace with your father. You've dipped your toe and possibly more than that in the water of at least two possible relationships. Would it be too dramatic to compare your new mindset to Saul's insight on the road to Damascus? Anyway, I'd say that substantial progress has been made. What do you think?'

'Putting it like that, I'd have to blush.'

'And agree with me?'

'Yes.' Timles looked hard at him, the curious darker rims of his irises seeming to make his gaze more penetrating. Peter could see Tina's eyes in them and for an odd moment he felt that she too was watching and listening to him.

'But you still have a difficult decision to make about a personal relationship?'

'You read me like a book - your book in fact!'

'You know, you're a different person today, Martin. The turn around seems remarkable. But then, when you were offered the contract with us, I always felt you had something special to offer. And although you probably still don't believe it, you have something special to bring to a personal relationship as well as working ones.'

'Give me some pointers.'

'If I remember right, your three counsellors, Tina, Anne and I have already given you all the pointers you need. My advice was, beyond the obvious matters of chemistry and intelligence, the more things you can successfully see yourselves doing together, the more satisfying - and durable - your relationship will be.' Timles looked at his watch.

'Look, I must bring our chat to a close. Do give Pete my condolences when you see him and tell him not to worry. We will help him whatever the University decides.' Timles stood up and made to leave, but turned back at the door.

'Oh, and I don't think we need another mentoring session, Martin. Whatever *you* decide to do next, I'll support your decision too. But remember Shakespeare's advice: *Love looks not with the eyes, but with the mind; and therefore is winged Cupid painted blind!*'

He winked conspiratorially and closed the meeting room door.

Part Four

LOGGING OFF

Happiness during any computer session is when you complete your work, log off and shut down your computer; Misery is when the computer interrupts your work, logs you off and shuts down itself.

Michael John Geisow

Happiness is not a state to arrive at, but a manner of travelling.

Margaret Lee Runbeck

CHAPTER TWENTY-ONE
Martin

Martin was in good mood when he signed in at the Woodlands on Friday. He noticed that there were dust sheets down along the corridor opposite his office and a power tool was in use in one of the rooms. Clearly contractors had started making changes in the building. No doubt there'd be an email that he had failed to open from Noura giving precise details and timings of the works. But it was easier just to talk to Julie on reception.

'What's going on, Julie?' Martin nodded towards the noise.

'Obviously you haven't been reading your email, Mr Wright.' Julie gave him her stock disapproving look which somehow also managed to be slightly suggestive.

'Guilty as charged; now don't keep me in suspense.'

'The contractors are preparing Tina's old room for our new therapist.' Martin was astonished. He didn't know that his new assistant would get their own room.

'I thought my new assistant would share my own surgery. Surely he wouldn't need a separate room as large as Tina's?' Julie shook her head in disbelief.

'And I thought the old Martin had returned. Clearly he's still not with us. We're not getting another physio or a Reiki therapist; the new person is a sighkiatrist or something. And anyway, why should you assume your assistant will be a "he"? Wouldn't a "she" be more appropriate to assist with your sort of work? Nicer for you too, I'd think.' Julie gave him her best wicked grin.

'What about that female physio company rep. who came to see you a few weeks back. If *she* took the post, you'd probably need your "do not disturb" light on most of the day.' Martin felt his face warm slightly. Julie didn't know how close to the truth she was with that remark. Wanting to change the subject he asked about his boss.

'I thought Dr. Timles was using Tina's old room as his operations centre? And what's this about a psychiatrist? That would be a pretty high powered appointment for a Centre like this. Are you sure about that?' But Julie was no longer looking at him.

'You'll have to ask Noura all these questions, Mart. I've got a visitor.'

Martin glanced behind and saw someone opening the entrance door. He turned away and left reception. A minute later he was standing in Noura's office.

'Is Dr. Timles here today, Noura?'

'I think he's due in later. Do you want to schedule a meeting with him?'

'I didn't know we'd advertised for a psychiatrist.'

'We haven't. It's a psychotherapist. Apparently it's part of Michael's new plan for the Centre. I understand he had a strong recommendation and interviewed the person concerned on-line.' Noura looked more than a little disapproving.

'And they'll be working in Tina's old room? I thought that was Dr. Timles's HQ.'

'Yes the new member of staff will be using the old Reiki suite. And you must know Dr. Timles has been using the Centre meeting room for some time now.' This was all in my last emailed memo, you know.' Noura looked even more irritated.

'Sorry Noura, I had some problems with my computer but it's fixed now.' He hoped she wouldn't pursue this transparent excuse further, but she was already looking at her wall clock. Martin took the hint.

'I'd better get back to my room. I've got to check my email now it's up and running again.' Noura's mention of email made Martin think of his Internet muse; Anne. He decided to use the hour before his next client to talk to her, if she was available. Closing and locking his office door, he fired up his computer and logged on to InterconNet. Moments later Anne responded to his request for voice contact.

'Hello Martin, how are you today?'

'Hello Anne. Your cheery greeting was almost instant. I can scarcely believe you're always there for me when I log on. Is it convenient to talk now?'

'It's OK.' Martin hesitated. In spite of his promise of confidentiality to Timles, it was going to be difficult to keep avoiding the subject of what the Woodlands was doing. In any case, Anne was a full time InterconNet user and might well become an external user of *LIFELINES* at some stage. He would certainly like to see that.

'Can I speak in strict confidence to you?'

'That's always been our understanding hasn't it?'

'Things are moving quickly at the moment. Our Centre's owner had a new computer system put in here at the Woodlands and we're all supposed to be working with it. The idea is that the staff here network better with each other and with external contacts. We expect eventually to be able to deliver much better therapies to clients.'

'It sounds exciting, but very ambitious. Are you involved in all this?'

'Very much so. I'm getting all our therapists on the network, organising training and eventually helping to set up a bridge between our own therapeutic work and work in other centres.'

'That *is* challenging.'

'Well for me at least there's a second big challenge ahead.'

'I'm guessing now. That's what you want to talk about this morning?'

'Do you remember that I mentioned my Reiki therapist?'

'Tina?'

'Yes. Well I finally summoned the courage to ask her for a date. She came for a meal at my flat and we talked about relationships.'

'I take it you're no longer seeing Tuula then?'

'I don't want *that* kind of relationship. It seems that before I even consulted her Tina had been thinking I'd make a good partner.' There was a long delay before Anne's voice responded. It might have been his imagination, but she sounded a bit sharp.

'So are you now worried that her unusual treatment of you in her flat amounted to a covert physical inspection of the goods before she told you that you might be suitable?'

'Ouch! That never even crossed my mind. No, she was talking about a *business* partner. Well, a personal one too I think, but her priority is definitely business first. To Tina, her work is like being in love, she enjoys it so much. And she says, in so many words at least, that a man and woman who work *and* play together, stay together.'

'What was your response to that?'

'I'm afraid I stalled for time by saying that we should go out together and get to know each other under more normal circumstances.'

'Are you concerned that Tina might want to fast track an arrangement where you become her live in business partner and emotional support?' Anne seemed to be pushing him to come up with answers this morning. He wondered if she had a client appointment scheduled soon. But he couldn't fault her grasp of his situation.

'I suppose if something like that had been on her mind while we both working at the Woodlands, she was already waiting for things to happen.'

'And in the end decided to make them happen?'

'Well to be fair, I did ask her if Reiki could help me with my depression. I didn't realise she had a potential future for us already mapped out.' Again there was a delay before Anne replied.

'But are you attracted by her?' Martin remembered his last consultation with Anne.

'Yes, but that's my problem isn't it? I'm attracted by young, good looking, high flying career women.'

'One of your problems perhaps. As Tom Jones once sang: "It's not unusual". But Martin, you've already told me that when your partner puts their career before their relationship, it can be uncomfortable and sometimes unfortunate. I'm talking about Helena of course.'

'So you aren't going to tell me what to do then, are you?'

'I think you already know the answer to that. My role is to help you to make important decisions; not make them for you.' Martin realised he'd reached the end of this line of questioning, but he didn't want to stop talking to Anne.

'Are you still OK for time Anne?'

'Yes, OK for now.'

'This morning I was told our Centre's getting a new member of staff, a psychotherapist.' Anne paused once again before replying.

'Actually, I do know about that, Martin. They're a postgraduate from our Psychological Sciences faculty here. She's a close friend as it happens. There aren't so many of us reading for a higher degree at present.' Martin was at first surprised by this, but then it seemed obvious. One of the first places for Timles to look for someone like that would have been the

University.

'I thought we'd be getting a replacement for Tina, but never saw any adverts for another post.' Anne responded quickly to that one.

'My friend says she was recommended by someone in the Computer Sciences Faculty who knows your boss.'

'Pete Swales?'

'No. She said his name was Chris. I wasn't told his surname.'

'Oh I can see it now. Chris Johns. He's the Reader in Computer Sciences; Pete's supervisor. Chris and Pete were asked by the owner to help with the Woodland's new network.' But Chris sadly died recently. A heart attack. Pete's now taking over as our University liaison. Martin didn't mention Tuula's involvement.

'Is the University a part of all this then?' Martin hesitated, again recalling Timles's caution not to go into details about what was planned for *LIFELINES*. He'd probably already told Anne more than he should.

'I'm afraid that's not a question I can answer right now. But what can you tell me about this new psychotherapist?'

'Well, you'll probably meet her soon and she'll be able to tell you more herself. You may soon have two people to act as that "bridge" as you call it between your Centre's work and therapies elsewhere.'

'What's her name?'

'Serena.' An old fashioned name. It seemed familiar; he thought Chris or perhaps Peter had mentioned it once. Anne was talking again.

'Martin, look, I must sign off now. I have a meeting scheduled and I have to prepare for that. Perhaps we can have a longer chat later?'

'OK, thanks Anne.' After the connection closed, Martin felt a curious sense of loss and a mild annoyance that Anne was obviously helping others. He was disappointed that although they were talking to each other her voice was being changed by InterconNet as a further measure of identity protection. He wondered if Anne would ever agree to a video link like Tuula had showed him. Well, not *quite* like Tuula had done, obviously. In a selfish way he already felt a special relationship with this unseen therapist. Although the anonymity of their connection helped him be open with Anne, it also created a sense of intimacy. He had to admit that he was uncomfortable about sharing Anne with others. He determined to ask this Serena for more information about Anne when she appeared at the Centre.

He didn't have to wait long. After he accompanied his next patient to the reception desk to fetch a booklet for him, a tall, slim, dark haired young woman was standing there. Something about her seemed quite familiar. As his physiotherapy patient left clutching the Centre's new brochure, Julie interrupted his thoughts.

'Martin. Good timing. Our new staff member has arrived for a tour of inspection. Noura's missing and Dr. Timles has got delayed somewhere.' She turned to the visitor.

'We're sorry that the Centre's owner and manager are both unavailable but our physiotherapist, Martin Wright, will be delighted show you round and answer your questions. Martin, this is Serena Peddy our new sigh kiatrist.' The visitor smiled.

'Psychotherapist actually. I'm not medically qualified. Not yet at least.' She extended a hand. She was about Martin's height with quite pronounced cheek bones. As her eyes connected with his own, the archivist in Martin's head suddenly retrieved the missing memory. That night months ago in the Green Dragon when he first met Peter. This was the woman who had been chatting with them. She had caught his eyes just before she left. Peter had told him her name; Serena Peddy. So this was Anne's friend, the nearest he had come to his mysterious on-line counsellor. Martin pulled himself hurriedly back to the present.

'Oh, Sorry, still thinking about my last client. Welcome to the Woodlands Centre, Serena.'

'Thank you. Actually I'm not due to start here yet. Dr. Timles suggested I come for a short tour and meet some of the staff. He said that your administrator would show me round. I'm supposed to be having lunch with Dr Timles at 1pm.'

'Well it's almost unheard of for our administrator—Noura Munday—to miss an appointment. So her absence must be for a very good reason. But I'd be delighted to show you round.' Serena followed Martin away from the reception desk.

'Noura Munday's such a curious name. It almost sounds like…'

'Black Monday. Yes, that's what all the staff here call her; behind her back of course. Martin checked himself.

'Oops, I probably shouldn't have told you that.' Serena smiled conspiratorially.

'Well I won't breathe a word.'

'Would you mind if I start with my clinic? That's the area I understand best of course.'

'Physiotherapy? The Woodlands has a good reputation for sports medicine at the University. You're listed in the health information sheets given to all students. I'm keen to see what facilities you have here. Although I deal with mental health and well being, physical health is a key factor. And the other way round too, of course.'

'Well my own facilities are getting a face lift soon and we're advertising for a physiotherapy assistant.'

'It's good to hear you're expanding here. You must be very busy.'

'Well at present, I'm not over subscribed, but the Centre's owner wants me to help with a new IT project to raise the Centre's profile. This means someone else to assist me treat aches and pains. Over the next year he's expecting to have many more clients. Presumably your post is part of the new plan?' Serena just smiled and commented:

'One of the post grads in our department comes for treatment here; she's heavily into sport.' Martin remembered Anne saying that she also had an on-line client who had come to the Woodlands for physiotherapy. That was hardly a co-incidence though; a high percentage of his walk-in and regular clients came from the University faculties or its associated organisations and suppliers. They stopped outside his office and Martin opened the door for his visitor. Once inside he invited her to sit while he described his own work and attempted to summarise what went on elsewhere. But he could no longer restrain his curiosity about Anne.

'Do you know a postgraduate called Anne Eres in your department?'

'Anne; yes she's also expecting to complete her Ph.D. course very soon. In fact her *viva* is scheduled around the same time as mine. She doesn't mix very much with the other postgraduate students in the Department, but I've met her in tutorials and seminars of course. Is she a friend of yours?' Martin thought carefully before answering. He had agreed that his conversations with Anne were confidential. He assumed that applied to what she told him about herself as well as what he confided in her.

'Well a Computer Science postgraduate I met in my local got me signed up to a special kind of social network experiment he has running at the University. It's called InterconNet.' He paused and looked at Serena to see if that was something she knew about, but she gave no sign of recognition. He continued:

'I came across Anne on this network and noticed she was from your department. We've been in touch since then on-line and I was interested in her research work…' Martin left the sentence hanging. He decided not to elaborate further in the hope that Serena would volunteer something more about Anne without further prompting. Serena nodded.

'I do know about InterconNet. A number of my friends are also members. But as with Face Book and other public social networks, people are spending more time on it than they should. In fact it's quite a cult at the University.' Martin could see she was now being polite, but was losing interest in the present line of conversation.

'I'm sorry. Getting sidetracked. I didn't know that Michael Timles had appointed a psychotherapist, although I can see it fits in perfectly with the direction he's now taking our Centre. Look, I'm afraid I'm not the best tour guide for the Woodlands because until recently, perhaps like your friend Anne, I've kept myself to myself at the Woodlands.'

'Until recently? Is that to do with the changes here?' Martin smiled ruefully.

'It's more to do with friendly advice I've been given from a number of different quarters.' Serena seemed to detect his ambivalence and smiled encouragingly.

'Well, we're both working closer to conventional as opposed to alternative heath care. So I hope when I do start here we'll be networking with each other in reality, rather than virtually like your InterconNet contact.' Martin picked up her intended sympathy and warmth. He felt certain that this stranger was going to be an asset to the Woodlands Centre and someone he would want to get to know better.

'I'd like that too, but here's a well intentioned piece of advice, Serena. Don't compare and contrast "complementary medicine" with the "mainstream" version when you speak to Michael Timles. That would definitely not be the thing to do.'

'Well Martin, thanks for the advice.' The next 45 minutes passed amazingly quickly. After spending rather a lot of it describing and demonstrating his physiotherapy work he did a reasonably good job of explaining what went on elsewhere. Timles and Tina's book, which he'd now read twice, helped him to connect the more alternative approaches with the appropriate positive states of mind conducive to healing. Serena was apparently fascinated by this and constantly asked questions as she was shown round the Woodlands. They ended up back in his clinic. Martin spotted his copy of *Universal Therapy* and showed it to Serena.

'Did Michael give you a copy of this book? He and his daughter Tina have just published it. Tina used to work here; she's a Reiki therapist.'

'Oh yes, Dr. Timles gave me that. Said it was required reading for the job. I've dipped into it. But there's a couple of chapters missing.' Martin was surprised.

'What do you mean?'

'No chapters on psychotherapy or physiotherapy!' She grinned.

'You hadn't got a *me* here when it was written of course, but I'm surprised they didn't get *you* to write about the role of belief. For treating carpal tunnel syndrome, for instance.'

Martin blinked and was about to comment on her curious reply, when Serena glanced at her watch and stood up.

'It's nearly 1 pm now, perhaps I'd better go back to reception.' Martin felt disappointed he hadn't been the first to introduce Serena to his boss's remarkable book. And he was not much wiser about his on-line therapist Anne. He would probably not have another chance to talk to this very personable new member of the Centre for some time. But then she only lived locally. Why not meet up for a drink and carry on their interrupted discussion?

'Look, I wasn't expecting to act as a representative and guide today, but I'd really like to hear more about your role with us.'

'I realise I've been dumped on you unexpectedly, but it couldn't have worked out better as far as I'm concerned. I'm sure I've had a much nicer introduction than your "Black Monday" would have given me.' Martin widened his eyes and put a finger to his lips and glanced at the walls as if to signal silently that the room might be bugged. Serena widened hers too and put her hand over her mouth. 'Sorry it just slipped out!' Their conversation had gone surprisingly rapidly from the formal to the familiar.

'The thought of us taking on a full time psychotherapist here is exciting. It means I'll feel less isolated as the only NHS recognised therapist and talking to you might help me with a difficult personal decision I have to make.' Martin was thinking about the disturbingly different and even opposing futures Tina and her father had shown him.

'You see I'm afraid I've been guilty of ignoring my Centre colleagues and now you're here especially, I want to make a fresh start.'

'And you'd like to "get fresh" with me?' Serena grinned cheekily. Martin was initially startled by this, but realised from her expression that the Centre's latest recruit had a wicked sense of humour.

'I was going to suggest we might meet for a drink one evening.'

'I'd like that. Where do you normally go?'

'Well for some time it's been the Green Dragon pub near the Centre. In fact I'm sure I saw you there some months back, talking to Peter Swales and several other students.' For a moment, Serena looked uncomfortable.

'You may have done, but don't you think it's become a bit…'

'Gay?'

'I was going to say noisy, but I do agree with your "alternative" assessment.' She hesitated.

'Well yes; I am free tonight, but then I have an awful lot of things to tie up before I start here. It would be great to have time for a chat before that happens. You can give me more grass roots information than your big boss and from what you've said on your guided tour, you could use an ally from the "mainstream" as you call it.' Martin quickly reviewed his extremely limited repertoire of places to eat.

'How about a chat over dinner at the Bear in Read?'

'The old Inn by the Thames? I've been there once. Nice food. At least there was when I was there before'

'Should we say 7:30, Serena?' The intercom interrupted them. Julie intoned in her posh voice:

'Dr. Timles in reception for Miss Peddy.' Serena stood up quickly.

'At 7:30 then. I'll meet you there. Thanks once again, Martin.' After The Bear Inn had confirmed availability of a table for two that evening, Martin returned to his scheduled appointments. He left the Woodlands that evening in a state of some excitement which he couldn't satisfactorily account for. It wasn't about the quality of the Inn's food, good though that was. He thought about what he would tell Serena about the Woodlands.

He would have to moderate the claims in Noura's excessively glossy Woodlands brochure. But Serena, being psychology trained, could probably see though those anyway. And, thanks to Timles and Tina's book, he was no longer anxious about displaying a lack of knowledge of the treatments the other therapists were providing. Which left only one explanation for the nerves. But it seemed irrational to feel that way about someone you had only just met. Martin found their reserved table early, but he didn't have long to wait. He stood up when he spotted Serena enter the pub and waited for her to settle herself, before he sat again.

'Thanks for waving. It's pretty full isn't it? Did you have to book this table for us?' She made it easy for Martin to relax and enjoy small talk while they chose drinks and discussed the menu. Poised give asked a potted history of the Woodlands, he was surprised that Serena seemed to want to talk about herself instead.

'I know you're expecting me to give you the 3rd degree about the Woodlands and all who sail in her, but I'd like just to unwind tonight. You might not have realised it, but you did a pretty good job of filling me in about your own practice and what else goes on at the Woodlands during my guided tour. But you don't know much about me and we'll probably be working quite closely. You told me your boss wants Centre staff to network more. Well, when you have to tell one of your patients you can't do anything about them being too short or having one leg longer than the other, you can send them to me.' Martin laughed at this.

'Actually many of my patients are super fit, but have injured themselves trying to stay that way. I'm sure *those* are clear candidates for your own services.' Serena laughed too, then asked:

'Do you *mind* if I go on a bit about me tonight? You know, as a psychologist, I spend most of my time thinking about and listening to other people. Either that or talking shop to fellow psychologists. It would be a novel experience to unburden myself to a physiotherapist!' The wine had arrived and Martin filled their glasses.

'I'd like to hear about you and I'm pleased you found my tour helpful. I hadn't practised it so if I did it again it would probably end up being completely different.'

'All the nicer for being off the cuff. Well Martin, here goes; I'm not from these parts originally. My family home's in Sussex. At school, I was interested in Law. When I left school I did some further studies at an FE college and was lucky enough to get a job as a legal secretary; family connections you know.' Serena gave a conspiratorial wink and sipped her wine.

'As a young girl in a law firm, it wasn't long before I attracted the attention of one of the senior partners. And by that I don't mean he thought he could fast track my legal career. Of course it turned my head and I was soon infatuated. But it wasn't long before I found out that my solicitor heart throb was also having an affair with another legal secretary. I was distraught. This other woman was older, wiser and certainly more dangerous to compromise. Although I couldn't see it at the time, she was far more likely to shipwreck his career than I was.' Serena paused.

'Is this too much information?'

'No, please go on.'

'Well. I was getting wiser too and I was becoming aware that other married partners in the firm were having affairs as well. It seems to be endemic in the legal profession. Anyway, I wanted out. Getting another job proved to be tough. I couldn't get a good reference from the law firm - but I bet the "other woman" would have been able to extort a fantastic testimonial and a golden handshake if she'd wanted to! Well, family help again got me a part time post in a joint practice dealing with patents and trademarks.

This time my boss was female and the other patent attorneys were so weighed down with paperwork and that they had no time for anything on the side except coffee.' Serena's story was interrupted then as their meals arrived. Once they had settled to eat and commented on the cooking, she was able to continue.

'Feeling bruised by my experience at the hands of people I had trusted, when I wasn't at work, I did some day and evening courses in psychology and personal coaching. Over the next few years I managed to enrol in the Open University and get a degree in psychology. I was still working part time for the patent outfit. In fact although they were experts on inventions and logo design, they were starting to pick my brains about some of their clients! Anyway, I finally set my sights on a career as psychologist and enrolled full time on a Ph.D. course at Tamford. And finally, at the end of this month, I've my viva exam and a new job. It's been a long haul. It hasn't left me much time or energy for socialising, so as you heard earlier today, I'm still *Miss* Peddy' Serena gave a rueful smile.' Martin nodded and grinned.

'Well, I'm still *Mr* Wright.' Serena's face brightened immediately.

'And always will be, of course. But, with a name like that, I'm sure there must be a *Mrs* Wright somewhere.'

'Actually I had a partner for a number of years, before we split up some time ago, but I've never married.' They ate in silence for a while, lost in their own thoughts. Martin saw Serena's glass was almost empty.

'More wine?'

'Half a glass; I'm driving afterwards. Not far though; I'm still living in the Uni halls of residence, until I've had my *viva* and wrapped up any number of admin things.' She put down her knife and fork.

'What about your own career. Are you planning to stay at the Woodlands?' Martin hesitated. This was a very pointed question right now. Tina and her father had both shown him different futures. Both were intriguing for very different reasons and both were uncertain.

'Strange you should ask that, because I have to make a choice between the Woodlands and another option that has come up. Right now I don't quite know which way to jump. I don't have to make my mind up immediately, but eventually I'll have to decide.' Serena looked quite worried.

'Well I hope you won't leave just as I start working. If you did, I could find myself as isolated at the Woodlands as you told me that you've been.' Martin found, to his shocked surprise, that his hand suddenly rested gently on Serena's. It was just a touch. He didn't let it linger. They were both quiet for a moment then the conversation returned to their earlier pleasant small talk. Eventually, Serena announced that she should get back to her room in the Halls of residence. She reached for her purse but Martin stopped her. Once again his hand moved to hers; this time in gentle restraint rather than empathy.

'I've got a tab at the bar. This is my welcoming treat. Please let me, Serena.' She smiled, opened her purse, but extracted a white business card instead of cash.

'Look, I'll give you my contact details in case we should need to get in touch before I start officially at the Centre. Mind you, I expect your Black Monday has already ordered some for me.' Martin showed mock concern.

'For goodness sake don't get in the habit of calling her that.' They both stood up. Serena pressed his hand and looked back and waved once she reached the door. When she had gone, Martin looked at the card she gave him and turned it over to read:

Serena D. Peddy

Psychological Sciences
University of Tamford
Room C43 Earley Hall
Email: serendipity@tamford.ac.uk

It was true, then that all students these days had business cards. She was in the same block in the Halls of Residence as Tuula. He wondered whether, like Anne, Serena had also met Tuula. Probably. All of the Uni people he had encountered so far seemed to know about Tuula. She was larger than life, that was certain. Martin recalled Pete's own impressive business card. He thought it was probably still in his wallet. Leafing through the jumble of loyalty cards and till receipts he managed to find it, looking distinctly tired. He turned it over to look at what Peter had scrawled on the back: "Her name is Serena Diane Peddy, can u believe? Perhaps you might meet her on-line!! Call me if you're interested (in my offer). Pete".

Martin sat down heavily. What was it that Times had said in an early counselling session? It had struck him as slightly odd then and he had recalled it again when he next logged onto InterconNet. Times had been talking about Martin's discovery of Anne on InterconNet and about his starting therapy sessions with her. It was something like: *I'd say that you have a made a happy chance find there.* That was the meaning of Serendipity. But Times had been talking about his on-line psychotherapist; Anne Eres. The other way round! If you reversed An(ne) Eres you got Serena. *Serena* was his mysterious on-line psychotherapist.

She had to be. It all fitted. All these weeks he had been confiding very personal information to the new member of the Woodlands staff. Times must have known who Anne really was. His appointment of her and his "happy chance find" remark could not have been co-incidences. Peter and probably Tuula knew too. Even Tina may have known if her father had told her.

Martin's thoughts were whirling. He stood up and paid his tab at the bar. On the way back to his flat, he went through the strange events of the past months in his mind. His overhearing Serena talking with Peter and two other students in the bar of the Dragon. He could remember some snatches of their conversation; recalled now because he was straining so hard to overhear:

'...*Well I'm broad-minded but that*...
...*would it actually be legal?*...
...*wouldn't you need Uni ethical committee approval?*...
...*and you aren't going to tell your supervisor?*...'

The discussion had obviously been about a research project. But whose? It had to be to do with InterconNet. And after that Peter had invited him to join him for a drink '..*You don't recognise me do you?...Frozen shoulder?*' He still couldn't recall Peter as a Woodlands patient. From there the discussion led to looking for relationships on-line and then to signing up to Peter's research project; InterconNet. He had forgotten until now that Peter had quite openly said he would be recording all Martin's activity on-line as part of his research project. Serena/Anne had a research project too; she was finishing it at the end of the month.

Perhaps her own research had switched to using InterconNet without her own supervisor's knowledge. There had certainly been *legal* issues involved in Peter's element of the InterconNet research programme, were the *ethical* ones the small group in the Dragon had talked about to do with Serena's involvement as a psychotherapist? Was it InterconNet or Peter Swales who had positioned their network nodes so close together? Peter *had* said he had been in serious trouble with his supervisor about the project. Back at his flat. Martin stared at the computer on his coffee table. Minutes later he was logged onto InterconNet. He opened Anne's network node and requested contact.

Anne Eres is presently off-line. Do you wish to leave a message?

Martin clicked "No" and on a whim, read through her profile once more. Chris had told him that each member could only see how they described themselves (and were free to update that at any time). But that was not what InterconNet showed others. The software constantly adjusted member's profiles as it monitored their interactions with others on the network.

It was through this impartial "policing" of content that the validity and quality of the information displayed was continually improved. That was one of the things that made InterconNet far more powerful than the Internet's main social networks. Only Peter Swales and Tuula Pippi appeared exempt from the programme's editing and censorship. Anne's profile was essentially as he remembered it from his first reading. She stated as before that she had joined the InterconNet community to help other network members, but her previous caveat to visitors at the foot of her profile about "not looking for romantic opportunities" was missing.

Martin closed her contact dialogue box and walked over to his balcony window to look out over the dark streets, towards a dim purple haze that was all that remained of the sunset. Was the deletion of that last sentence her own work or InterconNet's? Did it mean she had *deliberately* decided not to be a lonely on-line presence? Or had that change been decided by Peter and Chris's clever software? By giving Martin her business card Anne/Serena must have known that working out her true identity was only a matter of time.

Did the absence of that last sentence have anything to do with meeting him? She seemed so self assured but surely she must have felt a bit apprehensive about meeting him face to face. It looked very much like she had been using him as part of her Ph.D. work without his knowledge. As a psychologist she *had* to be asking herself whether he would feel flattered or angry. In truth the feeling uppermost in his mind was embarrassment over what he'd revealed about himself. But what to do now? He wouldn't appear very bright if he didn't let her know he'd guessed who she was. But what was the most sensitive way to do this? Martin recalled the first four principles of Reiki:

At least for today: Don't be angry; Do not worry; Be grateful; Be kind.

He returned to his computer and opened Anne's contact window once more.

Anne Eres is presently off-line. Do you wish to leave a message? He did. *Welcome to the Woodlands, Serena Look forward to working with you, Martin.* He closed Anne's InterconNet node and logged off the system. As he did so a text chirped on his mobile. It was from Tina.

Hi Mart
Sorry to have been out of touch for another week yet again. Everything went well in Sheffield and 'sis' is fully restored to health. I'm back now and I wondered if tomorrow evening would be a good time to meet? I promised ages ago to cook for you in my own flat and I'd love to wow

you with my cuisine! Unless your heart is set on the Dragon, of course.
Love Tina
xx
Friday 22:00

Martin stared vacantly at the text for a long while trying to work out what message lay beneath it. Take up the "Reiki sessions" from where they left off? Explore a possible personal or business relationship? Or both? Tina was in every sense a remarkable woman and either or both possibilities would be flattering. But now he'd just met another extraordinary woman. One who now knew as much or more about him than Tina. He decided to sleep on it; if he could. The following morning was a Saturday and the Woodlands was closed. He decided to walk to the Centre to see if its familiar working environment could clear his head. Once in his office, he turned on his computer intending to log on to InterconNet, half hoping to see some response from Anne/Serena to his last message. There were two emails.

From: Tuula Pipi
To: Mart (Physio)
Subject: Sorry I've have been 'offline'

Hi Mart!
It was pretty s**t of me not getting back in touch after our great trip to the coast, but life and work just took me over after that. You may or may not know that I'm back at my post in Helsinki. Actually, Pete came with me to do a presentation on InterconNet to my company. I won't go into details, but they aren't buying (literally and metaphorically!) the idea that we pitched to them.

But Pete let slip that your big boss does want to use the programme he and I set up at your Centre. He mentioned something about Healthcare use, but quickly clammed up. I've had time now to go over what Pete - and you - have told me. I reckon I can see where your boss is going with his version of InterconNet and it's not just keeping staff and patient records! I would like to meet your boss - Timles? - and offer my help. I've already written to him, but you can confirm when he asks, that I developed a special version of InterconNet myself. I have the expertise - and energy - he's going to need. To get what I think he wants do to off the ground, it won't work trying to tackle healthcare with a big H. Start small, build a wide user base and get the money coming in to fund expansion. I'm suggesting something right up your street; exercise for

health and well being. Loads of sites already on the 'Net, but InterconNet would leave them all standing (or sitting!).
I don't have a place at Tamford any more so I wonder if I could stay with you while I'm back in Reading - unless InterconNet has already fixed you up with someone else of course! I'd like to get your feedback on my idea and it would be a lot more fun (for both of us!!).staying with you rather than an hotel
Get back to me on this one soon!
Tuula

Subject: No longer anonymous!
To: Marin Wright
From: Sendipity

Hello Martin
Looking forward to working with you too.
I now owe you a big explanation and an even bigger apology for keeping you in the dark, discussing your most personal feelings with you and then appearing as a new member of the Woodlands staff. You will have probably guessed by now that I have used some of our discussions (anonymously of course) as part of my research work. It appears that I'm the third woman to do that to you recently, but at least my name doesn't begin with T!
When Pete Swales invited you to join InterconNet - to help him with his own Ph.D. work - you told me that looking for a real world relationship motivated you to accept. I'd like to talk more with you about that, this time as Serena, rather than Anne. But if you'd now prefer just to talk shop and draw a veil over our virtual relationship, I'll have to accept that decision.
However, I really hope you will agree to come over to my room in the Uni Halls and let me explain myself further and make amends. I could also show you how my avatar was created from my own photos - if, as a physiotherapist, you're interested. My room is more deluxe than others you may have "experienced" as I do duty as a block warden. If you do come, I'd love you to tell me more about the Woodlands and the mysterious Dr. Timles. In return, apart from a full and frank explanation about everything that has been going on, I will definitely lay on your favourite beer. Oops, I forgot it was Anne you confided in. Serena has to earn that privilege.
If you're not at work, I'm in all day today. Looking forward to hearing from you soon.
Serena
C43 Earley Hall
University of Tamford

* * *

****

Martin stared vacantly through his office window and shook his head, trying to clear his thoughts. He stroked his index and forefingers against his temple - somehow that seemed to help. Emotions ranging from elation to anger occupied his mind in succession. Yes, his life had moved on - or rather had been moved on; yes, he had shaken off those numbing feelings of disconnection and aimlessness; of worthlessness even. But his improved state of mind had been brought about in such a peculiar manner. At the kerbside immediately opposite the Woodlands Centre, a white van pulled up. Its signwriting announced: "FRESH START Ltd. Clear your personal space! Office and domestic cleaners" Martin felt the irony of its advertising message and half wondered if that too had been planned for him in advance by his alternative therapists. He felt angry at the way he'd been manipulated; like an experimental animal in a research lab. Even though everyone concerned, especially Martin himself, had gained from the exercise, it was still demeaning that he was the last one to realise what had been happening. In arriving at his present, happier frame of mind, he had been more like a mouse in a maze guided to an exit by small rewards, than a man taking calculated risks and choosing his own direction.

But which was more important? The means of arriving at a good place in life or the arrival itself? Once again, he went over what had happened and tried to imagine what answers his self-appointed mentor, Timles, might soundlessly provide to the questions in his head. But of course, his mentor would start by asking Martin questions; powerful ones, as he would often remark. Martin closed his eyes. Timles appeared behind his spacious desk, his hands steepled indicating that a virtual session was starting.

Why did you decide to visit Tina Elves's very alternative practice?

Martin considered this. He recalled that in desperation, he'd decided to explore an unconventional route to feeling better about himself. It had been he that had initiated this, even though Tina already had been more than willing to help him. He remembered his surprise at discovering Tina to be such a complex and interesting woman and not just another therapist peddling healing he once considered valueless.

What was the outcome of your visits to her?

Tina had led him to discover his own sensuality and think more sensitively about the needs and feelings of others. This alone had made her attractive, even though he was still uncertain about a personal relationship with her because of what she did. Yes, she had encouraged him to look for a new partner with whom to share his new found interest at work and in life generally. But if not Tina then who?

The peerless on-line image of Anne Eres floated before him. She had gained his admiration and, now that he recognised it; desire. She had acted as an ultimate go-between, discussing and impartially advising on relationships, then had disappeared into the 'net. But could he ever fully dismiss her compelling image from his brain? Then there was now Serena, Anne's alter ego. Timles broke into his reverie:

I agree that the maze you have been in was artificial and created by others, but you had a goal when you entered and you exercised freedom of choice throughout. Isn't 'real' life just a bigger maze, within which you choose your own route? And if you arrive at last at an exit, does it really matter much how you got there?

Martin thought: that man really is able to read minds and then reflected: idiot, this time he *is* in my mind and he is just echoing my own thoughts.'

Timles's disembodied voice continued:

So in the end, what was it that rescued you from wandering fruitlessly in your own dismal labyrinth which had no exit? Martin was just asking himself the same question, when the calm, familiar voice in his head seemed to answer it for him.

It was that very healing power you always dismissed as ineffective, wasn't it? Martin had to admit that his obvious recovery had been, in a way, through alternative therapy.

Timles's vision was fainter now, but another question assembled itself in Martin's head.

It's not complete yet is it, Martin? You have a key decision to make. For two people, the most important one of all.

Timles's vision faded, leaving Martin alone once more with his critical choice. This time it was the complete absence of advice from his mentor or anyone else that helped him make it. It was time for him to take back some control of his future. Serendipity, sensuality or sex! All offering the prospect of companionship and career advancement. Three exits, not one as his mental vision of Timles suggested. But which one to take? ***Just for today don't worry . . .***

Bibliography

Some of the ideas in this story have been inspired by the following publications. If there are concepts in this novel that interest the reader, then they are invited to browse the books listed below. Most of the references are accessible to general readers. One or two are more technical but have been included as they deal with what the author considers to be important issues about our present human condition.

Connected *The Amazing Power of Social Networks and how they shape our lives* Christakis, N & Fowler, J. (2011) Harper Press.

An exploration, with many examples, of how on-line social networks are changing our communications with others and influencing our behaviour, relationships and even our health.

Wikinomics *How mass collaboration changes everything* Tapscott D. and Williams A. D.(2006) Penguin Publishing Group.

A demonstration of how mass on-line collaboration combines the brain power of millions of individuals, world wide, to bear on such challenges as inventing new products, designing medicines, locating mineral resources and much else. Changing the model of private, corporate research and development of products and services into open source shared discovery and invention.

Staying Sane: *How to Make your mind work for you* Persaud, R. (2001) Bantam Books.

A psychologist and psychiatrist's analysis and self help manual on how to develop strategies to maintain a healthy state of mind in the face of present and future personal challenges and crises. This is in direct contrast with a huge literature on identifying mental 'dis - ease' and exploring its treatment 'after the horse has bolted'

The biology of belief *Unleashing the power of consciousness, matter and miracles.* Lipton, B. H. (2005) Hay House Inc.

Showing how the cells of our bodies process information received from the outside world. An exploration of how our biology is controlled, not by our DNA and genes but by external influences on our cells, especially positive and negative thoughts which arise from happenings outside our direct contr

Holistic Medicine: *A meeting of East & West* Altenberg, E.A. (1998)Japan Publications Inc.

Traditional medicine around the world. A comprehensive work covering global alternative medicine choices for combating and preventing illness and maintaining good health. Compares conventional and alternative medicine and covers nutrition and herbal (natural) treatments.

Life 3.0*: Being Human in the Age of Artificial Intelligence* Tegmark, M.(2017)Penguin.

Examines the fast developing reach, current and potential capability of artificial intelligence (AI) software. Considers its influence on people, jobs and even self-worth. Will machine 'minds' soon overreach the capacity of human ones?

Emergence: *The connected lives of ants, brains, cities and software* . Johnson, S. (2001) Allen Lane The Penguin Press.

Synergy: An exploration of how the whole is much greater (and more unpredictable than the sum of its components. We can in design, assemble and run, computer systems, cities and (possibly soon) brains but we cannot predict what will happen until these complex, interacting things are in operation. The results *emerge* over time.

Millennium: *Tribal wisdom and the modern world* Maybury-Lewis, D.(1991) Penguin Books

Deep thoughts on the knowledge of all aspects of social living as seen in distinct tribal communities. This highly local knowledge (which of course includes medicine and health care) reflects traditions that have been passed on for thousands of years. Key to these societies is respect for nature and the intention to work with it rather than exploit it unsustainably as most of the developed world now does. Tribal ways of living is vanishing, to be replaced by global notions of health wealth and prosperity. But there is much for modern society to learn from its own 'roots'.

* * *

Molecules of Emotion: Why you feel the way you feel Pert, Candace (1997) Simon & Schuster UK

In a work of popular science, neuroscientist Candace Pert examines the chemical links between mind and body and the role. A unique book which actually bridges the divide between "mainstream" and "alternative" medicine just as Michael Timles is trying to do in my book!

Plato's Revenge: *Politics in the age of ecology* Ophis, W. (2011) M.I.T. Press.

Almost echoing the examination of tribal society reported in *Millennium* Ophis argues for political administrations that prioritise sustainability, social welfare and ecology over growth and the die-hard expressions of international rivalry we see now. His arguments are inspired by recalling Plato's attempts to envision a better society and cover politics, biology and physics. Ophis appeals for a "wiser savage".

Becoming Human*: Evolution and Human Uniqueness* Tattershall, I (1998) Oxford University Press.

A beautifully written and thought-provoking work by a renowned palaeontologist that examines our evolution and the emergence of the human mind, unique in nature. Especially good at considering the emergence of our marked altruistic behaviour and how that has shaped human society. Goes a long way to explain both 'where we came from' but also 'where we may be going'. Two of the principle questions humans have asked themselves throughout our time on earth.

The Extended Phenotype: *The long each of the gene* Dawkins, R. (1982) Oxford University Press.

An academic work included here because it considers the 'memes': essentially non-genetic cultural behaviours passed on through the generations, still influenced by and influencing our genes. Modern biological research focuses increasingly on the influence on us of 'epigenetics': factors that lie outside our DNA. Society, social interactions and our future evolution are affected by this (this is also examined in *The Biology of Belief*). This older work is included here because considers the 'social interactions' of chemicals within the cells of which we are composed. Human society is built on layers of social interactions: between individuals, between their constituent cells and within the cells themselves. To build better societies, individuals and bodies we need to free ourselves from dogma and ideologies and open our minds to learn and accept what we are.

About the author

Michael has enjoyed a diverse technical, scientific and publishing career. His background is in fundamental medical research and the production of biopharmaceuticals in industry. With a broad interest in life science and medicine, he has published both his own original research papers and many commentaries in the leading science journal *Nature*. Later he diverged into conference organisation and publishing, both on- and off-line for a variety of public and private sector clients. In his spare time and holidays he has been an evening class tutor explaining the landforms and natural history of the English National Parks and a leader of Alpine mountain tours for the travel company *Rambers Holidays*.

He is an ardent DIY enthusiast, having renovated a succession of properties and he and wife Jill have spent the 2020/21 COVID19 lock down months turning an overgrown plot into a productive garden. After publishing facts on and off line for many years, this is his first venture into fiction.

Printed in Great Britain
by Amazon